Val McDermid is a top ten bestseller, translated into more than thirty languages, with over two million copies sold in the UK and over ten million worldwide.

She has won many awards internationally, including the CWA Gold Dagger for best crime novel of the year and the the Stonewall Writer of the Year Award. In 2011, Val was the recipient of the Pioneer Award at the 23rd Annual Lambda Literary Awards.

In 2010, she was awarded the prestigious CWA Cartier Diamond Dagger. This followed her induction into the Hall of Fame at the ITV3 Crime Thriller Awards in 2009, the same year in which she was elected to an Honorary Fellowship at St Hilda's College, Oxford.

Also by Val McDermid

A Place of Execution
Killing the Shadows
The Distant Echo
The Grave Tattoo
A Darker Domain
Trick of the Dark
The Vanishing Point

TONY HILL NOVELS

The Mermaids Singing
The Wire in the Blood
The Last Temptation
The Torment of Others
Beneath the Bleeding
Fever of the Bone
The Retribution

KATE BRANNIGAN NOVELS

Dead Beat
Kick Back
Crack Down
Clean Break
Blue Genes
Star Struck

LINDSAY GORDON NOVELS

Report for Murder
Common Murder
Final Edition
Union Jack
Booked for Murder
Hostage to Murder

SHORT STORY COLLECTIONS

The Writing on the Wall
Stranded
Christmas is Murder

NON-FICTION

A Suitable Job for a Woman

CROSS AND BURN

VAL McDERMID

Little, Brown

LITTLE, BROWN

First published in Great Britain in 2013 by Little, Brown

Copyright © Val McDermid 2013

Lines from 'Hammersmith Winter' from the collection *The Wrecking Point*
(Picador) reproduced with kind permission of Robin Robertson.

The moral right of the author has been asserted.

*All characters and events in this publication, other than those
clearly in the public domain, are fictitious and any resemblance
to real persons, living or dead, is purely coincidental.*

A CIP catalogue record for this book
is available from the British Library.

Hardback ISBN 978-1-4087-0456-1
Trade Paperback ISBN 978-1-4087-0455-4

Typeset in Meridien by M Rules
Printed and bound in Great Britain by
Clays Ltd, St Ives plc

Papers used by Little, Brown are from well-managed forests
and other responsible sources.

MIX
Paper from
responsible sources
FSC® C104740

Little, Brown
An imprint of
Little, Brown Book Group
100 Victoria Embankment
London EC4Y 0DY

An Hachette UK Company
www.hachette.co.uk

www.littlebrown.co.uk

For my friends by the sea – thank you for
taking me in and bringing me home.

Acknowledgements

Somewhere in my youth or childhood, I must have done something good. I can't think of any other reason why I am so lucky in the support systems that enable me to put this book in your hands. Some of them are experts who give up their time and expertise; some of them are my own backroom team; others go above and beyond the call of professional duty.

So I'd like to say thanks to Professor Dave Barclay for his DNA expertise; to Catherine Tweedy for her fascinating exposition of fingermarks; to Professor Sue Black for her unerring ability to astonish me; and to those who prefer to remain anonymous. Thanks to Marie Mather whose generous donation to the Million for a Morgue campaign is the reason why she appears in these pages.

The character of DCI Alex Fielding was first created by Patrick Harbinson for *Wire in the Blood*, the TV series based on the Tony Hill and Carol Jordan novels. I have appropriated her for my own purposes with the kind permission of Coastal Productions.

Unstinting gratitude to Kiri, who organises my life; to Carolyn, who makes it beautiful; to Tony, who keeps me on the fiscal straight and narrow; and most of all, to Kelly, Cameron, the cousins and their mums, who save me from myself. Not to mention the dog.

Finally, a big shout out to the professionals: Jane and the team at Gregory & Co, David Shelley and his crew at Little, Brown, my copy editor Anne O'Brien, Amy Hundley and her colleagues at Grove Atlantic, and all the booksellers, librarians and bloggers who have helped my books find their readers.

Lucky me.

The hardest thing in life is to know which bridge to cross and which to burn.

David Russell

But you're not here, now, to lead me back
To bed. None of you are. Look at the snow,
I said, to whoever might be near, I'm cold,
Would you hold me. Hold me. Let me go.

'Hammersmith Winter'
Robin Robertson

1

Day one

He woke every morning with a prickle of excitement. Would today be the day? Would he finally meet her, his perfect wife? He knew who she was, of course. He'd been watching her for a couple of weeks now, growing used to her habits, getting to know who her friends were, learning her little ways. How she pushed her hair behind her ears when she settled into the driver's seat of her car. How she turned all the lights on as soon as she came home to her lonely flat.

How she never ever seemed to check in her rear-view mirror.

He reached for the remote controls and raised the blinds on the high skylight windows. Rain fell in a constant drizzle from an unbroken wall of featureless grey cloud. No wind to drive the rain, though. Just a steady downpour. The sort of weather where people hid under umbrellas, heads down, paying no attention to their surroundings, faces invisible to CCTV.

First box ticked.

And it was a Saturday. So she'd have no appointments booked, no meetings arranged. Nobody to notice an unplanned absence. Nobody to raise an alarm.

Second box ticked.

Saturday also meant the chances were much higher that her plans would take her somewhere suitable for their meeting. Somewhere he could follow the first steps of the carefully worked-out plan to make her his perfect wife. Whether she wanted that or not. But then, what she wanted was irrelevant.

Third box ticked.

He took a long slow shower, savouring the sensual delight of the warm water on his skin. If she played her cards right, she'd get to share it with him, to make a pleasant experience even more rewarding for him. What could be better than starting the day with a blow job in the shower? That was the sort of thing that a perfect wife would be thrilled to perform for her man. It had never occurred to him before, and he happily added it to his list. It had never occurred to the first one either, which was typical of her many failures to meet his high standards.

New tick box added to the mental list. It was important to be organised.

He believed in organisation, in preparation and in taking precautions. An outsider, looking at how much time had passed since that bitch had thwarted him, might have thought he'd given up on his quest. How wrong that outsider would have been. First, he'd had to deal with the mess she'd made. That had taken a ridiculous amount of time and he begrudged her every second of it. Then he'd had to be clear about his objectives.

He'd considered trying to buy what he wanted, like his father had done. But pliable though the Asian women were, it sent the wrong message to turn up with one of them on your arm. It screamed inadequacy, perversion, failure. The same went for mail-order brides from the former Soviet empire. Those harsh accents, the chemical blonde hair, the criminal tendencies ingrained like grime – that wasn't for him. You couldn't parade one of them in front of your work-mates and expect respect.

Then he'd looked at the possibilities of internet dating. The trouble with that was you were buying a pig in a poke. And he didn't want to poke a pig. He sniggered to himself at his cleverness, his skill with language. People admired that about him, he knew. But the even bigger trouble with inter-net dating was that there were so few options if things went wrong. Because you'd left a trail a mile wide. It took effort, skill and resources to be truly anonymous online. The risk of exposure with one split second of inattention or error was too high for him to take. And that meant if it all went wrong, he had no way to make her pay the proper price for her failure. She'd simply retreat to her old life as if nothing had happened. She'd win.

He couldn't allow that. There had to be another way. And so he'd conceived his plan. And that was why it had taken so long to reach this point. He'd had to develop a strategy, then examine it from every possible angle, then do his research. And only now was he ready to roll.

He dressed anonymously in black chain-store jeans and polo shirt, carefully lacing up the black work boots with their steel toecaps. Just in case. Downstairs, he made himself a cup of green tea and munched an apple. Then he went through to the garage to check again that everything was in order. The freezer was turned off, the lid open, ready to receive its cargo. Pre-cut strips of tape were lined up along the edge of a shelf. On a card table, handcuffs, a taser, pic-ture cord and a roll of duct tape sat in a row. He put on his waxed jacket and stowed the items in his pockets. Finally, he picked up a metal case and headed back to the kitchen.

Fourth and fifth boxes ticked.

He gave the garage one final look, saw he'd trailed in some leaf debris last time he'd been in there. With a sigh, he put down the case and fetched a brush and dustpan. Women's work, he thought impatiently. But if everything went right today, soon there would be a woman to do it.

2

Day twenty-four

Dr Tony Hill shifted in his seat and tried to avoid looking at the wreckage of her face. 'When you think of Carol Jordan, what comes into your mind?'

Chris Devine, still formally a detective sergeant with Bradfield Metropolitan Police, cocked her head towards him, as if to compensate for a degree of deafness. 'When you think of Carol Jordan, what comes into *your* mind?' Her voice had a deliberate teasing quality. He recognised it as a bid to deflect him from his line.

'I try not to think about Carol.' In spite of his best efforts, the sadness seeped to the surface.

'Maybe you should. Maybe you need to go there more than I do.'

The room had grown dim as they'd talked. The day was dying outside but the light seemed to be leaching out of the room at a faster rate. Because she couldn't see him, it was safe for once to let his face betray him. His expression was the opposite of the lightness of his tone. 'You're not my therapist, you know.'

'And you're not mine. Unless you're here as my mate, I'm not interested. I've told them I'm not wasting my time with a counsellor. But then, you know that, don't you? They'll have told you the score. You're still their go-to guy. The rabbit they pull out of the hat when all the other magic tricks have fallen flat on their arse.'

It was amazing she didn't sound more bitter, he thought. In her shoes, he'd be raging. Lashing out at anyone who sat still long enough. 'It's true, I do know you've refused to cooperate with the therapy team. But that's not why I've come. I'm not here to try and counsel you by the back door. I'm here because we've known each other for a long time.'

'That doesn't make us friends.' Her voice was dull, all animation stripped from the words.

'No. I don't really do friendship.' It surprised him how easy it was to be candid with someone who couldn't see his face or his body language. He'd read about the phenomenon but he'd never experienced it at first hand. Maybe he should try wearing dark glasses and feigning blindness with his more intransigent patients.

She gave a dry little laugh. 'You do a decent facsimile when it suits you.'

'Kind of you to say so. A long time ago, someone called it "passing for human". I liked the sound of that. I've been using it ever since.'

'That's pitching it a bit high, mate. What does the length of time we've known each other have to do with the price of fish?'

'We're what's left, I suppose.' He shifted in his chair, uncomfortable at the way the conversation was going. He'd come because he wanted to reach out, to help her. But the longer he sat here, the more he felt like he was the one who needed help. 'After the dust has settled.'

'I think you're here because you hoped that talking to me

would help you understand whatever it is you're feeling,' she pointed out with a note of sharpness. 'Because I took the hit for her, didn't I? That's a closer bond than we ever had in all those years of working together.'

'I thought I was the psychologist here.' It was a weak response, barely a parry to her thrust.

'Doesn't mean you can figure out what's going on in your own head. Your own heart, come to that. It's complicated, right, Doc? I mean, if it was only guilt, it would be easy, right? That'd make sense. But it's more than that, isn't it? Because there's a dark side to guilt. The rage. The feeling that it's just not fair, that you're the one left carrying the weight. The outrage because you're left with a sense of responsibility. That sense of injustice, it's like heartburn, like acid burning into you.' She stopped abruptly, shocked by her own figure of speech.

'I'm sorry.'

Her hand moved towards her face, stopping millimetres from the shiny red skin left by the acid booby trap that had been targeted at someone else. 'So, what does come into your mind when you think about Carol Jordan?' she persisted, her voice harsh now.

Tony shook his head. 'I can't say.' Not because he didn't know the answer. But because he did.

3

Even from behind, Paula McIntyre recognised the boy. She was a detective, after all. It was the kind of thing she was supposed to be capable of. All the more so when the person in question was out of context. That was where civilians fell down. Without context, they generally failed. But detectives were meant to make the most of their natural talents and hone their skills to the point where people were once seen, never forgotten. *Yeah, right,* she thought. Another one of those myths perpetuated by the double-takes of TV cops confronted by the familiar in unexpected circumstances.

But still, she did recognise the boy, even from the quarter-profile of her angle of approach. If she'd entered the station via the tradesmen's entrance – the back door from the car park – she'd have missed him. But this was her first day at Skenfrith Street and she didn't know the door codes. So she'd taken the easy way out and parked in the multi-storey opposite and walked in the front door, coming up behind the teenager shifting from foot to foot before the front counter. There was something about the set of his shoulders and the angle of his head that suggested defensiveness and tension. But not guilt.

She paused and tried to get the measure of what was going on. 'I understand what you're saying. I'm not stupid.' The boy's voice was miserable rather than aggressive. 'But I'm asking you to understand that this is different.' He lifted his shoulders in a small shrug. 'Not everybody's the same, man. You can't just go with one size fits all.' His accent was local but, in spite of his best attempts, unmistakably middle-class.

The civilian staffing the counter muttered something she couldn't make out. The boy started bouncing on the balls of his feet, all wound up and nowhere to go. He wasn't the sort of lad who would kick off, she thought she knew that. But that was no reason not to try and placate him. Keeping a lid on things wasn't the only point of getting to the bottom of what was bothering the punters.

Paula stepped forward and put a hand on the boy's arm. 'It's Torin, isn't it?'

He swivelled round, his face startled and anxious. A thick mop of dark hair framed the pale skin of a teenage boy-cave dweller. Wide blue eyes with dark smudges beneath, a prominent wedge of nose, a narrow mouth with incongruous rosebud lips under the faintest shadow of what might one day become a moustache. Paula cross-checked the mental catalogue against her memory and ticked all the boxes. No mistake here.

The tightness round his eyes relaxed a little. 'I know you. You've been to our house. With the doctor.' He frowned, struggling for a memory. 'Elinor. From casualty.'

Paula nodded. 'That's right. We came round for dinner. Your mum and Elinor are mates from work. I'm Paula.' She

9

smiled at the small grey man behind the counter as she produced her ID from her jacket pocket. 'Detective Sergeant McIntyre, CID – DCI Fielding's team.'

The man nodded. 'I'm telling this lad, there's nothing we can do for him till his mum's been missing for twenty-four hours.'

'Missing?' Paula's question was drowned by Torin McAndrew's frustrated riposte.

'And I'm telling this . . .' He breathed heavily through his nose. '. . . this man that you can't treat every case the same because everybody's different and my mum doesn't stay out all night.'

Paula didn't know Bev McAndrew well, but she'd heard plenty about the chief pharmacist from Elinor Blessing, her partner and the senior registrar in A&E at Bradfield Cross Hospital. And nothing she'd heard tended to contradict Bev's son's adamantine certainty. None of which would cut any ice with the civilian behind the counter.

'I'm going to have a chat with Torin here,' she said firmly. 'Have you got an interview room?' The man nodded towards a door on the other side of the barren waiting area. 'Thanks. Please call up to CID and let DCI Fielding know I'm on the premises and I'll be up shortly.'

He didn't look thrilled, but he did pick up the phone. Paula gestured with her thumb towards the interview room. 'Let's have a sit-down and you can tell me what's going on,' she said, leading the way.

''Kay.' Torin followed her, shuffling his oversized trainers across the floor in the typical slouch of an adolescent who's still not quite accustomed to the margins of his body.

Paula opened the door on a tiny boxroom with barely enough space for a table and three steel-framed chairs upholstered in a zingy blue-and-black pattern. *Seen worse*, she thought, ushering Torin to a seat. She sat opposite him, pulling from her shoulder bag a spiral notebook with a pen rammed down its metal spine.

'Right then, Torin. Why don't you start at the beginning?'

Being stalled at the rank of Detective Constable had been the price Paula had willingly paid for membership of DCI Carol Jordan's Major Incident Team. So when that squad had been wound up, she'd applied for the first three-stripe job that had come up with Bradfield Metropolitan Police. It had been so long since she'd passed her sergeant's exams, she was afraid they'd make her resit.

This wasn't how she'd imagined her initiation into the rank of Detective Sergeant. She'd thought doing preliminary interviews would be someone else's scut work now. But then, that was the thing about being a cop. Not much ever turned out the way you imagined.

4

The blackout blinds did exactly what they were supposed to. And that was good, because pitch-black meant you didn't get shadow tricks setting your imagination on fire. The one thing Carol Jordan didn't need was anything to stimulate her imagination. She could manage quite enough on her own without any extra provocation.

It wasn't as if she was a stranger to bloody crime scenes. Most of her adult life had been punctuated by images of sudden violent death. She'd been confronted with victims of torture; banal domestic violence gone overboard; sexual sadism that was nothing to do with middle-aged, middle-class fantasy; pick your brutality of choice and Carol had seen its end result. Sometimes they'd kept sleep at bay, driven her to the vodka bottle to blur the outlines. But never for more than a few nights. Her need for justice had always stepped in, transforming horror into a spur to action. Those images became the engine that drove her investigations, the motivation for bringing killers to face the consequences of their crimes.

This time was different, though. This time, nothing diminished the power of what she'd seen. Not time, not drink, not distance. These days, there seemed to be a film running on a perpetual loop in her head. It wasn't a long film, but its impact wasn't dulled by repetition. The weird thing was that it wasn't simply a rerun of what she'd seen. Because she was in the film. It was as if someone had been right behind her with a hand-held camera, making a jerky home movie of the worst moment of her life, the colours slightly off, the angles somehow wrong.

It began with her walking into the barn, the view over her shoulder the familiar interior with its inglenook fireplace, exposed stone walls and hammer beams. Sofas she'd once lounged on; tables where she'd discarded newspapers, eaten meals, set wine glasses down; hand-stitched wall hangings she'd marvelled at; and a sweater she'd seen her brother wear a dozen times, casually thrown over the back of a chair. There was a crumpled T-shirt on the floor near the dining table, where the remains of lunch still sat. And at the foot of the gallery stairs, two uniformed bobbies in their high-vis jackets, one looking appalled, the other embarrassed. Between them, a concertina of fabric that might have been a skirt. Disconcerting, but not terrifying. Because film couldn't convey the stink of spilt blood.

But as Carol approached the wooden stairs, the camera panned back to reveal the ceiling above the sleeping gallery. It was like a Jackson Pollock painting whose sole palette was red. Blood; sprayed, slashed and streaked across the stark white plaster. She'd known then that it was going to be very, very bad.

The camera followed her up the steps, recording every stumbling step. The first thing she saw was their legs and feet, marbled with blood, drips and smears on the bed and the floor. She climbed higher and saw Michael and Lucy's bloodless bodies marooned like pale islands in a sea of scarlet.

That was where the film froze, locked on that single terrible frame. But her brain didn't stop running just because the film had. The blame circled and rattled in her head like a hamster on a wheel. If she'd been a better cop. If she'd taken matters into her own hands instead of relying on Tony to come up with answers. If she'd forewarned Michael that a man on the loose had his own twisted reasons to wreak vengeance on her. If, if, if.

But none of those things had happened. And so her brother and the woman he loved had been butchered in the barn they'd restored with their own labour. A place with walls three feet thick, where they had every right to feel safe. And nothing in her life was untainted by that single terrible event.

She'd always found much of her self-definition in her work. It was, she had thought, the best of her. A clear channel for her intelligence, it offered a place where her dogged determination was valued. Her ability to recall verbatim anything she'd heard had a practical application. And she'd discovered she had the knack of inspiring loyalty in the officers she worked with. Carol had taken pride in being a cop. And now she had cut herself adrift from all that.

She'd already handed in her notice with Bradfield Metropolitan Police when Michael and Lucy had been murdered. She'd been about to take up a new post as a Detective Chief Inspector with West Mercia. She'd burned her bridges there and she didn't care. She'd also been planning to take a deep breath and share the sprawling Edwardian house in Worcester that Tony had unexpectedly inherited. But that dream was over too, her personal life as much a victim of a brutal killer as her professional life.

Homeless and jobless, Carol had returned to her parents'

house. Home, according to popular mythology, was where they were supposed to take you in when all else failed. It seemed her judgement had missed the mark there too. Her parents hadn't turned her away, that much was true. Nor had they openly blamed her brother's death on her choices. But her father's silent misery and her mother's sharpness had been perpetual reproaches. She'd stuck it out for a couple of weeks, then she'd repacked her bags and left.

All she'd left behind was her beloved cat Nelson. Tony had once joked that her relationship with the black cat was the only functional one in her life. The trouble was, that was too close to the bone to be funny. But Nelson was old now. Too old to be stuffed in a cat carrier and traipsed round the country from pillar to post. And her mother was better able to be kind to the cat than she was to Carol. So Nelson stayed and she went.

She still owned a flat in London but it had been so long since she'd lived there, it no longer felt like home. Besides, the difference between her mortgage payments and the rent from her long-term tenant was all she had to live on until the lawyers were done picking over the remnants of Michael's life. Which left her with a single option.

According to Michael's will, in the absence of Lucy, Carol inherited his estate. The barn was in his sole name; their house in France had belonged to Lucy. So once probate had been granted, the barn would be hers, blood and ghosts and all. Most people would have hired industrial cleaners, re-decorated what couldn't be cleaned, and sold the place to some off-comer ignorant of the barn's recent history.

Carol Jordan wasn't most people. Fractured and fragile as she was, she held fast to the determination that had dragged her through disasters before. And so she'd made a plan. This was her attempt at carrying it out.

She would remove every trace of what had happened

here and refashion the barn into a place where she could live. A kind of reconciliation, that's what she was aiming for. Deep down, she didn't think it was a likely outcome. But she couldn't come up with anything else to aim for and it was a project that would keep her occupied. Hard physical work during the days to make her sleep at night. And if that didn't work, there was always the vodka bottle.

Some days, she felt like the writer in residence at the DIY warehouse, her shopping list a liturgy of items newly discovered, laid out on the page like a sequence of haikus. But she made sense of the dense poetry of home improvement and mastered unfamiliar tools and new techniques. Slowly but inevitably, she was erasing the physical history of the place. She didn't know whether that would bring her soul any ease. Once upon a time she would have been able to ask Tony Hill's opinion. But that wasn't an option now. She'd just have to learn to be her own therapist.

Carol snapped on the bedside lamp and pulled on her new working uniform – ripped and filthy jeans, steel-toed work boots over thick socks, a fresh T-shirt and a heavy plaid shirt. 'Construction Barbie', according to one of the middle-aged men who frequented the trade counter at the DIY warehouse. It had made her smile, if only because nothing could have been less appropriate.

While she was waiting for the coffee machine to produce a brew, she headed through the main body of the barn and stepped out into the morning, seeing the promise of rain in the low cloud that shrouded the distant hills. The colour was leaching out of the coarse moorland grass now autumn was creeping up on winter. The copse of trees on the shoulder of the hill was changing colour, its palette shifting from green to brown. A couple of tiny patches of sky were visible through the branches for the first time since spring. Soon there would be nothing but a tracery of naked branches, stripping the only cover from the hillside. Carol leaned on the wall and stared up at the trees. She breathed deeply, trying for serenity.

Once upon a time, the highly evolved sixth sense that keeps talented cops out of trouble would have raised the hairs on the back of her neck. It was a measure of how far she'd come from the old Carol Jordan that she was completely oblivious to the patient eyes watching her every move.

5

Rob Morrison glanced at his watch again, then pulled out his phone to double-check the time. 6:58. The new boss was cutting it fine if she wanted to make a good impression on her first day. But before he could settle into his smugness, the clatter of heels on floor tiles alerted him to an arrival from the street door rather than the underground car park. He swung round and there she was, mac shimmering with raindrops, shoes splashed with dirt. Marie Mather, his new opposite number. Director of Marketing to his Director of Operations.

'Morning, Rob.' She shifted her laptop bag to join her handbag over her shoulder so she could free up a hand to shake his. 'Thanks for taking the time to get me settled in.'

'Might as well start off on the right foot.' He squeezed out a half-smile that took the sourness from his face. 'Since we'll be yoked together like horses in the traces, pulling the mighty chariot that is Tellit Communications.' He enjoyed the flash of surprise as the extravagance of his sardonic comment sank in. He liked to upset people's general assumption that a man who ran the operations side of a mobile phone company must be a stranger to culture. 'You didn't drive in?'

She shook the sparkle of rain from her thick blonde bob and gestured with her head towards the street outside. 'We're only five minutes' walk from the tram terminus so I always get a seat. It's a better start to the day than fighting the rush-hour traffic.' When she smiled, her nose wrinkled, as if she'd smelled something delicious. In terms of aesthetics, Rob reckoned she was a distinct improvement on Jared Kamal, her predecessor. 'So. What's the drill?'

'We'll sort you out with security passes. Then I'll take you up to the main floor and give you the guided tour.' As he spoke, Rob steered her over to the security desk, a hand on her elbow, aware of a spicy floral aroma that clung to her in spite of the tram and the Bradfield rain. If she was as good at her job as she was at brightening the place up, Rob's working life was set to improve exponentially.

Minutes later, they emerged from the lift straight on to the main sales floor. At this time of day, the lighting was dim. 'Staff operate the lighting levels at their own pods. It gives them the illusion of control and it gives us a quick and easy way to spot who's actually working.' Rob led the way across the room.

'Somebody's early.' Marie nodded towards a pool of light in the far corner.

Rob rubbed his hand over his chin. 'That's Gareth Taylor.' He arranged his features in a standard expression of sorrow. 'Lost his family recently.' Personally, he was over Gareth's grief. Time to move on, get a life. But Rob knew he was in the minority on that one so he kept quiet around the water cooler, content to grunt supportively when colleagues went into one of their 'Poor Gareth' spasms.

Marie's expression softened. 'Poor bloke. What happened?'

'Car crash. Wife and two kids, died at the scene.' Rob forged onwards, not a backward glance at his bereaved colleague.

Marie broke stride momentarily then caught up. 'And he's in here at this time of the morning?'

Rob shrugged. 'He says he'd rather be here than staring at the walls at home. Fine by me. I mean, it's been three or four months now.' He turned and gave her a dark smile. 'We're fucked if he starts claiming his TOIL though.'

Marie made a noncommittal noise and followed him into a generous cubicle at the end of the room. A desk, two chairs. A couple of whiteboards and a paper recycling bin. Rob gave a cynical little bow. 'Home sweet home.'

'It's a decent size, at least.' Marie put her laptop on the desk, tucked her bag in a drawer and hung her coat on a hook on the back of the door. 'Now, first things first. Where's the coffee and what's the system?'

Rob smiled. 'Follow me.' He led her back into the main office. 'You buy tokens from Charyn on the front desk. Five for a pound.' As they grew closer to his workspace, the light from Gareth Taylor's pod revealed a door tucked away in a nearby alcove. It led to a small room furnished with a pair of coffee machines. Rob gestured at a series of bins that contained little plastic pods. 'You choose your poison, slot the pod in the machine and pay for it with a token.' He rummaged in the pocket of his chinos and produced a red disc. 'Have your first one on me.' He handed it over as if conferring a great honour. 'I'll let you get settled in.' He glanced at his watch. 'One or two things I need to deal with before the hordes arrive. I've arranged a meeting with key personnel at half eight in the small conference room. Ask anybody, they'll direct you.'

And that was it. He was gone, leaving Marie with an array

of beverage choices. She opted for a cappuccino and was pleasantly surprised by the result. She stepped back into the main office, where there were now three or four illuminated work stations. She decided to start getting to know her staff and moved towards Gareth Taylor, consciously applying a warm smile.

He glanced up as she approached, his expression startled. His fingers flew over the keyboard and as she rounded the corner of his partition, she had the impression of a computer screen quickly refreshing. It looked like Tellit resembled everywhere Marie had worked, with employees who liked to feel they were scoring points by doing their own thing in company time with company resources. Human nature, the same all over. It was a tendency that didn't bother Marie, so long as productivity was acceptable and nobody took the piss.

'Hi. I'm Marie Mather. The new marketing director.' She held out a hand.

Gareth accepted the handshake with no enthusiasm. His hand was cool and dry, the pressure firm but not aggressive. 'I figured that's who you must be. I'm Gareth Taylor, one of the screen and phone grunts.'

'I prefer to think of you as frontline staff.'

Gareth raised his eyebrows. 'Doesn't change the reality.'

'You're in early.'

He shook his head, sighing. 'Look, I know Rob will have given you the bullet points. Coming to work is the only consistent thing in my life right now. I don't want sympathy. I'm not like him with his "pity me, my wife left me" shtick. I just want to be left alone to get on with things, all right?' His voice was tight with frustration. She could only imagine how hard it was to deal with other people's well-meaning interference on top of such a devastating loss.

Marie leaned forward and peered at his screen. 'Message received and understood. So what are you working on?'

She'd hoped he might at least smile. Instead, he scowled. 'It won't mean anything to you till you've got your feet under the table. I'm implementing a strategy to switch silver surfer customers to long-term contracts. And I think we're doing it wrong, so maybe you might want to come back and talk to me about it when you're up to speed.'

There were two ways of taking Gareth's brusque response. For now, Marie elected to avoid confrontation. 'I'll look forward to that.' She sipped her cappuccino. 'I'm always happy to hear from my team.'

Tonight, when she relaxed with a glass of white wine while Marco cooked dinner, she'd enjoy telling him about this encounter. As they often did, they'd set up some light-hearted wagers about how it would go with her new colleagues. Would she win Gareth over or would he be determined to remain alienated? Would Rob's obvious desire to flirt cross the line to the point where she'd have to bring HR into the picture? She and Marco loved to play their little game of speculation, sometimes even using their fantasy workplace lives to spice up their own bedroom games.

It was harmless fun, Marie thought. Completely harmless.

6

Torin's adolescent inability to disguise his anxiety was immediately obvious to Paula. Luckily for her, maintaining a cool façade under pressure took more skill and effort than he had at his command. Normally she'd have offered him a drink to settle him down, but Skenfrith Street was alien territory for her and she didn't know how long it would take her to rustle something up. The last thing she wanted was to keep her new boss waiting any longer than absolutely necessary.

Technically, she should probably have sorted out a so-called appropriate adult before she questioned Torin. But she reckoned she was more than appropriate enough. And it wasn't as if he was being interviewed about a crime. Paula gave Torin an expectant look. 'When did you start to worry there might be something wrong?'

'I don't know exactly.' He frowned.

'What time does she usually get in from work?'

He raised one shoulder in a shrug. 'About half past five,

but sometimes she'll do the shopping on the way home, so then it's more like quarter to seven.'

'So it's fair to say that by seven, you were beginning to worry?'

'Not worry, exactly. More like, wonder. It's not like she's not got a life. Sometimes she goes out with one of her mates for a pizza or a movie or whatever. But if she's doing that, she usually tells me in advance, in the morning. Or she texts me if it's more, like, spontaneous.'

Paula wasn't surprised. Bev McAndrew had struck her as a sensible woman. 'So did you text her?'

Torin nodded, chewing the corner of his lower lip. 'Yeah. Just, you know, what's for my tea, will you be back soon, kind of thing.'

Standard teenage-boy stuff. 'And she didn't respond?'

'No.' He fidgeted in his chair, then leaned forward, his forearms on the table, his hands clenched together. 'I didn't know what to do. I wasn't really worried, more, like, pissed off.' He gave her a quick up-and-under glance, checking whether he was going to get away with a mild swear word in front of a copper.

Paula smiled. 'Pissed off and hungry, I'm guessing.'

Torin's shoulders relaxed a degree or two. 'Yeah. That too. So I looked in the fridge and there was leftover cottage pie from the night before, so I nuked it and ate it. And still nothing from my mum.'

'Did you call any of her friends?'

His head reared back slightly in a gesture of incomprehension. 'How would I do that? I don't know their numbers. They're all in her phone, not written down anywhere. I mostly don't even know their names.' He waved a hand in the air. 'And there's no way to look up, like, "Dawn from work", or "Megan from the gym", or "Laura that I was at school with".' He had a point, she realised. It used to be when someone went missing, you checked their address book, their diary, the list of numbers by the phone. Now everybody carried their whole lives around with them and when they disappeared, so did the means of tracking them.

'No relatives you could call?'

Torin shook his head. 'My gran lives in Bristol with my auntie Rachel. Mum hasn't spoken to my dad this year, and anyway, he's doing a tour of duty in Afghanistan. He's an army medic.' A note of pride, Paula thought.

'What about work? Did you think of ringing there?'

He glowered. 'They only answer the outside line during regular opening hours. In the evening, the pharmacy's just for hospital emergency prescriptions. So even if I'd rung, nobody would have picked up.'

Paula cast her mind back to her own early teens and wondered how unnerved she'd have felt if her staid and respectable parents had gone inexplicably AWOL. In the circumstances, she thought Torin was doing pretty well not to lose control in the face of what probably felt like pointless questions that only served to slow down the process of finding his mother. It was that understanding of other people's points of view that had helped Paula develop her skills as an interviewer. Now she needed to keep Torin on side, make him feel someone cared about his plight so she could extract enough information to do something useful.

'So what did you do?'

Torin blinked fast and furious. Ashamed or upset, Paula wasn't sure which. 'I went on my Xbox and played Minecraft till I was tired enough to go to sleep. I didn't know what else to do.'

'You did well. A lot of people your age would have panicked. So what happened this morning?'

'I woke before my alarm went off. At first I thought it was Mum moving around that had woken me, but it wasn't. I

25

went through to her room, and the bed was still made.' He chewed his lip again, dark eyes troubled. 'She hadn't come home. And she just doesn't do shit like that. One of my mates, his mum sometimes stops out all night without telling him. And that geezer on the front counter there, you could tell he was thinking, "Poor mutt, his mum's a slapper and he's the last to know it."' He was on a roll now, words tumbling into one another. 'But I'm telling you, my mum's not like that. She's really not. Totally. Not. Plus it's, like, a house rule. We always text each other if we're going to be late. Like, if I've missed the bus or somebody's parent's late picking us up. Or she's been held up at work. Whatever.' He ran out of steam abruptly.

'And so you came down here.'

His shoulders slumped. 'I couldn't think of anything else to do. But you lot don't care, do you?'

'If that was true, I wouldn't be sitting here with you, Torin. Usually, we wait twenty-four hours to start a missing person inquiry, it's true.' *Unless there's a vulnerable individual in the picture.* 'But not when it's someone like your mum, someone who has responsibility for a child or an old person, for example. What I need to do now is take down some details about you and your mum so I can set the ball rolling.'

A tap at the door interrupted Paula's flow. Before she could say anything, the front-counter officer stuck his head round the door. 'DCI Fielding wants to know how long you're going to be.' He didn't do any kind of job of hiding his self-satisfaction.

Paula dismissed him with a pitying look. 'I'm interviewing a witness. It's what I'm trained to do. Please tell the DCI I'll be with her as soon as I've finished here.'

'I'll pass the message on.'

Torin gave him a look of contempt as the door closed. 'You in the shit now? For talking to me?'

'I'm doing my job, Torin. That's what matters. Now, I'm going to need some background information.'

It didn't take long. Torin, fourteen. Pupil at Kenton Vale School. Bev, thirty-seven, chief pharmacist at Bradfield Cross Hospital, divorced eight years ago from Tom, currently serving at Camp Bastian. Torin and Bev shared a semi-detached house at 17 Grecian Rise, Kenton, Bradfield. No known reason why Bev wasn't where she should be. No history of mental illness or depression. No known financial pressures, other than the ones everyone in the public sector lived with these days.

Paula jotted down mobile numbers for mother and son then put her pen down. 'Have you got a picture of your mum?'

Torin fiddled with his phone, then turned it to face her. Paula recognised Bev from the picture, which wasn't always a given with smartphone snaps. It was a head shot, apparently taken on a sunny beach. Thick blonde hair, mid-blue eyes, oval face with regular features. Pretty but not drop-dead gorgeous, a face animated by a cheery smile complete with laughter lines. Seeing the picture reminded Paula that she'd found Bev attractive. Not that she'd exactly lusted after their dinner host. More of a private acknowledgement that Bev was her type. In the same way that Carol Jordan was. A particular configuration of features and colouring that always caught her attention. Not, interestingly, a match for Dr Elinor Blessing. Paula knew her partner was beautiful; her heart always rose at the sight of her fine black hair with its threads of silver, and the laughter in her grey eyes. But it hadn't been Elinor's looks that had tweaked Paula's attention when they first met. It had been her kindness, which trumped blonde every time. So yes, there had been a moment when she'd appreciated Bev's appeal. And if she'd noticed it, chances were that she wasn't the only one.

27

'Can you email that to me?' She flipped to a fresh page in her notebook and wrote down her mobile number and email address, tore it out and passed it to Torin. 'Has she got any scars, or birthmarks, or tattoos? It makes it easier for us to check with the local hospitals in case she's had an accident and been brought in without her handbag.'

He glanced at the scrap of paper Paula had given him then met her eyes again. 'She has a tattoo of a bluebird on her left shoulder. And she's got a scar on her right ankle where she broke it and they had to put a pin in.'

Paula made a quick note. 'That's very helpful.'

'What are you going to do about my mum?'

'I'll make some phone calls. Talk to her colleagues.'

'What about me?'

It was a good question. Torin was a minor and she knew she should phone the social services department and get a case worker assigned to him. But Bev might prove Paula's professional unease unfounded. She might still turn up, embarrassed and awkward after an unpredicted night on the tiles. Then unpicking the process set in train by the social workers would be a nightmare for mother and son. She'd be stigmatised as an unfit mother and he'd be classified 'at risk'. It might even have an impact on her job. Paula didn't want that on her conscience. 'Why don't you just go to school?'

'Like normal?'

She nodded. 'Text me when you get out of school and we'll take it from there. Hopefully, she'll have turned up at work and that'll be the end of it.' She tried to reassure him with a smile that matched her voice.

He looked dubious. 'You think?'

No. But, 'Chances are,' was what she said as she stood up and eased him out the door. She watched him as far as the front entrance, his shoulders hunched, his head down. She wanted to believe Bev McAndrew was fit and well and on her way home. But convincing herself would have required a triumph of hope over experience, and Paula didn't have it in her.

She turned away, momentarily nostalgic for her old team. They would have understood exactly why she was bothering with Torin and his barely missing mum. But that was then. Instead she had DCI Fielding to face. She'd heard good things about Fielding's conviction rates and this was definitely a team she wanted to hitch her wagon to. But already she'd kept her new boss waiting. It was far from the perfect start she'd hoped for. Hopefully, it wasn't too late to redeem herself. She'd simply have to try that little bit harder.

7

The tram rattled across the high Victorian viaduct, sleek modern lines a contrast to the soot-stained redbrick arches. It was, Tony thought, a powerful metaphor for the whole area surrounding the Minster Canal Basin. Opposite the viaduct was the ruined apse of the medieval minster itself, its stained limestone tracery all that had been left standing when a stick of Luftwaffe bombs had reduced the rest of the building to rubble. A dozen years ago, the viaduct and the minster had bookended a higgledy-piggledy scrum of random buildings, half of them empty and decaying, their window frames rotten and their rooflines sagging. The canal district had been the least lovely and least loved of inner-city Bradfield's precincts.

Then a bright spark on the city council had discovered an EU fund aimed at reinvigorating depressed and deprived inner-city environments. These days, the canal basin was the hub of a lively area. Craft workshops, indie publishers and software developers worked cheek by jowl, flats and studio apartments occupied the upper floors and a sprinkling of bars and bistros provided somewhere for locals and visitors to mingle. One of Bradfield Victoria's premier league stars had even lent his name to a Spanish tapas bar that he occasionally deigned to grace with his presence.

The basin itself had become a mix of permanent residential moorings and short-stay marina slots for the narrowboats that provided holidays and day trips where once they'd shifted cargoes round the country.

Attractive though it now was, it had never previously crossed Tony's mind as a possible home. He'd sat outside one of the waterside pubs with Carol Jordan once, when they'd been pretending to be normal people who could have a drink and a conversation that didn't involve the interior life of fucked-up individuals. Another time, he'd shared a clutter of tapas with a couple of American colleagues who'd come to look round the secure mental hospital where he worked. More than once, he'd walked the canal from one side of the city to the other while he mulled over a complex case. There was something about walking that freed up his mental processes to consider options other than the obvious.

So, he was familiar with the basin. Yet he'd never wondered what it would be like to live on the water in the heart of the city until it was all that was left to him. His former house in Bradfield was gone, sold to strangers when he thought he'd finally found a place he could with conviction call home. And now that was gone too, a burned-out shell that was an uncomfortable metaphor for what had happened to the life he'd imagined he could lead there. Everywhere he looked, bloody metaphors galore.

Tony crossed the cobbled area that separated the tapas bar from the houseboat moorings and swung aboard a pretty narrowboat whose name, *Steeler*, unfurled on a painted gold-and-black ribbon across the stern. He unfastened the heavy padlocks that held the hatch closed and clattered down the steep steps to the cabin below. As he passed, he threw the switches that activated the boat's electricity supply, generated by an array of solar panels. Even gloomy Bradfield skies provided enough energy for one person whose power needs were far from extravagant.

He'd been surprised by how readily he'd adapted to living in so confined a space. Life with a place for everything and everything in its place had proved unexpectedly soothing. There was no room for anything inessential; living like this had stripped his material life down to the bone, forcing him to reconsider the worth of stuff that had cluttered his life for years. OK, he didn't love the practical necessities like emptying the toilet tank and topping up the water reservoir. Nor was he entirely at ease with the camaraderie of the water, a connectivity that seemed to draw together the most unlikely combinations of people. And he still hadn't mastered the heating system. Now the nights were getting colder, he was growing fed up with waking in a freezing cabin. He was going to have to settle for the action of last resort – sitting down with the manual and actually reading the instructions. But in spite of all the inconveniences, he had grown comfortable in this calm, contained world.

He dumped his bag on the buttoned leather banquette that ran along the saloon bulkhead and put the kettle on for a cafètiere of coffee. While he waited for the water to boil, he booted up his laptop and checked his email. The only new message was from a cop for whom he'd profiled a serial rapist a few years before. Half-hoping it was an invitation to work with him again, he opened it.

Hi Tony. How are you doing? I heard about the business with Jacko Vance. Terrible thing, but without your input it could have been so much worse.

The reason I'm writing is because we're organising a conference to promote the use of offender profiling in high-visibility cases. Not just murders, but other serious offences too. It's getting harder to persuade top brass and police authorities that it's cost-effective in these times of austerity all round. We're trying to make the case that it's a front-end expense that saves a lot of back-end costs. I thought Carol Jordan would be the perfect keynote speaker, given how closely she's worked with you over the years. But I'm having some difficulty tracking her down. BMP tell me she's no longer on their books. They informed me she was transferring to West Mercia. But they say she's not on their strength. I tried the email address I had for her, but it bounced back at me. And the mobile number I had for her isn't working any more. I wondered if maybe she was deep undercover, but either way I reckoned you'd know where I can get in touch with her.

Can you give me some contact details? Or if that's not practical, can you at least ask her to get in touch with me?

Thanks in advance,

Rollo Harris,

Detective Chief Superintendent,

Devon & Cornwall Police

Tony stared at the screen, the words blurring. Rollo Harris wasn't the only one who didn't know where Carol Jordan was, or how to get in touch with her. Most people who knew them both would have struggled to believe it, but Tony hadn't spoken to Carol for the best part of three months. And he wouldn't have known where to find her if

33

he'd felt able to break that silence. The last thing she'd said to him after the hunt for Vance was done was, 'It's not all that's over, Tony.' And it appeared she'd meant it. She'd cut herself loose from his life.

At first, he'd managed to keep track of her. Although her final weeks at Bradfield Metropolitan Police had been classified as compassionate leave, she was obliged to let her employers know where she was. And because Paula McIntyre knew better than most how close the bond between Carol and Tony had been, she'd kept him in the loop. Carol had rented a service apartment in Bradfield for a month, then she'd moved into her parents' house.

Then she stopped being a DCI with BMP and, according to Paula, within days she was no longer under her parents' roof. 'I called her mobile and it wasn't working. So I rang her parents' number and spoke to her dad. He wasn't very forthcoming but he did admit she wasn't living there any more. He either didn't know or he wouldn't say where she is,' Paula had told him. Given the quality of Paula's interrogation skills, Tony reckoned David Jordan probably didn't know where his daughter was living.

He couldn't help wondering how that had happened. Going home to her parents, in the circumstances, wouldn't have been his professional advice. Her brother was dead, murdered by a killer he and Carol had failed to catch soon enough. And grief generally imposed a need to distribute blame. Was it Carol's guilt or her parents' pain that had driven a wedge between them?

However it had played out, it hadn't ended well. Tony would have put money on that. And since Carol needed to hold him responsible for Michael and Lucy's death because he had been too slow to realise what Vance had planned, then it followed that she would blame him for the rift with her parents. Insult to injury.

Tony rubbed his eyes with a knuckle. Wherever Carol Jordan was hiding, he would be the last to know. Sooner or later he was going to have to man up and either do something about that or let it go for ever.

8

Gartonside was a district nobody had ever chosen to live in. Even when the narrow streets of basic brick terraces had been built back at the tail end of the nineteenth century, their original residents knew they were destined to be slums before the decade was out. Thin walls meant cold and damp were perennial problems. Cheap materials diminished privacy. Outside toilets and no bathrooms did nothing for the hygiene or health of the factory workers who filled the two-bedroom houses to bursting point. Gartonside became the cheerless port of call of the feckless, the hopeless and the city's newest arrivals. Only the immigrants ever escaped its dead-end streets.

Finally, in one of the last hurrahs of the twentieth century, Bradfield city council had decreed that Gartonside was to be bulldozed and replaced with a planned housing estate of more spacious houses with parking spaces at the front and tiny gardens at the rear. A decade later, the first phase – the emptying of existing residents and the demolition of their former homes – was not yet complete. There were still a handful of streets in the shadow of Bradfield Victoria's vast stadium where residents lingered on. And beyond them, a huddle of houses were boarded up, waiting for the wrecking crews to reduce them to rubble.

Paula's satnav still believed in the streets of Gartonside, which made her even later to the crime scene. By the time she reached Rossiter Street, the perimeter was well established with festoons of crime-scene tape and stony-faced uniforms in high-vis jackets. She added her car to the impromptu parking lot at the end of the street and logged into the scene. 'Where's DCI Fielding?'

The constable with the clipboard nodded towards a mobile incident room parked further down the street. 'In the van, getting suited and booted for the scene.'

That was a relief. Not quite as late as she feared. When she'd finally said goodbye to Torin and found her way to the CID squad room, Paula had been taken aback by the absence of bodies. Instead of the usual buzz of chat and phone conversations there was a preternatural quiet broken only by the mutter of laptop keys struck by a couple of heavy-fingered operatives.

The one nearest the door looked up and raised his unruly eyebrows. 'You must be the new skip, right? McIntyre, yeah?'

Paula was tempted to slap him down with a quick *Sergeant McIntyre to you*, but she didn't know the lay of the land yet so she settled for, 'And you are?'

He pushed a thick fringe of black hair back from his shiny forehead. 'Detective Constable Pat Cody.' He gave an expansive sweep of his arm. 'And this is Skenfrith Street CID. Only, most of the firm are on a shout. A murder, down Gartonside.'

So much for hopes of a quiet day. 'Is that where DCI Fielding is?'

Cody gave a twisted little smile. 'Got it in one. And she's not very happy that her new bag man isn't with her.' The caterpillar eyebrows rose again. He was enjoying himself.

Paula wasn't about to explain herself to him. 'You got an address for me?'

'Rossiter Street, Gartonside.'

'Do we have a number?'

He smirked. 'The numbers fell off those doors years ago. The houses are boarded up, waiting for the council budget to afford bulldozers. You'll recognise the crime scene from the activity.'

And so she had. Paula dodged the puddles and potholes and climbed the metal steps into the mobile incident room. As she entered, a tiny woman wrestling her body into a white protective suit paused to look her up and down. 'McIntyre?'

Clearly the standard form of address in this firm. 'That's right. DCI Fielding?'

'That's me. Nice of you to join us. Get suited up, quick as you like.' There was something bird-like about Fielding. It wasn't simply her size or her fine-boned appearance. Her eyes darted around, even as she climbed into her suit, and there was a quick jerkiness to her movements that made Paula think of a blackbird raiding the earth for worms.

'I was taking a witness statement. Misper.' Paula checked the pile of J-suits. Fielding had snaffled the only small. She settled for a medium and began the inconvenient process of getting into it.

'That's a bit beneath your pay grade.' Fielding's Scottish accent was the honey-seductive rather than the half-brick aggressive sort.

'I happened to recognise the teenager who was reporting.

38

I've actually met his mother. I thought it would save time if I dealt with it since the front counter was sticking to the letter of twenty-four hours.'

Fielding paused with the zip halfway over her small bosom. She frowned, olive skin crinkling into a relief map of shallow furrows and ridges. 'That's because he's been trained to follow protocols. Protocols that are put in place so detectives like us don't waste our time on folk having a spur-of-the-moment night out.'

Paula shoved a second leg into the suit, annoyed by her trouser leg rucking up around the knee. 'I've always understood that when there's a child or a vulnerable adult left at risk by a disappearance, we take action straight away.' According to the grapevine, Fielding was a mother. She should get it.

Fielding grunted. 'Been a while since you've been at the sharp end, McIntyre. Major Incident Team's spoiled you.' She pulled a face. 'In an ideal world, you'd be right. But we're not in an ideal world. Cuts and redundancies have fucked us all up.' She frowned again, brown eyes glaring at Paula. 'We haven't got the bodies to jump in early on mispers. We leave that to uniforms. I need you here. Not fucking about on the tail of somebody who's probably chosen not to be where they're expected to be.' She held up a hand to shut Paula up before she could speak. 'I know. The reasons for those choices are usually fucking horrible. But we're not social workers.'

'Ma'am.' Angered but not chastened, Paula turned away and finished zipping herself into the suit. OK, Fielding had a point, but that didn't mean Paula had to hang up her humanity at the door. She'd check Bev's movements on her own time. Somehow. Still facing away from Fielding, who had the kind of physical presence that filled more space than seemed possible, she dragged the conversation away from her supposed transgression. 'So what are we looking at here?'

'Junkie squatters have been using one of the houses on and off for a few months now. They were at some music festival near Sheffield at the weekend. They got back a couple of hours ago and found the body of a woman in the middle of the living room.' Her voice muffled as she bent to pull on the blue plastic shoe covers. 'I suppose we should be grateful they phoned us instead of doing a runner.'

'Did they recognise her?'

'They say not.'

Paula raised the hood to cover her hair and pulled on the chilly blue nitrile gloves. 'Given that they phoned it in and didn't leg it, they're probably telling the truth. If they'd known her, they'd have been less likely to report it. People who live outside the mainstream tend not to trust us to do an unbiased job.'

Fielding cocked her head to acknowledge the comment. 'Good point. OK, let's do it.' She didn't mess around holding the door open for Paula, who caught it seconds before the spring slammed it shut. As they headed for the house, Fielding looked over her shoulder. 'I'd have liked a quieter start, so we could be clear about how it's going to work between us. I am aware this is your first assignment as a sergeant.'

'I worked as DCI Jordan's bagman on MIT, ma'am.' Paula was quick to stand up for herself. Fielding needed to understand she wasn't someone who could be pushed around. She needed to know she could count on Paula. 'I understand about having your back.'

Fielding's expression shifted, cold assessment giving way to acceptance. 'I'm proud of my team. We might not have the specialists you had at MIT, but we get more than our share of results. I've heard good things about you. Don't prove your friends wrong.'

It wasn't the most welcoming speech Paula had ever heard. But it was a start. And given how much she wanted her career to have a future, she'd make the most of it.

Just as soon as she'd found out what had happened to Bev McAndrew.

9

The carefully chosen furniture was gone now, carried off by the man and a van she'd picked from the small ads in the local paper. Actually, it had been two men and a van, and it had taken two trips to strip the barn of Michael and Lucy's possessions. Everything personal, Carol had packed in plastic crates from the DIY warehouse and stacked in the garage. All the rest was a memory, doubtless gracing the house of some lucky punter who was blissfully ignorant of its history.

The one part of the barn she'd left intact was the separate room that Michael had created at one end of the building. It was a studio-sized spare bedroom with its own toilet and shower, completely cut off from the remainder of the space by a new wall as thick as the traditional stone that protected the interior from the bitter weather. The reason for the sound insulation was that the room had doubled as Michael's office. Here, he wrote code and developed software for games and apps. Along one wall was a long table where an array of computers and games consoles still sat. As far as Carol was aware, this room was untainted by the presence of her brother's killer. When she came in here and closed the door, she could still feel as close to Michael as she had been when he was alive.

Back when she'd first come to Bradfield, they'd shared a loft conversion in the centre of the city. Outside their tall windows the city had hummed and throbbed, sparked and glittered. But inside, it had been a space where Michael had worked and they'd both lived. She remembered how she'd often opened the door to the rattle of gunfire or the electronica of a futuristic soundtrack. Once he realised she was home, Michael would always put headphones on, but he preferred to work with the sound effects blasting at him from all sides.

These days Carol had got into the habit of drinking her coffee and eating a bowl of cereal with tinned fruit in the room where she slept, music pouring out of the tall speakers that bookended the work table. Every morning, it was Michael's final playlist, the last music he'd been listening to while he worked. A mixture of Michael Nyman, Ludovico Einaudi and Brad Mehldau. Nothing she would ever have chosen. But she was growing comfortable with it.

She ate quickly, eager to return to the hard physical work that made introspection impossible. When she walked back into the barn, she was astonished to see a black-and-white Border collie crouching on the floor a couple of yards inside the door, pink tongue lolling between strong white teeth. Her heart leapt in her chest, a cascade of reproaches and terrors flooding her head. *How could you be so stupid? Leaving the door open, are you mad? This is how people die. This is how people have died. Dog means human, human means stranger, stranger means danger. Have you learned nothing, you stupid bitch?*

For a moment, she was frozen, incapable of figuring out

what to do. Then the old Carol Jordan kicked in. Slowly she stooped and put her bowl and mug on the floor. She knew where her tools were; she'd always had good recall. She retreated a little and moved sideways. Neither she nor the dog took their eyes off each other. Her left hand strayed outwards till her fingertips brushed the handle of the sledgehammer. As she gripped it, the dog's ears pricked up.

Carol swung the hammer up and held the shaft of the hammer across her body, hands apart. Then she launched herself towards the dog, roaring wordlessly at the top of her voice. Startled, the dog jumped up, backed off, then turned tail.

She followed it through the door, still raging at the blameless animal who was now, she saw, sitting at the heels of a strange man, peering round his legs with ears flat to its head. She skidded to a halt, not sure whether to feel foolish or frightened. He didn't look very frightening. She fell into her old habit of mentally creating an APB description in her head. A shade under six feet tall, medium build. Flat tweed cap over dark hair, silvering at the temples. Full beard, neatly trimmed. Narrow lips, fleshy nose, dark eyes nested with outdoor wrinkles. He wore a waxed jacket, open to reveal a brown suede waistcoat over a heavy cream cotton shirt with, God help her, a cravat at the neck. Toffee-coloured corduroys tucked into green wellies. He looked as if he should have a shotgun broken on his arm. A smile twitched at the corner of his mouth. 'You seem to have terrified my dog.' *Public school accent. The yap of the posh boys who don't know the price of milk.*

'I don't like trespassers.' Carol let the heavy hammer swing down till the head was resting on the ground.

'I do apologise. She's too curious for her own good.' This time, the smile was full on.

'The dog has an excuse, then. What's yours?' She didn't

care that she was being rude. After what had happened here, any local would cut her slack, confronted with a stranger on her own ground.

'I thought it was about time I came to introduce myself. I'm George Nicholas. I live in the house over the brow of the hill.' He turned and pointed behind him to his right.

'Would that be the bloody big house over the brow of the hill?'

He chuckled. 'I suppose you might call it that.'

'So you're the guy who owns all the land I can see apart from my own patch here?'

'Not quite all of it. But yes, most of it. And this is my dog, Jess.' He rumpled the fur on the dog's head. 'Say hello, Jess.' The dog sidled out from behind him and sat in front of Carol, raising a paw.

It was, she had to admit, a good routine. Completely dis-arming, if you were the sort of woman who allowed herself to be disarmed. Carol shook the dog's paw then crouched down to stroke its thick fur. 'You're a lovely girl, aren't you?' Then she stood up. 'I'm Carol Jordan,' she said, firmly avoiding a handshake by sticking her free hand in her trouser pocket.

'I know. I was at the funeral.' He looked pained. 'No reason why you would know that. I ... I was very fond of Michael and Lucy.'

'They never mentioned you.' It was a harsh response, but she didn't care. It was a lie too. Lucy had talked about going to dinner at the big house and Michael had teased her about abandoning her socialist principles.

'And why should they have,' he said easily. 'I gathered you didn't live in each other's pockets. But we were neigh-bours and we socialised from time to time and, for what it's worth, I liked them both very much. Like everyone around here, I was appalled by what happened to them.'

Carol cleared her throat. 'Yes. Well. It was appalling.'

Nicholas looked at his feet. 'I lost my wife three years ago. Drunk driver rammed her car on the motorway slip road.' He drew in a long breath and tilted his head back to stare at the sky. 'Obviously nothing like the scale of what happened here, but I do have some understanding of losing people one loves to sudden violent death.'

Carol tried to care, but she knew she didn't. Not really. She couldn't be bothered with people who tried to convince her they knew what she was going through. She was done with empathy. She'd watched Tony Hill being Mr Empathy for years and look where that had got her. Fuck empathy. Still. The obligations of good manners remained. 'I'm sorry,' she said.

'So am I.' He met her eyes again. This time, the smile was sorrowful. 'Anyway, I wanted to say hello. And to invite you to supper. Next week, perhaps? I've got a couple of friends from the village coming over on Tuesday, if you'd like to join us?'

Carol shook her head. 'I don't think so. I'm not very good company right now.'

He nodded, brisk in his understanding. 'Of course. Another time, perhaps.' There was an uncomfortable silence, then he glanced at the barn door. 'How are you getting on with . . .' His voice tailed off.

'I'm gutting it. Come and have a look.' Seeing his hesitation, she gave him a grim smile. 'It's all right, there's nothing left to see.'

He followed her inside to the hollow shell of the barn. Seeing it through his eyes, she understood the extent of what she'd done. Only the kitchen area remained unscathed. Everything else was stripped to the bare bones. The last job was the demolition of the gallery floor where Michael and Lucy had been murdered on their bed. She'd already ripped out the staircase. Today's task was to break down the supporting beam that held up the floor so she could set about the final stage of destroying it. She pointed to the sturdy timber. 'That's my next job.'

'You're not taking the whole beam out, are you?' He craned his head to follow the beam up to the A-frame joist that ran the width of the barn.

'If I take that out, the floor will start to collapse. It'll be much easier to break it down.'

Nicholas stared at her as if she was mad. 'If you take that out, your whole roof will collapse. That's a major structural beam. It's been there since the barn was built.'

'Are you sure?'

'I'm sure. I'm not an engineer, but I've been around old buildings all my life.' Suspicious, Carol followed his pointing finger as he outlined the structure of the hammer beam truss. 'If you don't believe me, get a structural engineer in to have a look. But please, don't get rid of it until you've taken advice.' He looked so distressed that she surrendered her instinctive mistrust of anyone trying to tell her what to do.

'OK,' she said. 'I'll work around it.' She crouched down again and ruffled the dog's fur. 'Looks like you did me a favour, Jess.'

'We're always happy to help,' Nicholas said. 'I'll be off now. No doubt I'll see you around?'

Carol made a noncommittal sound and followed him to the door. She stood and watched him leave her land and strike out across the rough pasture towards his home. It occurred to her that she'd been more friendly to the dog than to its owner. There was a time when that would have embarrassed her.

Not any more.

10

There was a terrible moment when Paula misunderstood what she was looking at. The shaggy blonde hair, the square shoulders, the legs that had always brought Anne Bancroft to mind; all markers for Carol Jordan. She'd never seen her naked except in fantasy, but her imagination was enough to blur the reality in front of her for a split second. Then she understood that the dead woman sprawled on the floor was not Carol Jordan. She was the wrong body shape. Too heavy in the hips and thighs, too squat in the torso. But it had been a head-swimming moment.

Fielding had caught it too, which wasn't going to help her respect for Paula. 'You all right, McIntyre? I'd have thought you'd be used to this by now.'

Paula coughed into her paper mask. 'With respect, ma'am, I never want to be used to it.'

Fielding turned away with a shrug. 'Fair enough.' She took a couple of steps towards the body, stooping for a closer look. 'He didn't want us to recognise her, that's for sure.

Look at that.' She pointed to the mash of flesh and bone that had been the woman's face. The naked body was a mass of bruises and abrasions. Paula had seen plenty of victims of violence, but she couldn't remember a body that had taken such a comprehensive beating.

Then another possibility flashed across her mind. She'd been slow to make the connection. But a description of this bludgeoned woman would also fit Bev McAndrew. Her breakfast coffee burned at the back of her throat and she side-stepped a CSI photographer for a better view. For the second time, relief made her weak in the knees. This wasn't Bev. Torin's mother was taller and slimmer, with bigger breasts. Whoever this woman was, she wasn't the missing pharmacist.

Paula looked around the room. It was a dismal place to die. The walls were stained with damp and mould and the floorboards were filthy with ground-in dirt. A sagging sofa faced a scarred coffee table whose missing leg had been replaced with a pile of crumbling bricks. Beer cans were piled at either end of the sofa and three ashtrays overflowed with cigarette butts and roaches. Empty blister packs of over-the-counter painkillers were scattered around among crushed boxes that had once held pizzas and burgers. The stench was a gruesome mixture of all the things she wished she'd never smelled.

Paula turned back to stare bleakly at the murdered woman. She longed for Tony Hill's facility for reading a crime scene and understanding something of the mind that had created it. But her skills were for interrogating the living, not the dead. She'd go through the motions at the crime scene, but she knew she'd always have to rely on other specialists for what it could reveal.

And right on cue, one of those specialists walked in on them. 'DCI Fielding. You have something for me, I've been told?' Paula recognised the warm Canadian drawl of Dr

Grisha Shatalov, the Home Office pathologist who generally worked Bradfield's homicides. He clapped Paula's shoulder softly as he passed her. 'Paula. Good to see you.'

Fielding stepped aside with what looked like relief on the little Paula could see of her face. 'She's all yours, Doc. Brutal, this one.'

'Taking someone's life? That's always brutal in my book.' Grisha hunkered down by the body. 'Even when it looks gentle.' He moved his hands over her body, gradually applying pressure and pausing to gauge temperature and rigor.

'Did she die here?' Fielding's question was brusque. It sounded to Paula as though her reputation for impatience was well-founded. There was clearly no place here for the exchange of pleasantries she'd always seen between Carol and Grisha. Straight to business and no messing around, that seemed to be Fielding's style. Like a lot of women in senior positions, she set out her stall to out-tough the men.

Grisha glanced over his shoulder. 'I'd say so. You've got blood spatter from the head wound, you've got lividity that looks to me like she hasn't been moved post-mortem. Chances are high she was still alive when he brought her here.' He looked up at the photographer. 'Are you done here? Can I move her?'

'She's all yours, mate.' The cameraman stepped away and left them to it.

Grisha carefully tilted the victim's head to one side. 'Look, here. You see this?' He pointed to a depression in the skull, blonde hair turned dark and matted with a mixture of blood and brain matter. 'A blow to the head with something long, rounded and heavy. A baseball bat or a metal pipe. I'll have a better idea once I get her to the lab. If nothing else had happened to her, chances are that would have killed her. But he made sure by giving her a good kicking.' He gestured at the bruises on her torso. 'Large, irregular rounded shapes, it's a classic bruise from a kick. And the colour, red shading towards purple. That tells us she was still alive when he gave kicking her to death his best shot.' He sat on his heels and considered. 'Either he's smart or he got lucky.' He paused expectantly.

'I've not got time for twenty questions,' Fielding groused. 'What do you mean?'

'He kicked her. He kept on kicking her. He didn't stamp on her. It would have been better for you if he had. You might have got a sole pattern from his boots.'

'Bastard.' Fielding sounded disgusted. 'Boots, not shoes?' Her face gave nothing away, but she folded her arms across her chest as if to defend herself from the violence.

'Given the extent of the damage – her face is wrecked, Fielding, look at it – my best guess would be steel toecaps. And that tends to boots rather than shoes.' Grisha pointed to her left ankle. 'Check out those abrasions. Looks like a restraint tell-tale to me. A shackle of some description. But one with a straight edge. Maybe designed for pipework rather than humans. That's why it's torn the skin the way it has. I'll check her wrists when I get her on the table.'

Before Fielding could say more, they were interrupted by another white suit. 'Guv, I thought you'd want to know. It looks like we've found her clothes and her bag. Stuffed behind the bath.'

'Good work, Hussain. Bag the clothes and get them straight to the lab. Paula, you go and have a look at the contents when we're done here. You're a woman, you'll have a better sense of what's what than these hairy-arsed lads.'

Paula bit her tongue. Only because she was glad to have first crack at the victim's possessions. But if Fielding thought she could defuse her by putting her in the little woman box, she was going to have another think coming. 'Ma'am,' she said.

'What about time of death?' Fielding was already on to the next thing.

Grisha took hold of the woman and gently rolled her on to her stomach. 'Let's see what she has to tell us.' He opened the plastic satchel he always brought to crime scenes and took out a thermometer. He parted her legs slightly so he could take a rectal temperature reading. Then Paula heard his breath hiss over his teeth. 'Jesus Christ,' he said. Grisha seldom showed any emotion, but the disgust was obvious in his tone.

'What is it?' Fielding demanded.

Grisha bent forward and stared intently between the woman's legs. He reached out gingerly with one finger. 'I thought I'd seen everything.' His voice was so quiet Paula could barely hear him.

'What is it, Grisha?' she asked, laying a hand on his shoulder.

He shook his head. 'It looks like he's superglued her labia together.'

11

By late morning, Marie had a list of questions for Rob Morrison. In her experience, there was no point in holding back out of a misplaced sense of politeness. She needed answers so she could make a start on the strategic developments she'd been hired to initiate and see through. Worrying whether Rob would take her enquiries as subtle criticisms wasn't helpful. If his finer feelings were going to stand in the way of progress, he'd better develop a thicker skin, she thought. And quickly.

So she double-checked the handwritten list she'd made – always better to write down a list of questions; they had a tendency to stick in the mind that way and they were less likely to fall through the cracks during the discussion – and bustled across the open-plan area to Rob's office.

Marie scanned the room as she went, taking note of who had their head down, talking on the phone or frowning at their screen, and who was staring into space or leaning back in their chair chatting to the person in the next carrel. She wasn't about to start anything as crude as a time-and-motion study any time soon, but it was never too soon to begin gathering impressions of the staff. Gareth, for example. He might well be one of the most productive employees, but right now he was paying no attention to work. He was half-turned away from his screen, chatting to a smug-looking bloke in a pink shirt and khaki chinos, hair immaculately groomed. Even from across the room she could make out the Ralph Lauren Polo logo. She'd have put money on him reeking of aftershave or cologne. She hadn't noticed him earlier when she'd been introduced to the floor, and she thought she would have if he'd been there. She knew his type and she didn't like it.

Dismissing him from her mind, she walked through Rob's open door to find him at his computer, mouse clicking as furiously as if he was in the throes of some annoying computer game. 'Have you got a minute?' she asked.

He immediately stopped what he was doing and before she could possibly have seen his screen, he closed the window he was working in. 'Sure. Is there a problem?'

'I need to go through some of our procedures,' Marie said, drawing a chair up at right angles to his desk. 'I want to be clear how we're doing things at present so I can work out where we can make strategic improvements.'

He nodded enthusiastically, rubbing his chin then tugging his earlobe. He was, she realised, one of those people who can't stop touching their face. It made her want to avoid touching anything he'd touched. He smoothed one eyebrow and scratched the side of his nose. 'Makes perfect sense,' he said.

They had barely made a start when Ralph Lauren Man swaggered into the room. He let his eyes slide over Marie, lingering on her breasts and her legs before turning his attention to Rob. 'Are you up for tonight?' he said, his tone almost accusatory rather than inviting.

Rob gave him what appeared to be a warning frown. 'Nige, I'd like you to meet Marie Mather, our new Director of Marketing. Marie, this is Nigel Dean. He's one of the boffins from upstairs. Software development for our data-gathering systems.'

Nigel inclined his head towards her. 'We're Big Brother,' he said. 'The one that is watching you, that is, not the one that you watch on your telly. We manage data for everything from your local supermarket to speed cameras to mobile phone networks. I could track you from your front door to the office without your knowing.'

Rob laughed nervously. 'Pay no attention to him, he likes to wind us all up, does Nige.'

Creep, she thought. 'I'll bear that in mind,' she said mildly, not making it clear which one she was responding to.

'I was just making sure Rob's coming along tonight. A bunch of us are going out to celebrate landing a tasty new contract. We're going to Honeypots, do you know it?'

You didn't have to be a lad about town to be aware of Honeypots, Bradfield's biggest and brashest lap-dancing club. Marie would rather have nailed her hand to the wall than spend an evening there. Not for the first time, she counted her blessings and was grateful for her Marco. 'I never go out on a school night,' she said.

Nigel raised one side of his mouth in a sneer. 'You ladies and your beauty sleep. Another time, maybe. On a Friday?'

Marie gave her sweetest smile. 'I'll bring my husband. He likes a good laugh.' She gathered her papers and stood up. 'Rob, perhaps we could finish this when you're free?'

Twat, she thought as she marched back to her office. It didn't seem to matter where you worked, you couldn't escape them. *More's the pity.*

12

The mobile incident room was bedlam with the volume turned down. A constant stream of police officers, CSIs and civilian support staff tramped in and out, covering all the bases from grim and grumpy to crass and chirpy. One look told Paula it was the worst possible place to examine evidence that might end up as a key plank in a court case. Clearing it first with Fielding, she left the crime scene and headed back to Skenfrith Street to find a quiet corner. And if she was honest, she wanted to put some distance between herself and the dead woman.

During her years with Carol Jordan's Major Incident Team, Paula had confronted a wide range of the hideous things human beings could do to one another. The things she'd seen had disturbed her nights and her days, but she'd always managed to put them in a box in her head where they couldn't contaminate the rest of her life. She'd known what it was to be at risk herself, and she'd lost colleagues to the job. It was only by chance that she'd escaped the act of violence that had destroyed Chris Devine's future during the hunt for Jacko Vance.

All of this horror she'd got through. Maybe a few extra drinks on the bad nights, a spike in her cigarette consumption on the bad days. Still, she'd absorbed the pain, dealt with the anger. Deep down, she'd learned to live with it. But today's victim had messed with her head. There was no escaping that. The brutal beating on its own would have been hard to stomach, but she'd have got past that without too much trouble. The other thing – she could hardly bear to articulate the act, even in her head – was somehow infinitely worse. It was as if her killer wanted to deny her everything that made her who she was. Wrecked face, ruined body, not even any use for sex. He'd rendered her utterly worthless. It spoke of a contempt that chilled Paula's heart. This, she suspected, was a murderer who wasn't going to stop at one.

The rest of the team would be gossiping and speculating about it. She knew what cops were like. And for a little while she wanted not to be part of that. Putting together a profile of the victim based on the contents of her bag would be a good enough excuse.

In the unfamiliar territory of her new base, she managed to find the canteen and set herself up with coffee and the comfort of Jaffa Cakes. And because the canteen staff always knew what was what, she acquired directions to a small meeting room on the fourth floor where nothing was scheduled for the rest of the day.

Gloved and masked, her coffee and biscuits on a separate table, she finally addressed the dead woman's life. The bag was businesslike – black leather, worn in but not scuffed, decent quality and capacious. It looked a bit like a scaled-down briefcase, with its neat compartments and pockets. Methodically, Paula emptied the contents on to the table, not pausing to study anything till she was sure the bag was completely empty. She was impressed with the relative absence of crap and made a mental note to clear her own bag of the accumulated detritus of everyday living.

She went with the obviously female stuff first. Lipstick, mascara, blusher, all own-brand from a chain chemist. Plastic folding comb with a narrow mirror in the handle. So, someone who cared about how she looked but didn't make a fetish of it.

Pack of tissues, only a couple left. A small tin that had once held sweets but now contained four compact tampons. A couple of condoms in a plastic pouch. Blister pack of birth control pills, three remaining. So, almost certainly straight, probably single. If you were in a relationship, you generally left those things at home, in the bathroom or the bedside-table drawer. You weren't going to spend the night in another bed on the spur of the moment.

Blister pack of strong painkillers. Paula frowned. She didn't think you could get these off prescription. When she'd torn a muscle in her calf a few months before and she'd been in excruciating pain for a couple of days, Elinor had sneaked her a couple from the hospital, swearing her to secrecy. Paula had teased her about it. 'Is one of your post-op patients on paracetamol tonight, then?' Elinor had confessed that they were samples from a pharmaceutical rep.

'All doctors have a drawer stuffed with freebies,' she said. 'You'd think we'd know better, but we self-medicate like mad.'

Was the victim a doctor? Or someone who had a problem with pain? Paula filed the question away for now and returned to the bag's contents. Three pens; one from a hotel, one from a stationery supply chain, one from an animal charity. A bunch of keys – a Fiat car key, two Yales, two mortises. House, car, office? House, car, somebody else's house? No way of telling yet. A couple of crumpled receipts from a Freshco Express in Harriestown revealed a taste for pepperoni pizza, chicken tikka pies and low-fat strawberry yoghurt.

The iPhone would be the treasure trove. Paula woke it from its slumber. The screen saver was a fluffy tortoiseshell cat lying on its back. When she tried to open the screen, it demanded a password. That meant the phone would have to go off to the technical team, where one of the geeks would unlock its mysteries eventually. Not like on MIT, where their own IT specialist Stacey Chen was always on tap. Stacey would have coaxed every last morsel of data from the phone in record time, speeding the investigation on its way. But here in her brave new world, Paula's evidence would have to join the queue. No rush jobs here; the budget wouldn't take the strain. Frustrated, she wrote a label for the phone and bagged it separately.

All that remained was a slim metal case and a fat wallet. She flicked open the case to reveal a short stack of business cards. Nadia Wilkowa was apparently the North West Area Representative for Bartis Health. There was a web address as well as a mobile number and email address for Nadia. Paula took out her phone and rang the number. The bagged iPhone did a jittering shimmy across the table before the voicemail cut in. 'Hi, this is Nadia Wilkowa.' There was a faint East European accent, but it had been almost completely painted over by polite Bradfield. 'I'm sorry I can't talk to you right now, but please leave a message and I'll return your call as soon as I can.' A welcome confirmation.

Paula flipped open the wallet. Three credit cards in the name of Nadzieja Wilkowa; loyalty cards for Freshco, the Co-op and a fashion store group; a book of first-class stamps with two remaining; a tight bundle of receipts and forty pounds in cash. No photographs, no convenient address. She took a quick pass through the receipts. Car parking, petrol, sandwich shops, fast-food outlets and a couple of restaurant bills. She'd pass them on to the officer in charge of doling out assignments to the team. Someone else could go through them in more detail, preferably after they'd got her diary off her phone.

And that was it. It was all very well to live an orderly life, but it didn't help detectives like Paula when you ended up dead. What they really needed was a home address. She opened the internet browser on her phone and navigated to Bartis Health's home page. Their offices were located in a town in Leicestershire she'd never heard of. Their business model appeared to be based on producing cheap generic versions of drugs whose patents had expired. Plenty of uptake but tight margins, Paula suspected.

She called the number on the contact page. The woman who answered the phone was rightly suspicious of her request for information but agreed to call back and ask to be connected to the extension perched on a corner table. Paula had little confidence in the capabilities of the system, but she was happy to be proved wrong less than five minutes later. 'Why are you asking about Nadia? Has something happened? Surely she's not in any kind of trouble,' the woman asked as soon as they were connected.

'Do you know Nadia well?' Paula was careful with her tense.

'I wouldn't say well. I've met her a few times. She's a very friendly, open sort of person. And they think very highly of her here. But what's happened? Has she been in an accident back home?'

'Back home?'

'In Poland. She emailed ... let me see, it must be three weeks ago? Anyway, she said her mother had been diagnosed with stage three breast cancer and she asked if she could have compassionate leave to go home and be with her mother for the surgery. Because her mother's on her own now, with her dad being dead and her sister in America. It was inconvenient, but you don't want to lose somebody that's as good at her job as Nadia, so the boss said yes, she could have a month.' The woman stopped for breath.

Baffled, Paula said, 'You're sure about that?'

'I opened the email myself,' the woman said. 'And I had to email her only last week with a query about a customer's repeat order. She answered me the same day. She said her mum was making a slow recovery but she'd be back next week.'

It made no sense. Had Nadia made an unscheduled early return? Or had her killer sent the emails, pretending to be her, covering up the fact that she'd never left Bradfield? Was it an elaborate sham, a scam to cover Nadia's disappearance? But the woman was talking again, cutting through Paula's racing thoughts. 'So has something happened to Nadia? Is that why you're calling?'

Paula closed her eyes and wished she'd asked someone else to make this call. 'I'm very sorry to have to tell you that Nadia has died in suspicious circumstances.' It was true without being anywhere near the whole truth.

A moment's silence. 'In Poland?'

'No. Here in Bradfield.'

'I don't understand.'

'We're still making inquiries,' Paula said, stalling.

'That's terrible,' the woman said, her voice faint. 'I can't believe it. Nadia? What happened?'

'I'm afraid I can't go into details. But we need help. We don't have any addresses for her. Home or work. Or a next of kin. I was hoping you might have access to that information?'

'Let me get Nadia's personnel file on the screen,' the

woman said. 'She worked from home, so there's no office as such.' One less place to take apart looking for answers to the questions raised by Nadia's death.

Ten minutes later, Paula had every scrap of information Bartis Health knew about Nadia. There wasn't much, but it was a start. She had an address in the Harriestown district. She also knew that Nadzieja Wilkowa was twenty-six years old and had worked for Bartis for eighteen months. She had a degree in pharmacology from the university in Poznan and spoke excellent English. She visited head office every two or three months. Her territory covered the North of England and she had been one of the company's most successful sales reps. The next of kin she'd given was her mother, with an address in Leszno. A place Paula had never heard of, let alone been able to point to it on a map. She wasn't sure of the process involved in informing overseas next of kin, but she knew there would be one. At least that was one death knock she wouldn't have to deal with herself. Or the interview to ascertain whether Nadia had been in Poland recently.

Paula checked her watch. What she should do now was pass on Nadia's phone to the techies, scoop up a couple of junior detectives and turn over her flat in a bid to find how her life intersected with her killer. But she was conscious of the promise she'd made to Torin McAndrew and that she'd done nothing to fulfil it. She had a few hours before the boy would be texting her. Nadia was dead, and Torin was very much alive.

In one sense, it was no contest. But Paula had been drilled by Carol Jordan that her duty was to speak for the dead. And as well as speaking for the dead, she also had a responsibility to the living. A killer was walking free and it was her job to find him before he killed someone else. What could be more important than that?

13

Bev felt as if she was swimming upwards through something thick and heavy. Not heavy like mud. More like milkshake or emulsion paint. Her limbs felt weighted down, the world impenetrably black. It slowly dawned on her that her eyes were closed. But when she opened them, nothing changed. Her head throbbed when she moved it, but she forced herself to turn it back and forth, yet still there was absolutely nothing to be seen. The thought drifted through her muzzy brain that this must be what a black hole was like. Black, black and more black beyond that.

Slowly the wooziness lifted, enough for her to understand that this darkness was something to fear, not simply wonder at. As the fog of unconsciousness dispersed Bev tried to make sense of where she was and what had happened to her. Her head hurt and there was a sickly sweet taste at the back of her throat. The last thing she remembered was opening the boot of her hatchback to stow a couple of bags of groceries she'd picked up on the way home. After that, nothing. A blank. A terrifying blank.

She had no way of knowing how long she'd been unconscious. Minutes? No, surely more than minutes. Wherever
she was, it wasn't the car park at Freshco. Hours, then? How
many hours? What was Torin thinking? Was he afraid? Was
he angry with her? Did he think she'd abandoned him and
gone off to have fun without letting him know? What
would he do without her? Would he raise the alarm or
would he be too scared of what might happen to him without her? The thoughts scampered in her head like a hamster
on a wheel. Christ, she had to get a grip.

'OK. Don't think about Torin. Put it behind you and move
on.' She said the words aloud then wished she hadn't.
Wherever she was, the acoustic was dead, her voice flat and
muffled. Still determined to keep her fear at arm's length,
Bev decided it would make sense to discover the limits of
her location. She was sitting down, on a smooth surface.
That realisation led to another. She wasn't wearing her
trousers, socks or shoes any more. Her hand crept down her
body. She was wearing her own bra, but the lower underwear definitely wasn't hers. Skimpy lacy panties were not
her style. Lace made her itch, and she liked loose-fitting
cotton against her skin. She refused to think about what that
meant.

It was just flesh, when you got right down to it. She'd had
no knowledge, no emotional engagement with anything
that had happened while she was unconscious. In a sense,
she told herself, it was no more a violation than any surgical
procedure carried out under general anaesthetic. Most
people would freak out if they had to witness what was
done to their bodies on the operating table. Ignorance
wasn't only bliss, it was what allowed them to be grateful for
the surgeon's knife. Bev could manage ignorance, she was
pretty sure of that.

She explored the surface she was sitting on. Smooth, cool

but not cold. When she moved her leg, it was warm from where her flesh had been resting. She extended her arms slowly, but couldn't straighten them. Then she slid down till her feet hit the far end of her prison. She moved one foot around and realised there was a sort of step there. Finally, she returned to a sitting position. There were a few inches between her head and the immovable top of what she had to admit to herself was a box. A metre wide, a metre and a half long and a little over a metre high. Plastic lined. A softer plastic seam round the top that made it light-tight, and presumably airtight too. With what felt like a step at one end. The only thing she could think of that fitted the description was a chest freezer.

She was locked inside a chest freezer.

Bev wasn't someone who panicked easily, but realising where she was set her heart pounding in terror. If the person who had put her here wanted to kill her, all they had to do was flick a switch and let hypothermia do the job for them.

Or just wait till the air ran out.

14

The middle of the afternoon wasn't the best time to get the undivided attention of anyone in the pharmacy at Bradfield Cross Hospital. Especially on a day when they were short a member of staff. But then, from what Paula had gathered from Dr Elinor Blessing and from Bev herself, there wasn't a spell during the working day when the pharmacists and their assistants weren't run off their feet. The accurate filling of hospital prescriptions was a process that never let up. Sometimes Paula thought the advancement of human learning came down to nothing except more sophisticated ways not to feel the pain.

Bev's deputy, Dan Birchall, looked like a member of a minor boy band run to seed. The lineaments of a handsome young man lurked beneath the slack fleshiness of his face, the neatly trimmed beard unable to disguise the jowls forming along his jawline. He still moved with a certain grace, almost dancing between the shelves and cabinets. But it was a dance whose tempo was starting to slip and whose steps looked a little more desperate with every passing year. 'You're Dr Blessing's lady, aren't you?' was his response when Paula introduced herself. It wasn't a line that endeared him to her.

'I'm looking into the whereabouts of your chief pharmacist, Ms McAndrew.' Paula smiled. There was no mileage in anything other than working the witness for whatever he might know. 'Her son has reported her missing.'

Dan rolled his eyes. 'Right,' he said, stretching the word as far as it would go. 'Well, suddenly, something makes sense. We've been at sixes and sevens all day, wondering what was up with Bev. Because Bev would never just not show. Totally not her style.'

Paula pulled up a lab stool and sat down, indicating he should do the same. But he remained on his feet, leaning against the counter with ankles crossed and arms folded. It made her wonder what he had to hide. If she'd been Tony Hill, no doubt she'd have worked it out already. But her gift was for interrogation; she was accustomed to taking the long way round. 'So you've had no communication from her?'

He shook his head. 'Not a word. Not a text, not an email, not a message. At first, I assumed she'd been caught up in traffic. Except Bev somehow always manages not to get caught up in traffic.' He rolled his eyes again. 'That's Bev. So organised she listens to the travel news with breakfast. But once it got to half past nine, I thought there was no way Bev would be an hour late without calling in. So I tried her home number and her mobile. I got the answering machine and the voicemail.' He spread his hands. 'What else could I do?'

'Did it occur to you to go round and check she was OK?'

He gave her a peevish look. 'Why would I do that? It's not like she lives alone. If anything had happened to her, Torin the Wonder Boy could have called for help. Besides—' He waved impatiently at the bustle in the dispensary. 'Look at this place. We were already one down. I couldn't walk away from the rest of the team. We only took half an hour each for lunch as it was.' He seemed more irritated than worried. Paula hoped that whatever had happened to Bev wasn't the kind of thing that would make his annoyance come back to haunt him.

'I appreciate that. You've got patients to consider.'

Dan pounced on the get-out. 'Exactly. People rely on us.'

'So, when did you last see Bev?'

'Yesterday. A bit after half past five. She was through in the office.' He pointed to a cubicle tucked away in the far corner. 'I was going for a birthday drink with Bob Symes, one of the porters. I asked her if she fancied joining us, but she said she had some paperwork to wrap up and then she had to go to Freshco on the way home. So I left her to it.'

'Was there anybody else still working?'

'Well, the duty pharmacist, obviously. She comes in at five and she's on till half past midnight. The night-duty dispenser does midnight till eight thirty.' He flapped a hand dismissively. 'But you won't be interested in the hell that is our staffing roster.'

Paula made a note on her pad. 'I'll need the details of the duty pharmacist.'

Dan nodded. 'No problem. Vahni Bhat, that's her name. I'll give you her numbers when we're done. She'll be in tonight, if you want to see her.'

'Thanks.' She looked around. Two young women and an older man were focused on what they were doing, paying no attention to her and Dan. Paula didn't often find herself in a workplace where the staff were so overwhelmed with their own tasks that they ignored a police inquiry in their midst. 'Was Bev particularly close to anyone here at work?'

Dan scratched his beard and frowned, his eyes sliding

away from hers. 'I wouldn't have said so. Don't get me wrong, we're good enough mates here. And heaven knows, I've worked with Bev for a million years. But we don't live in each other's pockets.' Still he wasn't meeting her eyes, using the pretext of keeping an eye on his colleagues to avoid her. 'Come the end of the working day, we all do our own thing. Bev was very family orientated. Torin came first with her.' A little edge there, she noted. Had Dan wanted Bev to be more interested in him? Or had there once been something more than friendship between them? It was hard to tell. Paula thought she might run that one past Elinor and see whether there had been any gossip.

'You called him Torin the Wonder Boy. What's that about, Dan?' Paula kept her tone light, almost teasing.

One corner of his mouth twisted downwards in a rueful grimace. 'I tease her because she's always going on about how great he is. I've got a kid of my own, Becky, but I don't make out she's the smartest, the prettiest, the most talented. The way Bev speaks about Torin, you'd think nobody ever had a kid before. That's all.' He shrugged and smiled, sharing a look of complicity with her. 'No big deal.'

'He knew enough to report her missing.' Paula looked around the room. 'So as far as you're aware, Bev had no plans for yesterday evening?'

'What she said to me was, Freshco and then home.'

'Would she have said if she'd had plans?'

Another shrug. 'She'd sometimes say if she was going to a movie or the football with Torin or something like that. Or if there was something on the telly she was looking forward to. But it wasn't like she'd routinely tell me what she was planning on doing. To be perfectly honest, it's always full on in here. You have to concentrate. It's not like being on a factory production line, where you can chat about all sorts while you work. Here, if we screw up, people get more sick.

69

Sometimes they can die. So we don't go in for much casual chit-chat.'

'Do you know if she was seeing anybody?'

'If she was, none of us knew anything about it. Look, you live with Dr Blessing. You must know what it's like. A hospital is a rumour factory. And this place is gossip central.'

'I thought you didn't have time for chit-chat?' Paula took the sting out of the barb with a teasing tone and a knowing smile.

'Not when we're dispensing. But at the counter, when they drop off and pick up, that's where all the info passes back and forth. And I haven't heard a whisper about Bev seeing anyone. After the divorce, she went out with a couple of blokes, but both times she felt like it was going nowhere so she knocked it on the head. She's been on her own for a couple of years now, as far as anybody here knows.' All at once it seemed he was protesting too much.

'And you? You went for a drink with Bob the porter? Did you see Bev later?'

Dan became very interested in the contents of the shelves next to him. 'Actually, in the end I didn't go. I wasn't in the mood. I went for a drink on my own on the way home.'

'Do you remember where?'

'The Bertie.'

'You mean the Prince Albert?' Paula knew the place. It was a busy barn of a pub on the edge of the city centre, always packed because of its cheap beer.

He nodded. 'That's the one.'

'Not exactly a place for a quiet drink.'

He made a face. 'Nobody bothers you, it's too rammed for people to strike up casual conversations. I like it when I want to be alone in a crowd.'

And nobody remembers whether you were there or not. Another avenue closed off. 'Had Bev fallen out with anybody that you know of? Any colleagues? Other staff? Patients? Somebody outside of work.'

Dan looked blank. 'She never said anything. I mean, we all get into a bit of a ruck at the counter from time to time. The punters aren't always sweet reason on a stick. But Bev's generally pretty good at calming things down. She doesn't provoke people.' He gave a wry smile. 'Not like me. I'm not good at taking their crap. Sometimes I just walk away, and that's when Bev steps up to the plate and pours oil on the troubled waters.'

'So, no boyfriend, no enemies. Did she seem at all uneasy lately? Rattled, frightened?'

Again he scratched his beard. 'Not her style. Bev's not a scaredy cat. I'd say the only thing she'd be scared of would be something happening to Torin. And nothing's happened to him, has it? Not from what you were saying.'

Apart from mislaying his mother. 'If I'd said to you last night that Bev would go missing, is there any part of you that would have thought, "Yeah, that makes sense".'

Without hesitation, Dan shook his head. 'No. Bev's totally reliable, totally organised. If she was going to do a runner, she'd do it in such a way that nobody would notice it was a runner until she was history.'

Paula could think of nothing more to ask Dan. Though she had a feeling there might be more later. She stood up and fished her card out of her pocket. 'Text me Vahni Bhat's number, would you? And let me know if anything occurs to you. Anything unusual, or anything Bev said. We're treating this seriously, Dan.'

'OK. Tell Torin we're thinking of him.'

That would be the easy part, Paula thought, checking her watch. She'd sent a pair of DCs to Nadia Wilkowa's flat, promising to join them there. Unless Nadia had lived in a monastic cell with no possessions, they'd still be there, poking through her underwear drawer and kitchen cup-boards. Which gave her a small window of opportunity to conclude some more unorthodox arrangements.

She sent a quick text to Elinor, asking for five minutes in the fifth-floor coffee shop that she knew was near the wards where her partner would be dealing with post-op patients from the morning. Paula was halfway through a mug of hot chocolate when Elinor appeared, businesslike in white coat and stethoscope. Time had done nothing to diminish the physical jolt of pleasure Paula still felt whenever they were reunited. Even if only a few hours had passed. It was crazy, it was adolescent, but she didn't care. When she'd met Elinor, her life hadn't held much joy. Now, the reason for getting up in the morning overwhelmed any argument on that score.

Elinor made straight for Paula's table, missing out a visit to the coffee counter. She leaned over and kissed her on the lips as she sat down. 'Not that it isn't always a delight to see you, but I genuinely only have five minutes,' she said.

Paula held up both hands in a gesture of apology. 'Sorry. I'm tight for time too. But it's important.'

'Give me the ten second version.' Elinor reached for the mug and took a swig, shivering with pleasure. 'Sugar rush, I love it.'

'Torin McAndrew reported his mother missing this morning. She's not in work, nobody's heard from her and—'

'Bev's missing?' Elinor interrupted.

'Apparently.'

'But she wouldn't leave Torin. Paula, something serious must have happened. Have you checked the hospitals?'

'First thing I did. And the custody records. She's not been in an accident and she's not been arrested. Believe me, I'm taking an interest.'

Elinor clapped her hand over her mouth. She knew only

too well the sort of cases Paula generally ended up dealing with. Anyone would be horrified at the thought of a friend ending up at the heart of one of those. 'What can I do?'

'Who's her best mate?'

'Probably Dan.' Elinor answered without hesitation. 'He's straight, but he's so camp he might as well be a gay man. There was a moment a couple of years ago where it nearly spilled over into more than just good friends. But they both backed off. She didn't want to risk his marriage and really, neither did he.'

'Was it mutual, the backing off?'

Elinor paused, thinking. 'To the best of my recollection. I've been in their company a few times since and I didn't sense any awkwardness between them.' She gave Paula a sceptical look. 'You're not thinking Dan's got anything to do with Bev going missing, are you?'

'I'm not going to apologise for covering all the bases, Elinor. But there's something a lot more pressing than what kind of guy Dan is. Here's the thing. I can't leave Torin home alone. I know he stayed there last night without Bev, but he didn't really believe she'd be out all night. He doesn't have any family near at hand. And I don't want social services taking him into emergency care.'

'You want him to come and stay at ours?'

Paula couldn't help smiling. 'This is why I love you,' she said. 'You have such a generous heart.'

'Obviously. I chose you.' Elinor tapped Paula's hand with a finger. 'How do we do this?'

'He's going to text me after school. Can I send him over here? Can you find him a quiet corner where he can do his homework till you're ready to leave? I don't want him going to a friend's house and letting slip that his mum's disappeared and he's staying with a couple of big old lezzas he hardly knows.'

Elinor thought for a moment. 'Sure, I'll come up with something. And you? What about you? When will you be home?'

Paula sighed and shook her head. 'I'm not sure. We caught a murder this morning. We've barely got started.'

'Just as well I'm an easy-going soul,' Elinor said.

'I know. Sometimes I think I behave like the worst of my male colleagues. I'm sorry.'

'The difference is, you know you're doing it. And I get to stake out the moral high ground.' Elinor grinned. 'It's OK, Paula. We both pay the price of caring about what we do. I'd love you less if you took your job less seriously. What's the new boss like?'

'Too soon to know. But she's not Carol Jordan, that's for sure.'

'That's not exactly informative.'

Paula picked up her bag. 'Later. You have patients, I have my back to cover.' She stood up, put a hand on Elinor's shoulder and kissed the top of her head. 'I'll send Torin over. See you when I see you.'

15

The rain had sloped out of a steel sky all day, relentless and depressing. He'd noticed it only intermittently, there being no window in his eyeline at work. Rain would have been a nuisance when he'd been waiting for the last two. There hadn't been anywhere unobtrusive to shelter. But this time, there was no problem. On the other side of the street from Tellit Communications HQ was a row of fast-food outlets. Subway, McDonald's, an indie café that promised the best roast in Bradfield. As if. He'd started off in McDonald's with a cheeseburger and made it last half an hour. Next, he stretched a chocolate chip cookie and a Diet Coke to forty minutes. Where the hell was the woman? Didn't she have a home to go to?

The irony of that last thought forced him to stifle a giggle. The home he was planning for her was very different from the one she'd be going back to tonight. If she played her cards right, if she made him happy, she could have a new life as well as a new home. If not, she could pay someone else's debt and join the others. His first one and the one before that, the one who should have been his one and only. Of course, he knew he might not need this latest one. But chance had dropped her in his path and he wasn't a man who failed to answer when opportunity knocked. He had a feeling the one he had now wasn't going to measure up and it was as well to be prepared for that eventuality.

He crumpled his napkin into a ball and stood up, about to move on to the café when he spotted her, tripping down the hallway from the bank of lifts. She crossed the foyer with an unexpected spring in her step. Most people dragged themselves wearily out of the office after a long day, but this one had a bounce to her. That was what had caught his eye in the first place, before he even registered she was a perfect fit. She looked like someone who was heading towards something worth waiting for. He made a point of storing that lustrous image away in his memory. That was what she'd have to replicate for him, if she was going to have any chance of survival.

She paused on the threshold, opening a folding umbrella. He pushed through the customers to the door, eyes fixed on his target, heedless of the complaints of the ones who'd been in his way. They were irrelevant. All that mattered was keeping her in view. By the time he made it on to the street, she was halfway to the corner. He moved a little faster, closing the gap, but careful not to get too close. He pulled his beanie hat further down over his forehead, tucked his chin into his scarf and checked the glasses with their clear lenses were still in place. It was amazing how much difference small things made to a man's appearance. People noticed the externals, not the essentials. Not that he was planning on doing anything that would get him noticed. But there were closed-circuit cameras everywhere in the city centre. He wasn't taking any chances.

She turned left at the end of the street, into the early evening bustle of Bellwether Square. Again, he speeded up, not wanting to lose her in the crowd. She wasn't tall and he worried that he might lose sight of her. It wouldn't wreck his plans, not in the long term. But it would be an inconvenience and he hated inconvenience. He needed to find out where she lived and he didn't want to waste another evening on something so basic.

She veered off to where the tramlines formed one side of the square and walked up the ramp to a tram stop, closing her umbrella as she gained the shelter of the canopy. He hung back until she'd chosen her spot on the platform, then daringly walked right up behind her. She didn't even glance at him as he approached, head down against the weather. It amazed him how these women walked in the world with no understanding of the threats that were everywhere. Sometimes he felt he radiated power as tangible as the heat rising from a log fire. How could they be oblivious to him? Dogs bared their teeth at him, cats hissed when he held out his fingers towards them. But women were so out of tune with their environment, they just didn't pay attention.

She'd pay attention to him soon enough, he promised himself that.

Now he was so close he could distinguish each blonde hair on her head. Sufficiently close to tell that she was a natural. No tell-tale roots here, which was as it should be. If he'd been betrayed by the thinnest line of brown, he'd have walked away. Because he was only interested in perfect matches. He wasn't some kind of inadequate who would settle for second best. He'd been deprived of what was rightfully his, but that didn't mean anything would do.

The tram glided into sight, the rain making its blue-and-claret livery gleam under the street lights and restaurant neon of the square. She'd chosen her spot perfectly, right opposite one of the opening doors. He stepped in behind her. She turned left, he turned right and slipped on to a jump seat where he could see her but she couldn't see him unless she turned her head. He sighed in satisfaction. Soon he'd know everything he needed to.

She didn't have a clue.

Marie Mather congratulated herself on getting a seat on the tram. She'd spent just over eleven hours inside Tellit Communications. For a first day, she reckoned that showed more than willing. It would probably be gone seven by the time she got in. But unlike most working women, she wouldn't be dashing home to put dinner on the table. Marie was lucky enough to be married to a man whose Italian mother had compensated for her lack of daughters by teaching Marco everything she knew about cooking. He mostly worked from home these days, designing furniture for an online retailer, so Marie came home to freshly prepared dinners that made her feel cherished every time.

It would be something special tonight, she was certain of that. Perhaps Marco would have splashed out on a leg of lamb or a steak. Or maybe even a truffle to grate over a risotto or a pasta dish. Her mouth was watering at the thought.

She spent the twenty-minute tram ride turning over the day's encounters in her mind. All in all, not a bad start to a new job. She knew she was there to shake things up and already she could see possibilities for change. But Marie had no plans to rush into anything. She'd feel her way in gently, get under the skin of the organisation and then start a quiet revolution that would leave them reeling. Oh yes, she had plans for Tellit.

The tram drew into the terminus, its electric motor making a sound like a soft moan of contentment. There were only a handful of travellers left on the tram, bunching together by the doors till the tram came to a smooth halt. And then she was off down the platform, heels clattering on the concrete. The rain had finally stopped, she realised as she reached street level. The air still felt thick with damp, but there was no need for an umbrella now.

Marie hurried down the street, her mind on her job, her sense of self-preservation entirely asleep. Then, struck by a sudden desire to finish the evening with a box of chocolates in front of the TV as she passed the newsagent on the corner, she wheeled round to return and almost cannoned into a man who was only a few feet behind her, his head down and shoulders hunched against the cold. Her heart leapt in shock. She'd had no notion anyone was that close.

He barged past her without a word and she was surprised by her relief when she entered the shop. *Silly woman*, she chided herself as she left a few minutes later, reassured by the empty street and the box of Ferrero Rocher tucked into her bag. Nothing more than a typical bad-mannered city encounter; what could be more normal than that?

She rounded the corner into the street where she and Marco lived, completely unaware that the man she'd almost bumped into was standing in the shadow of the house on the opposite corner, taking very careful note of Marie's destination and wondering how many more times she'd be walking through her own front door.

16

Of course there wasn't a legal parking space in the Minster Canal Basin. Cursing, Paula slotted the car into a disabled slot and propped a sign saying 'police' on the dashboard. It went against the grain, but then so did getting soaked to the skin on semi-official business. She consoled herself with the thought that not many disabled people would fancy negotiating the cobbles of the canal basin in monsoon conditions.

As she headed for Tony's floating home, she wondered fleetingly whether she should have phoned ahead. He didn't exactly have a vibrant social life, but it wasn't unusual for him to take long walks through the city. They were, he'd told her, a cross between sociological observation and thinking time. 'Watch and learn, that's what psychologists need to do,' he'd said in an uncharacteristically frank exchange about the way he approached his work. 'And then you have to apply what you've learned to what you observe.'

'You're better at it than most,' Paula had commented.

'It's not rocket science. It's mostly common sense mixed up with a bit of compassion and empathy. You could do it, you know.'

She'd laughed. But he'd continued, absolutely serious. 'You're already doing it. I've watched you interviewing witnesses and suspects. You might not know the theory, but your practice stands comparison with most of the clinical psychologists I've seen in action. Maybe you should think about applying to the national faculty and training to be a police profiler.'

'No way,' she'd said. 'I get my buzz from being on the front line. I don't want to be a backroom person like you.'

He'd shrugged. 'Your choice. But when you do get to the point where you've had enough of the grind of procedure and the pettiness of the top brass, it's an option.'

What Tony had suffered in the course of his work cast a bitter light on the conversation now. Paula had seen the destruction at first hand, and she was grateful that she had routine and procedure to cling on to among the wreckage. She wasn't sure if she was doing the right thing by coming here, but her instincts, both professional and personal, had led her inevitably to his door. Or hatchway, she supposed you'd have to call it. At least it wasn't a late call. Shortly before seven, Fielding had sent the team home. 'There's no budget for overtime and until we've got something back from the lab and the CCTV, you're all just spinning your wheels.' Paula had been stunned. Overtime had never been an issue on her old squad. They got on and did what had to be done when they were in the thick of it. The theory was that they'd take it easier in the quiet spells. Only there never had been any quiet spells.

She stood on the quayside, momentarily flummoxed by the etiquette. When she'd been here before, they'd arrived together and she'd simply followed Tony aboard. But it felt somehow intrusive to climb aboard and knock on the hatch. Logically, it was no different to walking up someone's path to knock on the door. Yet it felt wrong.

'Get a grip, woman,' she muttered, stepping aboard the steel-hulled narrowboat, not quite prepared for the definite movement of the deck beneath her feet. She almost stumbled, caught herself and rapped on the hatch. The top section swung open almost at once and Tony's startled face appeared below.

'Paula. I thought you were a drunk.'

Her smile was grim. 'Not quite. Not yet. You get a lot of drunks dropping by?'

He busied himself with opening up to let her in. 'Sometimes. Usually later than this. They think it's amusing to jump on and off boats. It can be disconcerting.' He spread the doors wide and beckoned her in with a grin. 'And I wasn't expecting you.' His face clouded in a frown. 'Was I?'

Paula squeezed past him down the galley and into the saloon. The TV screen was frozen in a scene apparently set in a deep mine. A games console lay discarded on the table. 'No. It was a spur of the moment decision.' She took off her damp coat and hung it on a hook on the bulkhead then sat down on the buttoned leather banquette that surrounded three sides of the table.

'Well, it's always good to see you.' He sat down opposite her, then stood up almost immediately, remembering the social conventions of dealing with a visitor. 'Do you want a drink? I've got coffee and tea. Orange juice. Some of that Indian lager, goes well with takeaways.' He gave a wry smile. 'And white wine and vodka. Though there's not been much call for those lately.'

Carol Jordan's drinks of choice. 'I wouldn't mind a lager.'

Two steps and he was by the fridge. Tony pulled out two

bottles, reached up for two glasses and was back at the table in a matter of seconds. The bottle opener was in a shallow drawer under the table. It was convenient, no denying that. 'So, what brings you here?' he said, pouring a beer for his guest.

'I've had a strange day.' Paula raised her glass. 'Cheers. And I wanted to talk about it with somebody who under-stands what I'm talking about. Because I've started on a new team and—'

'And your new boss isn't Carol Jordan and you don't have Chris and Stacey and Sam and Kevin to bounce things off.'

'All of that, yes. And I know you're not on the payroll any more and I know you don't owe BMP anything. But I suppose I've got used to using you as a sounding board—'

'Even when the boss says no.' That wry twist to his mouth again. They both remembered only too well the times they'd sneaked behind Carol Jordan's back for what they saw as the right reasons.

Paula scowled. 'OK, I don't have her scruples about exploiting you. I think if you want to help, we should let you. And if you don't, all you have to do is say no.'

'I know. I wasn't having a go at you, Paula. I've got skills and I prefer to use them rather than keeping them nicely polished on a shelf.' This time his smile was uncomplicated but sad. 'Besides, you're the nearest thing I've got to a friend. If I can't help my friend, what's the point of me?'

Paula shook herself like a dog emerging from a river. 'Oh, for fuck's sake. Listen to us. What a pathetic pair.'

'We are, aren't we? Best get some work done and stop auditioning for *Oprah*. So, what's been strange about the day? Apart from it being the first day on your new firm.'

And so she told him about Torin. About the unaccountable absence of Bev McAndrew and her rescue of the boy from the uncertain clutches of social services. 'I spoke to the duty pharmacist who did the handover with her last night. Bev said nothing about any plans for the evening other than picking up some shopping on the way home. I've tracked down a couple of her female friends. Neither of them have heard from her.' She ran her finger round the rim of her glass. 'I'll be honest, Tony, I don't like it.'

He leaned back and studied the low roof of the cabin. 'Let's consider the possibilities. Not an accident or an incident involving the emergency services.'

'I told you. I checked.'

'I know you did, I'm just running through the options. Amnesia? Hard to believe she could have gone twenty-four hours without attracting the attention of somebody who would do the responsible thing. And besides, real amnesia is incredibly rare. Usually memory loss is connected to a head injury which would have landed her in hospital. And you've ruled that out.'

'She's dead, isn't she?'

He held up a hand, palm towards her. 'You jump to that conclusion because it's what you know. In your world, murder is something that happens on a weekly basis. But that's not how it is for most of us. Even if you consider six degrees of separation, most of us get closer to Kevin Bacon than we do to a murder victim. We need to look at more likely scenarios first.'

'Like what?' Paula's jaw had a stubborn set. She knew what was coming and she'd already dismissed the other options.

'A boyfriend – or a girlfriend – she's gone off with spontaneously.'

'She's straight. But everybody I spoke to says she hasn't been seeing anyone in the last couple of years.'

Tony leaned forward. 'How likely does that seem to you? You described her as bright, funny, attractive. I'm assuming she's late thirties, early forties. A bit young to be going for the life of a nun, I'd have thought.'

Tell that to Carol Jordan. How many years have you two been avoiding getting your act together? Paula kept her face straight and said, 'What is it the straight women say? By the time you get to thirty-five, all the best blokes are taken or gay.'

'And by the time you get to forty, the divorces kick in and they're looking for a second bite of the cherry. I can imagine plenty of reasons why Bev might not be shouting from the rooftops about a new man. Maybe it's someone at work. Maybe it's someone who's married. Maybe it's one of Torin's teachers.'

Someone at work? Dan who protested too much? 'She'd tell her best mate. Women do.' *Unless it was her best mate ...*

'Have you never had a secret love?'

Paula laughed, embarrassed. 'Of course I have. I'm a lesbian. Half my life I've felt like Doris Day. But I always told my best mate.' Then she caught herself, hand to her mouth. 'Except when it was her girlfriend. Oops, I'd forgotten that.'

'See?'

'Yeah, but I didn't have a kid. You're forgetting about Torin.'

'I'm not. I wanted to remind you that assumptions always have exceptions. You once had a good reason for a secret. So might Bev. But even allowing for a secret, you're right. It doesn't on its own account for her disappearing without a word. She wouldn't abandon Torin without a word. Some mothers would, there's no getting away from that. But what you know of Bev personally, from her colleagues and from Torin himself, doesn't make that a credible proposition?'

'She'd never leave him high and dry,' Paula confirmed. 'I'd say that, in some respects, he's quite a young fourteen.'

'But if she is seeing someone, that someone might have

their own agenda here. And he might have prevented her from contacting anyone.'

Paula took a deep breath. 'What you're really saying is that whether it's a boyfriend gone rogue or a stranger stalker, Bev isn't on the missing list from choice.'

Tony pinched the bridge of his nose between finger and thumb. It was a gesture she'd seen many times before. 'I think it's inescapable, Paula. I think she's been taken. What's the official status of the inquiry?'

'I processed Torin's statement this morning. If they do things at Skenfrith Street like we used to do them, it'll be actioned in the morning. I'll brief Fielding on what I've done so far – she'll kick my arse for going off on my own, but at least the formal stuff will get started. Like tracking her mobile.'

'Everybody knows about mobiles these days. If it's switched on, it'll be nowhere near where Bev is.'

'Have you got any bright ideas?'

He shook his head. 'You're always looking for the point of intersection. Where did Bev cross paths with the person who took her? Was it a stranger who plucked her off the street? Or was it a sexual scenario that went somewhere she didn't want to go? Let's face it, Paula, after *Fifty Shades of Grey*, women are a lot less wary of being tied up by men they don't necessarily know that well. If you had Stacey, you could get her to go through Bev's home computer. That would be a good place to start. Can you get Stacey?'

Paula looked disgusted at the thought of what had happened to Stacey Chen, the terrifyingly effective analyst she'd worked alongside in Carol Jordan's Major Incident Team. 'They've got her working on computer fraud. She says it's like sending a Lear jet on the school run. All the forensic computer work in CID gets farmed out to private companies now.'

'She should quit the force and set up in competition to them.'

'Don't think she hasn't thought about it. But running a company would interfere too much with the programming she does in her spare time. That's where the real money comes from in Stacey world. Besides, if she wasn't a cop any more, she wouldn't have the licence to go poking around in other people's hard drives.'

'Could you ask for a copy of the hard drive before it goes off to the specialists? Would that work for Stacey?'

'Good idea. I'll ask her. And if it was a stranger?'

'You don't need me for this bit, Paula. This is nothing but old-fashioned coppering with new-fashioned methods. Interrogating the CCTV, looking for her car on the number-plate-recognition software records, examining her Facebook page and her Twitter feed, seeing who she's connected to on LinkedIn, checking her phone records. A profiler's no use to you at this stage. I need data, and that's what you haven't got. All I've done is confirm your worst fears.'

'I need a smoke,' Paula said, standing up abruptly.

'Just go out the back.'

'Come with me, would you? I want to take you through the rest of my day.'

'Will I need my coat and my keys?'

Paula's smile promised dark mischief. 'Only if you fancy a bit of transgression.'

Tony grabbed the waxed jacket that was hanging next to Paula's coat. 'For a lesbian, your knowledge of the way to a man's heart is remarkable.

17

Carol had never really grasped the concept of survivor guilt. She'd always believed that being a survivor was a good thing, something to be proud about, not ashamed of. Her past was dotted with struggles to get past bad things that had happened to her; if she'd been pushed, she'd have said she was gratified not to have caved under their weight. That was something else that had changed.

Now she understood the guilt and shame of being the one left behind. Loss had removed the old underpinnings of her beliefs and changed how she viewed the world. She would happily stop dead in her tracks if it meant Michael and Lucy could have their lives back. After all, they had been making a better job of living well than she was. They'd put something back into the world, restoring the barn. And the work they did. Well, the work that Michael did. Lucy's commitment to criminal defence work had always baffled Carol. She'd spent too many days sitting in court, disgusted at the barristers who exploited legal technicalities and twisted the words of witnesses, all in the service of getting nasty little shits off the hook of their own criminality. She'd tried not to argue with Lucy over the dinner table, but sometimes she couldn't restrain herself. 'How can you defend people you know are guilty? How can you feel satisfaction when they walk free from court, leaving their victims without any sense of justice?'

The answer was always the same. 'I don't know that they're guilty. Even when the evidence seems overwhelming, it may be misleading. Everyone's entitled to a defence. If you people did your job thoroughly, they wouldn't be walking free from court, would they?'

It was an argument whose speciousness left Carol almost speechless with rage. A desire for justice was what drove her, what made it possible for her to tolerate the horrors of her job at the sharpest of sharp ends. To see it constantly thwarted by hair-splitting lawyers who generated doubt where none should exist was the ultimate insult to the broken lives and broken bodies that occupied her memory. She'd always been with Dick the Butcher on that one. 'The first thing we do, let's kill all the lawyers.'

Except, of course, she hadn't been. Not really. Not when it came to the woman her brother loved. The woman who had transformed him from a single-minded geek to a relatively civilised human being. A transformation Carol had never managed for herself. Would never have to manage now.

It would have been bad enough if it had been some chance event that had cut their lives so brutally short. But there had been nothing chance about it. They'd been deliberately slaughtered with one aim in mind. To make Carol suffer. The man who had come to the barn with murder on his agenda didn't care about Michael and Lucy. The corrosive hatred in his heart was directed at Carol and he understood only too well that the best way to destroy her was to kill them in her stead. They were murdered because they were connected so intimately to her. No other reason.

And it should never have happened. They should have figured out – no, Tony Hill, forensic psychologist and offender profiler, *he* should have figured out what might happen. She had the resources at her command to have protected them. But she never had the chance to put those resources in place. It had never occurred to her that anyone could be so twisted. It should have occurred to Tony, though. Most of his professional career had been intertwined with people who were seriously twisted. She hoped he felt as gutted by their deaths as she did.

Two deaths on her hands would have been grounds enough for crippling guilt. But for Carol, there was more. One of her team had been maimed and blinded in a hideous booby trap that had been set for Carol and sprung by Chris Devine. Chris, a former sergeant in the Met, who had moved to Bradfield because she believed in what Carol was trying to do with her Major Incident Team, a raggle-taggle band of specialists who didn't quite fit in for one reason or another but who had learned to work together and grown into a formidable outfit. And Chris at the heart of it, the most unlikely of mother figures holding them all together. Chris, whose career was now at an end and whose life had been wrecked beyond mending because of a simple act of helpfulness.

When Carol thought about Chris, she felt ashamed. She'd been so wrapped up in her own pain, she hadn't paid the debt to friendship. Others had sat with Chris through her pain, talking to her, reading to her, playing music to her. Others had taken their turn supporting her through the first difficult steps towards regaining some of what she'd lost. Others had been there for her while Carol had busied herself elsewhere.

No doubt Tony would have some clever explanation for her inability to face Chris. But it wasn't complicated. It was guilt, pure and simple. Chris's fate was what had lain in store for Carol. She'd dodged the bullet. And as with Michael and Lucy, someone else had paid the price for her determination to see justice done.

Carol swung the sledgehammer through the gallery floorboards in a steady rhythm to accompany her thoughts. She'd paid heed to George Nicholas's suggestion about the beam and she'd set a ladder against the gallery and attacked it from above. Strictly speaking, scaffolding would have been a better option, but that exceeded her DIY skills and she was determined to see this through herself, no matter how long it took. She was done with getting a man in to solve her problems for her. She paused for breath, chest heaving with the effort, sweat running down her back.

Her encounter with George Nicholas kept cutting into her familiar mantra of guilt and shame. It had reminded her that there was a world beyond her self-regard. A world she used to inhabit. A world where people sat round tables and talked together, drank together, laughed together. She'd had a place in that world and she suspected walking away from it was not entirely healthy. She'd deliberately set herself apart so she could begin the process of healing. But how would she know if she was getting any stronger if she lived like a hermit? Reluctantly, she reminded herself she'd tried that once before and it hadn't been the answer. What had brought her back to life had been engaging with the world.

Maybe it was time to start again.

The closest Carol had ever previously come to a police convalescent home was sticking a twenty in the collection box at social events. She had no idea what to expect. When

91

she'd called Chris's Police Federation rep to check her
whereabouts, she'd half-expected her to be back home.
'She's at the convalescent home in Ripon,' the helpful rep
had told her. 'She's working with the physios there on her
range of movements. Scar management, that sort of thing.
They wanted to keep her in hospital longer, but because we
were able to provide specialist care, she's been able to start
living a more normal life.'

Carol cringed inwardly at the words, unable to imagine
how anyone would begin to cope. 'Has there been any
improvement in her sight, do you know?'

'I believe not. They're talking about lining her up with a
guide dog. But that'll be a bit down the road.'

Carol thanked her and ended the call, wondering whether
she had the strength for this. But building a bridge between
her and Chris was the first step to regaining her humanity.
She'd called ahead to ask about visiting times and been told
that visitors were expected to leave by nine o'clock. So she'd
finished work in the late afternoon, showered the sweat and
dirt away and put on one of her business suits for the first
time in months. She stretched the process out as long as she
could, taking time out for a large glass of cold pinot grigio.
Then another. But finally there was nothing for it but to set
off across the rolling green landscape to the tiny cathedral
city.

The convalescent home was on the edge of town, not far
from the ruined grandeur of Fountains Abbey. It was hidden
at the end of a twisting drive, obscured from sight by a
shrubbery that looked mature enough to have been planted
by the original owners of the sprawling Victorian villa that
formed its heart. There were modern two-storey wings on
either side of the main house and small chalets dotted the
fringes of the wide lawns, all linked by well-groomed paths.
Lights burned in several windows, but the curtains were

already drawn in the downstairs rooms. If she hadn't known what she was coming to, Carol would have been hard pressed to identify its purpose from outside.

A heavy Gothic door stood open into a substantial porch. The doors leading inside were modern, however, and slid open as they detected her presence. Inside was more like a hotel foyer than a hospital facility. A way, Carol thought, of communicating to people that this was a step on the road to something approaching normal life. It even smelled like a hotel rather than a hospital, a vague floral scent like supermarket pot pourri hanging in the air.

In keeping with this image, the young woman behind the curved reception desk wore a cheap business suit that was slightly too tight across the bust. She smiled in greeting. 'Good evening. How can I help you?'

For a moment, Carol was nonplussed. She'd been introducing herself by rank for so long she'd almost forgotten the art of plain announcement. 'I'm here to see Chris Devine,' she said. 'Sergeant Devine.'

'Is Sergeant Devine expecting you?'

Carol shook her head. 'I'm her commanding officer,' she said, slipping uneasily into the persona she'd abandoned months ago. 'DCI Jordan.' She took a slim leather wallet from her pocket. She wasn't sure whether BMP had forgotten to tell her to return her ID or nobody had had the nerve to ask for it. Either way, she'd hung on to it. She wasn't a sentimental woman. She could only suppose that at some level, she'd kept it because it might come in handy. She didn't want to think about what that might mean. Right now, she was happy just to milk it. She flipped the wallet open and let the receptionist take it in.

The woman tugged her jacket down, as if attempting a parade-ground attention. 'Have you visited us before?'

'This is my first time. Can you direct me to Chris's room?'

The directions were straightforward. Carol smiled her gratitude and set off towards one of the modern wings. Her normal brisk pace slowed as she neared her destination. By the end she was dawdling, pausing to look at the vibrant abstract paintings that hung on the corridor walls. Outside Chris's door, she ran a hand through her hair and wished she'd had a large vodka. She clenched the fist of her left hand so tight she could feel her short fingernails digging into her palm. And gently rapped on the door.

A voice that didn't sound like Chris said, 'Come in.'

Carol opened the door and stepped across the threshold. She'd barely registered that the figure in one chair was Chris when the woman in the other chair jumped to her feet, a look of welcoming enquiry switching in an instant to one of hostility. 'I'm sorry, I think you've got the wrong room,' Sinead Burton said, her voice warm and polite, her face the diametric opposite. She held a finger to her lips. 'Can I show you the way?' She crossed the room, practically pushing Carol out through the door. 'I'll be back in a minute, love,' she called over her shoulder to Chris, who had turned her head towards them, her face a twisted pink and purple mask. Carol had tried to prepare for it, but still it shook her.

Sinead closed the door firmly behind her and shooed Carol down the hall with her hands. As soon as they were far enough from the door not to be overheard, she started on Carol, her voice tight with suppressed anger. 'What the hell are you doing here? I thought you had the good sense to stay away. What the hell are you playing at?'

Carol backed away. Her previous encounters with Chris's partner hadn't prepared her for this. 'I wanted to say sorry,' she stuttered.

'You wanted to say sorry?' Sinead's Irish accent grew more pronounced as her anger rose. 'You don't think it might be a wee bit late for that? My wife nearly dies instead of you and it takes you all these weeks and months to get round to saying sorry? Talk about a day late and a dollar short. Jesus.'

Carol felt tears closing her throat. But she knew she had to hold it together. It was obvious that tears would cut no ice with Sinead. 'I know. Believe me, I know. But I couldn't handle it.'

Sinead cut straight across her. 'You couldn't handle it? What the hell do you think it's been like for her? The excruciating pain. The loss of her sight. The loss of her face, for God's sake. Couldn't handle it? You should have crawled on your hands and knees the day after and begged for her to forgive you.'

'I'd just lost my brother and sister-in-law,' Carol said.

'It's not a bloody fucking *competition*.' Sinead's voice was cold and hard as stone. 'You should have been here right from the start.'

Carol swallowed. 'I know that, Sinead. Nobody could feel more guilty and ashamed than I do.'

'As you should. Well, you're not welcome here. You haven't earned the right to be here. I don't care how hard it's been on you, it's been a hundred times harder on her. Other people have been here for her, you know. Paula and Kevin, they come a lot. Sam stops in, and even Stacey the geek. And you know who comes regular as clockwork? Tony. He's been coming right from the start. And believe me, he's a man who wears his guilt on his sleeve. But the one person she wanted to hear from, the woman she respected more than any other officer she ever worked under, the person she ended up sacrificing herself for – you couldn't be bothered to show your face. Well, fuck you, Carol Jordan. You don't get to stroll in now Tony's done the hard stuff for you. So are you going to walk right out of here or am I going to get security on to you?'

95

Carol wanted to slump to the floor and sob till her throat was raw. Instead, she simply nodded. 'I'm sorry.' She turned and walked back the way she'd come, desperate to make it to her car before she fell apart.

Sinead's last words hit like a handful of hail in her face. 'And don't fucking come again.'

18

Tony paused in the cramped hallway that smelled faintly of smoked paprika. 'Are we going to get in trouble?'

'Only if you grass me up. I did log the keys out officially. I told Fielding I wanted another look. I'm not mad – I'm not going totally off the reservation.'

'Fair enough. You said you had a set of the crime-scene photos,' he reminded Paula. 'Can I see them before we go in?'

'This isn't where she was killed,' Paula said, opening her bag to get the folder of photos she'd printed off before leaving the CID office. 'There's nothing to suggest the killer was ever here.'

'I realise that. But until we know how and where he acquired Nadia, I don't want to rule out any possible connections.'

'I hate that word.' Paula pulled out the folder.

'Connections?' Tony sounded confused.

'"Acquired" – it's so cold. So clinical.'

'I am a clinician. This is supposed to be scientific, not emotional.' He shrugged, doing his 'helpless' face. 'But you're right, it is cold. Would you prefer me to talk about "intersections"? That always sounds like a traffic report to me.' He took the proffered photographs and slipped them out of the folder. In the dim light of the hallway, he flipped through them quickly, taking a first impression of the body and its surroundings. Then he tugged a pair of owlish black-rimmed specs from his inside pocket and put them on. 'I'm getting old,' he said. 'I can't see detail without my glasses.' Taking his time, he studied each photograph from different angles. 'I once had a tutor, quite a young bloke, who thought wearing glasses made people take him more seriously. One day, I was sitting behind him when he took them off to polish them and I realised they were plain glass. Whether it was vanity or insecurity that drove him to it, it cost him my respect. And because I was young and smart-arsed, I told my fellow students what I'd spotted. So the trick he'd used to earn gravitas ended up making him look a fool.'

'And there endeth the sermon for today,' Paula said. 'What about my crime scene?'

Tony sighed. 'I'm wasted here. All that hard-won wisdom, and where does it get me?' He selected a full-length shot of Nadia's body. 'What did Grisha say about the damage to her body?'

'He said he'd given her a good kicking. Probably with steel-toecapped boots.'

'What about stamp marks? Did he say anything about that?'

'He made a point of saying the killer got lucky because he couldn't see any stamp marks.'

'And that's the dog that didn't bark in the night,' Tony said. 'He didn't stamp on her, which is the natural thing to do when you're frenziedly attacking someone and they fall on the ground. You kick and you stamp. So right there, you've got a contradiction. Battering her face to a bloody pulp, to the point where she's unrecognisable, that looks like frenzy. As if the killer is out of control. But the fact that he very carefully doesn't stamp on her suggests his actions are deliberate. He's thought this through. He doesn't want to leave forensic traces. He doesn't want to get caught.'

'So why the overkill on the face?'

'I'm not sure yet. The textbook answer is, to depersonalise her. To objectify her. To make her less than human so what he's doing isn't really murder, because she's a thing not a person. But that doesn't feel right here somehow. Because the other business, the sealing up of the labia, that's very personal. That's making a statement of possession. "I'm done with you but nobody else can have you." That's what that says to me. It's not a generalised statement of misogyny, it's specific, it's aimed directly at her. And that runs directly counter to the notion of smashing her face to depersonalise her.' He frowned at the photograph, turning it this way and that. 'I don't know, I'm going to have to think about this.'

'Good. I like what happens when you think about things. Now, are you done with the pics? Because I'm getting claustrophobia here. Any chance we could move into a room-sized space?' She handed him a pair of nitrile gloves.

Three doors led off the lobby. Tony opened the nearest one and revealed a poky, windowless bathroom with a shower cubicle, a toilet and a tiny sink. The lingering smell of toiletries couldn't quite hide the fetor of damp. 'Later,' he muttered and hastily pulled the door to.

The next door led to a room that comprised living room, dining corner and kitchen. The separate components could have made for a comfortable, welcoming space if they hadn't been crammed into half the area they actually required. Instead, it felt crowded and confined. 'Deceptively poky. Isn't that what the estate agents never say?' Tony looked around, taking in the pockets of clutter that had infiltrated the few available spaces. Piles of magazines, stacks of DVDs, cardboard boxes half-full of drug samples and promotional giveaways – pens, mouse mats, coasters. He squatted beside the DVDs and scanned the titles. 'No sign of anybody else's taste here. *Bridesmaids, How to Lose a Guy in 10 Days, The Wedding Singer, Eight Women, Juno, Notting Hill, There's Something about Mary, Amelie, My Best Friend's Wedding.* The fairytale reimagined for the twenty-first century.'

'Fairytales for straight girls. Nothing in Polish?'

Tony stood up and grunted as his knees cracked. 'No. She was probably trying to improve her English. Given her job.' He crossed to the dining table, where there was a laptop-shaped space between a stack of papers, an all-in-one printer, scanner and copier, and an A4 pad with a few lines of scribbled notes. 'Did forensics take the laptop?'

Paula nodded. 'They did. I'll ask them for a copy of the hard drive in the morning. If I'm going to talk Stacey into looking at Bev's hard drive, I might as well get her to see what she can find on Nadia's computer as well.'

But Tony wasn't listening. Now he had advanced into the kitchen area, he'd spotted a corkboard on a short section of wall that jutted into the room. The board had been obscured from sight when he'd been in the main part of the room. He made straight for it and stared at it, frowning as if he was cataloguing the contents for the crime-scene equivalent of Kim's Game. 'This is more like it,' he said.

Three takeaway menus – Indian, Chinese and catch-all pizza, kebab and burger. He turned and glanced round the kitchen area. 'She cooked. You can smell it, you can see it

100

from the pans and the knives and stuff. And there's vegetables in the rack. Onions, potatoes, carrots, garlic. OK, the onions and potatoes are sprouting and the carrots are as wrinkled as a Shar Pei's scrotum . . . '

'That's probably because, one way or another, she left here three weeks ago,' Paula interrupted.

He nodded. 'She worked hard, she worked late. She didn't always have time to cook.'

'Maybe she couldn't be bothered.'

'Take a look in the cupboards,' he said, anticipating open packets of ingredients, jars of herbs and spices, tins he'd have no idea what to do with.

Paula revealed exactly what he'd expected. 'You win. She cooked.' She picked an open cardboard box off the shelf and peered inside. 'Now I know the Polish word for lentils.' While she was on this theme, she opened the fridge. It smelled of over-ripe cheese and bad fruit and the plastic bottle in the door shelf was solid with spoiled milk. 'Well, that's one question answered. I don't believe she ever went to Poland. She'd never have left all this food to go off in the fridge. She certainly didn't come home at the weekend just in time to be abducted. At the very least she'd have binned this rotten stuff.'

Tony turned his attention back to the corkboard. A postcard from Ibiza. He unpinned it. 'Sun shining, booze cheap, plenty guys!!! You should have come. Ashley xxx' He replaced it. Business cards from a computer repair shop, a Polish deli in Harriestown, a dressmaker specialising in alterations and a taxi firm. The police would check them all, he knew. Chances were high that they would lead nowhere. Although Ashley might be able to colour in some of the background to Nadia's life.

There were a couple of flyers for upcoming pub gigs by local bands, a bus timetable for the 183 from Harriestown to

Bellwether Square and a cartoon about Polish builders. Finally, he turned his attention to the photographs. A dog-eared and faded colour snap of a wedding party – bride and groom and two presumed sets of parents. 'Her mum and dad?'

'No reason to think otherwise.'

Next, three women, arms around each other, in a night-club or a fun pub, all mugging drunkenly at the camera. The kind of photograph half the women in Britain under thirty had on display, commemorating some celebratory night out with the girls. Tony was about to pass on, but something nagged at him. He took the photo off the board and studied it more closely. 'The one in the middle,' he said. 'She looks familiar. I can't place her. She's not someone I know. But I've met her somewhere.' He looked up at Paula, whose expression was unreadable. 'Do we know who she is?'

'Oh yeah, Tony. We know exactly who she is. She's the victim.'

His confusion was obvious. 'That's Nadia Wilkowa?'

19

B ev had no way of measuring how long she'd been conscious inside the freezer. She'd started trying to count the minutes, going from one elephant to sixty then back again, but she couldn't keep track. Her mind was too busy skittering from one awful possibility to another. And beneath them all, the constant thrum of anxiety about Torin. How would he be coping without her? How would he cope if she never got back to him? Would he go to the police? Would they find her in time? She tried to push the worst of her imaginings away from her, but there was no escaping it. This wasn't the kind of predicament that generally had a positive ending.

As well as losing all sense of time, Bev had also given up on dignity. She'd grown uncomfortably conscious of her full bladder but she'd held it in for as long as she could. Then she'd asked herself why she was bothering. She was locked in a chest freezer wearing nothing but a pair of pants that didn't belong to her. There was nothing dignified in any of that. How could it be worse to be sitting in a puddle of her own piss? If it – literally – pissed off the person who'd put her in here, then score one to her.

When the light came it was a physical shock. Without warning, the lid of the freezer suddenly lifted and a blaze of brilliant white light stunned her optic nerve. All she had time for was to cross her forearms across her face in a timeless gesture of self-defence and supplication before excruciating pain shot through her body and reduced her muscles to jelly. Completely disorientated, Bev felt herself lifted through the air then dumped face down on the floor. As her senses gradually returned, she was aware of rough cement against her skin. There was some kind of cold cuff round her left ankle and she felt her hands being secured behind her. She opened her mouth to scream but before she could make a sound, a terrible blow to the ribs knocked the air out of her. Strong hands turned her on her back and punched her in the side of the head. Colours flashed behind her eyes and thick pain throbbed through her head. 'Shut the fuck up, bitch,' a man's voice said. It was all the more terrifying for being matter-of-fact.

And then there was some kind of wide sticky tape smacked into place across her mouth. Bev had no choice but to shut up. She looked up at the man who was doing this to her. Blue overalls, scuffed black work boots. Quite tall, brown hair, blue eyes, bulbous nose, long straight mouth, square chin. Her first thought was to memorise these unremarkable features. But in a split second her determination gave way to dismay. She'd watched enough crime series on TV to know that if they let you see their face, it was because they were planning to kill you. A wordless moan came from behind her gag and this time he slapped her hard. 'If you did what you were told, I wouldn't have to hit you, would I?' His tone was reasonable, as if he were explaining to a child why they shouldn't stick their hand in the fire.

He grabbed her shoulders and pushed her into a sitting position. Then he gripped her upper arms and yanked her to her feet. She heard a metallic rattle as she struggled upright and looked down. A shiny metal cuff was secured to her ankle with a heavy padlock. A sturdy-looking chain trailed backwards from the padlock. He forced her forward and the chain came too, a heavy drag on her ankle.

From somewhere, Bev dredged up a shred of determination. What about all those cases where girls and women had been taken captive and ended up escaping? She could be one of those. She wasn't a quitter, she was a survivor. Whatever it took, she could find it in herself. Without making it obvious, Bev checked out the room she was being marched across. Cement floor, workbench, blank walls covered with hooks that held tools and garden equipment. A garage, then. He was pushing her towards a door that stood ajar in a side wall. He shoved her hard through the door, making her stumble and fall. Polished stone tiles, wooden cupboards, a fridge. A kitchen, then. Bev tried to get to her feet, but with her hands fastened behind her, it was impossible. She heard the rattle of the chain then slid across the floor as he pulled on it. The skin round the cuff tore, giving her a new centre of pain.

When she came to a standstill, he kicked her thigh, so hard she felt the muscle numb. 'You're mine now,' he said. 'Do you understand? You're my wife. If you do what you're told and you behave like a good wife should, everything will be fine. But if you give me any grounds for complaint, I will hurt you. Is that clear?' He spoke with an educated Northern accent, at odds with his working man's outfit. She couldn't pin his origin down precisely. Never mind. It was something else to store away for the future. Bev didn't know how, but it might be useful.

He picked up the slack in the chain and waved it at her. 'You see this? The other end is chained to the wall. There.' He pointed to a solid metal eye screwed into the door frame. 'Don't even think about it. Four screws, each one three inches long. You've got free range for the length of your chain. There's no knives within reach. Nothing you can hurt me with. And I've got this.' He took a slim black object from his trouser pocket. 'It's a taser. That's what I used on you when I took you out of your kennel. Remember how that felt? Well, that was just a taster. A taster of the taser.' He smiled at his own cleverness. 'I can disable you from twenty feet away.'

All at once, her hands were free. He stepped smartly clear of her. Bev looked round to see him dangling a pair of pink furry handcuffs, the novelty kind sold in sex shops. His lips were turned up in a parody of a smile. 'Don't be under any illusion, Bev. I don't want to hurt you, but if you make me, I will.' He backed away from her, putting some distance and a breakfast bar between them. He pulled out one of the high stools and set it against the far wall. She wasn't good at estimating distances, but even she knew they were less than twenty feet apart.

Bev looked around her, trying to work out whether she had any options. A dining kitchen in a modern house. The rear wall had been opened out to lead into a conservatory. All the blinds were drawn and they were effective. She couldn't even tell if it was day or night. She couldn't see out and nobody could see in.

She was shackled at the far end of the room, nearest to the garage door. She could reach the appliances – cooker, hob, dishwasher, fridge. But she wouldn't make it past the island in the middle of the cooking area. All the doors of the ground-level cupboards had childproof fasteners. There might be potential weapons inside but they would take too long to get at, she reckoned. By the time she'd unfastened the locks, he'd be on her, taser knocking her over, boots flying.

The worktops were clear of appliances and there was no sign of chef's knives or utensils that had anything approaching an edge. On a thick wooden chopping board sat a fillet steak, half a dozen chopped mushrooms, a sliced onion, a plastic bottle of olive oil and three new potatoes. On the stove was a heavy frying pan and a small saucepan. A wooden spoon rested against the frying pan. She couldn't quite take it in. Did he want her to cook his dinner? Had he gone to all this trouble to have her wait on him? She'd seen plenty of crazy people at her hospital counter but this was madness of an order she had never previously encountered.

'So get on with it.' He sat on the stool, looking perfectly normal and relaxed, apart from the little black box that rested casually on his thigh. She wasn't fooled, though. She knew he was alert for the slightest reason to hurt her again. She shrugged and spread her hands wide, as if to indicate she wasn't sure what he wanted.

'Cook the fucking dinner,' he shouted, exploding into sudden loud anger. 'I can't make it any more clear, can I?'

Bev lowered her eyes. *Avoid confrontation.* She picked up the saucepan and crossed to the sink. There was just enough play in the chain to allow her an awkward reach to the taps. She half-filled the pan with water and returned to the stove. It was a gas hob, similar to the one she had at home, but she pretended to struggle with the ignition. Maybe he'd grow impatient and come over to light the gas himself then she could deck him with the frying pan.

'What's the problem?' A mocking drawl from the other side of the room. 'Are you too stupid to light the gas? Do I have to beat the instructions into you?' The sarcasm darkened to threat as he tapped the taser against the breakfast bar.

Scrap that idea. Bev lit the gas under the pan and dropped the potatoes in. She poured a little oil into the frying pan and put it on a medium heat. Fear and incredulity were taking turns in her head. Why would anyone pick her if they were looking for the perfect wife? She hadn't been that good a wife when she'd had a husband, and Tom at least had professed to like his women with a mind of their own. If her kidnapper had bothered to find out anything about her, he'd have learned pretty quickly she was never going to make housewife of the year. Well, if she was going to stay alive, she'd better start working at it. She stared at the bleeding meat, trying not to think how it got that way. Thank goodness she was a half-decent cook, according to her ex, her son and her friends.

When the potatoes came to the boil, she added the onions to the hot oil and stirred them around with the spoon. At least the frying onions killed the smell of piss that hung around her. But how in the name of God was she supposed to know how he liked his steak? There was a world of difference between blue and well done. She picked up the steak and turned to face him, shrugging a question at him.

He laughed, sounding genuinely delighted. 'Medium rare,' he said. 'Good girl. The last one didn't even ask. She turned my steak into shoe leather. Useless cow.'

The last one. Bev blinked back tears as she turned her attention to the stove, trying not to show a reaction to those distressing words. She remembered a poem she'd learned at school that had the same murderous chill. What was it? 'That's my last Duchess painted on the wall, Looking as if she were alive.' Scary then, scarier now. Blindly, she tossed the mushrooms in the pan, mixed them with the translucent onions and cleared a space for the steak. She slapped it into the pan and started counting in her head. When she got to a hundred and eighty, she flipped it over and began the count again. She lifted a potato and tested it by squeezing. Almost there.

Bev was startled by the sound of a plate hitting the granite top of the island behind her. She whirled round. He was on the far side of the island, just feet from her, pushing a dinner plate towards her. For a mad moment, she thought about grabbing the pan and swinging for his head, but common sense prevailed. She wasn't fast enough, he wasn't close enough. If she was going to make it home to Torin, she needed to choose her ground well.

Instead, she picked up the plate and turned back to the stove. She switched off the heat under the pans, drained the potatoes as best she could at full stretch, then served up the meal. She placed it on the island then stepped away, lowering her eyes, determined to offer him no excuse to criticise. Bev tried not to hate herself for becoming so cowed so quickly. It was a strategy, she told herself. A strategy for staying alive.

He took the plate to the breakfast bar and started eating. After a couple of mouthfuls of steak and vegetables, he glared at her. 'You cooked the steak properly.' He ate another chunk of meat, frowning. Then he cut into a potato and his face cleared. 'You stupid bitch,' he snarled. 'How can you not know how to cook a potato? Fucking children in primary schools know how to cook a potato. These are like bullets.' He picked up a potato, took aim and hurled it at her. Bev tried to dodge it, but it caught her on the shoulder, surprisingly painful, then skittered across the floor.

'Pick it up, you lazy slut,' he yelled. She tried but it was beyond the limit of her chain. 'You can reach it if you lie down, you thick cow,' he said, turning back to his steak.

Bev did as she was told. She had to stretch full length, straining with her fingertips to reach the potato, driven on by his sadistic grin. But she finally managed to tease it within reach. She picked it up and pushed herself to her feet. She held the potato up, raising her eyebrows in a question.

'Shove it up your arse for all I care,' he said, finishing off his steak and pushing the plate away from him. 'Now, what does a good wife do to please her husband after dinner?' As he rounded the breakfast bar, she could see his erection tenting the front of his overalls.

Oh Christ. It was going to get a lot worse before there was any chance of it getting better.

20

Paula watched Tony cross the cobbles and climb aboard *Steeler*. She waited till he was safely below and the hatch was closed. Not because she feared for his safety but because she wanted a few moments to gather herself before she headed home.

When he'd recognised Nadia Wilkowa in the photograph from the corkboard, Paula had assumed that he'd made the same mistake she had. That he'd been tricked by the superficial resemblance to Carol Jordan into thinking that he knew a woman who was in fact a stranger. When she'd said, 'We know exactly who she is. She's the victim,' she'd thought she was kicking a misapprehension into the long grass.

He'd looked confused. 'That's Nadia Wilkowa? Then I must have encountered her at some point.'

'You don't think it's your mind playing tricks?'

'What do you mean, my mind playing tricks?'

'Tony, she looks like Carol.'

He'd taken a step back, as if she'd poked him in the chest. 'You think so?' He looked again. 'No, you're wrong. The haircut's the same, but that's all. Look.' He thrust the photo at Paula. 'Her face is a different shape. Cheekbones, totally different angles.'

'The jawline's similar, so are the eyes.'

Tony shook his head stubbornly. 'She's . . . I don't know, ordinary. You wouldn't look twice at her in a crowd.'

Paula turned away. 'For a moment, for a split second when I first saw the body . . . I thought it was her, Tony. The hair, the legs, the line of the shoulders. Then I realised the body shape was wrong.'

'But her face was wrecked, Paula. If you'd seen her in life, you wouldn't have taken her for Carol. You're overlaying your first impressions on this picture. And she doesn't look like Carol.' His voice changed, bitterness creeping in. 'Believe me, Paula. I am the man who sees Carol Jordan everywhere. And I don't see her in this woman's face.'

Paula turned in time to catch the shadow of grief cross his face. She put a hand on his arm. 'I'm sorry.'

He gave a harsh little cough of laughter. 'I don't even know where she's living. All those years when I knew where she was sleeping every night, even when she was undercover. Even when she went to ground after Germany. And now, I don't even know what bloody country she's in.' He hung his head and sighed. 'The one time I needed to be good at my job, and I failed her.'

'You couldn't have known what was in Vance's mind. Nobody could.'

He raised his head, his eyes wide and angry. 'My job is to work with probabilities, Carol. That doesn't mean discounting the improbabilities. And I didn't even give them house room during that investigation. I was blinkered because I was convinced I knew Jacko Vance so well.'

The silence between them was like the air before a thunderstorm. 'You just called me Carol,' Paula said.

He looked thunderstruck. 'God help you, then, Paula.' His voice was husky with emotion.

'I miss her too, Tony.'

Hesitantly, he reached out and put an arm round her shoulders. They seldom touched, he and Paula. Never hugged as a greeting or as a farewell. This was a moment that mattered to them both. 'She's got no bone to pick with you, Paula. She'll be back in your life one of these days.'

She leaned her head on his shoulder and tried not to cry. After a while, she cleared her throat and stepped away. 'You really think you know her? Nadia?'

Tony pinched the bridge of his nose. 'I think so. It's not coming, though. I'm going to have to tuck it away and make my subconscious do the work when I'm asleep. What we do know about her, looking at this picture, is that she liked to go out and have fun, and she had mates to do that with.'

'How do you know it's not just a one-off and she's been stuck with Brittney and Bubble from Accounts for somebody's camera-phone shot at the company Christmas party?' Although her tone was teasing, deliberately trying to shift the mood, Paula genuinely wanted to know.

'None of them is self-conscious or awkward with each other.' He swung round and flicked through the menus. Tucked away behind the rest was another shot, on ordinary printer paper. 'And look, there's another one of the three of them. Different night, different outfits, very relaxed on a banquette.' He was right. She'd missed that on her first cursory look at the board. 'You need to find these women and speak to them. But you don't need me to tell you that.' He wheeled away and headed for the hallway. 'I don't know what I'm doing here, pointing out the obvious to you, Paula. Is this the investigative equivalent of the pity fuck? "Poor Tony, I should give him something to think about."'

Her first reaction had been to feel insulted. 'Of course it isn't. It's not about you. I want to crack this case and I don't have anybody to bounce ideas off, OK? It's about me, feeling lost without my old team. I'm sorry if you think I'm wasting your time. I wanted another pair of eyes that I could trust, that's all.'

'I'm sorry.' He sighed again. 'I'm not at my best right now. Let's take a look at the bedroom and see if there's anything there that rings my bell.'

But there hadn't been. The room was neat, no piles of laundry on the floor, no half-worn outfits thrown over the single chair. The duvet cover, a bright abstract, was the only splash of colour in the room. It had been straightened up, the pillows plumped. There was nothing in the wardrobe that didn't fall into the category of work, casual or night-on-the-town. No fetish outfits, no fantasy props, no sex toys. On one bedside table sat a paperback with a Polish title. It looked more chick lit than Booker Prize. Beside it, a half-empty sports bottle of water and a pair of glasses. Three pairs of understated earrings nestled in a tiny wooden tray beside a small gold crucifix on a fine chain. 'The kind of girl every mother wants her son to meet,' Paula muttered.

Tony snorted. 'Maybe not mine.' He opened the dressing-table drawer. A box of tissues. A tub of peach-flavoured lip balm. A scatter of condoms and a half-squeezed tube of lubricant. 'Sexually active.' He picked up the lube and tested the cap. 'But maybe not recently. See, it's hardened round the cap.'

'Or maybe she'd been having the kind of sex that doesn't need lube,' Paula said drily. 'It happens.'

'So I'm told.' He turned to the small chest of drawers in the corner. The top drawer contained a wide selection of inexpensive make-up. Second drawer, practical but pretty lingerie. Third drawer, T-shirts. Bottom drawer, a couple of thick sweaters. 'I think Nadia might have been on the intersection of nice and dull. Which is interesting, because that's a combination that reduces her risk factors significantly. Most victims have chaotic elements in their lives. That's usually how their killers cross their paths. But Nadia seems the opposite of chaotic. Which makes your job that bit harder.'

And that had been the sum total of Tony's insights. She'd tried not to feel disappointed, but she couldn't escape the realisation that she'd hoped for more. She'd wanted something to drive the investigation in a new direction, something that would show her new boss that she was someone worth watching.

Paula straightened up in her seat and started the engine. She'd stop off at Skenfrith Street on her way home and put a rocket up the uniforms. Get them to take Bev's disappearance seriously, not just stick it on the back burner and hope it would simmer away to nothing.

'It's like the bloody Marie Celeste in here,' she said aloud as she tried to find someone to direct her to the duty inspector's office. She ended up descending to the custody suite in the basement in the hope of finding signs of life. A radio was playing softly, a low mutter that sounded like sport commentary. The custody sergeant, a craggy-faced tough in his thirties, looked up from his paperwork and raised his eyebrows.

'Have you lost your way?' He stood up, wary but not unfriendly. 'We've not met, have we?'

'DS Paula McIntyre. I'm the new face on DCI Fielding's firm. I was looking for the duty inspector, but there doesn't seem to be anybody about upstairs.'

He gave a snort of laughter. 'Are you not from round here?'

'I've lived in Bradfield all my adult life. Why? What's so special about Skenfrith Street? Don't you do crime outside school hours?' Paula kept her tone light, but she wished Sergeant Banter would cut to the chase.

'Bradfield Victoria are playing Manchester United at home. Every warm body is at the game, in case of any crowd trouble. Including the duty inspector.'

'Are they expecting crowd trouble?'

This time, he laughed properly. 'Nay, lass. But they're expecting a bloody good game of football. Now, is there owt I can help you with?'

Paula shook her head. Whatever the uniform branch were doing about Bev Andrews' disappearance, they clearly weren't doing it tonight. 'I'll speak to them in the morning. I hope you have a quiet night,' she added on her way out.

'Fat chance. There'll be drunks galore later, whatever the scoreline is.'

There was nothing for it but to go home empty-handed and see how Elinor was getting on with Torin. Maybe the boy would have thought of something that might open up a more promising line of inquiry. Something that would command attention more than a bloody good game of football.

21

There must be an algorithm that described the twist in the space-time continuum that occurred when a teenage boy was in the room, Paula thought, pausing on the threshold of her living room. Adolescent lads seemed to occupy a space out of all proportion to their actual size. The room usually seemed spacious when it was only occupied by herself and Elinor. It didn't even feel crowded when they had friends round. But with Torin sprawled on the sofa, legs stretched across the rug, shirt untucked and tie at half mast, it seemed to have shrunk. She'd have to find a *Doctor Who* geek and ask.

Elinor was in her favourite armchair, legs curled under her, knitting in her lap. The pair of them were watching *Shaun of the Dead*. Paula wasn't sure it was the best viewing for a boy whose mother was missing, but presumably Torin and Elinor had chosen it between them.

As she entered, Torin straightened up, his face stripped of teen anomie, naked anxiety exposed for anyone to see. 'Has my mum turned up?'

'I'm sorry. I've got no more news.' Seeing the crestfallen look on his face, Paula wished she had something else to offer. She perched on the arm of the sofa. 'I know you're going to want to shout at me for even asking, but are you totally sure she didn't say anything to you about any plans to meet someone?'

He glared at her. 'I told you. No. And even if she had and I missed it, she'd still have texted me to remind me. She always does. She says I never listen, so she always does a back-up.' His lower lip trembled and he looked away, covering his mouth with his hand. 'But she's wrong anyway. I do listen.'

'I'm sure you do, Torin,' Elinor said. She paused the DVD.

'So what are your lot doing to find her?' Torin demanded, belligerence a cover for his fear. His shoulders hunched defensively inside his thin shirt.

'The information I took from you this morning will have been put on the computer and circulated nationally. Tomorrow, they'll get started on the painstaking stuff of tracking down friends, checking out any activity on her bank accounts and credit cards.'

'Why are they waiting so long? Why aren't they doing it right now?' His voice was a howl of outrage.

Because it's not a priority. Because they'd rather be at the football. Because nobody else is worried about her the way you are. 'Because these things are all easier to do during normal working hours,' Paula said. Elinor's raised eyebrows told her what her partner thought of that pale excuse. Guilt-tripped, Paula said, 'I'll tell you what I'll do, if you like. I'll go round to your house tonight and put together all the stuff they'll need so they can get started right away in the morning. How does that sound?'

He chewed the skin on the side of his thumb. 'OK, I suppose.'

'Where does she keep stuff like bank statements and her passport? Do you know?'

'There's, like, a boxroom between her bedroom and the bathroom. It's a cupboard really, but my dad fitted it out like an office. Built a desk in and everything. All our official stuff's in the bottom drawer.'

'Thanks. I'll need to pick up some clothes for you too, if you're going to stay with us. Is it OK for me to go into your room?'

He looked mutinous but he nodded. 'OK, I suppose.'

'Do you want to stay here with us, Torin? It's up to you. If you've got a mate you'd rather stay with, or another friend of your mum's? You can say what you want, you know.'

'Do you not want me here, then?'

Paula could have wept for him. 'You can stay as long as you need to. As long as it's what you want.'

'It's OK here.' He jerked his head towards Elinor. 'She doesn't make a fuss. And if I'm under your feet, you'll crack on, get some answers so you get your space back, right?'

'Fair enough.' She tried to hide her surprise at his insight. 'Can I have your keys?'

'Not so fast,' Elinor said. 'You haven't eaten, have you? We saved some pizza for you. So before you go over to Bev and Torin's, you're going to sit down and have some dinner.'

Paula didn't even bother trying to protest. And if she was honest, as she headed back out into the night, she was glad she'd taken the time to eat. Not just because it recharged her physical batteries but because it gave a face to the task ahead. That was something she'd learned from Carol Jordan. Until then, she'd listened to the colleagues who said you couldn't afford emotional involvement with cases because it would burn you out. Working with Carol, she'd come to understand that you deliver a better quality of justice when you care. Yes, the price was high. But why do the job if you didn't care about the outcome?

It felt strange, letting herself into a house where she'd been a guest. Usually when she was searching premises or interrogating in someone's space, as she had been with Tony earlier, she was coming to it fresh. Here, she'd have to put aside the embarrassment of raking through the life of someone she knew and liked. For Bev's sake, she couldn't put personal squeamishness ahead of scouring the house for anything useful.

Of course, the house should have been searched already by whoever had been given her original notes. Paula suspected that Bev had been identified as low risk, the lowest rung on the ladder of missing persons. A by-the-book classification – 'no apparent threat of danger to either the subject or the public' – that would allow the officer concerned to put Bev on the bottom of the pile for someone else to pick up on the morning shift. They might not search the house at all at this stage. If Paula had been in charge, she'd have opted for an assessment of medium risk and not simply because Bev was a mate. The manual said, 'The risk posed is likely to place the subject in danger,' and she thought Bev slotted right into that category. Women like Bev did not go missing voluntarily. She tried not to dwell on the single sentence capitalised and highlighted in its own box near the start of the missing person protocol – 'If in doubt, think murder.'

There was a corner of her professional mind that had already been thinking precisely that.

She made a note of the time in her pocket book and stepped inside. The first phase was the Open Door search. Her former colleague Kevin Matthews used to call it the 'Don't-discount-the-bleeding-obvious search'. They all remembered unnerving cases where missing kids had turned up hidden in obscure corners of houses and flats, sometimes off their own bat. But more often at the hands of others. So Paula made her way through the house, checking every room and cupboard, every cubbyhole and boxed-in space big enough to accommodate a woman of Bev's dimensions. And as anticipated, she drew a blank.

She expected the next phase to be more productive. Now she would sweep the house in a quest for anything that would give her the inside track on Bev's life. Notes, diaries, phones, photos, computers. Torin had his own tablet with him; he'd said Bev never used it and he never touched her laptop, not now they'd got a wireless printer he could command from his own machine. She'd already spotted the laptop on the desk in the cubbyhole office Torin had described, but she didn't want to fuck that up for the techies. Time to call in a favour.

Paula took out her phone and checked the time before she keyed in the call. Half past nine wasn't too late to call a woman who spent her spare time communing with the digital world. To her surprise, it took four rings before Stacey answered. 'Paula, hello, what's going on?'

If Paula hadn't known her better, she would have said Stacey sounded flustered. But that wasn't her style. She'd never seen the former MIT's computer analyst anything less than cool under pressure. And Paula didn't think a call from her qualified as pressure. 'This and that. Started today in my new firm at Skenfrith Street. And you?'

'Don't ask. I'm doing stuff that a GCSE student could manage. It's not a productive use of my skills.'

'I thought as much. That's why I was wondering if you might be interested in doing a favour for me?'

Stacey gave a prim little laugh. 'It did cross my mind that might be why you're calling. What do you need?'

'I've got a misper. It's a bit complicated. I know the

woman concerned so I'm doing the prelims myself. I'll have to hand the laptop over to the CSIs. And they'll take for ever and they won't fillet it the way you will.' Paula let her voice tail off.

'And you want me to come over and make a shadow hard drive and analyse it, all without leaving a trace for the CSIs to find?' Stacey was back to her usual calm deadpan.

'Pretty much, yeah.' And then Paula heard what sounded like a male voice in the background. 'Have you got company? Is this a bad time?' Then it hit her. 'Oh my God, it's not Sam, is it?'

'It's OK,' Stacey said briskly. 'I'll pick up an external hard drive and meet you there. Text me the address. I'll see you soon.' And she ended the call. With anyone else, it would have been rude. But with her, it was just Stacey.

While she was waiting, Paula scouted out the kitchen and living room. A calendar fixed to the side of the fridge revealed the routines of normal life. Football practice, chess club, a school in-service day, a couple of sleepovers for Torin. A dental appointment for Bev. A trip to the movies, a gig for Torin, some friends for dinner. She flicked back a couple of months; it was much the same. A wood-framed blackboard fixed to the wall acted as a memo board. 'Spaghetti, bacon, milk, nutmeg' to one side, 'School trip deposit, tickets for Leeds fest, dry cleaning' on the other. Drawers and cupboards revealed nothing she wouldn't expect to find in a kitchen. The living room was no more productive. There wasn't even a notepad beside the phone. Nobody wrote down messages any more. They texted each other instead.

Paula was on the point of heading back upstairs when Stacey arrived. The daughter of Hong Kong Chinese parents, Stacey had proved to be a computer prodigy, seeming to grasp the finer elements of programming as readily as if they were a child's building blocks. She'd set up her own software company while she was still at university, coming up with a couple of boilerplate programs that had made her enough money never to have to work again. Then she confounded everyone by joining the police. She'd never explained her motives but over the years Paula had learned enough about her colleague to suspect that what Stacey loved was the licence to poke around in other people's data without fear of being arrested for it. She was also convinced that Stacey was firmly ensconced somewhere on the autism spectrum, so socially awkward was she. But towards the end of the MIT, it had dawned on Paula that Stacey was carrying a torch for another colleague, Sam Evans.

Sam's naked ambition and lack of team spirit had been obstacles to friendship as far as Paula was concerned. She didn't trust him to have her back when the shit came down, and that was a problem in a close team. Nevertheless, she'd nudged Stacey in the direction of making her feelings known. Life was too short not to go for the things that mattered. Of course, Stacey had said nothing since. They'd gone out for a meal a couple of times since the MIT disbanded, but Stacey had stolidly avoided talking about Sam. However, she had changed her hairstyle to something much more flattering and her clothes had definitely become more interesting than her standard uniform of beautifully tailored business suits. She was wearing more make-up too, emphasising the dark brown of her almond-shaped eyes and giving a palette of colour to unlined skin that looked surprisingly healthy considering how little daylight it ever absorbed. For the first time since Paula had known her, Stacey looked like a woman who thought she deserved to be loved.

Now, as they climbed the stairs, Paula said again, 'Did I interrupt something? Was that Sam's voice I heard in the background?'

Behind her, Stacey sighed. 'He was at my place for dinner. OK? That's all. Same way you'd come to my place for dinner.'

Paula smiled triumphantly, knowing Stacey couldn't see her face. 'Stacey, I've known you, how many years? And how many times have I been to your place for dinner? That would be a big fat zero. We always eat out, remember?'

'You could have come if you'd wanted to.'

At the top of the stairs Paula turned and pulled a face at Stacey. 'You are such a liar. Look, I'm actually glad you're seeing him.'

'Dinner. I didn't even cook,' Stacey said firmly. 'I had it catered.'

'It's a start.'

Stacey looked around the landing, her lips pursed, hands on her hips. 'So where is this computer? And who is this woman?'

Paula pointed to the cubbyhole door and gave Stacey the key points. She was done by the time Stacey was settled in front of the laptop. Stacey swung round in the chair and stared at Paula, frowning. 'You've taken in a teenage boy? You?'

'What? You mean, as in "the lesbians"?'

'No,' she said impatiently. 'You know I'm not like that. I mean you, as in, never shown any interest in parenting.'

Paula rubbed her tired eyes. Just what she needed. A discussion on her maternal instincts, or lack thereof. 'I'm not parenting, for fuck's sake. I'm taking in a stray. For the time being. Besides, Elinor's the one doing the hands-on. Look at me. Here I am. Not on a sofa with Torin. OK?'

Stacey turned back to the screen and pressed the power button. 'Fine. So long as you remember the prime directive of mispers. If in doubt . . . '

'Think murder. I know. We'll cross that bridge when we

come to it. Now, can you shove over enough to let me at that bottom drawer? Apparently that's where all the paperwork is.'

Stacey obliged but there was still barely room for Paula to crouch beside her. She opened the drawer and found it almost filled to the brim with folders, envelopes and loose papers. 'You'd be better taking the whole thing out and sitting down on the landing with it,' Stacey muttered, her head already in what she was doing. 'It never ceases to amaze me – how can you not password your computer? Especially when you share your home with a teenage boy? Are you listening, Paula?'

'No, I'm not.' Paula finally wrestled the drawer free of its runners and backed out of the room. She took it through to Bev's bedroom and sat on the edge of the rumpled duvet. Unlike Nadia Wilkowa, Bev wasn't a neat freak, which made Paula feel a little better about her own untidiness. She'd seen enough of the mess left by lives cut unexpectedly short to have learned the lesson of what's left behind but it still hadn't been enough to make her change her ways.

But at least Bev was careful with the paperwork. The top folder contained birth certificates for her and Torin, plus her marriage certificate and the divorce decree. The next envelope held National Insurance numbers, National Health Service numbers, a note of blood groups and Torin's red record book from babyhood. A folder of bank statements and another of credit card bills. Bev was one of those people who paid off her balance dutifully every month.

Then came the passports. Wherever Bev was, it wasn't abroad. At least, not by conventional means. There was a will leaving everything to Torin and granting guardianship to her ex-husband; an exchange of lawyers' letters arranging the terms of Tom's contact with his son; a bundle of Christmas and birthday cards to Bev from Torin; a folder of

Torin's school reports; and finally, right at the bottom, a battered old address book.

Stacey appeared in the doorway, waving a small silvery box in the air. 'A copy of Bev's hard drive. And nobody will ever know I was in there. I'll take a quick look tonight and forward her emails on to you. The rest I'll let you have as soon as I can.' She glanced at a slim gold watch that Paula reckoned must have cost a few months' salary. 'If I shoot off now, I'll still have time for dessert.'

'Good luck with that.' Paula shovelled everything back into the drawer except the address book. 'Thanks for this, Stacey. It's looking darker and darker.'

'I'm sorry, for your friend's sake. I'll be in touch.' She half-turned to go then paused. 'Have you heard from the DCI, by the way?'

Paula shook her head. 'Not a word. I don't even know where she is or what she's doing.'

'I expected her to come home to BMP once the dust had settled.'

'Ha. You have to be joking. The brass don't want her. She makes the bureaucrats look like a bunch of useless wankers. No, they were thrilled when she handed in her notice so she could move to West Mercia. But she never turned up. She resigned before she even started.'

'I know. That's why I thought she'd come back. For the sake of familiarity. And Tony, of course. He's still at Bradfield Moor, isn't he?'

'Oh yes. They were over the moon when he said he wasn't leaving after all. He's living on a narrowboat down at the Minster basin. But he hasn't heard from her either.'

Stacey slipped the hard drive into her pocket. 'Maybe she's the one you should be treating as a misper.'

22

Day twenty-five

Fielding definitely had presence, Paula decided. She appeared different in almost every respect from Carol Jordan, but the one thing they had in common was the ability to hold the attention of a room full of hard-arsed coppers. Nobody was whispering to their neighbour or texting their girlfriend while Fielding was running a briefing. She might be petite and pretty, but when she started talking you forgot those fleeting fantasies and focused on what she was saying. It reinforced Paula's desire to make the right mark on this firm.

It was a kind of performance. DCI Fielding did her briefing on PowerPoint. She had one of those soft Scottish accents that took the harshness out of her words and made her audience want them not to stop. 'The body of Nadzieja Wilkowa, known as Nadia, was found yesterday morning in a squat in Rossiter Street, Gartonside.' A picture of the exterior of the house. 'She had been beaten to death.' A shot of the body in situ. Fielding clearly didn't believe in sparing the squeamish or the hung-over. 'A blow to the head from a pipe or a baseball bat, then battered and kicked. We think she was killed here, judging by the blood spatter. Our killer's finishing touch was to superglue her labia together.' An explicit photograph that made Paula feel angry and nauseous. 'As we can see, her genital area had been shaved. When we find a boyfriend, I want to know if the shaving was her usual practice or if it's something our killer likes to do.'

The next shot showed the bathroom. Fielding used the laser pointer as she went through the key information. 'The victim's clothes and bag were stuffed down here. Not really hidden, just out of the way. It's possible he may have made her wash in the bath. Or washed her himself. The water to the property has been cut off, but the squatters have rigged up a rainwater catchment system that provides a limited water supply. There was a puddle of water in the bath.'

Back to the exterior shot of the house. 'Gartonside is no-man's-land. So there are no cameras on the approach to Rossiter Street or the surrounding area. I'm thinking the killer knew that. He seems too careful an offender simply to have got lucky. One of the many interesting questions is how he knew that the squatters would be gone for the weekend. Black, Hussain, I want you to talk to them. Find out exactly who knew they were going to be away. And who knows they live there.' She flashed a smile at the two detectives, the kind of smile that Paula reckoned made you feel the love.

'Nadia was a sales rep for a pharmaceutical company. Not one of those multinationals that are always coming up with new miracle cures that make you constipated or increase your risk of breast cancer. A small British company that does generic versions of common drugs. The kind of stuff your GP puts you on when she's trying to save the NHS a bob or two. She'd been working for them for eighteen months. No complaints, she was a good worker. A bright girl. Did well.' A photo of Nadia in life, her shaggy blonde hair tousled and her smile reaching her eyes. 'Although she was Polish she spoke exceptionally good English, her employers say. But still.' She scanned the room. 'Stach-niewski, you've got the right kind of name. Talk to the Polish community, put some feelers out, see whether she was known in the pubs and clubs and grocery stores.' A lanky ginger-haired officer nodded gloomily. 'Oh, and Stach? Give the Polish cops a call and see if you can find out whether Mrs Wilkowa has cancer. Because, three weeks ago, an email was sent from Nadia's account to her employers, stating that her mother had been diagnosed with cancer. She asked for a month's compassionate leave. The company didn't want to lose her because they thought she was a good worker so they agreed. Last week, they emailed her with a query about a client account. They got a reply, answering the query and also indicating that she would be back next week, as originally planned. Now, we don't know at this point whether she ever went to Poland, though DS McIntyre reckons she wouldn't have left her fridge full of perishables if she had. Black, check with Immigration and the Borders Agency to see whether there's any record of her leaving and returning. And talk to the airlines that fly to Poland out of Manchester and Leeds/Bradford, see if she's on any of their passenger lists. It's probably a waste of time, but we have to cover the ground. We don't want some defence counsel ambushing us down the line over things we left undone.' Everyone nodded sagely, like a roomful of car parcel-shelf ornaments.

'What's really interesting is that her killer managed to extort from her enough information to make the emails possible and plausible. As far as we can tell, she made no attempt to turn those messages into a cry for help.' Fielding paused, her professional demeanour slipping for a moment into an expression of pity. 'Her phone is passworded, which is a nuisance, but the techies tell me they'll have her call records today and hopefully we'll get into the phone for texts and messages very soon. We got luckier with the computer. Apparently the password was her birthday, so easy peasy for the CSIs to crack. Inspector Gardner is co-ordinating the actions, so he'll be setting a bunch of you on to the tedious but important job of working your way through the emails and the tweets and the Facebook contacts. I know it's boring . . .' She paused, giving them her best sympathetic smile. 'But it's also potentially crucial. Nadia crossed her killer's path somewhere and we have to find out precisely where and when. The answer could be buried in one of those emails. I'm counting on you not to let anything significant disappear in the slipstream of boredom.'

Bloody hell, she's talking like a poet now. Slipstream of boredom, for fuck's sake. Paula kept her face straight. She didn't want to draw attention to herself in case she got lumbered with the emails. 'Another group will be backtracking on all her recent appointments. I want anything you can squeeze out of them. And I would like alibis, please. I know this is a nightmare assignment because of the number of contacts involved, but we have to lift up every stone and expose the white bellies and the creepy crawlies beneath them.

'And finally. The CSI working on the computer has also identified two women who seem to be her closest pals. DS McIntyre, you and I will take them. I'll be doing a press conference later this afternoon. Till then, the ID is still under wraps.' She turned off the screen. 'That's it for now, everybody. I'm counting on you. And so is Nadia. Let's do it for her and her family.' Fielding finished with a dazzling smile. She knew how to use her charm, that much was obvious from her performance, Paula decided. But judging by her failure to turn it on for Grisha at the crime scene, she used it only when it was going to earn her clear advantage. Making her team love her was a priority; getting the pathologist to go the extra mile hadn't been.

Paula made her way through the bustle of officers discussing the briefing to Fielding's side. 'Morning, McIntyre,' Fielding said absently, flicking through a bundle of papers. 'Give me ten minutes to deal with this lot and we'll head out.'

'I need to talk to the duty inspector in uniform first, ma'am.' Paula was at her most conciliatory. 'The misper I caught on my way in yesterday. I have to brief them, make sure they're taking it seriously.'

Fielding's perfectly groomed eyebrows rose. 'Any reason why they wouldn't take it seriously?'

Paula knew she had to tread carefully. She was the new girl here; she had no idea where the political lines were drawn in this nick. 'No reason. But I know the misper, ma'am. Her son gave me the key to their house. I wanted to pass it on personally. Just so they know I've got an interest. And so I can give them a backgrounder.'

'Have you been poking your nose in where you shouldn't, McIntyre? You're not with the MIT any more. We respect each other's boundaries in this nick. Have you not got enough on your plate with a murder that you have to do uniform's job for them?' Fielding didn't bother to lower her voice. The officers nearest them pretended not to notice, but Paula knew it was all sinking in. She could feel her ears burning.

'Like I said. I know the misper. Her son is staying with us for the time being.'

Fielding froze in the middle of turning a page. 'Are we talking minor here?'

'He's fourteen.'

Fielding stared at her as if she was mad. 'What were you thinking? You should have called social services. Or a relative. Last time I looked, you weren't on the list of appropriate adults.'

Righteous indignation was in danger of trumping good sense. 'His nearest relatives are in Bristol. His dad's in the army, in Afghanistan. I considered he was less at risk in my spare room than in an emergency placement.' She paused. 'Ma'am.' She couldn't make Fielding out. Where was her compassion? This woman was a mother. If anyone should understand Paula's reasoning, it was someone who had a kid of their own.

Fielding gave an exasperated sigh. 'Go and brief the duty inspector, then. And make it quick. We've got a murder here and that takes precedence over everything else.' She waved a hand at Paula in a gesture of impatient dismissal. Paula was halfway to the door when Fielding called after her. 'And if you plan on carrying on with the child-minding, for Christ's sake get consent from the relatives. I don't want to have to arrest you and your girlfriend for unlawful imprisonment.'

Someone guffawed, another sniggered. Welcome to Skenfrith Street, Paula thought bitterly. The home of modern policing.

Dean Hume, the duty inspector, had the mangled ears, thick neck and asymmetric nose of a rugby player who had never shirked in the scrum. His scalp had a five o'clock shadow that revealed his male pattern baldness and his eyes nestled in tired grey folds of skin. He inhabited a tiny glassed-in cubicle in a corner of the main squad room. His computer monitor was the size of a bedside cabinet and it was surrounded by stacks of file folders. His white shirt was already wilting under the pressure of work. When Paula explained why she was there and what she had discovered at Bev's house, he looked as thrilled as Fielding had. 'You used to be on the MIT team, right?'

Paula was starting to get tired of this. 'That's right, sir. DCI Jordan's firm.'

'You were a bit of a law unto yourselves there.' To her surprise, Hume smiled. 'Got some good results, though.'

'We did, sir. We thought we were bloody good value for money.'

He grunted. 'Shame the brass didn't agree. The thing is, Sarge, we're a bit more by the book here. DCI Fielding runs a tight ship. And she gets results too. So if you're going to go off piste, you'll need to be discreet about it.' It was a warning, but in the friendliest of terms.

For the first time since she'd arrived at Skenfrith Street, Paula felt part of a team. Shame it was the wrong team. 'Thanks, sir. I'll bear that in mind. As far as Bev Andrews is concerned, I typed up a full report of my actions and the information I gathered. It should give your officers a head start. Who should I email it to?'

He gave her the details of his sergeant. 'From what you tell me, it's not looking too clever,' he said. 'I'll have a word with media liaison and see if we can get something in the *Sentinel Times* tonight. And we'll have to talk to the lad again.'

'I doubt he's got anything else to give.'

Hume nodded. 'I'm sure you're right. I heard you're the whizz kid when it comes to interviews. But we've got to cover all the bases. You can sit in as the appropriate adult if you like?'

Paula's smile was grim. 'I don't think DCI Fielding's going to cut me any slack on that score. My partner is probably your best bet.' She scribbled down Elinor's details and handed them to Hume. 'She's a doctor at Bradfield Cross.'

'Thanks. Any developments, I'll let you know.'

Paula stood up to leave. But Hume hadn't quite finished. 'And, Sergeant – leave this to us now. None of your maverick MIT tricks, please? Nobody's got your back here. Where DCI Fielding's concerned, you're on your own.'

23

B ev's first return to consciousness inside the freezer had been bewildering; the second was excruciating. Every time she took a breath, her ribs hurt, sharp pain like a handful of daggers stabbing her in the chest. Gradually, as she grew more aware, she understood that if she kept her breathing shallow and moved as little as possible, the pain ceased to be all-consuming. But that left room in her nervous system for the other agonies to make themselves felt. There was a dull ache in her lower back. Kidneys, she thought. Her head throbbed and when she moved her jaw, lightning shot from the point of her chin to the top of her skull. A fire burned between her legs, spreading up into her groin. The pinkie on her left hand was hot and swollen. Probably broken. The least of her worries.

She'd been determined to do whatever it took to survive, to make it home to Torin. But it had quickly dawned on her that her captor was as determined to find fault as she was to obey his every whim. She'd fallen into the hands of a man whose only satisfaction came from causing pain. It wasn't enough just to rape her. He had to make the excuse of her inadequacy to hurt her. He'd subjected her to humiliating sexual acts, all the while maintaining the sick pretence that she was a failing wife. God help any genuine wife who had fallen prey to this monster, Bev thought, shuddering involuntarily, a groan of pain seeping from her bruised lips.

He'd ripped the tape from her mouth while he'd been fucking her in the kitchen. He said he wanted to hear her appreciate his sexual prowess. But if she made any other kind of noise, she'd be sorry. Tasering would be the least of her worries.

Then he unchained her and dragged her upstairs. He fastened her to another metal eye in a room furnished with nothing but a bed covered with a rubber sheet. He punched her hard in the face and forced her on to the bed, tying her by her wrists and ankles so she was spread-eagled across it. He'd left her alone briefly, then returned with a can of shaving foam, a pair of scissors and a plastic razor. 'If you move, I'll cut you to ribbons,' he said, as matter of fact as if he'd been asking for sugar in his tea. Then his hands had been on her, snipping away at her pubic hair, carefully trimming it to the skin. Her flesh crawled at his touch, but she bit her lip and forced herself not to flinch. Next came the shaving foam, then the rasp of the razor against her most tender skin. Bev had never shaved herself; being blonde, she hadn't even needed a bikini wax for sunshine holidays. The feeling of air against her bare skin was strange. But at least he was careful and he didn't hurt her. She wondered why, when his sole aim till then had been to punish her.

The respite didn't last long. This time, he made her beg. Hating herself, she did as she was told, though not convincingly enough to avoid another beating. When he'd finally reached the point where he couldn't raise an erection, that had been her fault too. Bev refused to remember what had come next. Some things didn't bear thinking about. She thought she'd passed out in the end.

Now she was back in her box. Her kennel, he'd called it. As if she was an animal. Bev had seen plenty of anger in her life. But she'd never come across such a sustained level of aggression directed at a stranger. Not even rape victims. From what she'd seen in the hospitals where she'd worked, women were only beaten this badly, this systematically, by their partners. This was domestic violence gone rogue.

And she was caught at the heart of it.

Tears seeped from her swollen eyes. She'd tried to hold on to the promise of seeing her son again. But Bev was no fool. She knew she couldn't withstand another night like that. She'd seen his face. She could identify his home.

She wasn't going to make it out of here alive.

24

Tony had always liked the room where he visited Dr Jacob Gold. Nothing in it reminded him of anywhere he'd spent any significant amount of time; it was emotionally neutral. The walls were lemon yellow, broken up by four large paintings of beaches, seascapes and tidal estuaries. Two armchairs at an angle to each other sat on either side of a gas fire, separated by a striped rug in muted colours. In the shallow bay window sat a chaise longue with another armchair close to its head. A low table sat in the centre of the floor displaying an exotic collection of polished seashells.

It was the kind of calm space that was perfectly suited to the supervision sessions most psychologists saw as a key part of their professional lives. The relationship was all about helping them to develop skills and become better practitioners, which was something Tony took seriously. The problem he had with supervision was that he didn't have a whole lot of respect for most of the supervisors he'd encountered. He was well aware that his was an unconventional mind. It wasn't arrogance to acknowledge he was also smarter than most of the people doing his job. Then he'd heard Dr Gold speak about damaged lives at a symposium. This, he thought, was the man for him. He'd approached him afterwards, but Dr Gold had refused. 'I don't do supervisions,' he'd said in a tone that left no space for discussion.

That had never stopped Tony. 'I know why,' he said. 'Compared with your patients, practitioners are boring. Well, I'm not. I'm the one passing for human.'

Dr Gold frowned, turning his attention properly to the little guy in the ill-assorted clothes and the bad haircut. That had been back in the days before Carol had made some subtle changes that Tony had barely noticed happening. 'Who *are* you?'

'You remember that serial killer in Bradfield last year? Young male victims?'

Something shifted in Dr Gold's expression. 'You're the profiler.' Tony nodded. There was nothing more to be said. Either Jacob Gold would bite or he wouldn't. They stood, eyeing each other up, heedless of the conference bustle around them. 'Come and talk to me next week. I'm based in Leeds. You can contact me via the university.'

And so it had begun. After that first session, Tony knew he'd found someone who could help him live with himself and his work, his achievements and his mistakes. Luckily for him, Jacob Gold had also discovered someone worth breaking his own rules for.

Tony had always conceived of the role of supervisor as analogous to that of the priest in confessional. As he understood it, the theory of Catholic confession was that you went when you had sins to confess; that the priest helped you to see the error of your ways; that you

139

underwent a penance to remind you of the way, the truth and the light; that you departed, ostensibly to sin no more; and that whatever you brought into the box stayed between you and the priest. And presumably, God. Though He never seemed to intrude much on the practical proceedings of the Church.

Tony made an appointment with Dr Gold once or twice a year, when some aspect of his clinical practice was troubling him, when he felt he wasn't dealing well with some element of his professional life, or, more rarely, when his personal life was throwing him conundrums he couldn't readily solve. A fifty-minute hour under Jacob's gentle probing usually suggested a solution to whatever he'd brought to the session. At the very least, it brought Tony a degree of clarity. The equivalent of Catholic penance was the process of digging away at the roots of the issue during their session. And of course, he would leave with the firm intention of making the changes that would resolve his difficulty.

And often he would fail.

But that was part of the process too.

Tony knew he should have talked sooner to Jacob after the debacle with Jacko Vance. He was conscious that he'd been avoiding it. Jacob, who wore his supervision lightly, had clearly been well aware of the media coverage and had left a message of support. Which, in the terms of their relationship, had been the equivalent of shouting, 'Oi, get your arse down here, pronto.'

But he was here now, and that was what mattered. Today, he'd chosen the armchair rather than the chaise longue. Jacob sat across from him, long legs crossed, an elegant notebook open on his lap, Mont Blanc pen lying in the crack between the thick cream pages. 'How are you?' It was the question that always began their sessions. Unless Jacob had been living on a desert island with no access to the electronic media, he had to have a pretty good idea, given the coverage of the recent events in his life.

'Well, let me see.' Tony steepled his fingers in front of his chest. 'BMP decided they no longer need my services, my new home was burned to the ground, people died because I wasn't good enough at my job and Carol walked out of my life because she needs someone to blame for her brother's murder and in her head, I'm that someone. By the same argument, another colleague would have grounds for blaming me for the fact that she's been blinded and disfigured for life from acid burns, but she's forgiven me and I'm not sure, but that almost feels worse. I'm living on a boat with my books in storage, but on the positive side, one of my former police colleagues came round last night looking for my insights. Apart from that, Mrs Lincoln, how did you enjoy the play?' His tone was light but he knew that wouldn't fool Jacob. Hell, it wouldn't fool a block of wood.

'And which item in this catalogue of disaster is the one that costs you most peace of mind, would you say?'

The trick with these sessions, Tony had found, was to try to answer without pausing for thought. His discomfort generally came from thinking too much. Trying something different was one of the reasons for supervision. So he replied at once. 'Carol. I failed her. And she's out of my life. I don't even know where she's living. What she's doing to get through the days. And I miss her. Every single day, I miss her.'

'What makes you think you failed her?'

'I'm supposed to be able to work out what's going on inside the heads of people with aberrant minds. But on this case, I was thinking in straight lines. It's as if I forgot I was dealing with someone whose defining characteristic was wrong-footing everyone around him. I didn't explore the possibilities properly. I had half my mind on other things and I didn't drill down deep enough. And people died. Among them Carol's brother and his partner.' Tony hung his head, the sense of failure as vivid as it had been at the time. 'If I'd been rigorous, they would have been warned. And the chances are, they'd be alive today.'

'You know this is magical thinking, don't you? You're claiming control over circumstances you can't control.'

'Don't, Jacob. Don't try and get me to let myself off the hook. I know I didn't do my job well enough. I'm not looking for excuses. I'm looking for a way to move forward from the consequences.'

Jacob picked up his pen and made a short note. Just a few words. 'To move forward, you have to accept the truth of a situation. Not persist in myth-making. Wouldn't you say?'

'It's not myth-making. It's acknowledging failure.'

Jacob's considering expression didn't alter. 'He was a clever man, your opponent?'

'Yes. An exemplar of Narcissistic Personality Disorder. An arch-manipulator.'

'So, a man perfectly capable of second-guessing whatever tactics you might have chosen to employ against him?'

Tony gripped the arms of his chair. 'Maybe. You're saying he would have found a way to circumvent whatever defences I'd constructed?'

'He had the advantage. He was working in the shadows. In the interstices. It's impossible to guard against someone like that if they are clever enough and determined enough. He was determined to have his revenge. Or so it seems to me. Does it seem so to you?'

It was an invitation to a shift of perspective. Tony wanted to grasp it, but that very desire made him suspicious. 'I think I should have stopped him.'

'You don't think you might be taking responsibility for the actions of another?'

'I know I didn't kill Michael and Lucy. I know I have no direct responsibility for what happened. But I can't escape the indirect responsibility. It's what Carol believes too.'

'If Carol didn't hold you responsible, do you think you would feel this level of guilt? This is not the first time that victims have died in the course of an investigation you've been party to. I've sat in this room and listened to your grief on that score. But all I have heard from you in terms of responsibility is a wish that you could have done better or done differently. Not this scourging guilt.'

And this time, Tony had no instant reply. At last, he said, 'Adler would have had a field day with this, right?'

'How might he have characterised this, do you think? How would you characterise it if a patient presented with this shift in their belief system?'

'I'd think it was hubris. I had a friend once. She knew me when I was a teenager. She was kind to me, but she thought I needed toughening up. She used to say, "You're like a man with a big nose who thinks everybody's talking about him. Well, they're not, and the sooner you thicken that skin of yours, the happier you'll be."'

'Was she right, do you think?'

Tony gave a rueful chuckle. 'I don't think I ever learned the lesson. I've always thought that was why I had such powerful empathy.'

Jacob nodded, so slight a movement that Tony wondered whether he'd imagined it. 'And still you haven't answered the question. If Carol didn't hold you responsible, do you think you would feel this level of guilt?'

'Probably not.' The honesty was hard but there was no point in being here if he didn't try.

'And if this source of feeling bad about yourself was reduced or removed, do you think the other things that are causing you difficulties would be made easier?'

'That's one of those questions that provokes only one answer,' Tony said, an edge of annoyance in his voice.

'And that may well be why you need to ask it.' Jacob sighed. He closed his notebook and put it on the floor next to him, pen aligned with the end. 'Tony, I've been your supervisor for many years. I like to think I have formed a good idea of how you function. I know you have made an accommodation with aspects of your personality that many people would find problematic. I also know you want to move forward in your practice and in your personal life. For a long time, Carol Jordan has been the centre of your emotional life. At times, she has appeared to be the only component of your emotional life. Would that be a fair assessment?'

Tony's shoulders were tightening involuntarily. He had an uneasy sensation in his stomach. Jacob had never spoken to him in these terms. He'd probably never actually said so much in the whole of a session before. 'I do have other friendships,' he said, hearing his own defensiveness. And who were those other friends, when the chips were down? Paula? Alvin Ambrose? Cops who had been colleagues and had grown into more than that. But not the kind of friends most people had. Nobody he went to the football with. Nobody he was on a pub quiz team with. Nobody he'd kept up with from his student days. Nobody he went hillwalking with. Not even anybody he regularly gamed with online.

'The only one you've been bringing into this room for years is Carol.'

'You think it's going nowhere, don't you? You think it's holding me back? Trapping me in the same place?'

Jacob breathed heavily and pushed his gold-rimmed glasses up to the bridge of his nose in a rare moment of fidgeting. 'It's not what I think that matters. But we both know there is significance in you even asking those questions in those terms.'

Tony's expression was bleak, his eyes blank. 'In so far as I've ever loved anyone, I love Carol.' Even to say it was a wrench, like something twisting in his gut.

'What would happen if you let that feeling go?'

He shook his head. 'You don't just let feelings go.'

'You can allow time to release you from them. Grief and mourning are part of the process, but there is a process. When you clear out the attic, it's amazing what you make room for.' Jacob sighed again. 'It's not my job as a supervisor or as a therapist to tell you what to do. But I will say this: living with so much pain is neither healthy nor necessary. You need to look at your life and decide what really serves you. And what you should let go.'

'You've helped me understand one thing today. If it had been anyone else's brother, I would feel bad about it. But I wouldn't be taking all the weight. I need to think about what that means for me.'

'You don't have to carry this alone. You can always bring it here. And as you reminded me, you have friends. You will find comfort.' Abruptly, he stood up. 'Would you wait a moment?'

Jacob left the room without a backward glance. Baffled, Tony stared at the closed door. Jacob had never walked out of a session before, no matter how challenging it had become. What was going on? Had his supervisor heard something outside the room that he'd missed? He fretted over what had happened, finding that easier than returning to his own problems.

And then Jacob was back, carrying a slim hardback book with an olive-green and cream jacket. He handed it to Tony. *Rings on a Tree* by Norman MacCaig. 'I don't know how you feel about poetry. But I find it helpful as a way of interrogating myself and my own process. There is a poem in this collection, "Truth for Comfort". I think it would be a good place for you to start.'

'You want me to cure myself with *poetry*?' He couldn't help his incredulity showing. Jacob, that rigorous psychologist, suggesting poetry was like Elinor Blessing suggesting crystal healing as a cancer treatment.

Jacob smiled, settled into his chair. 'There is no cure for what ails us, Tony. But I think we can manage something better than palliative care, don't you? And so, how is work?'

That was one of the things Tony liked about working with Jacob. He didn't linger once the patient had understood his next step. 'I'm on a part-time contract at Bradfield Moor again,' he said. 'They seem happy to have me back. And I like the work.' He outlined the bare bones of his clinical practice, explaining his thinking in a couple of interesting cases.

'And the profiling?'

'Bradfield don't want me any more. They say it's about economy, but I think it might have something to do with the fact that I haven't hit it off with their new Chief Constable. James Blake and I, we're chalk and cheese.' Before Jacob could say anything, Tony held up one finger. 'Which I am not blaming myself for. It's one of those things. I'm doing bits and pieces with other forces, but there really are cuts that are affecting outside experts like me. They see us as a luxury they can't afford. And with them training up their own so-called experts . . .' He puffed out his cheeks and blew the air out. 'I miss the work. I like it and I'm good at it.'

'You are.' Jacob took off his glasses and polished them. It was weird to see him shifting around so much. 'And I have been thinking about that too. A man who has found his calling should be able to practise it, wouldn't you say?'

Tony grinned. 'Some might say it's better to have no call for someone with my particular skills.'

'There is, I think, nobody with your expertise and experience in the field. It's time you shared that, Tony.'

He held his hands up, defensive. 'Oh no. No more teaching. I'm not doing dog-and-pony shows again.'

'I'm not talking about the academic life. I'm talking about writing a book. Taking the reader through your custom and practice. Showing and telling how you profile, how you resolve cases. How you work with the police, how you make your arguments. There is nothing comparable out there, Tony. You could create a future generation of profilers in your image. If the police are going to train their own, don't you think they should be informed by best practice?'

Tony shook his head, almost laughing. 'I'm not a writer. That's not my skill set.'

'You're a communicator, though. And publishers have editors to make your prose pretty. Don't make a decision now. Go away and think about it. It may provide you with a double satisfaction. Working through those old cases might help you work through your other process. Cleansing, not wallowing.' Jacob looked at his watch. 'Our time is up.' He stood up and pointed to the book of poetry. 'Think about what we've talked about. Remember what they say about bridges. The hard thing is to know which ones to cross and which ones to burn. Make some changes, Tony.'

Tony gave a wry smile and scrambled to his feet. 'Physician, heal thyself?' But even as he spoke, he knew he was trying to make light of what might be the most difficult choice of his adult life. Was it really time to cut Carol Jordan out of his heart for good?

25

A quick pass through Nadia Wilkowa's Facebook page had indentified the two friends in her memo-board photos as Ashley Marr and Anya Burba. Anya was a teaching assistant in a primary school in Todmorden, a twenty-minute drive from Bradfield. Ashley was closer, a receptionist in a GP-run health centre in Harriestown, a ten-minute walk from Nadia's flat. Fielding decided Ashley would be their first target. The head receptionist wasn't thrilled when they asked to interview her, but Fielding made it clear she wasn't going to argue the toss. With a great deal of emphatic breathing, the receptionist showed them into a tiny room with four chairs and a table. 'It looks more suited to a poker school than anything medical,' Paula muttered as the woman left them alone so she could fetch Ashley.

'Let's hope Ms Marr doesn't have a poker face,' Fielding said. 'Right then, McIntyre, let's see what you're made of. You lead off on the interview.'

Paula was gratified at Fielding's confidence in her. But

there was no opportunity for her to say so. Ashley Marr
stuck her head round the door, looking more confused than
worried. 'Are you the police? Are you sure you've got the
right person?'

There was no mistaking the woman in the photo. Ashley
looked in her mid-twenties. She had a round, cheerful face
framed with a mop of auburn hair. Her large green eyes
were widely spaced and coupled with a neat little nose and
a small mouth, they gave her the look of a happy kitten.
Her black jeans and pink jumper were both tight, as if she'd
put on a few pounds since she'd bought them. Paula gave
her a welcoming smile. Best to keep things relaxed and
informal till they got the young woman settled, then hit
her with the bad news. 'Come in, Ashley. I'm Paula
McIntyre and this is Alex Fielding. We're police detectives
here in Bradfield. Have a seat, please.' Paula waved her to
the chair furthest from the door and sat down at right
angles to her.

Ashley perched on the edge of the chair. 'I don't understand. I haven't done anything. What's all this about? Do I
need a lawyer? They always ask for a lawyer on the telly.'

Paula inwardly cursed the ubiquitous inaccuracies of TV
drama. 'You really don't need a lawyer. It's nothing you've
done, Ashley. We need to talk to you about one of your
friends.' From her bag, she produced a copy of one of the
photos from Nadia's kitchen. She pointed to Nadia. 'Do you
recognise this person?'

Ashley looked scared. 'It's Nad. My mate, Nad. Nadia.
What's happened to her? Why are you here?'

'I'm afraid I've got some very sad news, Ashley.' Paula
reached across the angle of the table and put a hand over
hers. 'Nadia's dead.'

The colour drained from Ashley's cheeks, making her pale
freckles distinct as a rash. Her hands flew to the sides of her

head and she looked stunned. 'I don't believe it. Not Nad. You must have made a mistake. It's her mum that's got cancer, not her.'

'There's no mistake, Ashley. I'm very sorry. I know this is a terrible time for you, but we really need your help.'

'Can we get you a cup of tea or a drink of water?' Fielding leaned forward and for a moment, Paula could see that she'd be the kind of mother you could rely on.

Ashley shook her head. 'What happened? How can she be dead? She's in Poland, she texted me only the other day, saying the weather was crap where she was and how she was looking forward to coming home.' Her hand flew to her mouth. 'She never texted me on Monday, is that when she died?' Paula felt Fielding's quick glance at her. The squatters had returned on Tuesday morning to find Nadia's body in their living room. It looked as if the killer saw no need to pretend Nadia was alive after he'd murdered her. He simply wanted to prevent anyone raising the alarm while she was still with him.

'We think someone took Nadia,' Paula said. 'He kept her prisoner. And then he killed her.'

'In Poland?'

'We think she never left Bradfield,' Paula said.

'But she texted me. She said she had to go home at short notice because her mum had cancer and she thought she was going to die. I said to Skype me when she got there but she said she couldn't because her mum didn't have internet access. So we texted.' She pulled her phone out. 'Look, I'll show you.'

'That's really helpful, Ashley. And we'll need a copy of those text exchanges between you. Did anything strike you as odd about anything she said in her texts? Or the way she said it?'

Ashley frowned. 'Everything was just normal. That's why

none of this makes any sense. Are you sure you've got the right person?'

Paula's heart went out to her. 'I know this is a terrible thing for you to hear, but we're sure. And we need all the help we can get. The sooner we get it, the more chance there is that we'll catch whoever did this to your friend. So we'd like to ask you some questions. Do you mind?' It was heartless, to demand such a thing when the woman was still in shock. But necessary.

Ashley's eyes brimmed with tears and she started to shake. Paula put an arm round her shoulders and let her sob. Her eyes met Fielding's. Any suggestion of sympathy had disappeared. Her boss made a rolling gesture with her hand; hurry it up. *Fuck that.* Paula let Ashley cry, finding a packet of tissues in her pocket to wipe her eyes and blow her nose when the first storm had passed. 'I'm s-s-sorry,' Ashley hiccuped, smudged mascara giving her racoon eyes.

'Don't be. She was your friend. It's right to feel upset.' Paula sat back but kept a hand on Ashley's arm. 'So, tell me when you last saw Nadia.'

Ashley gulped and swallowed, then managed to speak. 'It was a Saturday.' She counted back, her lips moving silently. 'Three weeks ago. We went down Manchester to go shopping at the Trafford Centre. They've got, like, a load of cool shops there. We met up with Anya – that's our other mate, Anya Burba. She's Polish, like Nad. Anyhow, we met up at Burger King at noon and had a burger then we went round the shops.' She stopped, smitten by memory, her bottom lip quivering.

'Did you buy anything?' Paula sounded chatty, interested in the shopping rather than the sinister.

'I got some purple jeggings and a sequinned top to match. Nad got two blouses for work. A yellow one and a blue one. They had, like, a white pinstripe. They were really pretty, she looked lush in them. Anya, she got some stuff out of Body Shop. Bath stuff. She'd live in the bath, give her half a chance. Then we went to the food court and had chips and Cokes. Then Anya gave me a lift home. 'Cause Nad decided she wanted to see this movie that me and Anya didn't fancy.'

There was always a moment in an interview when the witness said something whose significance wasn't obvious to them. The trick was not to show that it mattered. Paula had to struggle to keep her hand from gripping Ashley's hand tightly, as if she could squeeze information from her. 'What film was that?'

Ashley shrugged. 'Dunno, really. It was something French. Nad, she speaks French as well as English. It had subtitles, like, but I'd rather watch the telly or go down the pub. If I wanted to read all night, I'd buy, like, a magazine.'

'So Nadia was planning to go to the cinema alone?'

'Yeah. She did that sometimes. She was into films, way more than me and Anya.'

It made sense. Paula remembered a couple of French films in the stack of DVDs in Nadia's flat. 'And she was happy to go by herself?'

'Yeah, why not?'

'And you're sure she hadn't made plans to meet anyone there?'

Ashley shook her head. 'It was a spur of the moment thing. We went and had a look at what was on, to see if there was something we all fancied. And when Nad spotted that French film she was made up.' Her face crumpled. 'That might have been the last thing she ever did before he got her, right?' Tears dribbled down her cheeks again.

'We don't know, Ashley. Now, here's how you can help us even more. I want you to cast your mind back to that Saturday. Were you aware of anyone following you? Was there anybody you kept catching sight of?'

Ashley frowned, concentrating on recall. 'Nothing springs to mind. We were just out having a laugh and a shop, we weren't paying attention to anybody else.'

'And you didn't get into a ruck with anybody? Nobody hit on you?'

She shook her head. 'Nothing like that. Like I said, we weren't interested in anybody else.'

'You didn't see any guys you fancied, then?'

Ashley gave her a shrewd look. 'Not that we did anything about. We were looking, like. When we were sitting down eating, we were checking out the talent. But not in any serious way. Just, like, "he's hench", or, like, "he's got a nice bum". We never spoke to any of them and they never spoke to us. It was totally, like, normal.'

'What about boyfriends? Was Nadia seeing anybody?'

Ashley looked down at the table. 'Not any more.'

Paula caught Fielding's eye. They were both like pointers who had caught a whiff of prey. 'She'd been seeing someone?'

'Yeah, but it's been over and done for months.' She looked up and cottoned on to Paula's interest. 'It's not what you're thinking. She was going out with this Polish bloke, Pawel. She started seeing him soon after she moved over here. When it was all done and dusted, she said she thought she'd fallen for him because she was feeling homesick and he made her feel safe. She was going out with him when I first met her. He was a nice bloke, he was working as a hotel receptionist. Anyway, one night they were out in Leeds and they ran into this other Polish woman who totally freaked out. She called Nad a slapper. Well, she said it in Polish, but that was the gist of it. She said Pawel had a wife and two kids in Gdansk and Nad was a dirty whore. All at top volume in the middle of a bar. Well, Pawel tried to make out it was a case of mistaken identity, but the woman wasn't having it.

She whipped out her phone and took a photo of the two of them and said if he didn't get his sleazy arse home to Gdansk, she would send it to his wife so she'd know what a bastard she'd married. And that was that, pretty much.'

'She dumped him?'

Ashley shrugged. 'One of those things where you're not sure who got the shaft in first. She dumped him or he dumped her on his way to the airport. He went back to Poland and she said she was taking a break from men.'

'And did she? Take a break?'

Ashley looked mildly shifty. 'Pretty much. She had a one-night stand with one of the doctors at Bradfield Moor after a Christmas party, but they were both off their chops. No hard feelings the next morning, but neither of them was interested in taking it further.'

'There's a set of keys on Nadia's keyring that don't fit her flat. Do you know whose keys they are, Ashley?'

She nodded, her face bleak. 'They're Anya's house keys. She's, like, totally dozy, always locking herself out. So she gave a set to Nad because Nad's dead organised and that way Anya wouldn't be screwed the next time she left her keys sitting on the breakfast bar.'

It made sense. Paula pulled the photo of the three women towards her. 'Looks like you three like to party. Did you ever get anybody bothering you? Taking an unhealthy interest in Nad?'

Ashley chewed the skin at the edge of her pinkie nail. 'We like a night out,' she said eventually. 'We have a few drinks, but we're not like some of those mad bitches that get so off their faces they don't know their own names by the end of the night. We're not silly little girls, Detective. We have a laugh but we don't take stupid risks. That's why I can't believe Nad's gone.'

'What about drugs? Did Nad ever do drugs?'

Ashley sighed and rolled her eyes. 'Everybody over thirty thinks our generation's permanently off our tits. Look, I did E when I was a teenager. A few times, when I was out clubbing. I did coke half a dozen times when I was twenty. But I don't do that shit now. I've got a good job, my own flat, my own car. I'm not going to flush all that down the toilet. And Nad was the same. She came over here to make enough money to go back to Poland and have a good life. She wasn't going to risk all that for one daft night. No way.' She gave a twisted little smile. 'We're the good girls, Detective.' Then the bravado crumbled and tears spilled again. 'Shit like this, it's not supposed to happen to girls like us.'

Except that this time it had.

26

Fielding was already on the phone as the door of the health centre swung shut behind them. She talked as she walked, moving surprisingly fast for such a small woman. Paula almost had to break into a trot to keep up.

'Get a car round here now,' Fielding said briskly, heading for the car. 'Yes, Harriestown Road Health Centre. Pick up Ashley Marr and take her to the Trafford Centre. She can identify where Nadia parked her car on arrival that Saturday ... Yes, that's right, three weeks ago. Nadia said she was going to watch some French film at the multiscreen that same evening. I need another team down there, finding out when the film ended and checking out the CCTV for routes from the multiscreen to where the car was parked ... I appreciate that ... Pull them off the diary contacts, this is the strongest lead right now.'

Fielding ended the call as she got into the passenger seat. 'What's Ashley not telling us?'

Paula eased into a space in the steady flow of traffic. 'You think she's holding on to something?'

Fielding popped a piece of nicotine gum into her mouth. 'There's always more. They don't always know it, but there's always more.' She rubbed one eye with a knuckle and stifled a yawn, skin stretching taut over her fine bones. Paula realised she wasn't the only one who'd been up late the night before. 'Another thing,' Fielding added. 'Why is he going to all this trouble to cover up the fact that he's taken her? All the texts and the emails?'

'I wondered that too. The only thing I could think of was that most private security cameras recycle their recordings, whether it's tape or digital. They only keep them for a certain length of time. Maybe he was worried about the CCTV at the Trafford Centre and reckoned a month of blue water between the abduction and the alert would keep him in the clear.'

Fielding brightened up for a moment, her brown eyes alert and shining. Then she scowled. 'So why kill her after three weeks if you've bought yourself some extra time?'

'I don't know,' Paula admitted. 'Maybe he didn't mean to kill her when he did. Maybe she did something to make him lose his temper. And then once she was dead, he just wanted rid.'

Fielding gave a little snort of cynical laughter. 'Aye, right enough. You wouldn't want a corpse lying around making the place look untidy.'

'They are a nuisance,' Paula said. 'It's always easier to deal with them sooner rather than later, before they start decomposing and leaking all over your car boot.'

'Yeuch. But you're right, McIntyre.'

'Thank you. Todmorden, then? Anya Burba?'

'Sure.' There was a moment's silence, then Fielding said, 'I had respect for Carol Jordan. I imagine you learned a lot, working for her.'

It was a statement, not a question. In Paula's head, she'd worked *with* Carol Jordan, not *for* her. Not that there had been any doubt who was in charge. It was more that Carol had always acknowledged the different skills in her squad and had made sure they all understood that MIT was greater than the sum of its parts only when they played as a team. A team of mavericks, admittedly, but a group of people who saw the personal advantage of being part of a successful unit. Paula didn't sense that same collegial spirit in Fielding. She was very clearly the boss and apparently everything went through her. Paula knew which style she preferred. But her preference was irrelevant. She had to work with what she had. Not to mention that Fielding's methods also seemed to get results. 'We all came out of MIT better cops than when we went in,' she said, trying not to make it sound like a challenge.

'I'm glad to hear it. You're my bagman from choice, not necessity. But on this firm, we don't go off on our own, McIntyre. We do things through the proper channels. We clear on that?'

Paula kept her eyes on the traffic and her face expressionless. 'Yes, ma'am.'

'Is that what you called Jordan? "Ma'am"?' It wasn't quite a straight question.

Paula wasn't comfortable with where this was going, but she wasn't willing to start lying over something so apparently trivial. 'No. I called her "chief". She wasn't very keen on "ma'am".'

'No more am I. Ma'am's what you call the queen. It's fine in formal situations, fine from the grunts in uniform to remind them who's in charge. But it makes me feel a bit of a twat coming from my own officers. My lads call me "boss", but "chief" would be fine.'

So, it was a power play. *Call me 'chief' or I'll assume you rate me lower than Carol Jordan.* Paula had never had a conversation like this with a senior officer before. Was that because men just assumed they'd be treated appropriately according to their rank but women had to fight for that right? Whatever. She'd try to avoid calling Fielding anything. If she had no choice, she'd go with boss. If it was good enough for the lads, it was good enough for her. She was saved from answering by the beeping of Fielding's phone.

'Text from the pathologist,' she said, bringing it up on her screen.

'What's Grisha got to say?'

'He's finished the post-mortem. I need to call him.' She plugged her phone into the car jack so she could make the call on speaker and keyed in the number.

'Shatalov speaking,' came from the tinny speakers.

'DCI Fielding. I got your message. What have you got for me?'

'I completed the post-mortem on Nadzieja Wilkowa. Cause of death was internal bleeding from multiple blunt trauma injuries.'

'Not the head injury?'

'The blow to the head was probably sustained first, given the bleeding around the site, but it's doubtful whether that would have been enough to kill her on its own. I'd say she was beaten with a tapering cylindrical object such as a baseball bat. And she was kicked repeatedly. So much so that the skin was torn and bleeding. That's not all. There was a considerable amount of old bruising at various sites all over her body, consistent with regular assaults over a period of up to two weeks.'

'Not longer than that?'

'Bruises generally fade completely after two weeks. So any predating that will have disappeared.'

There wasn't much to say to that, Paula thought. But Fielding found something. 'On the scale of beatings you've seen, where would this figure? Top five? Top ten?'

A moment's silence then, his voice flat, Grisha said, 'I have only ever seen one body more severely beaten than this. And that was the victim of a biker-gang punishment beating.'

'Thank you. What about sexual assault? I mean, before the superglue, obviously.'

'I treated the superglue with solvent so I could examine the genital area. I would say she had recently had violent sexual intercourse, vaginally and anally. There are internal tears that would suggest a pretty brutal rape scenario. Again, there's old bruising in the genital area, and some internal tearing that is partially healed.' He let out a heavy sigh. In all the years she'd known him Paula had never known Grisha to be blasé. Being confronted with the terrible things humans did to each other still caused him distress. 'No semen. Either he used condoms or a foreign object.'

'A foreign object?' Fielding's question was clinical.

'A dildo. Maybe even the baseball bat he used on her head. It's impossible to say.'

'Then theoretically it could be a woman?'

Grisha gave a hollow laugh. 'Theoretically it could be a woman, yes. She'd have to be pretty strong, to move your victim around. But yes, it could be a woman.' Silence, while they all thought about that one. 'One other thing,' Grisha said. 'It was hard to pick up at first because of the bruising and the damage to the skin. But I found three instances of two puncture wounds close together. One on her right shoulder, one on her left thigh and one on her stomach, by the navel. The one on her shoulder was almost totally healed. All that's left are the purple-pink marks of scar tissue.'

'Knife wounds?'

'No. Much smaller and shallower. There are some tears to the skin in four of the cases. I can't be sure but I think they might be damage inflicted by taser probes.'

160

'You think he's tasered her?' Fielding sounded intrigued.

'I can't be certain, I don't have much experience in this area. I'll need to do some research. But yes, that would be my cautious opinion at this point.'

'That would explain how he acquired her without any report of a struggle somewhere public ... ' Fielding's voice tailed off as she thought through what she'd just heard.

Paula took her chance. 'Hi, Grisha. It's Paula here.'

'Hi, Sergeant Paula. How're you enjoying your promotion?'

'I can't remember when I last had this much fun without laughing. Grisha, what have we got on time of death?' Fielding gave her a dirty look, as if she'd been caught speaking out of turn.

'I'd say between nine in the evening and four in the morning. Can't do better than that, sorry. Stomach contents are no help because there are none. The small intestine's also empty, so it looks like it was at least twelve hours between her last meal and the time of death.'

'No question that he kept her before he killed her, then?'

'Looks that way. And that he beat her regularly while he had her.'

'That fits with our thinking,' Fielding snapped. 'Thank you, Doctor. I appreciate your help. When will we have your full report?'

'My secretary will email it to you as soon as she's finished the transcript. Good luck with your investigation. This is a bad one, Inspector.' And he closed the connection.

'Nothing there we couldn't have predicted,' Fielding said, her tone suggesting that Grisha had failed them.

'Apart from the possible taser wounds.'

'Well, he had to have some way of subduing her and that's one of the more straightforward methods.' Fielding wasn't giving any ground.

'Three separate times, though. And only one of them in a place where the taser would get you from behind. That's interesting. And what Grisha said? It does support our theory that she never went to Poland.'

Fielding grunted and started typing texts into her phone. There was none of the batting around of ideas and possibilities that Paula had grown used to in the MIT. All of her colleagues had thrived on speculation, trying out theories and testing them against the evidence. Whatever was going on in Fielding's head, she was keeping it to herself.

Anya Burba was stashed behind the closed door of the head teacher's office. Her sharp features were swollen with tears, her make-up streaked and ugly. 'Ashley texted me,' she said as soon as the head left them alone with her. 'I couldn't believe what she says. How can Nadia be dead? How is this possible? You must have made a mistake.'

'Sorry, Anya. There's no mistake. I'm very sorry for your loss.' Fielding's sympathy was underscored with briskness. 'We need your help so we can find the person who did this.'

They sat at a round table in a corner of the office. It was strewn with children's artwork. Anya cleared it impatiently to one side with a sweep of her arm. 'Stupid art competition,' she said, her voice shaky. 'How did she die?'

'We can't go into details, I'm afraid,' Fielding said.

'Was it quick? Tell me she didn't suffer.'

Paula reached out and touched her shoulder. 'There's a lot we don't know, Anya. But Nadia was your friend and we need you to share what you know about her so we can stop this happening to somebody else.'

She shivered and wrapped her thin arms round her body, pushing her small breasts upwards. 'Please God, not that.'

And so Paula worked her way through the final Saturday

again. Anya confirmed what Ashley had told them, and had nothing to add. But when she turned to the subject of Nadia's ex-boyfriend, Anya turned slightly in her seat, away from Paula, and abruptly became noncommittal.

Whatever was making her uncomfortable, Paula was determined to get to the heart of it. 'There's something more, isn't there, Anya? Something you don't want to tell us?' Her voice was gentle. 'Nothing you say can hurt Nadia now, Anya. But I think she'd want you to tell us anything that could help bring her killer to justice.'

Anya shook her head. 'It's nothing. It's not connected to her death. It's just . . . nothing.'

'Anya, I'm trained to make connections that nobody else can see. But if you don't give me something to work with, I can't make anything. Please, tell me what you know.'

Anya blew her nose noisily. 'Pawel – he has no wife and children.'

If she'd been intent on stopping them in their tracks, she'd succeeded. Even Paula, the consummate interviewer, faltered. 'What? What do you mean, no wife and children?'

Anya looked embarrassed. 'The row, in the nightclub? The woman? I was at the bar, getting drinks. I was on my way back when it happened, the woman shouting and accusing Pawel and taking their photo. I think if I had been with them, it wouldn't have happened. Well, it wouldn't have happened then.'

This was making no sense. 'I don't understand,' Paula said.

'I know this woman. Maria is her name, I don't know her family name. She isn't even from Gdansk. She worked in a bar in Lvov, where I used to live. I couldn't figure out what was going on. I didn't say anything at the time, because I wanted to get the truth. So next evening, I went to the coffee shop where she works now. It's out at the university,

163

we never go there normally. And I told her, I know you're lying about Pawel. Tell me what's going on or I bring Anya here and make you tell her.' She fiddled endlessly with the cheap silver rings on her fingers.

'And what was it she told you?'

Anya looked haunted and hunted. 'I want to go outside, I need to smoke.' She jumped to her feet and headed for the door. The detectives followed her as she ran down the hallway and out the front door. They rounded the corner of the building and saw her slip behind a steel container. By the time they caught up, she had a cigarette at her lips, her fingers shaking uncontrollably. Paula took her lighter from her pocket and held the flame to Anya's cigarette, taking the opportunity to have one of her own in spite of Fielding's frown. 'What was it, Anya?'

'She knows Pawel. She used to be a waitress at the hotel where he works. He paid her money to make a scene in the club so he could break up with Nadia.'

Paula was completely baffled now. Fifty ways to leave your lover, and still people were coming up with new ones. 'I don't get it. Why couldn't he just tell her it was over?'

'He has a new job in Cornwall. A promotion. He thought if he told her, she'd want to come with him. And he didn't want to be tied to her. So he thought the best way was to make her hate him.' She exhaled a stream of smoke and gave a twisted smile. 'Worked perfectly. And poor Nadia had no idea.'

'You didn't tell her?'

Anya gave her an incredulous look. 'Why would I tell her? I love Nadia. She already knew he was shit. She didn't need to know precisely what kind of shit. It would only have made her feel bad about herself, like she was some piece-of-crap person he couldn't wait to get rid of. No, I didn't tell her. I didn't tell anybody. Not even Ashley.' Her chin came up, defiant and defensive. 'So you see? Is nothing to do with somebody killing her. Pawel, he is in Cornwall, being the big shot assistant manager. He didn't have to kill her to get rid of her, just pay someone to tell his lies for him.'

She had a point, Paula thought. 'And you're sure Nadia had no suspicions?'

Anya shook her head. 'She trusts people, Nadia. She always thinks the best of people. I think that's why she is good at her job. She treats people like she expects the good from them, and that makes us better, I think.'

There was nothing wrong with Anya's psychology, Paula thought. Carol Jordan worked in a similar way. Expect extraordinary things from your people and they'll go flat out to give you what you hope for. Paula was beginning to think she'd have liked Nadia Wilkowa. 'Ashley told us that Nadia carried a set of your keys. Is that right?'

She nodded. 'Always. On her own keyring so they were always with her.' She kicked at the ground with the pointed toe of her shoe. 'I am hopeless. Always forgetting my keys and locking myself out like an idiot.' Her face crumpled again. 'Now who will I trust to take care of me?'

They talked to Anya for as long as it took her to smoke another two cigarettes, but by then she was shivering with cold and even Paula thought there was nothing more to be had from her. They said goodbye in the car park, Paula double-checking she had the correct details for the woman Pawel had paid to lie for him.

'We'll have to check out this Maria,' Fielding said. 'We've only got Anya's version of events.'

'Even so, it's hard to think of any twist on the circumstances that gives Pawel or Maria a motive. Or would provoke the kind of fury that drove this killer. If anybody's got a possible motive in this scenario, it's Nadia.'

'But as we know, McIntyre, motive is the least important

piece of the jigsaw. Give me means and opportunity and the complete absence of a decent alibi and I don't give a toss about motive.'

'Juries like motive,' Paula said. 'People want to know why.'

'As my mother always used to say to me, want doesn't get. Facts, McIntyre. Facts.'

'I take it you're not an advocate of psychological profiling, then?'

Fielding frowned. 'There's no budget for anything you can't reach out and touch any more. What I believe is neither here nor there. Solid evidence, that's what we need to focus on. So we'll get someone to talk to this Maria and we'll get Devon and Cornwall to pay a visit to Pawel the Shit to see what he's been up to lately. Because, frankly, we've got bugger all else happening for us. Drop me at Skenfrith Street, then swing by the lab and see what the CSIs have got for us. Seeing a human face sometimes acts like a kick up the arse.' She sighed. 'Remember the good old days when we were in charge? When we wanted a quick turnaround, all we had to do was tell them to get their fingers out? Now, they're their own bosses, they claim to rank equal to detective constables in the pecking order and if you want them to move faster than techtonic plates, it costs you about as much as a small family car. Bastards.'

It was hard to disagree. Privatising the Forensic Science Service had turned lead investigators into accountants, sitting down with a calculator to work out which tests their budget could run to. Juries weaned on *CSI* knew all about forensics, and when the prosecution didn't reel out all those juicy test results, they assumed it was because the tests didn't support the case. Not that the tests had never been done because there wasn't enough money in the kitty and the tests they *had* done should have been enough to satisfy those sitting in judgement. When you weighed that in the balance, it was hard to argue that Tony Hill was a luxury they should afford.

'I'll see what I can chase up,' Paula said.

'Good. Because I'm not holding out too much hope for the CCTV footage after all this time. This guy's smart. We need to be smarter, McIntyre. We need to be smarter.'

27

It had been a bloody awful day. Paradoxically, Carol found that easier to endure than the other kind. It was what she felt she deserved. But so far this one had been particularly grim. After her abortive visit to Chris the night before, she'd driven home and blitzed the vodka bottle. She'd woken in the small hours with a raging thirst and a banging head. The pint of water she'd glugged down came straight up, along with the paracetamol she'd swallowed. She tried again, this time sipping the water, and managed to keep the painkillers down.

She'd gone back to bed, tossing and turning, sweating and cursing. Eventually accepting there would be no more sleep, she dressed in her work clothes, added a padded jacket and went outside, hoping the chill would make her feel better. A smudge of paler sky in the east took enough of an edge off the darkness for her to walk by and she set off up the field behind the barn to the skyline trees on the hill-top.

It was hard going, tufts of grass and uneven footing threatening to trip her every other step. But Carol struggled on, chest heaving, making herself suffer all the way to the top of the hill. Instead of being rewarded with a sunrise, all that dawn brought was a chilly rain and a lightening of the grey sky. By the time she got down the hill, her hair was plastered to her head and her cheeks were numb with the cold and wet.

She brewed coffee, but it only made her stomach burn and her heart race. Work was no help either. The day's tasks were dull and repetitive, offering nothing to distract her from revisiting her disastrous encounter with Sinead. A slip of a chisel gouged a slice in the ball of her thumb, which bled madly till she packed it with medicated lint and slapped a dressing on it. After that, it just hurt like a bastard. Somehow, she dragged herself through the morning without resorting to the vodka bottle, but it was never far from her mind.

At last, she finished clearing the first section of the gallery flooring and its underpinnings. She'd created a substantial pile of timber to haul outside and add to the heap she was stacking ready for the next bonfire. She was halfway to the door with the first armful when the unexpected thump of a knock made her drop the lot with a loud clatter.

Swearing under her breath, Carol hauled the door open. George Nicholas stood on the threshold, a sheepish smile on his face. 'I seem to have the knack of arriving at the wrong moment,' he said, looking past her at the scatter of timber on the floor.

'There aren't many right moments,' Carol muttered. She was annoyed at his presence. It made her aware of her vodka breath, her unwashed hair, the stale alcohol reek of her sweat. She was aware and ashamed of her disintegration. But not enough to do something about it, she thought defiantly.

'Might I come in?' He gave a plaintive glance upwards at the heavy drizzle that was still falling. She opened the door wider and stepped aside, waving her arm in a gesture of invitation. 'And the dog?' He pointed to the black-and-white collie at his heels.

'Hello, Jess,' Carol said. 'Always happy to see you.'

Nicholas stepped inside. He snapped his fingers and the dog followed, then lay down, head between its paws, eyes on Carol. 'Actually, this isn't Jess.'

'That shows you what I know about dogs.' Carol closed the door on the weather.

'An easy enough mistake. This is Flash. Jess is her mother.' George took off his tweed cap and shook the rain from it. 'I don't suppose there's any chance of a hot drink?'

Carol felt her smile had been forced from her. 'You're a brave man, Mr Nicholas. Not many people who know me would be so bold.'

'Not brave. Cold. And please, it's George.' Confident, but not arrogant.

'Tea or coffee? The coffee is good, the tea is basic.'

'In that case, I'll take the coffee.'

Carol headed for her living quarters to brew up. She'd barely got the kettle on when she heard the clank and clatter of wood striking wood. She stuck her head round the door to see Nicholas shifting the splay of fallen wood into a neat pile by the door. 'You don't have to earn your coffee,' she said.

He gave her an amused glance. 'I'm here to ask a favour. I need all the capital I can get.'

Her heart sank. She didn't want to do anyone a favour. She didn't want him to owe her anything in return. Besides, she couldn't imagine any favour she'd be inclined to grant George Nicholas.

By the time the coffee was brewed and poured into a pair

of mugs, most of the wood had been stacked by the door. 'Thanks,' she said ungraciously.

'You're very welcome.' He looked around, as if expecting a chair to have materialised while his attention had been elsewhere. Failing that, he sat on the floor with a pleasing disregard for its lack of cleanliness. Carol leaned against the wall. The dog stayed put, her eyes shifting from one to the other.

'So what's this favour, then?' She pushed her sweaty hair from her face with the back of a dirty, bloodstained hand.

Nicholas pointed to the dog. 'I kept a couple of Jess's pups from her last litter. We've expanded our holding of sheep and we need more working dogs. Jess is a terrific sheepdog, but she can't be everywhere. The idea was that we'd train up the pups so they would fill the gap.'

Carol took a cautious sip. This time, it tasted good. Finally she had the hangover on the run. 'Makes sense. I don't see where I come in, though. You may not have noticed, but I don't actually have a flock of sheep out there.'

'That's entirely the point.' Nicholas looked pained. 'This is an embarrassing thing to have to confess, but Flash is afraid of sheep.'

Carol snorted with laughter. 'You're making that up.'

'No, honestly. As soon as they bleat, she runs away. If it wasn't so pitiful, it would be funny. I'd heard this sometimes happens, but I never believed it either.'

'A sheepdog that's afraid of sheep? That's hysterical.'

Nicholas looked at the dog, shaking his head and smiling sadly. 'But once you get past funny, it's bad news for the dog. The options for a working dog who can't work are pretty limited. Keeping her as a pet alongside a working mother and brother is a bad idea, or so my shepherd says.' His face grew serious, his eyes downcast. 'And so it comes down to rehoming her or having her put down.'

171

'And you thought of me?' Carol made no attempt to keep the incredulity from her voice. 'I've never had a dog. I'm a cat person. The only reason my cat isn't here is that he's too old to adapt to this life.'

'It's never too late to become a dog lover,' Nicholas said. 'Come, Flash.' The dog got to her feet then settled beside him, head on his thighs. He buried his fingers in her fur, massaging the base of her skull. 'She's a lovely dog. Ten months old, fully house-trained. She does come, heel, sit, down and stay. And, as you saw, you snap your fingers and she comes to you and lies down. She's a perfect dog for a beginner. If she was a pure-bred collie, I wouldn't dream of offering her to you. Far too skittish, demanding and neurotic.' He gave a rueful smile. 'We thought we were breeding from another collie, but Jess must have sneaked out when we weren't looking. What we've ended up with is a collie crossed with a black Labrador. And that's a much more biddable option. Intelligent but soft as butter.'

'I don't want a dog.'

He grinned, taking years off. 'You just don't know you want a dog,' he said. 'They're great company. And better than a burglar alarm. Nobody burgles a house where there's a dog barking inside.' The unspoken history of what had happened here underpinned what he said. He had more sense than to refer to it directly.

'Won't she need a lot of exercise?'

'I can't deny that,' he said, scratching the dog's head. 'But so do we. Problem is, we don't take it. Here's the thing, though, Carol. Collies love to run. And you've got miles of moorland on your doorstep here. You can let this dog run in absolute security because you know for sure the one thing she's not going to be doing is worrying sheep.' He smiled up at her. 'Why don't you give her a try? Give it a week. See how you both take to each other? No obligation. If it doesn't work out, I'll take her back without a word of recrimination.'

'Back to be put down?'

Nicholas rubbed the dog's flank. 'Hopefully, it won't come to that. Look, Carol, I'm absolutely not going to guilt-trip you into taking a dog you don't want. That would be even more unfair to Flash than having her humanely put to sleep.'

'I don't know anything about dogs. What they eat, what they need.' She heard the whiny weakness in her response and despised herself for it. 'I'm not the person you're looking for.'

'They don't need much. I've brought her bed down in the Land Rover, along with a bag of dog food and a leash. She can sleep in there with you—' He waved towards the closed door. 'Or out here. Though she does prefer company. Human, if canine isn't available. Feed her twice a day, three-quarters of a bowl. You can add table scraps to her bowl if you want to, but don't feed her from your hand or you'll make a beggar of her. She needs at least one good run a day, preferably two. How hard is that to accommodate?'

'I won't be doing this restoration for ever.' It was a rear-guard action, and she knew it.

'You'll be doing it for a good while yet. Look, you can cross that bridge when you come to it. But I think a dog in your life would be nothing but positive right now.'

'How do I know she'll do what I tell her?'

'Try it. Call her. You might as well, Carol. What have you got to lose?'

28

Marie Mather was pleased with how the new job was going. She'd split the team into groups of half a dozen and she was working her way through short but intense briefing sessions, group by group. She encouraged frankness in the people who worked for her. That meant the first step was making them feel secure in their dealings with her. They had to believe there was common ground they all occupied, and a common enemy in their business rivals. Once they'd reached that point, they could be manipulated into all sorts of work practices and agreements. Having everyone facing in the same direction – that was how to make progress.

Rob had sat in on the first two group sessions. He claimed he wanted to see how she worked so he could make sure his tactics fitted in with her overall strategies. Marie suspected it was more to do with him wanting to stare at her legs, given that his eyes never left them and he didn't take a single note. It didn't matter; whether she won him over with the shapeliness of her calves or the competent way she wrangled her staff, he would be firmly on her side in no time at all.

So far, the staff seemed eager to impress her. That was the joy of an economy in the doldrums. Anyone who was in work was desperate to stay that way. Even people whose natural inclination was to be cross-grained whatever the situation generally knew enough to turn on a smiley face when it came to impressing the new boss. They all wanted to make sure that if the new broom was going to sweep clean they wouldn't be the ones in the dustpan.

Of course, there were always the exceptions. Gareth, for example, had made no contribution in his group session. He'd sat with folded arms, head cocked to one side, an expression of bored superiority on his face. She had tried to get him to tell the group what he had hinted at when they'd spoken the day before, but he'd only grunted and said, 'Best if I run it past you first. No point in getting this lot excited about something that isn't going to happen, is there?'

Maria had looked at Gareth's performance indicators and understood that he was one of their most productive workers. It was clear he knew that too. But she wasn't prepared to let him trade on it, to take his quarterly bonus as a given. If she didn't turn the screws a little to show him who was boss, he could easily become a thorn in her flesh, stirring up unease at the way she was going about things. So she'd smiled sweetly and said, 'I always think the more the merrier when it comes to thrashing out new ideas. We'll be having short group meetings every fortnight from now on. Gareth, I'd like you to write a proposal for the next meeting that outlines your ideas and the reasoning behind them. I'm sure we can find better ways to achieve our goals, and nobody understands that better than you. I'm counting on all of you to come up with constructive suggestions.

Gareth, I'm delighted you're going to lead the way on this one.'

He'd scowled at her, clearly baffled at being outflanked. But he'd said no more. And he hadn't had the chance to foment dissent round the water cooler because, like Rob and half a dozen others, he was using his accumulated time owing to take the afternoon off. Bradfield Victoria were due to play Newcastle United in the FA Cup, and their loyal fans were leaving work early to travel up to the North East for the game.

When lunchtime rolled around, Marie followed the football fans out. She wanted half an hour outside the office, looking at faces that weren't her responsibility, stimulating her mind with images of beauty rather than office cubicles. The city art gallery was a brisk three-minute walk from the office, and she particularly liked their collection of Scottish Colourists on the second floor. Twenty minutes of staring at the paintings of J. D. Fergusson and William McTaggart and she would be refreshed and renewed, ready to face the next bunch of employees who needed to be energised and inspired.

Marie sat on a leather-covered bench in front of a large canvas showing the impressionistic figures of two small children in white smocks kneeling among sea grass and pinks, behind them the tousled blues and whites of the sea, above them a sky filled with plump cumulus clouds. She took from her bag the carrot and home-made piccalilli salad she'd made that morning and munched her way through it, eyes fixed on the painting, drinking in the complicated build-up of brushstrokes that came together to create certainty in the mind of the spectator. She'd loved these paintings ever since she'd first encountered them in a small Scottish town where she'd been seconded to a branch of her previous employer. She'd escaped to the art gallery during the lunch hour and she'd been astounded by the effect they had on her. She'd hardly been able to credit that there was a whole collection of them in the very city where she lived. 'We're philistines,' she'd said to Marco, insisting he visit the gallery with her. 'Imagine not knowing this was right here on our doorstep.'

She knew that Marco didn't share her enthusiasm for the paintings. But he liked to come with her, to share her excitement. And somehow, it gave her a sense of security to know he was sitting on one of the benches, playing Angry Birds on his phone while she moved among the paintings.

But it wasn't Marco who was watching her that day. Marie ate her lunch, oblivious to the fact that she was being studied. On a similar bench in the next gallery, a man was apparently enjoying a pair of L. S. Lowry seascapes, a surprising contrast to the artist's usual subject of working-class life. However, the target of his attention was quite different. He was intent on Marie, fixated on every move she made. She was a neat eater, he thought. You wouldn't want just anyone eating their lunch in the midst of expensive artworks. But Marie was someone who could be trusted not to splash or drip or even leave a trail of crumbs behind her. He liked that about her. A woman who took care about how she ate in public would probably be fastidious in other ways. Not one of those sluts who couldn't look after a man properly.

The world seemed to be full of women who were rubbish at being a woman. It took a man like him to see clearly that something needed to be done about that. The trouble was his foolish optimism. Three times now he'd been mistaken. He'd had such high hopes of the latest one, but it was already obvious she wasn't capable of meeting his criteria. He'd been willing to deal with the consequences of his mistakes, but deep down, all he really wanted was a woman who would fulfil his dreams of womanhood. It wasn't as if he asked too much. The failure was theirs. Every time. And it was his right to set things straight. He was doing the world a favour by weeding out the ones who would never be fit for purpose.

He looked across at Marie and smiled. This time, he'd chosen well. She was smart, well turned-out and she knew how to behave in public. If she showed the same ability in private, he'd be very happy.

Otherwise, he'd keep on searching. It wasn't like it was a hardship.

29

The last time she'd been out to the Kenton Vale industrial estate, Paula was pretty sure the building that housed the private forensic lab had been a CD-pressing plant for the indie music business. But the world moved on. People downloaded music directly to their devices and criminal investigation was outsourced.

Gaining access would probably have been easier when it had been churning out CDs. In order to get inside, Paula had to display her ID to a camera, wait while it was checked against who knew what database, then press her right index finger against a small glass screen. By the time she had crossed the foyer to the reception desk, a laminated ID was waiting with her photo, her fingerprint and a QR code.

'Nice to see you again,' the woman behind the counter said with a friendly smile. 'I see you've been promoted. Congratulations.'

Given that the company had occupied completely different premises and that her last visit had been months ago, the welcome made Paula deeply uncomfortable. It tripped over the border of what she considered normal behaviour and landed somewhere in the intersection of *1984* and *Blade Runner*. It occurred to Paula that even her choice of references dated her. There was no longer any possibility of her passing for young or cool. Not that she'd be mourning that any time soon.

She managed an uneasy smile and said, 'I'm here to see Dr Myers.'

'He's expecting you.' She gestured to a door behind her with a waist-high pillar beside it. 'Hold your visitor ID against the glass panel and the door will open for you. There's a cubicle on the right where you can suit up. Don't forget the shoe covers. Dr Myers' lab is the second on the left. But don't worry if you forget.' She pointed to the ID. 'That's the only door your ID will open.'

Paula found Dr Dave Myers in a white suit and gloves, filling tiny test tubes from a large syringe, his big brown hands moving with surprising delicacy. He glanced up when she walked in and nodded. 'Gimme a minute, Paula, while I get this lot started.' He finished what he was doing and slotted the tray of samples into a tall fridge. While she waited, Paula looked round the lab. She realised she had no idea what most of the equipment was for these days, nor which reagents and stabilisers did what. It was a relief to spot a microscope in the middle of a bench. It felt like Neanderthal technology alongside the other analytical tools.

Amidst the lab equipment were bagged and labelled evidence bags sitting in plastic boxes to avoid any possibility of cross-contamination. Paula recognised Nadia Wilkowa's clothes from the crime scene; she was pleased to see they'd made it that far up Dave Myers' priority list.

He closed the fridge and gestured to a lab stool. Paula sat down and he perched next to her, pulling his protective mask down. 'New facial hair,' she said, nodding towards a geometrically precise soul patch beneath his lower lip.

He pulled a face at her. 'Male pogonotrophy is often culturally associated with virility and strength.'

'But in your case, we'll make an exception.'

'You're not growing more charming with age, Paula,' he said, clutching at his heart in a mockery of pain.

They'd known each other for years. When Paula had first joined CID, Dave had worked in the police lab, analysing the assorted traces humans left behind them at crime scenes. DNA analysis was in its infancy; Dave and his colleagues were on the cusp of a series of biological breakthroughs that would transform what they could glean from criminal carelessness. It would spawn TV shows whose relationship to reality would be, as always when it came to anything to do with criminal investigation, tenuous at best. It would create unrealistic expectations in both prosecutors and the victims of crime. But it would also produce the kind of evidence that was impossible to argue against. It would take criminals off the streets and put them behind bars. Most importantly, it would promote a conviction among the population that justice was being better served.

All of which came at a price. And when budgets were squeezed to the point of strangulation, bean counters made ruthless decisions about which categories of crime merited forensic intervention. Within those categories, there were very clear guidelines governing how much a Senior Investigating Officer could spend. If those guidelines were exceeded – and Paula had been involved in MIT cases where they had been smashed to smithereens in the interests of saving lives and nailing killers – the money had to be found elsewhere. So now a key part of any serious criminal investigation was weighing up how little they could get away with in terms of forensic expenditure. It was hardly satisfactory, in Paula's opinion. But nobody in the budget team much cared what the troops on the front line thought.

So, for officers like Paula, who had learned her priorities from Carol Jordan, cultivating relationships with individual forensic scientists and crime-scene investigators had become as essential as developing what the acronym-obsessed hierarchy termed CHIS – Covert Human Intelligence Sources. What used to be called 'snouts'. A CSI who was your friend could be persuaded to go the extra mile for you, to cut bureaucratic corners in processing crime-scene material, even to suggest what might be fruitful lines of inquiry and evidence-gathering. When you actually liked them, it was a bonus.

And Paula liked Dave Myers. They'd discovered early on that they shared the same tastes in music and comedy. Dave, ever the scientist, used to prepare monthly spreadsheets of upcoming gigs and email them to Paula. They'd spend half a dozen evenings a month in scuzzy pubs and crummy music venues sampling whatever took their fancy, occasionally branching out into bigger auditoriums when their favourites hit the big time. They'd kept up the habit for years, until eventually Dave married Becky and became a dad. Then Paula had teamed up with Elinor. Now they met up as a foursome every couple of months at a comedy club or a more salubrious music venue than in the old days. Dave no longer did the spreadsheets, but he still had the knack of picking good nights out.

'King Creosote,' he said now, crossing his lanky legs and leaning one elbow on the upper knee.

'Definitely. Email me the date.'

'It's at the Methodist Central Hall, so you'll have to smuggle in your own drink.'

'Not a problem. OK, Nadia Wilkowa. Where are we up to?'

'Crime scene's a mess of prints so we haven't even bothered processing the DNA. It's a waste of your money at this point, unless any of the prints throw up a person of interest. Obviously, if you hit a brick wall down the line, we'll revisit that decision with your guv'nor. Based on past experience, DCI Fielding doesn't like spending unless she's pretty damn sure it's going to move the case forward.' He made an apologetic face. 'She's keen on clear-up but she likes to keep the top brass happy too.'

'No bad thing these days.' Paula pointed towards the evidence bags. 'What about the clothes? Have you had a chance to examine them? We're looking at an underlying sexual assault.' She shrugged. 'Might be something there?'

'Harley went through them and I had a quick eyeball earlier, but I'm not hopeful. You know yourself how it goes when the killer's abducted his victim. He's usually careful and he usually gets her stripped as soon as possible. It's not like a street assault, where you've got DNA all over everything.'

'All the same . . . May I?' She nodded towards the bags.

'As long as you're gloved and masked,' Dave said. While Paula pulled a mask on, he brought over the bagged-up clothes, then turned back to his bench and started checking some bar charts on his computer.

Item by pathetic item, Paula went through the clothes. It looked as if Dave's assessment was correct. There was no obvious sign of disturbance or of unexpected staining. The last item out of its bag was a fitted dark navy jacket with a line of small buttons up the front. It was clearly not new, but Paula recognised the signs of someone who took care of her clothes. There were no obvious stains on the front of the jacket and the buttons were all firmly attached. The inside of the collar was worn but clean, the lining intact though sagging a little along the seams. Finally, she went to check the cuffs for stains. What she found startled her. 'Did you notice this, Dave?'

He looked up sharply, his brown eyes narrowing in a frown. 'Did I notice what?'

'There's a button missing on the left jacket cuff. Look, there's six on the right sleeve, but only five on the left.'

'I never counted,' he said, peering at the two sleeves where she'd laid them side by side on the bench. 'Harley did the preliminary pass, I only took a very quick look.' He took a magnifying glass from a drawer in the bench and studied the fabric. Then he turned the sleeve inside out and examined it. 'There's still some threads left, pulled through to the inside. That suggests a recent event, if she wore this jacket regularly.'

'She didn't have many clothes. Even if she rotated them regularly, she'll have worn this once or twice a week. So maybe this button came off when she was taken? Either in a struggle, or just the process of him getting her into his vehicle? What do you think?'

'It's possible.' As he spoke, Dave was reaching for a box of cotton swabs. 'And if there was a struggle . . .'

Paula finished the thought. 'Then maybe there's some blood.'

'Exactly.' He scanned the shelf above his work station and took down three bottles.

'What are you going to do?'

'A Kastle-Meyer test. To see if we've got any latent blood-stains. It's very accurate and you only need a trace for it to work.' He opened one bottle and dipped the swab in the liquid. 'Ethanol first. Pure alcohol, Paula. But not for the Methodist Central Hall. We use it to break down the cell walls and release the stain. Makes the test more sensitive.' He rubbed the swab over the threads on the inside sleeve and then took a second swab and applied it to the material on the outside.

The second bottle had a rubber bulb and dropper built into the cap. Dave added a globule of the contents to each swab. 'Phenolphthalein reagent,' he said. 'And finally, a single drop of what the laydeez use to bleach their moustaches. Hydrogen peroxide.'

'Don't be mean, you – holy shit, it's turned pink. That means blood, doesn't it?'

Dave nodded, a rueful smile on his face. 'It does. And how crap does that make me look, that it takes a plod to come into my lab and spot what my highly paid crew has missed?' Dave tried to sound as if he was taking it lightly, but Paula could tell he was genuinely pissed off.

'Like you said, Dave, you'd only given it a preliminary once-over. Someone would have picked it up down the line. All I've done is speed things up a bit.'

'Which DCI Fielding will be pleased about. We'll get on this straight away, Paula. You'll have a full sample and a database search tomorrow morning.'

'Thanks, Dave. Oh, and I meant to say, Grisha thinks the killer might have used a taser on her. Could you check for any bloodstains on her clothes on the right shoulder, the left thigh and the stomach in the navel area?'

He rolled his eyes. 'Now she tells me. I'll get somebody on it and see what we can come up with. Go on, get out of here before you end up busting the budget.'

Paula grinned. 'It'll be worth it when we catch the bastard.'

'Save it for Fielding,' Dave said. 'Times like these, I bet you miss Carol Jordan.'

Paula's good humour vanished, banished by his words. 'Every day. Every bloody day.'

The hours had passed in a blur of pain and discomfort. Sometimes Bev had drifted off into a kind of sleep, only to jerk into consciousness when the centre of hurt shifted and sent a new bolt of agony shooting through her nervous system. At one point, the pain in her head had been so intense it had morphed into nausea and she'd retched and coughed bile over her legs. Normally so fastidious, she had reached a stage beyond disgust and she didn't even try to shift away from the puddles of vomit.

When the light came back, it was just another source of distress, stabbing her eyes and making them water. The taser was almost a relief because it was so all-encompassing a sensation. She really didn't care when he grabbed her by the hair and dragged her out of her white coffin.

The shock of the freezing spray from the hosepipe smacked her back into consciousness as nothing else had done. All at once, Bev was herself again, her fight and determination reawakened by the sharp cold needles of water. She struggled on to hands and knees, squinting in a vain attempt to see past the deluge to the figure behind it. She screamed in rage, struggling to get to her feet.

He kicked her in the head so hard she felt her jaw separate from her skull, a tearing crack that made her recoil into a whimpering heap. Before she knew what was happening, he had rolled her in polythene sheeting, fastened it tight with packing tape and dumped her in the boot of her own car.

Hardly able to breathe, terrified and driven mad with pain, Bev McAndrew made her last journey. This time, when the light came back, she didn't even notice. And that was the closest she came to mercy.

30

The session with Jacob Gold had left Tony profoundly unsettled. He'd seen two patients at Bradfield Moor Secure Hospital that afternoon and he could barely remember any of the ground they'd covered. When his own mental state interfered with the quality of treatment he was delivering, it was clearly time to take seriously the uncomfortable conclusion he'd been irresistibly drawn towards.

After work he'd gone home to the narrowboat, determined for the first time to see it not as a poor fallback position but as a symbol of change and possibility. That he had adapted to living in a place and style he'd never previously contemplated was a positive thing, he told himself, summoning up an image of himself wagging a finger in his own face. And when he stopped to think about it, he had to admit how much he liked the compact nature of life on board. The only drawback was the lack of space for his books. But surely there had to be a way round that? Lateral thinking, that was what he needed. Maybe he could rent a nearby storage unit and use that as a book room, somehow? It wasn't as if he'd mind the walk. He gave a hollow chuckle. 'Chances are, I'd have worked out whatever it was I needed the book for by the time I got there,' he said aloud.

'It's not books you need right now,' he continued, opening the fridge and the storage cupboard next to it. 'It's food. What use is pasta sauce without pasta? Or milk without breakfast cereal? Or butter without bread?' Time for an emergency shopping trip. He grabbed one of the sturdy reusable carrier bags that Carol – *ouch, no, let her go, you can't get sentimental over a bloody carrier bag* – had made him buy when they'd ended up late-night grocery shopping in the middle of a case. There was a convenience store branch of a supermarket chain a couple of streets away; he'd be back inside half an hour.

But back to what? Unresolved thoughts chasing round his brain like a ball in a pinball arcade, empty chairs reminding him of his empty life, case notes for patients who frankly felt more stable than he did right now. He needed to fill the hours before sleep with something more constructive than brooding.

Tony put on his coat and set off into the evening, determined to walk Carol Jordan out of his system. What he needed was to occupy his mind with something else, something more challenging. He let his mind drift backwards, waiting for it to find a baited hook to snag on.

And there it was, as he rounded the corner of the tapas bar. Paula's missing woman. He fished his phone out and called her. As soon as she answered, he dived straight in. 'Paula, is your missing woman still missing?'

'And hello to you too, Tony. Yes, as far as I know. I haven't been directly involved today, but I would have heard if there had been any developments.'

'So the last anyone knows is that she was going to stop at Freshco on the way home? She left work as usual and nobody saw her after that?'

'I haven't heard anything to the contrary. Here's something else that might interest you. You know the murder I'm on? Nadia Wilkowa? We think he used a taser on her.'

'That narrows things down, doesn't it? I mean, it's not like spiking a drink in a crowded bar and waiting for it to kick in. It's up close and personal. And hc's acquired her somewhere relatively private. You can't taser someone in front of an audience. Not unless you're a cop. Plus, you've got to have your getaway lined up, because a taser, that's not like knocking somebody out. Your victim gets their body back in pretty short order, isn't that right? So you've got to have a plan, it can't be a spur-of-the-moment thing.'

'Are you done?' Paula's tone was mild, amused.

'Just thinking aloud, sorry.'

'No, it's fascinating, listening to your mind work. If I hear anything more about Bev, I'll keep you posted. But I thought you weren't that interested?'

He turned up his collar against the chill wind that hit him as he emerged from the shelter of the buildings around the basin. 'I'm trying to take my mind for a walk.'

'OK. Have you got it on a leash?'

'Very funny. I don't suppose you know which Freshco she used?'

'Not for sure, but the logical route from the hospital to home would take her past the big Freshco on Kenton Vale Road. You know the one I mean?'

'On the right as you're coming from town? Before the roundabout?'

'That's the one. Why?'

'I need some groceries.' And, having nothing further to say, he ended the call. As he replaced his phone in his pocket, he wondered whether his tendency only to use the phone for what was absolutely necessary was a hangover from his youth, when landline phone calls were comparatively expensive. His grandmother, who had done most of the hands-on work of raising him, had regarded the phone as a means of parting fools and their money and only permitted its use in what she considered emergencies. He remembered she'd lived in terror of losing her low-user rebate. And then when mobile phones had first been introduced, they'd been prohibitively expensive to call and to make calls from, reinforcing his grandmother's message of frugality. It couldn't just be a generational thing, though; he knew plenty of his contemporaries who chatted away on the phone with casual disregard for what it might cost. No, it had to be one of his own personal quirks. A notion that was borne out by the reaction of most of his friends and colleagues to his own reticence during their phone conversations. Carol had always – No. He wasn't going to allow his memories of Carol to take up space in his mind.

Kenton Vale Road was about two miles away. There wasn't a direct route; he'd have to zigzag across the outskirts of the city centre, but the map he carried in his head was up to the task. He could manage this more or less on automatic pilot while he did some real thinking.

What exactly would it mean, to cut Carol Jordan out of his life for good? Take it step by step. In practical terms, compared to how things used to be between them, she was already out of his life. For the past few years, they'd lived in the same building. His house had occupied the top two floors, her basement flat a staircase and a locked door away from him. They hadn't lived in each other's pockets, but he'd always had a general awareness of her presence and absence. He was like the Lord in the Psalms, preserving her going out and coming in.

Then he'd inherited the house in Worcester. For the first time in his life, he had somewhere to live that felt like home. The moment he'd stepped inside the big Edwardian house by the park, he'd finally understood what people meant when they said they belonged. Edmund Arthur Blythe's house could have been built around Tony, so perfectly did it match. And it was a homecoming that seemed to have room in it for Carol. Living together under the same roof; a tentative step closer that might lead further still.

Everything had always been tentative between them. Two wary people whose life choices had inflicted emotional scars and psychological damage. Neither of them the sort of person you'd choose to love. But they had grown to understand that what bound them together was a kind of love. Not the conventional sort that quickly morphed into sweaty bodies in tangled sheets. It was never going to end up there, not with Tony's inability to perform.

Instead, they'd fashioned a different sort of relationship that accommodated their professional and personal lives. They trusted each other in a way that neither trusted anyone else. Although they had never lived together, there was a connection in the dailyness of their lives that had made her absence very hard to bear.

But absent was what she had become. In her grief, instead of turning to him, she'd lashed out with all the pent-up violence in her heart. She'd made no bones about blaming him and the night she'd walked away from him had been the hardest he'd ever known. He'd tried to convince himself she would be back, but he'd been right to fail. She'd walked away from all of them without a backward glance. It was as if she had died, but in some shameful way that prevented people coming together to celebrate what she'd meant to them. The mourning was real, though.

Yet he had managed that first step beyond the rawness of

grief. He was living somewhere that had no associations with her. She'd been on the boat only once, when it had been moored in another city, and it wasn't a visit that had left a trail of happy memories. He wasn't beset by images of her everywhere he looked; this was his domain, and that made getting along without her a little easier.

The second step was accepting that it was over. Whatever name you wanted to give what had existed between them, it was done. There might have been a way back to their easy companionship and affection if she'd returned after a short break and been willing to draw a line under what had happened. Hard though that would have been, it would have at least privileged the living over the dead. Something he always advocated with his patients. Now he had to practise what he preached.

Tony trudged on, paying no attention to his surroundings except to look up at road junctions so he could check his directions. When he walked like this, it acted like the release of a brake on thoughts and emotions. He could brace himself and be stern, tell himself he had to stop hankering for what he'd lost and accept that it was gone. There was no point in wistful yearning. It wasn't going to happen.

He wasn't there yet, he knew. But wanting to get there was half the battle. Then he could take the final step and, as the sort of therapist he despised would say, move on. Accept that chapter of his life was closed and give it a new shape. Believe that there were people out there who could fill the spaces in his life and in his heart.

Yeah, right.

It was going to take a few more sessions with Jacob before he could convince himself that life after Carol Jordan was somehow going to be magically better than it had been before the slow build of their relationship. The truth was, she was the only woman he'd ever dropped his defences for.

She knew his dark places. She'd even survived his mother. How likely was it that he'd find another like her?

'Stop it.' His voice was as loud as a parade-ground command. It startled two teenagers minding their own business in a bus shelter, but he was oblivious to them. Luckily, he'd reached the main road in time to break his chain of thought. The supermarket was only a couple of hundred yards away and he began to rehearse his shopping list. 'Pasta, cereal, nice bread. Maybe some ham or salami. Tomatoes, that would be good.'

Rather than use the pedestrian entrance, he walked into the car park by the route Bev would have taken. In the early evening, the supermarket was busy, the car park a constant juggling of traffic. Nearest the store, cars jockeyed for position, looking for parking slots that meant they had only a short distance to walk. 'If you were in a hurry,' Tony mused as he walked, 'you'd be quicker to park in an outlying space and walk that bit further. Maybe that's what you did, Bev. You didn't want to deal with the hassle, just a quick in and out then home to your boy.' He stopped and looked around him. The car park was pretty well lit, but he wondered how good Freshco's CCTV coverage was. Out on the edges, it seemed the cameras were few and far between.

Tony continued into the supermarket, wondering about Bev McAndrew and Nadia Wilkowa. Two apparently blameless women gone missing, one dead already. No obvious source of conflict in their lives. He hoped he wasn't the only one considering whether to put two and two together.

By the time he got to the checkout, he had managed to fill his basket to the brim. Coffee, a couple of pizzas, apples, grapes, eggs, bacon and cans of beans had mysteriously joined his existing list. Dismayed, he realised he'd never fit all this in one bag. Worse, he'd have to lug it across town. There was no time for revision, not unless he wanted to be lynched by the people behind him in the queue, so he shelled out for another bag-for-life and walked back to the car park while he considered his options.

He didn't want to walk home. He'd done his thinking, it was starting to rain and his knee hurt, reminding him he was supposed to make an appointment with the consultant to talk about surgery. The very thought of what Mrs Chakrabarti had in mind made Tony sweat. He was on the point of calling a taxi when a double-decker bus lumbered through the car park and pulled into a bay only yards away from him.

According to the destination board, it was bound for Preston Street bus station. A mere five-minute walk from his mooring. It was a no-brainer. He waited while a handful of shoppers boarded ahead of him. He knew he didn't have the correct change; boarding the bus would involve sighs and moans from the driver, and not in a good way.

As he expected, the driver tutted and muttered all the way through the process of issuing a ticket and changing a twenty-pound note. Tony raised his eyes to the heavens, seeking patience.

What he found was something quite unexpected. Mounted above the driver's seat was the familiar CCTV monitor. Tony had never studied it before; if he'd ever given it any thought, he would have assumed it would show only the interior of the bus. But the reality was very different. The screen was split into nine sections, showing upper and lower decks, the entrance and exit doors and the rear of the bus, to make it easier for reversing, he presumed. What he hadn't expected was how much of the outside of the bus was under surveillance. A wide-angle lens revealed the whole width of the pavement, extending as far as the plate-glass windows of the store; another showed the roadway on the far side of the bus. Tony imagined that if it was blown up on a single monitor it would be possible to read number plates. Maybe even identify drivers.

'How often does this service run?' he asked the driver, who was dropping pound coins one by one into his waiting hand.

The driver gave a weary sigh. 'Every twenty minutes from seven in the morning till ten at night.'

'Is this the only bus service that runs into the super-market?'

'Do I look like Google? Go and sit down so I can get moving.'

'Can I stand here and watch the monitor?'

The driver pointed to a sign on the Perspex screen that protected him from his passengers. 'Can you not read? No passengers beyond this point while vehicle is in motion. That means sit down and leave me alone. You can do that, or you can get off.'

Tony perched on the edge of a double seat already occu-pied by a large elderly woman with two bulging bags that seemed to contain only potatoes and biscuits. 'Miserable git,' she said. Seeing his startled face, she giggled. 'Him, not you. There's two other buses stop at Freshco, love. The thirty-seven runs down through Kenton to Kenton Vale then back round to Colliery End. Every half-hour, I think. And there's a little ring-and-ride coach that serves the estate. It doesn't have a timetable, as such.'

'Thanks. That's very helpful.'

She looked at him curiously. 'It's a funny question, though. Why are you so interested in the buses?'

'It's a long story,' he said. 'And I can't really explain it. But it's all about different ways of looking at things. And how you don't always think about the things you think you know about.' He smiled. 'A lot of what I say doesn't make sense. But don't worry, I'm perfectly safe.'

She gave him an appraising look. 'Are you sure about that?'

He shook his head, rueful. 'Probably not.'

31

There was an air of excitement in the incident room when Paula got back to Skenfrith Street. 'What's up?' she asked one of the DCs on her way to Fielding's office.

'They keep their CCTV for a month at the Trafford Centre. Pat Cody's picked up the vic on it. And it looks like they've captured the killer on camera too.'

'That's great news. Is he emailing it across?'

He shook his head. 'He's got it on a memory stick. He's on his way over with it now.' He offered a tentative high-five and Paula returned it. Even if high-fives were childish American nonsense, building bridges was the key to settling into a new nick. Make friends with your underlings, build a bulwark till you've figured out how to make the DCI happy.

DC Black had something else to add. 'Devon and Cornwall got their arse in gear too. They've interviewed Pawel the Shit and the bad news is he's alibied rock solid for that Saturday and for Friday through to Tuesday morning this weekend. He was either at work or shagging the arse off one of the chambermaids. No way he had enough time between shifts to get up here and dump Nadia's body.' The news didn't come as a blow to Paula. She'd never had any conviction that Pawel had the heft for this kind of crime.

She found Fielding at her desk, intent on her computer screen. The DCI barely looked up when Paula walked through the open door after a token knock. 'Any news from the lab?' Fielding asked, fingers rattling over the keyboard with the fluency of a touch-typist. Her hair had lost some of its glossy perfection; she almost resembled a mere human who struggled with the hours and the demands of the job.

'Would you settle for a bloodstain on her jacket?'

Fielding stopped typing and gave Paula her full attention. 'Tell me more.'

'I noticed there were six buttons on one cuff but only five on the other.' Paula wasn't in the habit of playing up her own role in investigations, but she reckoned she still had a long way to go when it came to making Fielding understand how good she was.

'Have you been at the Sherlock Holmes again?' Fielding's tone was severe, but for the first time, she treated Paula to a sardonic smile.

Paula shrugged. 'I'm such a girl. Anyway, Dave Myers took a closer look and he reckons the button came off recently.'

'So it could have happened when she was taken.'

'Exactly. There was nothing to be seen, but the test for blood came up positive. We might have some of the killer's DNA.'

'That's a good start. Fingers crossed that we get the DNA.'

'And double-crossed that he's on the database.'

'How soon will Dr Myers have a result for us?'

'In the morning. I also mentioned Grisha's theory about the taser, so Dave's going to check whether there's any of Nadia's blood in the relevant places.'

'Good, that helps us build up a narrative for the jury. He stalks her, he walks up on her, he tasers her and boom! It's over. Juries always resist abduction unless there's a good struggle. But the taser ticks that box for us.' Fielding's laptop chirruped and she glanced at the screen. 'Is that all?' she asked absently.

'You know about the CCTV at the Trafford Centre?'

Fielding nodded impatiently. 'Yes. Give me a shout as soon as Cody's in the house. Well done, McIntyre. Go and get yourself a coffee before we look at the CCTV, it could be a long night.'

Never mind the coffee. Now she had a minute to herself, Paula wanted to catch up with whoever was dealing with Bev Andrews. It took her a few phone calls to establish who had been put on the case then track him down. She found PC John Okeke in the canteen, working his way through a double all-day breakfast. He was a big lad who looked like he needed the fuel. If she'd been his boss, she'd have been more inclined to assign him to crowd control than investigating a missing person, on the basis of his unnerving size alone.

She bought a couple of coffees and parked herself opposite him. He looked surprised, then she saw the wheels go round and gain traction. He chewed and swallowed then said, 'Are you DS McIntyre?'

'I am. And you've taken on Bev McAndrew's disappearance, is that right?'

He nodded. 'Not that you left me much to do. Thanks for the report. And for doing the search. You saved me a lot of time.'

'So where are we up to?' She half-expected him to find a polite way to tell her it wasn't her case and she should butt right out. But he was surprisingly willing to share.

'In terms of results, not much further forward. I went to the Freshco you said she usually shopped at and looked at their CCTV for the hour after she left work. She shows up on the cameras in store. She picks up some milk and bread and sausages. She comes out of the store and that's where we lose her. She walks into the car park and out of their coverage.'

'Don't they have the whole car park covered?'

'No. The area in front of the shop is well covered, but as soon as you get away from there, it's pretty sketchy. They cover the trolley return points, but once you're outside that ring of coverage, we're screwed. Sorry.'

Paula sighed. 'Bugger. Good thinking, though.'

He dipped his head in acknowledgement and bit into his toast. Chewed, carried on speaking. 'I talked to her colleagues again. She didn't show at work today, no messages, out of character for a very responsible boss, no worries or hassles that anybody knew about.'

Paula interrupted. 'What did you think of Dan the man?'

Okeke's eyes took on wariness. 'I thought he was straight up. Worried, a bit upset, but nothing that set my bells ringing. Did you think different?'

Paula pulled a face. 'Not really, no. I just felt he was a tad evasive.'

Okeke swallowed half a tomato. 'You have to factor in the way people get around cops. And around the opposite sex. I thought there might be more between him and Bev McAndrew than he was letting on, but he seemed more concerned than guilty to me.' He speared a mushroom. 'I know what you're thinking. "That's what people said about Ian Huntley during the Soham murder hunt." And it might have been what the punters and the hacks said, but I bet it's not what the cops said behind closed doors. We get a smell off the bad guys, don't we?'

'Not always,' Paula said, recalling the killer who had come so close to ending her life. 'But this time, I think you're right.'

He nodded, satisfied. 'I also did a formal interview with your nephew—'

'My nephew?' Paula squeaked.

Okeke looked surprised. 'I thought with you and his auntie being civil partners, you'd think of Torin as your nephew too. Did I get that wrong?'

Her first thought was that Torin was a cheeky little bugger, telling lies to keep out of the hands of social services. Then it dawned on her that he was alone and afraid and clinging to her and Elinor because he didn't really have anyone else. Hastily, she backtracked. 'No, no, you're fine. I never think of myself as an auntie, that's all. More like a big sister.' Her smile felt false. Okeke was trying to keep his face stern, but one corner of his mouth kept twitching in a half smile.

'Anyway, I spoke to Torin but he didn't have anything of substance to add to your report. To tell you the truth, I'm worried.' It didn't stop him shovelling another forkful of food in his mouth.

'We all are.' Paula sipped her coffee. 'What's your guv'nor saying?'

'If she's not turned up by tomorrow morning, he thinks we should do a media appeal. Not with Torin, obviously. Just a release with a photo and a request for sightings.'

Paula nodded. It was what she'd been going to suggest. 'What's your gut feeling?'

He wouldn't meet her eyes, concentrating instead on cutting up a sausage. 'Not good. Woman her age, no history of depression or abusive relationships, decent job, decent home, no significant debt that we can pinpoint. And a kid.' He took a swig of coffee. 'Women like that don't generally take off. And they definitely don't take off without their passport or their driving licence.'

'I didn't find the driving licence,' Paula said.

'It was in her desk drawer at work.'

'You think something bad has happened.'

Now he looked her square in the face. 'Don't you?'

Paula stared into her coffee. 'Yeah.'

'I'm sorry. But there's no point in pretending.'

Paula pushed her chair back and stood up. She wasn't a small woman but she was barely taller than Okeke sitting. 'Keep me in the loop, would you?'

He dabbed his lips delicately with a napkin and nodded. 'Likewise. If Torin remembers anything . . .'

Paula stood outside the back door in the lee of the building, huddled with the other smokers. She'd checked upstairs and Cody hadn't returned yet. One short encounter with Cody and she'd already have put money on him taking a detour via one of the outlets in the shopping-mall food hall. Out here by the car park, she'd see him when he finally showed up. She lit up and called Elinor's mobile, half-expecting it to go to voicemail. But she was in luck. 'It's your wife,' she said. 'Torin's auntie.'

'Ah,' Elinor said. 'It was his idea. He's desperate to avoid being taken into care. Even if it's only for a night or two. And your very charming colleague seemed willing to accept me as the half-sister of his absent father. He told me his family is also complicated.'

'And you call him charming. Sounds like you had PC Okeke eating out of your hand.'

'Police officers and their weak spots. I'm an expert. I'm presuming since you didn't begin this call in a burst of enthusiasm that there's no news?'

Paula tried not to sound as glum as she felt. 'In my job, no news is good news.'

'That's tough. Listen, I'm perfectly happy to keep Torin with us, but I think we've reached the point where we need to talk to his dad, to put this on an official footing. Not to mention his grandmother and his real auntie. Torin says there's a facility called ArmyNET that lets him communicate with his dad in real time, so we'll use that. Are you happy to let me take care of it?'

Again, Paula remembered why she loved Elinor. What was it Tony had once said to her? 'There's nothing clever about being clever. In the MIT, everybody's clever. What's really clever is being kind.' And nobody did kind better than Elinor. 'I would be in your debt. As usual.'

'I'll do it when I get home. Torin's going to a friend's house for tea and homework. He's going to text me so I can pick him up. How different their lives are from what ours were ...' There was a tickle of laughter in her voice.

'I'll catch you later. I might be late. I love you.'

'Love you too. Take care out there.'

Paula ended the call and, right on cue, her cigarette. She contemplated one more cigarette. She'd been good all day, not wanting to push her luck with Fielding. And she'd already been warned it might be a long night. 'Sod it,' she said, fishing out another and sparking up her lighter.

She'd barely taken her first drag when her phone rang. The *X Files* ringtone she reserved exclusively for Tony. 'Tony,' she said. 'How's things?'

'Has Bev McAndrew turned up?'

No small talk, as ever. 'No. Not a trace of her since she walked out of work.'

'I went shopping this evening. I thought I'd go over to the Freshco on Kenton Vale Road. You know how it is.'

She knew how it was. He liked to look at the scene, to think himself into the head of the victim and the perpetrator, to walk a mile in their shoes in a physical exercise of empathy. 'And what did you learn?'

'I learned a very interesting thing about buses,' he said.

'That doesn't sound very likely,' Paula said.

'Round the fringes of the Freshco car park, the CCTV footage is pretty poor. But that's exactly where the buses go.'

'You think someone on a bus might have seen Bev?'

'Of course they might have, but what matters is the buses themselves. They're festooned with cameras. And they show what's going on outside the bus as well as inside. Not close-up, really quite a distance from the bus. I thought maybe you'd get lucky and find some footage with Bev on it if she's not parked close to the store.' He stopped.

'That's brilliant. I knew they had cameras on the buses but I had no idea they filmed the outside.'

'Me neither. It's because you never go on buses.'

'You think we should be actively looking for Bev?'

'It's not my call. But according to you, you've already got one murdered woman with nothing apparently problematic in her life. Now you've got a second one missing. Have you found the intersection between Nadia and her killer yet?'

'Nothing definite. We think he may have picked her up in the Trafford Centre and taken her in the car park. But I haven't seen the footage yet.'

'And you've got another missing woman who might have been abducted in a car park. Plus they look kind of like each other, Paula.'

'You think? There's about twelve years' difference in age, their body types aren't that similar.'

'You don't want to see it because you're scared for your friend, Paula. But they're both blonde, medium height, medium build. They dress like professional women, not bimbos. They've driven themselves to the shops. One's dead and the other's missing. I know your precious Chief Constable once accused me of seeing serial killers round every corner, but sometimes I'm right, Paula. Sometimes I'm right.'

'More often than not, unfortunately. I'll pass this on to

the uniform who's looking into Bev's disappearance. And I'll talk to Fielding, OK?'

'I think you should. I'll back you up, if it helps.'

Paula choked on her cigarette smoke. 'Are you out of your mind? Have you forgotten how pissed off Carol got when I fed you confidential case info behind her back? Multiply that by ten and you've got DCI Alex Fielding.' She sighed. 'I miss Carol.'

'I'm trying not to.'

And he was gone, the phone a dead lump of plastic in her hand. Across the car park, she saw Pat Cody and another bloke get out of a car and hustle towards the building. 'Showtime,' she muttered, tossing her cigarette into a puddle and heading indoors.

'What have we got, Cody?' she asked, falling into step beside him.

He tapped the side of his nose. 'That's for me to know and you to find out.'

A flash of anger lit her up. If she let this go, it would shape how Cody and his mates treated her. 'Constable, you need to remember who the sergeant is around here,' she snapped. 'I'm in your line of command and when I ask you a question relating to an ongoing case, I expect an answer.'

Cody flushed. It wasn't an improvement. 'No disrespect intended, Sarge.' His heavy eyebrows lowered in a frown.

'He's always making daft jokes,' his mate chipped in, trying to defuse the atmosphere.

'And you are?'

'DC Carpenter, Sarge.'

'I love jokes, me,' Paula said conversationally. They climbed the stairs in a tight knot. 'Only thing is, they need to be funny. Bear that in mind, Cody, and we won't fall out. Now, tell me what we've got. Save the full briefing for the boss. Just give me the bullet points.'

He grunted, but told her what she wanted to hear. 'Nadia comes out of the cinema and walks out to the car park. Her car's a way off because she parked up earlier when the place was hopping. A bloke tails her across the car park. He's carrying a metal box, like a camera case. She opens her boot to put her shopping in the car. He comes up behind her. You can't really see what goes on but he tips her in the boot, puts the case in the boot, leans over her for a minute or so. Then he gets in her car and drives off.'

'We've asked the DCI to put a request in to the National ANPR Data Centre to track the car,' Carpenter chipped in, sounding more excited than anyone should at the thought of data mining. 'All the roads round the Trafford Centre are well covered. We should be able to track him without any problem.'

They walked into the incident room together, greeted by a few whoops of delight. Fielding came out of her office and gave a couple of handclaps. 'We're all set up, Cody. Get that memory stick plugged in and let's see what we've got.'

Everyone settled down to watch the interactive whiteboard and someone turned off most of the lights. 'Here we go,' Cody said. It was as he had said. Nadia emerged from the cinema and walked through to the car park a level below. As she stepped outside, she put her bags down to fasten her jacket against the cold. The line of small buttons took a few moments to close. Paula recognised the jacket from the lab. Pity there was no prospect of counting the cuff buttons at this level of definition. Nadia walked forward out of shot. Next out was a couple, the man with his arm round the woman's shoulders. They were laughing and talking, paying no attention to their surroundings, unaware that a third figure was walking close behind them, head lowered, hard to see. He stayed tucked in behind them till they moved out of shot.

'The next camera picks Nadia up on the diagonal. Here she comes. Bottom right,' Cody explained. Head down against the wind, Nadia was cutting across the almost empty car park at an angle. *How often have I done that without a second thought?* Paula felt a frisson of fear as the figure following Nadia entered the frame.

Fielding took centre stage now. 'Look at this guy. Study everything about him. Look at that case he's carrying. Commit him to memory.'

Which sounded great except that there wasn't much to commit to memory. It was dark, the lighting was designed to help people find their cars, not to allow CCTV operatives to make like Martin Scorsese. All you could definitively say about the stalker was that he was medium height, medium build, wore glasses with thick frames and owned a jacket whose hood, pulled forwards, almost completely obscured his face. He kept his head down; he was clearly well aware of the risks of being captured on pixels. The rectangular case in his hand seemed quite heavy, though that fact offered no clue to its contents. Nadia disappeared from the top left of the screen, followed by the man. Even the gender was a presumption, Paula thought.

The third camera was the one that had picked up the action. Nadia's car was close to the limit of its field of view, so again, there wasn't much detail to be seen. She unlocked the car as she walked, taking the keys from her handbag. As she opened the boot, the man suddenly speeded up. 'He takes something from his pocket,' Cody said, his voice rising with excitement.

'We think it's a taser,' Fielding said, watching Nadia put her shopping in the hatchback boot.

'Where's the confetti?' Hussain asked.

'Not all taser cartridges contain confetti,' Paula said. 'Usually it's only law enforcement who use it, so there's a record.'

206

'And she kind of crumples forward as he comes up from behind,' Cody continued.

It was over in next to no time. The kidnapper scooped up Nadia's legs and shoved them in the boot. He straightened up and took something out of his other pocket then leaned into the boot. 'What's he doing?' one of the others asked.

'Hard to say,' Cody said. 'We watched it a few times and couldn't make it out.'

'Packing tape,' Paula said. 'He's restraining her.'

Cody flashed a quick look at her. She couldn't tell whether he was impressed or pissed off.

'Could be,' Fielding said. 'We'll take another look after we've seen the rest of it.'

There wasn't much more of it. He finished whatever he was doing, closed the boot, walked round to the driver's door, got in and shortly after, drove out of shot. All of it without letting the camera have even a fleeting glimpse of his features. It was as if he knew exactly where he was being surveyed from, so effectively did he avoid the lens, Paula thought.

'Let's have it again,' Fielding said. This time, Cody slowed it down after the man tipped Nadia into the boot. It still wasn't clear what was happening; the man's body obscured what he was taking from his pocket. But Fielding conceded Paula was probably right. With a marker pen, she wrote what they knew about the man on the board. 'Anything else?'

A hand went up in the far corner of the room. A woman who looked like she wanted to disappear into the wood-work. 'Boss? I think he's got a limp.'

'A limp? How do you work that out, Butterworth?' Fielding was already moving away from the whiteboard.

'You can't see it in the diagonal shot because of the angle. And then he's running. But when he walks round to the driver's seat, it looks like he's limping.'

Fielding frowned. 'Play it again, Cody. Just the last bit. And slow it down.'

Cody did as he was told. And as they watched, it was clear that DC Butterworth had spotted something the rest of them had missed. The man was limping. Whether it was temporary or permanent, they had no way of knowing. But that Saturday night in the car park of the Trafford Centre, the man who had abducted Nadia Wilkowa had something wrong with his left leg.

32

Day twenty-six

The sun was a thin brilliant line across the top of the moors. For the first time in more than a week, the morning sky was clear, dark blue fading into eggshell as dawn broke. The light crept down the side of the hill, bringing the colours to life. White Edge Beck sparkled as the broken water caught the light and the rocks glistened. Early morning dog walking didn't get any better than this, Paul Eadis thought as he drove up the twisting single-track road to the National Trust car park. His two lurchers, caged in the rear section of his estate car, were restless, as if they too could sense a change in the weather.

He rounded the last bend. As usual at this time of the morning, the White Edge car park was empty, the only break in the skyline the stone rubbish bin and the hollow cairn where motorists were supposed to deposit a pound whenever they parked. Paul had never paid to park here; that was for tourists, and he considered himself a local. For five years now, he'd been running George Nicholas's dairy operation. He'd done more for the local economy in that time than most folk around here managed in a lifetime.

He turned off the road and parked in a random slot. Paul liked to pretend to himself that he was an enemy of habit; the truth was he fetishised variety in small things so he could kid himself he wasn't hidebound in the things that mattered. It was one of the things that made him such an effective herd manager.

Humming under his breath, he got out of the car and released the lurchers from their captivity. They took off with their usual enthusiasm. But in the business of closing the tailgate and locking up, Paul missed the sudden arrest of their headlong plunge for the moors. When he turned, expecting to see the dogs a distant blur of movement, he was astonished to see they'd stopped behind the bin, nosing at something on the ground. 'Bloody dead sheep,' he muttered, pulling leashes from his pocket and heading for the dogs.

But it wasn't a sheep.

Startled awake by an unfamiliar sound, Carol was out of bed and halfway to the door before she registered what she was actually hearing. A scratch at the door, followed by a soft whimper. Then a more insistent scratch. The bloody dog, that's what it was. She let out the breath she'd been holding and felt her muscles loosen as the adrenalin fled. 'OK, Flash, I'm coming,' she called through the door, hastily pulling on jeans, T-shirt and fleece. She opened the door into the main body of the barn and a bundle of black and white threw itself at her, threading a figure of eight round her legs, barking with delight at being reunited with the new human.

Carol staggered under the onslaught, laughing in spite of her grumpiness at being wakened on a schedule other than her own. She ruffled the dog's fur, then said, 'Sit,' in her most commanding voice. Flash obeyed, but looked over her shoulder at the door to the outside world, another soft whimper escaping from her mouth. 'You need to go out,' Carol said. She crossed the room barefoot, looking out for wood splinters and stone chips, then opened the door on a glorious clear morning, the chill in the air invigorating and inviting. Flash ran out into the yard, heading for the rough grass at the edge of the cobbled parking apron. Carol watched while she peed, concerned in case the dog made a run for her old home over the hill. But Flash simply trotted back to the barn after she'd finished, rubbing herself against Carol as she re-entered.

'Good dog,' Carol said. She headed into her room to put on socks and boots so they could go for a walk. 'Listen to me,' she grumbled. 'Already I'm talking to you as if you're going to answer.' The dog thumped her tail on the floor. 'It was at least a month before I started talking to my cat like that, you know. I'm turning into a weird old hermit.'

She grabbed her waxed jacket and the leash Nicholas had left her and headed for the hill. The dog stayed at heel until they climbed the stile into the rough pasture, then she ranged back and forth, scenting the air and the ground, but always checking to see where the human was. Carol was amazed at how quickly the dog appeared to have bonded with her. Flash had watched Nicholas leave with apparent indifference. No crying, no casting around as if wondering where he might have gone, nothing that remotely resembled pining. Instead, she'd followed Carol round, lying down with her head between her paws near where she was working. They'd gone for a walk along the lane in the afternoon, Flash docile on the leash, apart from a couple of tugs towards open ground.

In the evening, Flash had sat politely by while Carol cooked and ate, then she'd lain at her feet while she drank wine and browsed the news on her iPad. Come bedtime, though, Carol had shooed her into the main barn, pointing to the dog's bed and blankets, set next to the door behind which her new mistress would be sleeping. She drew the line at sharing her bed – or even her bedroom – with a dog. Nelson had been a relatively unobtrusive bed-sharer. She suspected Flash didn't know what unobtrusive meant.

She'd been mildly surprised that there had been no protest from Flash. According to Nicholas, Flash had been accustomed to sleeping in the utility room with her mother and litter mates. Carol had worried that the dog might be lonely. But she seemed perfectly content with her lot, and she showed no signs of wanting to escape from her new life.

'Didn't take me long to fall for you, did it?' she said, scrambling up the hill behind the happy dog, feeling notice- ably more cheerful than she had the previous day. Maybe it was the weather. But maybe the dog's *joie de vivre* was irre- sistible. 'What exactly did Michael tell George Nicholas about me that made him think I needed a dog? Because, damn it, he might be right.'

They covered the ground to the trees at the top of the hill in good time. The dog seemed as fresh as when they'd left and Carol recalled Nicholas's injunction about exercise. 'Come on then, we'll go through the trees and along the ridge,' she said, striking off at an angle through the mix of birch and alder that struggled against the prevailing wind on the shoulder of the hill.

Ten minutes brought Carol to the far side of the woodland and a breathtaking vista of the moors and the valley below. But this morning, the view she'd grown accustomed to had an added element. A familiar element, but one seen from a very different angle.

Over to the east, perhaps quarter of a mile away, spotlit by the newly risen sun, the roadside past White Edge car park was occupied by a string of vehicles though the car park itself was empty. She identified half a dozen police cars and Land Rovers, the ID numbers emblazoned on their roofs revealing them to be from the West Yorkshire force. One displayed the solid circle of a Dog Unit but the others were standard response units. There were also four unmarked cars and an ambulance. She could see what looked like crime-scene tape fluttering round the perimeter, and several figures were milling around something she couldn't identify. Something waist high, stone-built, possibly.

It was a crime scene. And a serious one at that. The only crimes that would merit this sort of police presence so early in the day were murder, attempted murder or serious sexual assault involving a high level of violence. The kind of crimes that had been her bread and butter, her meat and drink, and the icing on her cake for years. The kind of crimes she'd built a career on. The kind of crimes that both answered and thwarted her fundamental craving for justice.

It felt strange to be a distant spectator at the first stages of an investigation. For so long, she had been the person controlling the scene. Taking the decisions. Deploying the personnel. Driving everyone to do their best for the dead and the living. And now, she was just another rubbernecker.

'Flash, come,' she said, snapping her fingers for the dog, who was quartering the hillside a hundred yards away. Low to the ground, Flash moved swiftly to her side and dropped down beside her, tongue lolling out of her mouth. Carol crouched down and buried her hand in the thick mane at the back of the dog's neck. She didn't want to leave yet; her history wouldn't let her go. But she didn't want to be obvious to anyone scanning the landscape from below.

While she watched, another car came hammering up the road. And instead of West Yorkshire's 13 on the roof, this one carried the 51 that signified Bradfield Metropolitan

Police. What had brought BMP officers to a West Yorkshire crime scene? She knew from her own experience that there was little love lost between the detectives of the two forces. There would have to be a very good reason for BMP cops to be here this early in an investigation.

The BMP car pulled up by the entrance, double parking to let two people out. Even from that distance she could see they were women. Carol couldn't rely on the evidence of her eyes to identify them. But common sense told her the small, dark figure who had been in the front seat could only be DCI Alex Fielding. Her equal in rank, but her opposite in so many other aspects. Fielding was authoritarian and formal where Carol was more relaxed and inclined towards teamwork. Fielding was all about hard facts and never mind the story behind them; Carol loved working with Tony because he helped her to understand why. Fielding was married with a son, a hinterland of emotional connection that Carol had failed to establish. And now it appeared Fielding had a new bagman. Her former sergeant had been a lanky raw-boned Ulsterman who always talked about going home. Wherever he'd gone, the person filling his shoes looked very familiar. Carol couldn't have sworn to it, but she'd have put serious money on Fielding's new bagman being Paula McIntyre.

The realisation provoked a confusion of feelings in Carol. Outrage at Paula's skills being put at the service of so unimaginative a boss; a stab of regret that it wasn't her down there; an acceptance that that life was behind her; and a benediction to Paula, who could still manage to do what she would not.

Carol stood up, backing into the trees. This was no place for her. She'd turned away from all that was going on down there, and she was slowly growing better for it. Hard phys- ical work, all those books and movies she'd missed out on over the years, a dog for company. Somewhere in the middle of that, she'd finally manage to forgive herself.

Let other people speak for the dead.

When she turned to go, a spasm of shock flashed across her chest, stopping her breath and making her heart clench. A few feet away, a man stood watching her. How could he have come so close without her realising? And why was the dog not reacting? Carol was on the point of making a run for it when her brain clocked on and she understood what she was seeing. The reason for Flash's passivity was that the man standing in the shelter of the trees was George Nicholas. At his heels, Jess, cheerfully licking her pup's head.

He held up his hands in a placatory gesture. 'Sorry. I didn't mean to startle you. You were so intent on that lot down there—' He nodded towards the cars and cops in the valley below.

'What are you doing up here?' Carol didn't care how rude she sounded. She was rattled but not so much so that she could let go of instincts honed by years of policing serious crime.

'Same as you. Walking my dog. Nothing more sinister than that, I promise you.'

He looked innocuous enough in his waxed jacket and tweed cap, recently shaven face pink with the cold autumn air. But she knew only too well the viciousness and treachery that could lie behind so harmless an appearance. 'I thought she was a working dog? Doesn't that give her the exercise she needs?'

Nicholas smiled. 'What she needs and what she wants are two different things. Jess loves to run more than anything else. Answering her whims keeps me fit. If I didn't do this, I'd sit around getting fat. Usually we don't see anyone else up here. This morning, it's a bit like Bellwether Square. What are they doing down there, do you know?'

Carol shook her head. 'Something serious. A murder or a serious sexual assault, given the number of warm bodies and the presence of two forces.'

'Two forces? How can you tell?'

She pointed to the vehicles below. 'Different transport codes. West Yorkshire and Bradfield Met.'

'Your former colleagues. That must feel strange.'

Carol deliberately walked past him, not wanting to give anything away. 'It's exactly the sort of case I would have been called out to when I was still a serving officer,' she said. 'Being a spectator is . . . unexpected.'

'Nowhere's immune these days,' Nicholas said. 'My wife. Your brother and Lucy. And now this. The world has become smaller, Carol. And that means the unpleasantness infects places like this, places that used to be immune from the worst excesses of human behaviour.'

'You're wrong. This isn't some communicable disease that's spread out from the city. It's always been here. Lurking under the beauty. Wherever you are, somebody's inflicting horror on another human being. It's just that there are some environments where it's easier to get away with it. You can pretend all you like, but underneath your country idyll, the bad stuff is simmering and seeping in all directions.'

Nicholas tilted his head back and laughed. 'Christ, Carol, you make it sound like *The Wicker Man*. Look, why don't you come down and have breakfast with me? So I can show you that the big house isn't a dark, brooding presence on the far side of the hill? Come on. There will be fresh eggs and—' He pulled a paper bag out of one of his big side pockets and dangled it at her. 'Fresh field mushrooms. I picked them on the way up. And sourdough bread from Bentley's in the village.' He looked eager and open-faced. And if there was anything sinister about his presence on the hilltop, either because of her presence or that of the police, she would have the chance to ferret it out at close quarters.

'All right,' she said, making it sound as if it was as appealing as a colonoscopy. Nicholas lit up like a birthday boy. 'Come on, Flash.' The dog didn't need telling twice. Carol almost wished she could find so uncomplicated a response in her own heart. But those days were long gone. With one last look over her shoulder, she set off down the hill.

Let other people speak for the dead.

33

The call had roused Paula from the glorious depths of sleep. They'd gone to bed before midnight, but Elinor had wanted to revisit her conversation with Bev's sister Rachel. 'But after I IM'd with Torin's dad and he gave us his blessing, I'm still not sure I was right to encourage her to come up,' she'd said for what Paula reckoned was the eighth or ninth time.

'Torin's in limbo,' Paula said. For only the third time, she thought. 'He needs the stability he'll get from his family. He hardly knows us, love.'

'According to Torin, he hardly knows his aunt either. Be honest with me, Paula. Do you think Bev's coming home alive?'

Paula sat up and punched her pillow into shape. 'I honestly don't know. I think someone took her, but I have no way of knowing if she's being kept prisoner or ... We're in the dark here. I can't help thinking that Auntie Rachel arriving like the cavalry is going to feel like a worst-case scenario to Torin. In his shoes, I'd start giving up hope.'

'Maybe that's the best thing for him.' Elinor snuggled into Paula's side. 'Facing up to what's most likely to be the reality. And having his aunt here might help him with that.'

Paula yawned and patted Elinor's hand. 'It won't hurt for them to get to know each other better, that's for sure. If Bev doesn't come home, he's going to end up living with her. Or his gran. At least until his dad gets a home posting.'

Elinor gave a noncommittal grunt and kissed Paula's shoulder. 'Let's see what tomorrow brings.'

That was the last thing Paula was aware of until her phone began ringing. She looked at the time as she answered. Twenty-seven minutes past six. 'DS McIntyre,' she moaned.

'DCI Fielding here. West Yorkshire have got a body. The ID says it's Beverley McAndrew, your misper. I've got a squad car coming, I'll pick you up in twenty minutes. Be ready.'

'OK,' Paula said. But she was talking to no one. Still half asleep, she sat up and ran a hand through her dark blonde hair. She wanted to believe the phone call was a bad dream, but she knew it wasn't. Bev was dead.

Elinor turned over and murmured sleepily, 'Did your phone just ring?'

'It was Fielding. She's picking me up in twenty.' This wasn't the time to tell Elinor. It wasn't fair to expect her to go through breakfast with Torin hugging that terrible knowledge to herself. And it wasn't right to tell Torin anything until his mother's ID was confirmed.

'What's happened?' Elinor was alert now. She knew the ways of her lover's job too well.

'I think it's a break in the Nadia Wilkowa case.' Which was sort of true. Paula stood up, then bent to kiss Elinor. 'See you later.'

She barely made it out the front door in time, but she'd managed to be waiting for Fielding. To her surprise, her boss had handed her a cardboard cup of coffee when she climbed into the car. 'The body's up on the moors. I don't suppose there will be catering,' Fielding said drily.

'What have we got?' It was easier to listen than to talk ahead of her first coffee. And Fielding definitely seemed to be a morning person.

She leaned through the gap between the front seats so she could more easily talk to Paula in the rear. 'If I had a fiver for every dog walker who finds a body, I'd be sunning myself on a yacht in the Caribbean. Local farm manager out with his lurchers didn't make it past the car park. The body was stashed behind a stone rubbish container. West Yorkshire didn't specify whether it's a primary scene or a body dump. She's a match for Nadia Wilkowa. Battered unrecognisable, badly beaten, genitals glued shut.' She paused to take a swig from a water bottle. 'But that's not why they called us.'

'Why did they call us?'

'Her clothes and bag were dumped at the site, same as Nadia. In this case, they were stuffed in the rubbish bin. When they ran her ID through the computer, the misper alert came up. They rang John Okeke – he's down as the point of contact. Soon as he heard the details, he told their SIO to call me. So here we are.'

'But Nadia was kept for three weeks before he killed her. Bev's not even been gone three days. That's a hell of a difference.'

'The key elements of the MO are the same, McIntyre. There's more that links them than distinguishes them.'

'Her son's only fourteen,' Paula said.

'It's going to be rough on him,' Fielding acknowledged, then moved right along. Her face gave no clue whether she couldn't bear the thought or simply didn't much care. 'What was she like, Beverley McAndrew?'

'Bev,' Paula corrected her automatically. 'I didn't know

her that well – my partner, Elinor, knew her better than me. They both work at Bradfield Cross.'

'Yes, Bev was the chief pharmacist. Okeke sent me the file, I've skimmed the details. What I want is the human stuff. What was she like?'

'She was smart. Opinionated, but not pushy. Good company. Her and Elinor, they were very funny when they got talking about their colleagues. You'd be amazed how much pomposity goes on inside a hospital.'

'I doubt it. I've been a cop for twenty years. We've got plenty of pompous arseholes of our own. So, was she on your team?'

'You mean, was she a lesbian?'

Fielding pursed her lips and gave Paula a pissed-off look. 'Unless there's another team you're not telling me about.'

'As far as I'm aware, she was straight. Her marriage to Torin's dad didn't break up because she ran off with another woman.'

'Why did it break up?'

'She said Iraq changed him. He began drinking heavily and she felt scared all the time when he was around. He was never actually physically violent towards her or Torin, but he shouted a lot, he was always angry. She felt they were living on a knife edge. Ironically, once they got divorced, they got on better. He had a good relationship with Torin. Bev reckoned having to take responsibility for being a family man was one stress too many, given what he was dealing with on the front line.'

Fielding nodded. 'That's squaddies for you. The Army acts like their parents and that's an easier family to belong to than real live ones, with all their demands and issues. So have we checked that the husband is where we think he is?'

'I haven't. I expect PC Okeke made inquiries.'

'Check it with him. So what kind of social life did Bev

have post-divorce? Was she a party animal? Did she have boyfriends?'

'She'd been out with a couple of guys since the divorce, but nothing recent, according to her colleagues. From my observations, I'd have said she was someone who took her job and her role as a mother seriously, which didn't leave a lot of room for much else.'

'But you admitted you didn't know her that well. What about internet dating? Do you think she might have been into that?'

Paula shrugged. 'I wouldn't have thought she was the type. But what do I know? What is the type? Presumably forensics will be able to tell when they have a crack at her computer.'

'Though God knows when that will be.' Fielding looked gloomy. 'Remember when they told us computers would make everything quick and easy? So how come it takes for ever for the geeks to get them to spill their guts?'

'We never had that problem in the MIT,' Paula said. 'We had Stacey Chen.'

'Yeah, well, lucky you. The rest of us have to live in the real world. So who gets the kid? With the dad in Afghanistan and mum dead? Where is he now? With relatives? Or social services. You sorted that out, right?'

Fuck, fuck, fuck. Truth or lies? 'He's with friends,' Paula said, setting for the half-truth and moving swiftly on. 'He's got a maternal grandmother and an aunt in Bristol. I believe the aunt is coming up to Bradfield today.'

'Good timing. We need to go through Nadia Wilkowa's life again, see if there are any intersects with Bev McAndrew. That might bring us closer to finding how he acquired her. Pharmaceutical rep, pharmacist – not such an outrageous thought.' Fielding turned away and stared out at the moorland landscape. 'Christ, it's bloody bleak. Why the hell would you want to live out here at the arse end of nowhere? What do people *do* all day? There's nothing as far as the eye can see. Even the bloody sheep have given up.'

Paula had never had much faith in her sense of direction, but she was beginning to wonder about where they were heading. She took out her phone and opened the map app. A flashing icon marked their movement along the road. In the 'search' box, she typed in an address she recalled from the Jacko Vance investigation. The app took a moment to load, then it informed her that the barn where Vance had killed Michael Jordan was a mere seven miles away by road. Looking at the map, it was a lot less than that as the crow might fly if it had any interest in making the trip.

She had no idea whether Carol Jordan had visited her late brother's home since his death, but if she was going to be out this way again, it might be worth taking a swing by to see if there were any locals who could help to pinpoint Carol's location. Because she really didn't want to lose contact with the boss she had come to count as a friend.

Moments later, they were slowing down, driving alongside other parked police vehicles. They emerged into the bright morning, eyes narrowing against the sunlight, and identified themselves to the PC who was controlling and noting access to the crime scene. 'Where's the SIO?' Fielding asked.

The PC pointed. 'DCI Franklin's over by the body.'

'Which one is he?'

Paula's heart sank as she followed the PC's finger. 'The tall one who looks like a Neanderthal undertaker,' she said under her breath, barely loud enough for Fielding to hear. Her boss gave her a quick, raised-eyebrow look. 'I know DCI Franklin,' she said more loudly for the PC's benefit.

They set off on the short demarcated route leading to the cluster of men round the stone box, stepping with care on the metal trays laid down to protect the ground and any clues it might ultimately yield. 'Good description,' Fielding said, nodding towards the craggy man with the pronounced eyebrow ridge and distinctive beak of a nose. 'I take it there's some history there?'

Paula nodded. 'Mutual antipathy, it would be fair to say. We thought he was a patronising obtuse bastard. He probably thought we were a bunch of smartarses.'

'Some validity on both sides, I suspect.' Fielding forged ahead and called out, 'DCI Franklin? I'm DCI Fielding from Bradfield.'

He swung round, his scowl lifting as he took in Fielding's trim figure and groomed appearance. Then he saw Paula and his face clouded again. 'DC McIntyre,' he said, ignoring Fielding. 'They split you up, then, you and DCI Jordan?' He delivered each word in a Yorkshire accent heavy as a paving slab. The other officers around him stopped what they were doing to catch the cabaret.

'It's DS McIntyre,' Fielding said, to Paula's surprise. 'And you don't have to bother your pretty little head about the threat from DCI Jordan any more. I'm the person you have to deal with now.'

Franklin smirked. 'Is that right?' He stepped back and made a sweeping bow. 'Well, be my guest.'

As he moved aside, they were confronted with what remained of Bev McAndrew. It was as if Nadia Wilkowa had been transplanted from Gartonside to the high moorland of West Yorkshire. Only when she got past first impressions could Paula discern the differences. Bev's body type was different – she was an apple to Nadia's pear – and her shoulders were broader, the muscles more defined. But as far as identifying her from her features was concerned, it was a non-starter. Again, the victim's face was a mash of bloody tissue, the white of bone showing through on cheeks and jaw. Determined though she was to reveal no weakness in front of Franklin, Paula couldn't help biting her lip.

'She's the twin of the one we caught on Monday,' Fielding said, her voice blank of any emotion. 'I think that makes her ours.'

'Not to mention that this looks more like a body dump than a crime scene,' Paula added. If this was going to turn into a turf war, better to get all the cards on the table as soon as possible.

But the response from Franklin was not what she expected. He dug his hands into the pockets of his trench coat. 'And according to her ID, she's come from your patch. Be my guest, ladies. You want us to process the scene or do you not trust us?'

'It's not a question of trust. It's a question of chain of responsibility.' Fielding looked around the car park. 'I'd appreciate the loan of some uniforms to secure the scene till my team gets here.'

'Where's her possessions?' Paula asked. 'The stuff you ID'd her from?'

'Bagged up,' Franklin said. 'We're not fucking turnips. We do know how to handle evidence.' He looked over his shoulder. 'Grimshaw?'

A chubby detective in a white suit that clung to the contours of his body approached. 'Sir?'

'The victim's clothes and bag. You need to hand them over to the nice ladies from Bradfield.' Grimshaw grinned and rolled off towards the line of vehicles. 'Anything else I can help you with?'

'Cameras,' Fielding said. 'Where's the nearest coverage?'

Franklin slowly made a 360-degree scan of the surrounding area. 'There's nothing on this road. It's four miles north to a junction with a main road, five miles south-west, where you came from. There's a couple of speed cameras on each of those, but I doubt there's anything much in terms of number recognition till you get to the outskirts of Todmorden, Hebden or Colne. Sorry.' He turned and walked away, a jerk of his head telling his team to follow.

Paula watched them cross the car park and reconvene round the nearest car. 'Nice to see DCI Franklin staying true to himself.'

'Whatever you lot did to piss him off, it worked.' Fielding sounded less than thrilled.

'His bark is worse than his bite. He won't obstruct us.'

'He bloody better not.' Fielding took out her phone and made a call. 'I need a full homicide forensic team up here . . . PC Okeke has the directions . . . There's no doors, so I won't need a door-to-door team, just some uniforms to secure the scene. What I need is for you to plot this locus on a map then figure out which are the nearest roads with ANPR. Get the data and work out which vehicles disappear between cameras where there's a turn-off on to this road . . . Soon as.'

Grimshaw returned with a couple of sealed blue polythene evidence sacks and a sheet of paper at risk of being snatched by the bitter wind. 'You'll need to sign for this,' he said, sounding as if he was already arguing with a refusal.

Paula dug in her bag for a pen and scribbled a signature on the damp paper. 'Thank you,' she said politely, holding out her hand for the sacks. Grimshaw dropped them at her feet and headed back to his boss. She liked to think she'd never been that petty to anyone her boss despised. She couldn't be certain, however.

She picked up the sack containing Bev's handbag and its contents. Staring at her, tinted blue by the plastic, Bev smiled out from her hospital ID. Her throat tightened, and she blinked away tears. How was she going to tell Elinor her friend was dead? Worse, how was she going to face that moment when she had to tell Torin his mother was never coming home? The death of hope was always the hardest part of any investigation. Knowing the victim, feeling so personal a loss intensified Paula's sense of failure. But it was also a potent spur to action.

Paula examined the contents of the bag as well as she could through the plastic. A moorland car park wasn't the place to take them out of their protective covering. There was nothing that she didn't expect. But the mobile phone did give her a moment's pause. She pointed it out to Fielding, who was studying the body intently.

'What about it?'

'Nadia's phone was among her things too,' Paula said. 'That suggests her killer knew there was no threat to him from the phone. He knew we weren't going to find his name or his number on their phones. Doesn't that suggest a stranger or a stalker rather than somebody they knew?'

'Either that or he used a false name and a pay-as-you-go phone so it wouldn't matter.'

She had a point, Paula thought. 'But it would still be taking a risk. If we found messages from untraceable numbers on both victim's phones, we'd know we might be looking for someone in their lives. Surely to be on the safe side, he'd take the phones?'

Fielding shrugged. 'On balance, you're probably right. Unfortunately it doesn't take us any further forward.'

A little encouragement would go a long way, Paula thought. It almost made her not bother offering her other idea. But she couldn't let pettiness interfere with the hunt for Bev's killer. 'Another thing struck me,' she said.

Fielding looked up. 'What?'

'The lack of cameras. Here and around the crime scene in Gartonside. When you think how much of our road system is covered by ANPR or speed cameras, it's a bit of a coincidence that he dumped both his victims in places he could approach without any concerns about being recorded.'

227

'You don't think that's a stretch?'

'I think it's worth bearing in mind. We should ask Traffic how you could find out where the camera blind spots are and how somebody could find that out.'

Fielding nodded. 'Not a bad idea. But it feels a bit like clutching at straws. Let's see what the forensics give us on both victims and, if we're no further forward, you can talk to Traffic. I tell you what I'm more concerned about right now ...'

'What's that?'

'Franklin was a pushover about handing the case over to us. I'm wondering whether he knows something we don't.'

34

By the time their forensics team arrived with the uniformed officers who would see to it no unauthorised feet trampled the car park, Paula was chilled and bad-tempered. There was nothing useful for her to do at the crime scene, but she and Fielding had to stay put to make sure there were no gaps in the preservation of the scene that a defence counsel could later exploit. Fielding had retreated to the car and her mobile, but Paula had chosen to remain with the body. She knew it was pointless, but she felt the need for some sort of gesture. Keeping vigil was the least she could do.

The first of the support vehicles had no sooner appeared in the distance than her phone rang. 'DS McIntyre.'

'Hello, Sarge. It's PC Okeke here.'

'Hi, John. What can I do for you?'

'Well, I know the misper's turned into a murder investigation and your team will be handling things from now on. Just a couple of things. The dad is definitely with his unit in Afghanistan. And after our talk yesterday evening, I got the

229

bus company to release their CCTV footage. I hadn't finished going through it when I spoke to DCI Fielding this morning, so I thought I might as well complete the job.'

'Good thinking. That's one less action for our squad. Appreciate it. Any joy?'

'A little bit. I ran it through a few times, to make sure I wasn't imagining what I wanted to see, you know what I mean?'

'I know exactly what you mean.' She didn't want to hurry him but she wished he'd get to the point. 'So what did you see?'

'I think Ms McAndrew must have parked a row over from the outside of the car park. It looks to me like her car is just out of shot. As the bus drives by, I saw her walking up the space between the rows of cars, then she moves off to the side and out of shot. I'd say she's walking quite fast. She's got her head down because it's raining. Next thing is, a few seconds later, another figure comes up the same way. I'd guess it's a man, but it's hard to be sure. He's wearing a waterproof jacket with the hood up. You can't see his face at all, except a bit of light glinting off glasses. He was carrying a case. Looked like it was made of aluminium, like photographers have. About the size of a pilot's case. And he carried it like it was quite heavy. Anyway, he goes the same way as Ms McAndrew, only he speeds up as he gets closer. Almost running. You'd have to say he was following her. And then he disappears out of shot, right where she did. It's not a lot of video. Only about fifteen seconds.'

'You did well to get that, John. Now, how would you describe this figure? Was he tall, short? Build?'

'Not tall. Medium height, I'd say. Not more than five feet ten. He was slim to medium build. It was difficult to tell. I couldn't be sure how thick his jacket was. And like I said, he's got his hood obscuring his face. The only distinctive thing is I think he might have a bit of a limp. It's hard to be sure. The quality isn't great and the weather doesn't help.'

It was a tiny shred of corroboration, but Paula's heart leapt at Okeke's words. 'That's very interesting, John. Can you say which leg he's limping with?'

He paused for a moment. She could hear him breathing. 'I'd want to look again, to be certain. But I think the weakness was in his left leg.'

Bingo. Not that it was exactly a break in the case. But it would help if it came to issuing an appeal for witnesses. Unless the killer was smart enough to fake a limp to throw them off. They already knew he was forensically careful. If he suspected there was any chance of being picked up on camera, he may have deliberately chosen to create a false image. 'I'm going to need you to make a formal report of this, John. File it with the incident room team, but send a copy directly to me and to DCI Fielding. I don't want this to get lost in the white noise.'

'Will do. You'll have it within the hour.'

Smart lad, she thought, readying herself to brief the forensic team. Once they were here, they could move the body. The way Bev was lying, it was impossible to see either the scar on her ankle or the tattoo on her shoulder. Those identifying marks would enable them to formally identify the body without having to wait for DNA. And then it would be time to break the news to Torin. Paula thought her chances of dodging that bullet were nil.

She walked across to the roadway and lit a cigarette while she waited for the specialists to suit up. Fielding got out of the car and Paula took the opportunity to bring her up to speed on what Okeke had discovered. 'There's no doubt about it,' Fielding said. 'We've got a single perp and two victims that we know of. Chances are he's got a record for violent offences, which means as soon as we do get some forensic evidence, he should show up on one of the data-bases.'

'Let's hope so.'

'Once we get her turned and we confirm the tattoo and the scar, I want you to talk to the son. You know him, it'll be better coming from you than a stranger. Presumably you know where he goes to school?'

Paula nodded. 'Kenton Vale. You don't want to wait till the end of the school day? Or until his aunt gets here?'

Fielding looked at her as if she was mad. 'Paula, this is the twenty-first century. There's no such thing as a hermetically sealed investigation any more. I don't want this kid finding out his mother's dead from Twitter or Facebook. As soon as we know for sure, we need to move on it. Line up an appro-priate adult. What about the friend he's staying with? Presumably there's a parent in the picture?'

Now she was in the shit. 'Actually, the friends he's staying with are me and Elinor. My partner.'

Fielding surprised her again, given her child-minding jibe the day before. 'Why didn't you say so? It's no big deal, as long as the family's happy with that.' She sounded more exasperated than angry. 'Frankly, I'd rather he was safe under your roof than camping with some mate we know nothing about. Can you get your girlfriend to come and hold his hand?'

'It depends on her schedule. She's a registrar at Bradfield Cross; if she's got a clinic or ward rounds, she can't just walk away from it.'

'When does the aunt arrive?'

'Not until this afternoon.'

'I don't want you tied up till then. See what you can do.' She glanced at the white-suited CSIs, lugging their boxes of kit across the bleak car park. 'Looks like we're getting some action.'

She set off in their wake, but Paula's phone rang and she hung back to answer it. The screen told her it was Dave Myers. 'Hi, Dave. I hope you're ringing me with some good news,' she said. 'We've got another body and it's looking like the same killer. So any help would be really welcome right now.'

'I'm sure it would,' he said, sounding unusually down-beat. 'Can you swing by the lab? There's something I want to show you.'

'That sounds intriguing. You want to give me a clue?'

'Not on a mobile.'

Paula wasn't used to Dave in worried, cagey mode. 'Will it take long? I've got to drive into Bradfield soon, but I won't have much time to spare.'

'It won't take long. What might take longer is figuring out what to do about it.'

Forty-five minutes later, Paula was climbing into a white paper suit at the forensics lab once more. Once they'd confirmed it was Bev's body that had been abandoned in the moorland car park, Fielding had despatched Paula back to the city. On the way, she'd managed to get hold of Elinor and arranged to swing by for her after she'd seen Dave. The police car had dropped her at home so she could pick up her Toyota; she was running on her own clock again.

When she walked in, Dave was in front of his laptop, pecking at the keys with two fingers. She placed the two polythene bags on the counter beside him. 'A gift from West Yorkshire police. If there's any issues of contamination, blame them.'

Dave stood up and lifted the bags one by one, peering into them. 'They've been out all night?'

'We don't know when they were dumped. The clothes

and the handbag were shoved in a rubbish bin so they've been pretty well protected from the elements.'

'But who can say what they've picked up from the contents of the bin.' He sighed, prodding the clothes bag with a finger.

'The victim is Beverley McAndrew. She was a friend of Elinor's.'

'I'm sorry to hear that. Tell her I'll do everything I can.'

'You always do, Dave. So, what's this mysterious thing you want to show me that you can't talk about on the phone?' Paula said, perching on a stool.

'The blood sample I recovered from Nadzieja Wilkowa's jacket. I extracted DNA from it without any difficulty. And I ran it through the NDNAD. There was no hit. This sample belongs to someone who isn't on the national database. But I didn't stop there. I decided to run a familial DNA search. You know what that is?'

'It tells you if there's someone on the database who's a close relative to the person whose sample you're testing, right?'

'Right. There have been some spectacular results since we started using it. Cold cases being solved. They've even caught serial killers with it in America. Some people bleat about human rights and privacy, but personally I think it's my human right to live in a world where murderous bastards don't get to roam unmolested in my community.'

'Here endeth the sermon.'

Dave conceded with a rueful smile. 'Yes, but here beginneth the lesson. So, I ran a check for familial DNA. Basically, the computer analyses the alleles and comes up with a list of people who have a degree of commonality. So, number one on the list has most alleles in common, and so on, right down to number one thousand, three hundred and forty-nine, in this case. Now, experience shows that if you're going to get a familial match, it's going to be in the top thirty.

We've got a little formula that incorporates the genetic match, the ages of the people concerned and their geographical location, and that gives us a likelihood of a particular relationship. But even before I had to use the formula I spotted someone in my top three who lives within a dozen miles of where your sample was taken. When I looked more closely, what do you know? I got what I consider a definite hit.' He neither looked nor sounded happy about it. 'The family member is a woman. It's my opinion, based on the DNA analysis, that this woman is a close relative of the man – and it is a man, by the way – whose blood was deposited on Nadzieja Wilkowa's jacket.' He leaned across the desk and clicked a tab on his screen. Up popped a pair of the familiar DNA profiles, one above the other, with their jagged peaks at irregular intervals. 'See for yourself. Where the alleles align, that's the key factor. So, how close is this genetic relationship? Now, we all have around five alleles in common with any given person. But the direct relationship of mother to offspring means there would be at least ten alleles from the crime stain which must have come via the mum.' Dave tapped each of the allele peaks with the tip of his pen. 'Eleven, you see?'

'I believe you, Dave. And so will a court. You seem really anxious about this. I don't know why. It's not like it's ground-breaking science.'

'The integrity of the science is not what's bothering me. Well, it is, but not for the reasons you're thinking.'

Paula shook her head. 'I'm a simple copper, Dave. I can't do cryptic crosswords. Just tell me straight. What's the issue?'

He looked pained. 'The identity of the person on the database. It's a woman called Vanessa Hill.'

Paula gawped at him, her mouth open. She couldn't quite credit what she'd heard. 'Did you say "Vanessa Hill"?'

Dave nodded, his expression miserable. 'I did.'

'What's her DNA doing on the database?' Paula clutched at what she knew was a broken straw.

'She was arrested and charged over the stabbing, remember? Even though the charges were dropped pretty much overnight, the DNA stays on the record.'

Paula shook her head, disbelieving. 'Could it have been transferred by someone else? Planted, even?'

'It's very doubtful. The way it's soaked into the threads and the cloth around the button – it would be hard to replicate that unless you had a liquid sample. And if you were trying to fit him up, wouldn't you leave the bloodstain somewhere more obvious? We could have missed that, even on a detailed second pass. If you hadn't been counting buttons, it could easily have gone unnoticed.'

'There must be a mistake. You've got to run the test again.'

'I will, of course. But I'm confident the answer will be the same. And I'll also run a mitochondrial DNA test. That's the DNA that comes direct from the mother to the child. If that's a match, there's no room for doubt.'

'What if she had another child? A sibling he doesn't know about?'

'You're reaching, Paula. That hypothesis breaks down as soon as we test his DNA, unless it's his secret identical twin. Which starts to sound like *The Man in the Iron Mask*.'

Paula stared at the screen, willing it to metamorphose into something different. 'Can we keep this to ourselves?' She saw the look of horror on Dave's face. 'Not completely, obviously. But at least till you've double-checked that there hasn't been a cock-up with the test. Or with the database. And you've checked the mitochondrial DNA. And' – she pointed to the evidence bags she'd delivered – 'you expedite the evidence from this latest murder and see whether that gives us a more viable suspect.'

He sighed. 'I'm not happy with this, Paula. This is important evidence in a murder inquiry.'

'Evidence that we both know makes no sense.'

He rubbed his soul patch between finger and thumb. 'The science doesn't lie, Paula. The blood on that jacket – you can't get away from it. That blood came from Tony Hill.'

35

Marie was on her way back from the bathroom when she heard the raised voices. If she needed any help in working out where they were coming from, she'd only have had to follow the eyes of everyone who worked within earshot of Rob Morrison's office. Even with their headsets on, they could clearly still pick up the sound of aggravation.

As she got closer, she recognised Ralph Lauren Man's arrogant tones. 'And I'm telling you, we'll fall flat on our arses if we put this out to Gareth and his merry men in marketing now. It's going to take at least another six weeks before we're ready to roll it out to civilian punters.'

'That's not what you promised me two months ago,' Gareth protested. 'You said it was only a matter of tweaking the front end. Making the user interface more idiot-proof, you said.'

'And that's what will happen. It's taking a bit longer than anticipated, that's all. How many times do I have to put that in words of one syllable?'

'"Anticipated" is five syllables,' Rob muttered.

238

'What's all the bloody rush about anyway?' Nigel demanded as she pushed the door wider. He had his back to the door but even so, he should have registered the consternation on Rob's face and the amusement on Gareth's. 'Is it the new boss? You're crapping yourself over a woman? Do you think she'll even understand what we've put together here? Give me a break, she's only a bloody skirt.'

'A bloody skirt who outranks you, Nigel,' Marie said sweetly. 'And who fully intends to get to the bottom of why your department can't deliver its promises on time.' He spun round, fury on his face.

'What are you doing, sneaking up on us?' His right hand curled into a fist.

Marie shut the door behind her. 'I never sneak. I don't have to. Next time you decide to throw your toys out of the pram, do it behind closed doors, please. There's a room full of workers out there absolutely agog. Generating water-cooler gossip doesn't help any of us to achieve our goals. We're all after the same thing. Success is what makes the world go round. We'll get there much quicker if we help each other.' Her smile was as warm as she could make it. Even Nigel seemed to settle down, shifting across the room to lean against a filing cabinet with his hands in his pockets.

'Boys will be boys,' Gareth said.

'Speak for yourself,' Nigel sneered.

'I'd like to get to the bottom of this, but not while you're all wound up. Why don't you each write me a memo explaining what all the fuss is about? In words of one syllable, obviously.' She pulled the door open again and walked briskly to her office, feeling quite pleased with herself. There was nothing like finding out where the fault lines were in an office community. And then you could exploit them to the full.

Marie smiled. She had to admit, she enjoyed the exercise of power.

36

C arol was at the top of a ladder, prising a reluctant chunk of mortar from the stonework, when the dog started barking. She looked down to see Flash hunkering before the door, front paws splayed in front of her, haunches bunched and ready to spring, head jerking back and forth in a frenzy of noise. 'Shut up, Flash,' Carol yelled, only now realising that she didn't have a command for quieting the dog.

She climbed down as quickly as caution permitted and hurried to the door, clicking her fingers at the dog, who obediently stopped barking and fell in at her side. Whoever was on the other side of the door, she'd bet it wasn't George Nicholas. But apart from the postie, he was the only person who had visited since she'd moved in. Cautiously, keeping one foot firmly behind the door, she cracked it open.

If she hadn't recognised the looming presence on her doorstep, his size alone would likely have provoked her into setting the dog on him. Whatever command that was. But it only took seconds for her to make the connection. After all, this had been the place where she'd last seen DCI John Franklin.

The corners of his mouth lifted in a smile without warmth. 'DCI Jordan,' he said, dipping his head in a curt nod.

'Not any more,' she said.

'No, I know. I was ...' He tailed off, and this time, the smile had a twist of sardonic humour in it. 'I was using it as an honorific,' he said. 'Like when officers retire from the regular army and march around in their Barbour jackets and tweed caps calling themselves "captain". Cops like us, we never really think of ourselves as civilians, do we?'

'I don't think of myself as a cop, DCI Franklin. So what brings you to my door? And how did you know it was my door?'

Franklin ostentatiously turned his collar up against the wind. 'Are you not going to invite me in? This is Yorkshire, we believe in hospitality. Come in, sit down, have a cup of tea.'

'I don't remember that aspect of my relationship with West Yorkshire Police.' What she remembered was blood and death and nobody ever listening to a word she or Tony said. What she remembered was bloody-mindedness and prickliness and men who used words like bludgeons. What she didn't remember was cosy cups of tea and slices of parkin. The dog picked up on her mood, grumbling gently at her side.

Franklin's shoulders rose and fell in a huge sigh. 'Look, Carol – OK if I call you Carol?' She nodded. Better that than a title she didn't hold and didn't want. 'We got off on the wrong foot and I reckon we're a pair of stubborn bastards who don't like to back down. How's about we call a truce? We're practically neighbours.' He spread his hands in a generous gesture.

'Come in,' she said, sullen rather than welcoming. 'There's nowhere to sit.' The dog followed her as she walked to the middle of the room.

He proved her wrong by perching on a sawhorse. He looked around and she could see him calculating where he was in relation to what had happened here. She couldn't complain. If anyone had the right to curiosity about what she was doing to the place, it was the cop who had had to confront the bloodbath up on the gallery, where the blood of her brother and his partner had turned the walls and ceiling into a grotesque abstract painting. But he said nothing about the past or the present state of the place. 'I suppose a cup of tea's out of the question?'

'Only when you tell me how you knew I was living here.'

He gave a dry guffaw of laughter that took all the threat out of his heavy brows and sardonic mouth. 'This is my patch, Carol. And what happened here is notorious for miles around. I knew the day you arrived. There's not a soul living round here that doesn't know you're living in your brother's office and gutting the place. What they're all gagging to know is what you're going to do with it once you've stripped it to the bare bones.'

Carol folded her arms and gave him her best hundred-yard stare. 'What I plan to do here is nobody's business but mine.'

'Fair enough. But I answered your question. Now do I get a cup of tea?'

'My coffee's better.' It was a grudging concession.

'Happen. But I don't like coffee.' He thrust his hands in his coat pockets. 'Oh, go on, Carol, it'll not kill you.'

She turned on her heel and marched through to her private quarters, Flash at her heels. She didn't like anyone inside the barn, least of all a man like John Franklin. Behind that bluster and bullshit, there was a tenacious terrier toughness in play. Whatever his reasons for being here, it wasn't an act of good neighbourliness. Carol hastily made a mug of tea, and brewed some fresh coffee for herself.

When she returned, he was prowling round the perimeter, studying the exposed stonework and the original beams as if he knew what he was looking at. He'd lost weight since she'd seen him last. His suit hung loose on his big frame, his shirt billowing out above his belt. The lines round his eyes were more deeply etched, his cheeks hollow. 'Ta,' he said, taking the tea. 'You've pretty much rubbed out all your brother and his missus did here.'

'Apart from the far end. Where Michael worked. It's a kind of guest suite. Or granny flat or whatever. It's self-contained.'

'And Vance was never in there.'

Carol's mouth tightened. She said nothing.

Franklin looked as if he was about to say something then stopped himself. He changed tack, crossing to the sawhorse. 'You'll make summat of it, I expect.'

Carol leaned against the wall, one hand on the dog's head. 'Why are you here? Is it because of the body over the hill?'

She caught a momentary flash of surprise in his eyes. 'Still a copper at heart, Carol. How did you find out about that? You don't talk to anybody round here except George Nicholas, and he's not on the bush telegraph.'

She toyed with the notion of refusing to tell him. She didn't owe him anything. 'I was walking the dog up on the shoulder of the hill. I know what a crime scene looks like, even at that distance.'

He sighed in satisfaction, and not at the tea. 'Mr Nicholas picked the right day to give you the dog.'

'Depends on how you look at it. I've got no interest in dead bodies or crime scenes any more.'

'How do you know it was a body?'

'Too much activity for anything less. A body or a serious sexual assault, I thought. But there's other places on the way up there if you're after a bit of lay-by sex. So I assumed a body.'

Franklin drummed the fingers of his left hand on the saw-horse. 'Here's the funny thing,' he said. 'Well, two funny things. First is, she's from Bradfield. A misper, but according to DCI Fielding, she's a match for another body they caught earlier in the week. Looks like the same killer, so I've graciously handed it over to her.'

'Very generous of you. I don't remember you being so open-handed with that murdered teenager a while back. I had to fight you tooth and nail for that one. Or maybe you prefer brunettes. Blokes always seemed to be suckers for Alex Fielding's charms, as I recall.'

He shrugged. 'Never noticed she had any. I was too busy getting into Detective *Sergeant* McIntyre's ribs.'

Sergeant. She hadn't known that. It was hardly a surprise. Carol would have promoted Paula in a heartbeat if she'd had the budget for another sergeant. 'Still,' she said. 'You handed it over without a fight.'

'This one's Bradfield through and through. The crime scene we've got, that's a body dump if ever I saw one. There's no blood to speak of, no weapon, no nothing except her clothes and her bag with her ID. Just as well that was there, because there wasn't much left of her face. I can't recall seeing a body so badly battered.'

'Why are you telling me this? It's got nothing to do with me.'

He put the mug on the floor and stuffed his hands in his pockets again. 'See, that's the other thing. To my mind, it's got everything to do with you. Because she looks like you.'

For a moment, it was too bizarre to be frightening. 'A

woman with no face looks like me? Do you have any idea how mad that sounds?'

'Not as mad as you think. She's got the same hairstyle as you.' He took a second look and corrected himself. 'Well, the same hairstyle you had when a proper hairdresser used to cut it. And she's about the same height and build as you. I tell you, Carol, when I first clapped eyes on her, for a few seconds I thought it was you. The resemblance, plus the fact I knew you were living here, right over the hill? Well, it was an understandable mistake, let me put it that way.'

'Are you trying to scare me, DCI Franklin?'

He shook his head vigorously. 'Of course not. I'm trying to warn you there's a killer out there who likes women who look a lot like you. You live in a building that's already notorious for murder. A stone-cold killer's out there, looking for victims who fit his type. One that lives in a placc with these associations could be irresistible.' To her surprise, he looked away, staring up to where the bedroom gallcry used to be. 'One crime scene here was enough, thank you very much.'

Carol didn't know what to say to that. She turned and crossed to one of the lancet windows cut into the thick stone walls. She could see all the way up the moor to the trees on the skyline where she'd walked the dog earlier. 'I'll be on my guard.'

'That would be good,' Franklin said. 'Happen it's nowt to do with you, this body turning up on your doorstep. But if it's some evil bastard leaving a calling card, you need to take care.' He stood up and left his mug on the sawhorse. 'I'm glad you've got the dog.'

'She does appear to be a good guard dog.'

Franklin walked to the door. 'Aye. She won't let anybody creep up on you.'

Except George Nicholas. Carol squashed the thought as ridiculous and unworthy. 'Thanks for keeping me in the loop.'

He gave another harsh bark of laughter. 'I'm not in the bloody loop myself. DCI Fielding made that crystal clear. But if I hear anything you should know about, I'll let you know.' He opened the door and scowled at the sleety rain that had come out of nowhere, as it so often did up on the moors. 'You might want to give Sergeant McIntyre a bell. She's the one with her finger on the pulse.'

Carol watched him leave. She didn't believe there was a killer out there who was trying to put the fear of death into her by killing women who looked a bit like her. And until she did, there was no reason to put in a call to her old life. No reason at all.

37

'I wish we could have waited until his auntie Rachel was here,' Elinor said, buckling herself into her seat belt.

'Me too. But Fielding's got a point. It's not like the olden days where information was safe till the next edition of the newspapers hit the street. Now, all it takes is one inadvertent slip or one idiot from West Yorkshire keen to make a bob or two by slipping something to the papers and suddenly it's all over Twitter. Can you imagine what it would be like to find out your mother was a murder victim from your Twitter feed?' Paula eased out of the hospital ambulance bay and into the stream of traffic.

Elinor shuddered. 'I take your point.' She laid a hand on Paula's thigh in a companionable gesture. 'It must have been a horrible shock for you, being confronted with Bev like that.'

Paula sighed. 'To be honest, Elinor, it was almost a relief. Not seeing her like that, obviously, but for the uncertainty to be over. I've been pretty sure she was dead for the last twenty-four hours. She wouldn't have walked away from her life. She loved her son. No matter how bad things had been for her – and we've found no evidence of anything amiss in her life – she would never have abandoned Torin without a word. She had to have been taken. And stranger abductions never end well.'

'I couldn't help hoping that she was being kept some-where. That you'd somehow manage to find her alive. You read about these cases, where people have been kept captive for years and then they're rescued. And Nadia was held pris-oner for three weeks, according to this morning's paper.' She bit her lip. 'I really wanted to believe.'

Paula wished she had Elinor's optimism. In spite of years of watching patients fail to recover, she still approached every case as if a good outcome were possible. 'Those cases, though, they all involve very young women or young girls. They're at an age where they're compliant and impression-able. They can be bullied and manipulated. They haven't learned how to stand up for themselves against an adult. It doesn't work that way with women of our age. We're too bloody stroppy.'

'I suppose. What's it like, working a major case with a new team?'

Paula turned on to the main road that would take them to Kenton Vale School. It was clogged with traffic, cars and vans all doggedly trying to get from one side of the city centre to the other. Times like this, she wished she had a blue light to clamp on top of her anonymous little car. Put the fear of god in White Van Man and carve a path through traffic. 'It doesn't feel like a team yet. Fielding is keeping me close. I've not had the chance to bond with the rest of the squad. Plus there's the baggage of coming from the MIT. That's a red rag to a bull for some people. It's a no-win. If you do something smart, it's "Ooh, get you, who do you think you are?" and if you fall over your own feet, it's "Not as clever as you think you are, are you?" I'm only trying to keep my head down and do my job. And that's not easy in this case.'

'Why not?'

'Partly because everybody knows I knew Bev, so they assume it's going to be personal. And partly because . . . ' She momentarily lifted her hands from the wheel in a gesture of frustration. 'I can't really tell you. Just, something that's . . . problematic about the evidence.'

'Can you tell me how it's problematic?'

Paula blew out a puff of breath. 'It's a matter of interpretation. And I want to be clear about it before I lay it out for Fielding. It would have been a lot more straightforward with Carol. I could have counted on her and the rest of the team not to leap to the wrong conclusion. I don't know that I can do that with Fielding. And it's not the kind of thing I can keep to myself. Plus the only explanation for it is impossible. So I have to figure out a way through it.'

'You will.' Elinor's confidence wasn't rubbing off on her partner and she could tell. 'If you take the next left, you can escape the traffic and circle round the industrial estate and come at the school from the other direction.'

Paula gave her a quick glance. 'How do you know that? Have you been moonlighting as a cabbie?'

'When I first moved to Bradfield, I had a horrible little bedsit down by the canal. That was the quickest way to get there in the rush-hour traffic.'

'I never knew that.'

'My feminine mystique. I have to keep you on your toes somehow.'

They drove in silence for a couple of minutes. Paula was dreading what lay ahead. Breaking the worst possible news was something she'd done more times than she cared to remember; it never got any easier. As if she read her mind, Elinor said, 'No matter how many times I give people bad news, I still feel inadequate to the task.'

'I've never had to tell someone I know.' Paula turned in at the school gates.

'Sometimes I've grown to know a patient quite well. At least you have a sense then of how to approach it. Take Torin. Like you, he's already expecting the worst. There's no leading up to it gently. Direct but kind is the best way for him, I'd say.'

Not for the first time, Paula thought her partner was Blessing by name and a blessing by nature. She'd cut straight to the heart of what was troubling Paula and she'd resolved it. If only the inconvenient issue of Tony's DNA could be so readily settled.

The news barely caused a ripple with the head teacher, a man who clearly believed that emotional crises needed practical responses. Paula warmed to him straight away. He installed them in a cosy room with soft armchairs and a low table. 'Our main guidance suite,' he explained. 'I'll send someone for Torin's form teacher and have her bring him here. What about tea, coffee?'

'Just water. And a box of tissues if possible,' Elinor said, matching brisk with brisk. His secretary swiftly brought what they'd asked for and left them to wait. It felt like a long time, but it was only minutes before the door opened and a large-bosomed woman in her forties ushered Torin into the room.

One look at the pair of them and his face crumpled. All his efforts at toughing out Bev's absence crumbled away, leaving him lost. 'She's dead, isn't she?' It was a roar of anguish. His knees couldn't hold him and he crouched low on the floor leaning into the side of a chair, his arms over his head, racking sobs tearing through him.

Elinor was first to his side, kneeling on the floor next to him, pulling him close and folding her arms round him. She didn't speak. She just held him and let the wave of grief suck him under and drag him with it.

Slowly, the sobbing subsided. Between them, Elinor and Paula helped him into a seat while the teacher watched helplessly. 'We're not supposed to touch them,' she muttered to Paula, who managed to restrain herself. Elinor sat on the arm of the chair, a hand on Torin's shoulder.

He looked up at Paula, eyes swollen, cheeks wet with tears, lips trembling. 'What happened?'

She chose her words carefully. 'Someone took her against her will, Torin. And then he killed her. I'm so very sorry.'

'Did he hurt her? Was it over quick? Did she suffer?'

The first thing they always wanted to know. With murder, you couldn't lie because the details would eventually come out in court and they wouldn't thank you for misguided attempts to spare them. 'I won't lie to you, Torin. He did hurt her. But I don't think she was in pain for long.'

His face twisted with the struggle not to crack up again. 'Thank you,' he stammered. 'For being honest. Did he— Did he interfere with her?'

The other thing they always wanted to know. This was, for some reason, the place where you had to let them down easy, without actually lying. 'We don't know at this point,' Paula said.

Torin started shivering, like a dog left out in winter rain. 'I d-d-d-don't know what to do,' he moaned through chattering teeth. 'What about the funeral? Who sorts all that out?'

'Come home to ours,' Elinor said. 'Your auntie Rachel will be here this afternoon.'

'Perhaps your form teacher could collect your bag and your coat?' Paula said firmly. The teacher looked dubious but left the room anyway. Paula followed her out into the hallway. 'He's been staying with us,' she said. 'Elinor's a doctor. She worked with his mum at Bradfield Cross. We'll take care of him.'

'Shouldn't you contact social services? He's only fourteen.'

'You think he'd be better off in emergency care?' Paula shook her head in bewilderment. 'Listen, in my line of work, I see too many vulnerable kids screwed up by the so-called care system. Let's see what happens when his aunt gets here. Nobody'll get on your case for leaving him in the hands of a cop and a doctor, for heaven's sake.'

'There's no need to be like that,' the woman said huffily. 'We have a duty of care here.'

'I understand that. But let's not get into a ruck. Torin's just lost his mum. He knows us and he trusts us. There'll be a family member with him this afternoon. This is the best course of action. If you stand in my way, there's a simple solution. I can take him in to the police station for questioning and there's nothing you can do to stop me. That's not the option I want to take, but I will if I have to.' Paula heard the words coming from her mouth with a sense of shock. She hadn't known she was going to take so adamant a line in respect of a teenage boy she hardly knew. *Bloody hell*. What was happening here?

The woman pursed her lips and put her hands on her hips as if she was squaring up for a fight. 'Right,' she said. 'I'll get his stuff then.'

38

It was all in the planning. He'd always been good at planning. Flow charts, fault tree analysis, cause-consequence diagrammatics – he'd been using all of those before he even knew the correct terminology. The first lesson his father had taught him was that actions have consequences. B follows A as surely as night follows day.

He remembered little of his mother. She'd been a timid woman, unassertive and bland, always scurrying to meet her husband's requirements. But she'd been a poor excuse for a wife and mother, forcing his father to constant complaint. When words didn't work, he'd had to resort to slaps, then punches and kicks. That was the way the world worked. When you failed, you had to take your punishment.

Then one April afternoon, when he was only seven years old, he'd come home from school to find the house locked and empty. He'd banged on the door but there had been no reply. Even at seven, he knew better than to make a fuss.

He'd slipped down the side of the house to the back garden and settled down to wait on the doorstep. By the time his father came home from work a little after six, he was chilled to the bone but he didn't complain.

His father explained that he'd thrown his mother out. Just like a piece of rubbish, the boy had thought at the time. If people didn't live up to the appropriate standards, they had to face the consequences. His mother had let them both down, so there was no place for her in their family any more.

He missed his mother's cooking and holding her warm hand on the way to school in the morning. But not for long. His father explained the need to be tough and self-reliant, and he absorbed the lesson. There was no alternative.

Not long after he turned eleven, he was sent off for two weeks of the summer holidays to an outdoor activity camp in the Lake District. A trio of ex-Army fitness instructors ran it like boot camp. Most of the boys spent the first few days in a state of shell-shock. They'd never been yelled at so much, never been expected to take responsibility for themselves and others, never had to face tests of physical endurance like it. For him, it had been business as usual. He wondered what all the fuss was about.

When he returned home, he discovered he had a new mother. While he'd been gone, his father had travelled to Thailand and returned with what the boy later discovered was a mail-order bride. This time, his father had chosen a wife who came much closer to his idea of perfection. Sirikit was subservient, polite, hard-working and eager to please. She never answered back, she cleaned house like a dervish and she never complained, even when his father criticised her for minor infringements of his regime. And she was a great cook.

By the time he hit fourteen he realised something else

about Sirikit. Practically every move she made had the capacity to arouse him. Every meal became a kind of torture, his penis straining against the tight underpants he'd taken to wearing in a bid to control his rebellious body. Luckily, his father paid him almost no attention unless he'd broken the house protocols, which he hardly ever did these days.

As he lay in bed one night, engaged in his nightly ritual of wanking to mental images of Sirikit spreadeagled over the kitchen table, smiling flirtatiously over her shoulder at him, it dawned on him that this didn't have to stop with fantasy.

The next afternoon when he came home from school, he found her in the kitchen preparing dinner. He approached from behind, reaching round to grab her small taut breasts. He pushed himself against her, as hard as he'd ever been. She squealed and squirmed, trying to break free. But he was strong and held her tight. 'I'll tell your father,' she screamed at him. 'And he will kill you.'

'No, you won't,' he'd growled into her neck. 'Because if you do, I'll tell him you're making it all up to cover the fact that you tried to seduce me because you're tired of an old man and you want young flesh.'

She hissed at him. 'He won't believe you. I am his wife.'

'And I'm his flesh and blood. He bought you. The bottom line is you're a whore and I'm his son. And he'd love the excuse to beat the crap out of you.'

The fight had gone out of her then. She knew her husband too well. And so Sirikit became his. Until he left home to go to university. His father had made it clear to him that he was on his own now. He'd sold up and taken Sirikit to live in Thailand, where she couldn't be further tainted by independent Western women. He never sent his son so much as a birthday card. Clearly, he was done with parenting.

Really, he should have learned from his father's choices and found himself a younger version of Sirikit. But he'd grown beyond his father and his crappy job working for the council. He was a graduate, a man with possibilities his father had never known. He was better than his father. He'd find a perfect wife without having to buy one. He'd find one who wasn't a whore.

For a while, he thought he'd done just that. She'd come for a job interview at the office where he used to work. On paper, she was well qualified as a market analyst but she was so shy she could barely answer the questions he and his boss put to her. She was demure and deferential and she couldn't believe it when he asked her on a date as he showed her out after her failed interview. Even on that first date, her eagerness to please was obvious. He used every technique at his disposal to undermine her, and within weeks she was cowed and controlled. Her parents lived sixty miles away in York and the first measure of his success was to turn her from a devoted daughter to one who never called. In spite of her parents' unease, they were married six months after that first meeting. By the end of the year, he had separated her from all her previous connections. He deliberately kept in touch with the only one of her cousins who lived in Bradfield because he didn't want to be blindsided. Information was power.

As far as he was concerned, he'd achieved exactly what he set out to do. Digital technology provided so many more opportunities for power and control. She didn't have to go out shopping; everything could be delivered from the internet, from groceries to sex toys. She didn't even need a bank account. He okayed or vetoed all the online spending, paying with credit cards she had no access to. He gave her small sums of money to pay for things like bus fares when she had to take one of the kids to the clinic, but he made her account for every penny. And whenever she fell short of the perfection he demanded, he made sure she understood the magnitude of her failure. He instructed her in ways she would never forget; it encouraged her not to repeat her errors. And it was effective.

Until it wasn't. He didn't know how or why, but she started to stand up to him. In small, almost imperceptible ways at first. But then she'd outright contradict him when he was commenting on the TV news or something in the *Daily Mail*. He confronted her with her betrayal of their love, but even though he punished her, she persisted. He reached the point where he knew he would have to put a stop to her behaviour once and for all.

That was when she paid him the ultimate insult. She deprived him of what was his right.

And now he had to replace her. And if those replacements didn't come up to scratch, then he'd have to make sure they didn't dodge what she should have had.

39

By the time Paula made it to Skenfrith Street, Fielding was in the middle of briefing the squad on Bev's murder. Paula expected a bollocking for being gone so long, but when they eventually convened in her boss's office, Fielding simply asked whether Torin had remembered anything useful.

'I don't think there's anything useful to be remembered,' Paula said. 'There's no reason to believe the killer knew Bev ahead of the abduction.'

'You think it's random? He chooses women who look similar, who both work in the pharmaceutical business, both in car parks? You don't think he's maybe been planning this a while? Maybe stalking them?' There was a sarcastic edge in Fielding's voice that pissed Paula off. She wondered whether that was intentional, designed to spur her on to greater efforts.

'Even if that's the case, everything we know about this killer is that he's careful. I can't see him behaving in a way that would catch the attention of your typical self-absorbed teenager.'

'Don't assume, McIntyre. It makes an ass out of you and me.'

Paula couldn't believe Fielding had actually uttered such a dismal cliché. 'I'll talk to him again. See if he noticed anybody hanging around.'

Fielding nodded her approval. 'Any strange cars parked near the house. We've got a line in to the boy through you. We might as well make the most of it.' She moved papers across her desk then looked up. 'What about the lab? What did Dr Myers have to say for himself?'

'He wanted to run more tests. I dropped off the evidence bags from this morning's crime scene and he's got a team working on them as a priority.' Well, it was almost true. She was getting good at finding a path between truth and lies with her new boss.

Fielding reached for her phone. 'I'm going to call him, remind him the DNA is our number one priority. Because we don't want to lose sight of Nadia Wilkowa in all this. I need you to review her appointment diary and see if she had any connections at Bradfield Cross. I know most of her contacts were GPs, but anything that links her to Bev McAndrew's workplace gives us a link. And look at her Facebook page too, see if she's got any friends listed who work there.'

Paula was on her way out of the door when Fielding spoke again. 'Torin. What kind of name is that? It's not Polish, is it?'

'It's Scottish, I think. Bev's dad was from Scotland.'

'Oh. OK. Just thought I'd check there's not a Polish connection we're missing. Wood, trees, that kind of thing.'

Paula went to her desk and started working through Nadia's data. She'd barely begun when her phone beeped.

The text was from Dave and read simply, Summoned by AF. Sorry . . .

No point in feeling too glum, Paula thought. The DNA analysis would have to come out eventually. She'd been hoping she could figure out an explanation before it did. As if it was ever going to be that straightforward.

Twenty minutes later, Dave Myers walked in. He sketched a wave in Paula's direction but headed straight for Fielding's office. Under cover of checking Nadia's records, Paula kept a discreet eye on their meeting. The DCI's face gave nothing away at first. Then slowly, she moved back in her seat, shock and incredulity chasing each other across her face. And then a slight flush on her cheeks. Her lips parted and the tip of her tongue moved quickly from one side to the other. *Fuck, she's actually loving this.*

Now Fielding was leaning over the desk, clearly making Dave go through all the data, point by point. Finally, she stood up and opened her door, patting Dave on the shoulder as she passed. 'McIntyre,' she called. 'My office, now.'

Feeling numb, Paula did as she was bid. Fielding pointed to the chair next to Dave. 'Dr Myers has brought us some extraordinary evidence. Doctor, can you tell Sergeant McIntyre what you told me?'

She had to sit and listen to it all again. But she didn't have to feign her astonishment. Hearing it a second time didn't make it any more credible. 'And there's no doubt about any of this?' she asked when he'd finished.

'No. We double-checked. I know it's hard to believe, but I'd stake my reputation on the accuracy of these results. The DNA from the bloodstain on Nadia Wilkowa's jacket belongs to the child of Vanessa Hill.'

'Dr Tony Hill.' Fielding stood up. 'Thanks for coming in with this, Dr Myers. And now that we've got a viable suspect, you know what we're looking for from the Bev McAndrew evidence, right?'

Dave looked outraged. 'You'll get what's there. Nothing more, nothing less.'

'That's all I want. But where there's room for doubt, I expect your team to drop on the right side of the fence, Dr Myers. In times of financial constraints, we have to be sure we're getting the best value in our forensic services, after all.'

Dave looked murderous as he gathered his papers together. 'I'll email you a full report.' He gave Paula a pained look as he turned for the door.

Paula waited till she heard the snick of the catch close behind him. 'There's got to be a mistake,' she said. 'Nobody who knows Tony could imagine for a moment he could kill. And certainly not like this.'

'Are you sure about that? Don't they say the best profilers are the other side of the coin from the people they hunt?'

'Only people who like to come up with lazy sound bites.' Angry now, Paula didn't much care whether she pissed off her boss. Getting her to see sense about Tony was more important. 'Tony Hill has dedicated his working life to preventing this kind of crime. He's about redemption and rehabilitation, not killing women.'

'McIntyre, sit down.' Fielding's voice was firm but not hostile. Paula hadn't even realised she was standing. 'Put your personal feelings to one side and look at the evidence. His blood is on Nadia Wilkowa's jacket. He limps with his left leg. He knows how to leave a body forensically clean. And the victims, Sergeant. The victims. They both look like DCI Jordan. Who, if I'm not mistaken, has shaken the dust of Tony Hill from her shoes along with the rest of us.'

What Fielding said only made sense if you looked at the world reflected in a distorting mirror. But Paula could see how seductive that picture would be to senior officers keen for a quick arrest that the media would love. The wolf in sheep's clothing, the gamekeeper turned poacher, the healer undone by his love for the woman who'd abandoned him. 'And what if someone's framing him somehow? What then? I don't believe it.'

Fielding rested her elbows on the desk and her chin on her fists. She appeared to be on the verge of asking a purely philosophical question. 'I'd expected more from you than grasping at straws. But you're entitled to that view, McIntyre, paranoid though it might seem to some. The question is, can you put it to one side and do your job?'

Paula felt the hot flush of annoyance burn her cheeks. 'It's my job to bring the guilty to account. I've never let personal feelings stand in the way of that.'

'You see, Sergeant, this is where you have to nail your colours to the mast. Can you concede that Dr Hill might be guilty? Can you commit to pursuing this investigation without your friendship getting in the way? Can you arrest and interrogate this man? If you can't say yes to those questions, say yes and mean it, there's no place for you on this case. There's plenty of other crimes need a talented investigator. Plenty of other SIOs who could use a smart sergeant. But I can't use somebody who's a secret squirrel for the other side.'

Even through her suppressed fury, Paula found a moment to wonder where this woman got her vocabulary from. *Secret squirrel?* What was that about? 'I'll do what's necessary,' she said, her voice thick with anger. 'I'll go where the evidence takes me. I'm not afraid of the truth.'

Fielding gave her a long hard look, head cocked to one side, considering. 'I think I believe you, McIntyre.' She looked at her watch. 'I want to do this quietly. No big media ruckus. Presumably you have Dr Hill's phone number?' Paula nodded. 'What would bring him in here?'

'A request for help.'

'Perfect. There's no way that can be construed as entrapment. Text him now. Tell him you need his help, ask him to come here.'

Paula stared at her phone screen for a long moment then typed in, Need your help. Can you stop by Skenfrith Street later? She showed the screen to Fielding, who nodded. Paula sent the text. *This is how Judas felt.* She stood up. 'I'll get to work on Nadia's diary. I'll let you know as soon as he gets back to me.'

She sat at the computer, the screen blurred and meaningless. Her stomach churned and her hands felt cold and clammy. She felt disloyal and disgusted, but the treachery she'd chosen at least had the virtue of keeping her on the front line. From this position, she was best placed to help her friend. Maybe even to save him. She only hoped he'd see it like that.

40

Rachel McAndrew bore little resemblance to her sister. The dark business suit over a kingfisher-blue polo-neck jumper that she'd chosen to travel in was formal, in opposition to Bev's more casual outfits. Where Bev was blonde and smiling, Rachel was brunette and reserved. Elinor didn't want to rush to judgement – the woman had just lost her sister, after all – but she sensed in Rachel a more complicated and closed-off personality. Torin had insisted on meeting his aunt at the station and breaking the news himself. Elinor hadn't tried hard to dissuade him. She reckoned he had the right to make some decisions. She'd be there to support him, and his aunt if need be.

Rachel had leaked tears at the news, but she'd composed herself quickly. 'I feared as much,' she said, her Northern accent still noticeable after years in Bristol. 'I lay awake last night, trying not to give in, but I couldn't convince myself. She wouldn't walk away from her responsibilities, not our Bev.' She'd tucked her arm proprietorially through Torin's.

'Come on then, Torin, let's get back to yours and see what needs to be settled.'

Torin stood still, a stubborn cast to his jaw. 'I don't want to go home,' he said. 'Not yet. I'd rather be at Elinor's.'

'Torin, Dr Blessing's done enough. I'm here now, I can take you off her hands.' Rachel tried to draw him along with her, but he refused to move.

'You're both very welcome to come home with me,' Elinor said.

'That's what I want,' Torin said, stepping towards Elinor.

The atmosphere on the drive was awkward. Torin crouched in the back seat in silence while Rachel alternated between dripping tears into a tissue and turning to tell him how dreadful he must be feeling. Elinor had seldom felt more uncomfortable.

She left them in the living room while she made tea and opened a fresh packet of biscuits. It was the last one in the cupboard. Grief had done nothing to diminish Torin's adolescent appetite. Either that or he'd taken to comfort eating like a terrier to rabbits. She carried a tray through and found them sitting on opposite sides of the room.

Rachel dived in straight away. 'When can I see her?'

'I don't think that's a good idea,' Elinor said, aware of how little detail they'd given Torin.

'Someone has to identify her, surely?'

'You need to talk to my partner, Paula, about the details.'

'She's one of the people in charge,' Torin said. 'Paula's determined to find out who killed my mum.'

'She'll be home later,' Elinor added.

'Will she be able to tell us how soon we can make the funeral arrangements? We need to get all that settled.' Rachel took a box of sweeteners from her handbag and dropped one into her tea. She sat back in the chair, her legs tight together at knees and ankles.

'When someone dies like this, you can't have the funeral right away,' Elinor said, trying to find a sensitive way to explain the situation.

'Why not?'

'It's a question of evidence,' she said. 'After someone's arrested, they've got the right to have their defence team examine the body.'

'But that's terrible. That could be months. How can you do that to people?' Her voice rose in outrage. Displacement, Elinor thought.

'I think some families hold memorial services. To mark the passing of someone they love.'

'That's not what's important,' Torin said angrily. 'She's dead, that's what matters. Not what they do to her body. It's just dead meat now.'

Rachel's hand flew to her mouth, revealing perfectly manicured plum-coloured nails. 'Don't say that, Torin. That's your mum we're talking about.'

'It's not my mum. My mum's gone. What they've got at the morgue, it's nothing but a bag of flesh and bones. It doesn't matter. This is where she is now.' He clapped a hand to his heart, his face screwed up in his determination not to cry.

'Of course she's still in our hearts.' Elinor passed the biscuits to Torin. 'About your mother,' she said to Rachel. 'Will you phone her and break the news? Or is there a neighbour . . . ?'

'I'll phone her later. I told her I'd speak to her this evening, once I knew what was what. So, if we can't have a funeral, there's no real reason why we have to stay up in Bradfield, is there?' It was as if she couldn't wait to get away.

'Well, you'll have to register the death. And deal with the estate,' Elinor said.

'Because the sooner we get Torin down to Bristol and

settled in there, the better,' she continued, as if Elinor hadn't spoken.

Her words galvanised Torin, who straightened out of his slump and shifted to the edge of his seat. 'Bristol? I'm not going to Bristol.'

'Of course you are, don't be silly. We're your family, we're all you've got left now, with your dad off wherever he is. You'll come to Bristol and live with me. Or your gran, whichever you prefer. We've both got room.' She sounded matter of fact, as if it was open and shut.

'Why would I want to go to Bristol? All me mates are here. I go to school here. I sing in a band here. Tell her, Elinor. I belong here, in Bradfield. It's bad enough losing my mum without you making me lose everything else as well.' Now he was on the verge of tears again. He rubbed his nose vigorously with his fist. 'I'm stopping here.'

'You can't stop here. You're only fifteen—'

'Actually, he's fourteen,' Elinor said.

Rachel looked momentarily cross, but she quickly reversed into sympathy. 'Torin, you can't live by yourself. You have to see sense. A clean break's best all round. You can make a fresh start.'

Now tears were spilling down his face. 'I don't want a fresh start. I want to be where I belong, where the places I go remind me of her and me and our life. I don't want any kind of break. My dad said I could stop in Bradfield. If you make me go to Bristol, I'll run away, I swear.' He banged his mug down so hard that tea slopped over the table.

'I understand why you're so upset. I am too. I'm tearing up just sitting here. She was my sister, and my heart's broken.' Rachel delicately wiped a tear away with a tissue. 'I want you with us because you're part of her.'

'What do you care? You don't know me. You hardly see us from one year's end to the next. You came for exactly one weekend last year, you and my gran. If Mum hadn't dragged me down to bloody Bristol for half-term, that would have been it. So don't pretend we're close, because we're not. You don't know anything about me.'

'We'll learn,' Rachel said softly. 'We should have spent more time together, you're right. But you always think there'll be time, down the line. You never think it'll be too late, just like that. You never think. I can't make it up to Bev, but I can make it up to you.'

'I don't want you to,' Torin said plaintively. 'I need to be here. This is all I've got left.'

'But you're too young to be on your own, Torin.'

Elinor knew it was coming before he turned to her. 'You'd let me stay, wouldn't you, Elinor? I could rent out our house and pay you the rent. It wouldn't cost you owt.'

'You know you're welcome here, Torin. But your aunt has a point. Your family can give you support we can't. When you need to talk about your mum, about her past, about what she was like when she was your age, we don't know the answers to those questions.' Being so generous was surprisingly hard. To her amazement, Elinor felt an ache inside at the thought of Torin leaving them. She wanted him to stay. It was unfathomable. She'd never wanted children. But this boy had touched her in a way she hadn't imagined possible.

'We can phone. I can go there for my holidays. But please, Elinor, let me stay. I want to be here.' He buried his face in his hands and wept. Elinor waited for Rachel to make a move, but she didn't. So Elinor got up and perched on the arm of his chair and hugged him close. She'd be damned if she was handing the boy over to a woman who didn't have the instinct to comfort him in his distress. When he eventually got himself under control, he stood up and said, 'I'm going up to my room.'

'I'm sure this isn't what Bev had in mind,' Rachel said as he closed the door behind him.

'I think it will be up to Torin and his father to decide what's going to happen in the long run,' Elinor said. 'Either way, this isn't the time or the place. You're both in a very emotional state. I suggest Torin stays here for now. We've spoken to Tom and he's sanctioned Torin living here with us for the time being. You'd be welcome too. There's a sofa bed in the study.'

'I don't think so,' Rachel said. 'I've got keys for Bev's. I'd rather feel her all around me than be in a strange place with strangers.'

'Of course. The police have already searched it – my partner, Paula, did it as soon as we realised Bev was missing. It's been hard for her, being so closely involved in the case. But if you like, I can call her and check that the police have finished with it?'

Rachel shook her head. 'I'll take my chances. If there's a problem, I'll go to a hotel. I just want to get things sorted out. I was pretty sure I was coming to bury my sister. All I wanted was to organise a nice funeral and take Torin home with me. It looks like I won't be doing either of those things.'

'I'm sorry,' Elinor said. And she was, because, as Paula regularly pointed out, Elinor was the nice one. But part of her felt a deep satisfaction that Torin wanted to stay.

41

The first thing Paula said when she came to meet him in the waiting area at Skenfrith Street was, 'I'm sorry.'

Tony was puzzled. 'Sorry for what? It's not like I was doing anything else.'

Uncharacteristically, Paula made no quip about him being a sad bastard. Instead, she briskly ushered him through into the main part of the station and down a hallway lined with doors. The signs said 'Interview Room' followed by a number. 'I misled you. I had to. It's the only way I could stay on the inside.'

'I don't understand.'

Paula stopped in front of a closed door, number four. 'You will.' She opened the door and gestured for him to enter.

The claustrophobic room was painted battleship grey with a low ceiling covered with acoustic tiles. There was no two-way mirror, just bare walls and a video camera mounted in one corner. DCI Fielding was already sitting in one of the grey plastic bucket chairs arrayed on either side of the grey table with the recording equipment. She didn't even raise her head from the file in front of her when they walked in. All she did was wave a hand at the chairs opposite her.

Tony had been in plenty of police interview rooms, but always on the questioner's side of the table. Unsure of what was going on, he sat down facing Fielding and was even more disconcerted when Paula took the seat next to her. Paula took out a notepad and pen and arranged them in front of her. He could see there was a list, presumably of questions, but he couldn't read her handwriting upside down.

'What's going on, Paula?'

Fielding looked up. 'Let's get the tape running, McIntyre.'

Paula gave him an apologetic look but she pressed the buttons on the recording equipment. After the long beep sounded, she said, 'Interview commenced at six twelve p.m. Present are DCI Alex Fielding, Detective Sergeant Paula McIntyre and Dr Tony Hill. Dr Hill, it's our intention to interview you under caution in connection with the murders of Nadzicja Wilkowa, known as Nadia, and Beverley McAndrew, known as Bev.'

'Are you arresting me?' There would be no mistaking his incredulity on the recording.

'Not at this point, no. We simply wish to ask you some questions. You're entitled to have a lawyer present. Would you like to have a lawyer?'

The role reversal was so startling that Tony couldn't quite process it at first. 'What do I need to be lawyered up for? I haven't done anything. Apart from a couple of unpaid parking tickets. On you go, Paula. Ask anything you want.'

'You do not have to say anything. But it may harm your defence if you do not mention when questioned something which you later rely on in court. Anything you do say may be given in evidence. Do you understand?'

271

'What defence? I thought you weren't arresting me?'

'It's a form of words, Dr Hill. As you well know. This isn't the time or the place for levity. Two women are dead.' Fielding's eyes held no promise of warmth. He'd heard she didn't hold much of a brief for his dark arts; he hadn't realised how deep her dislike for his work was. And of course, she was ambitious, which could be a hard thing for a female cop to negotiate. Solving these crimes quickly and nailing them on a high-profile offender would do her nothing but good in the eyes of those to whom those things mattered. Was he about to become a scapegoat? It was an unnerving thought. The only option was to pretend he had no idea what was going on.

'Of course. I apologise. Please, I'm happy to answer your questions. Is this to do with the bus? Only, that was just by chance that occurred to me. I bought more shopping than I intended and I had to get the bus.'

Now it was Fielding's turn to look baffled.

'Tony,' Paula said. 'All in good time. The first thing I have to ask you is to cast your mind back three Saturdays ago. Can you tell us where you were that Saturday afternoon and evening.'

'Saturday three weeks ago?' Theoretically, it should be easy. A day when he had no appointments. A day when he could please himself. But with nothing to differentiate one Saturday from another, how could he say what he had actually done?

'Bradfield Victoria were playing Chelsea at Stamford Bridge, if that helps.' Knowing his love for the Vics, Paula had checked the fixture list ahead of the interview.

His face cleared and he smiled. 'Of course. Ashley Cole conceded a penalty and looked like he was going to cry. I thought about watching it live at the pub, but I didn't fancy fighting for a seat and all that relentless camaraderie. So I watched the game at home. I had a couple of beers. Then I walked up to the chip shop on Mistle Row and bought cod and chips for my dinner.'

'Will they remember you?'

'Three weeks on? I shouldn't imagine so for a moment. It was busy after the game, I didn't talk to anyone.' He gave a hapless little shrug. 'I didn't know I was going to need an alibi.'

'And afterwards?'

'I went back to the boat.' He smiled at Fielding. 'I live on a narrowboat on Minster Basin. I spent the evening alone. I'm finally catching up with Scandinavian *noir*, so I probably watched a couple of episodes of *The Bridge* or *The Killing* then chances are I played Arkham City or Skyrim on my Xbox.'

'Do you enjoy violent computer games?' Fielding butted in.

'I enjoy computer games,' Tony said. 'Nobody gets hurt. It's fake, DCI Fielding. Whatever the *Daily Mail* likes to think, the jury's still out on any direct correlation between gaming and IRL violence.'

'For the tape, what's IRL?' Paula asked.

Tony rolled his eyes. 'In real life.'

'Did you make any phone calls?'

'I shouldn't think so. You have my permission to check my records with my mobile provider though.'

'Did anyone phone you?'

He locked his fingers behind his head and leaned back, making it obvious that he was thinking. At last he said, 'I think that's the Saturday when the Clinical Director of Bradfield Moor Secure Hospital phoned me but I didn't pick up the call. I was in the middle of my game and I didn't want to be interrupted by work on a Saturday evening.'

'It might have been an emergency relating to one of your patients.'

Tony inclined his head. 'Not very likely, but yes, it might have been. But I'm not the only clinical psychologist on the staff. I'm learning not to be indispensable.'

'You're sure that's what you did that Saturday? You didn't go shopping?'

'I don't do shopping, not in the sense of a leisure activity. I buy most of what I need online, and I buy my food at the supermarket. And I don't go there any Saturday. I go week-days when it's quiet. Sometimes in the middle of the night, if I can't sleep. I went there yesterday evening. As you know, Paula, because I phoned you up afterwards to tell you to look at the bus CCTV to see whether you could spot Bev McAndrew.' He smiled at her, to remind her he was on her side.

'Like I said, we'll come to that. You didn't go to see a movie that Saturday, did you?'

He shook his head. 'No. I definitely didn't do that. I can't remember the last time I went to a cinema to see a movie. Either I stream them or I watch them on DVD. I hate the smell of cinemas. Popcorn and hot dogs.' His face echoed his disgust.

And so it crawled onwards. On Monday evening, when Bev had been abducted, he'd been at home, working on a parole report on his laptop. 'You can get some techie geek to check the time stamps on my computer.'

'Time stamps can be faked,' Fielding said dismissively.

The previous night, when Bev had been killed and dumped, he'd explained that he'd walked across town to Freshco and come home on the bus.

'Why did you go all the way to that Freshco? There are plenty of places you could have shopped closer to home,' Fielding asked.

Tony frowned, his eyes flicking back and forth between the two women. 'Because that's where Bev was most likely to have gone shopping after work. It was a reasonable hypothesis that her abductor might have acquired her there.'

'And how did you know all that?'

'Because Paula told me.' The 'duh' was unspoken, but Paula heard it loud and clear.

Fielding gave Paula a look of angry perplexity. Tony realised he might have dropped Paula in it even more than himself. Was this what all this was about? Was Fielding using him to destroy Paula?

'DS McIntyre?' Her expression was certainly severe enough for his theory to be on the money.

Paula wasn't conceding ground, however. She spoke clearly and confidently. 'I talked to Dr Hill after Bev went missing. I wanted to see if he had any suggestions that might help me trace her. I spoke as a friend of the family. Not as a police officer. It was barely a police case at that point.'

Fielding's grim expression indicated that Paula hadn't heard the last of this. 'So you decided to mount your own investigation, Dr Hill?'

'Not really. I needed a walk, I needed some shopping. Bev was at the back of my mind, that's all that was going on.' He leaned forward, his expression pained. 'Am I a suspect here?'

'At this point, we're just trying to resolve some issues,' Fielding said.

Tony wondered again what those issues were. Surely there were easier ways to bump Paula off the case, if that was what Fielding wanted? Perhaps he needed to be a little more proactive. With his skills, he should be able to control this interview. He tried his best conciliatory smile. 'Only, if I'm a suspect, why would I call Paula and suggest looking at the bus CCTV? Why would I help your investigation?'

Fielding sat back. 'If you figured it was going to come out

anyway – which it would have, once we had a full-scale murder investigation under way – you'd be diverting suspicion by pointing us in the right direction.' She let a tiny smile escape. 'Plus, aren't you profilers always telling us that killers like to inject themselves into the investigation? Seems to me that's one interpretation of what you did with DS McIntyre.'

Tony gave a self-mocking groan. 'Hoist by my own petard, eh?' He paused, frowning. 'What is a petard anyway? I've often wondered.'

'It's a bomb,' Fielding said. 'Stop trying to derail this interview, Dr Hill.'

'Busted,' he said, offering Paula a rueful look.

Fielding passed a couple of sheets of paper to Paula, who laid them on the table facing Tony. She tapped one. 'That's Nadia Wilkowa.' And the second. 'That's Bev McAndrew. Have you met either of these women?'

He had to admit, Paula was good. She'd asked the question in such a way that he could answer honestly without dropping her further in the shit. It was in nobody's interest right now for him to reveal she'd taken him to Nadia's flat. It would simply muddy the waters. He'd worn gloves so there would be no prints and he hadn't done anything to shed significant DNA there. Really, they should be in the clear. For now, at least.

'I'm not sure,' he said. He pulled Nadia's picture closer. 'She looks familiar. Actually, they both do. But I can't place either of them. I'm sorry.' He looked up, giving his best little-boy-lost. 'Bev worked at Bradfield Cross, right? They call me in for a psych consult from time to time. And occasionally I have meetings there. I might have run into her there. But I can't be certain.'

Fielding took another two pieces of paper from her folder and looked at them. 'You're an only child, is that right?'

'Why is that relevant?'

'Just answer, please.'

'Yes. I am an only child as far as I'm aware.'

'As far as you're aware?'

He shrugged. 'None of us can ever be certain of that. But I was brought up as an only child and I've no reason to think otherwise. Why do you care?'

Fielding set the two sheets of paper in front of Tony. The names had been blanked out with Post-it notes. 'Do you know what these are?'

He glanced down at the graphs with their jagged peaks. 'They look like DNA profiles.'

'This one came from the National DNA Database. And this one came from a bloodstain on Nadia Wilkowa's jacket. Even as a layperson, you can see the similarities,' Fielding said. 'Would you agree?'

'I've no expertise in this area,' Tony said cautiously. It was dawning on him that something more serious than fucking up Paula was going on here.

'The reason for the similarities is that there's a genetic relationship between these two people. What we call a familial relationship. A is the mother of B. Would you like to guess who A is?'

He met Fielding's level, triumphant gaze. 'No.'

'It's Vanessa Hill. Your mother. And this is presumably you. Can you explain how your blood came to be on the cuff of Nadzieja Wilkowa's jacket?'

It was as if someone had punched him hard in the chest. For a moment he couldn't breathe. Then the adrenalin rush of fear surged through him, switching his senses on full alert. His brain raced frantically, synapses firing crazily, rifling through his store of memories to find this woman. He knew he was innocent, so he knew the answer had to be in there somewhere.

He had no idea how long had passed before Paula said gently, 'Tony? Can you answer the question, please? Can you explain how your blood came to be—'

His expression was stricken. 'I've no idea,' he said, his voice dry and tight.

Fielding shook her head. 'I'd have thought you could do better than that.' She turned back to her folder.

Before she could ask another question, Paula's phone beeped. She glanced at the screen then showed it to Fielding, who nodded and got to her feet. 'Interview suspended.' Ushering Paula ahead of her, she left the room. Tony watched them go, feeling genuine fear for the first time since he'd arrived at Skenfrith Street.

'Fuck,' Fielding said as she closed the door behind her. 'He's got nothing. No rebuttal, no excuse, nothing. Now, let's see what your pal Dr Myers has for us.' The text from Dave Myers had simply said, Buy me a coffee. Seven minutes later Paula pulled in by the coffee stall that crouched under the North Stand of Bradfield Victoria's premier league stadium. Dave liked meeting here; it reminded him of American cop shows, glossing their dull lives with a spurious glamour. Seeing her car, he stepped away from the counter carrying two coffees in a cardboard tray. He looked worryingly glum. His face fell further when Fielding climbed out of the passenger seat.

He gave a wry smile and passed a coffee to each of the women. Paula leaned on the open driver's door and peeled away a section of the lid and enjoyed the aroma of the spicy dark roast the Italian owner preferred. She had a feeling there wasn't going to be much else to enjoy at this encounter.

'Nice of you to offer my sergeant a coffee, Dr Myers.'

'We go back a long way,' Paula said.

'So what do you have for us?'

'That evidence bag you left us this morning – there was a phone in there, right?'

'Yes. Presumably Bev's,' Paula said.

'It is hers. We checked.' He tugged at his soul patch. 'There's a partial thumbprint on the back of the phone.' He took a folded sheet of paper from his jacket pocket and handed it to Fielding. It was an enlarged photocopy of a fingermark, smudged down one side and slightly distorted where the thumb that made it had shifted slightly. 'Because I know you're in a hurry on this one, I gave it to my best fingerprint tech as a matter of urgency. She ran it through the AFIS database. Nothing came back from criminal records. But in Bradfield, we keep our own database of prints for elimination purposes. Serving police officers, CSIs, pathologists. And anybody else who regularly attends crime scenes or has contact with evidence.'

Fielding looked visibly brighter. 'I hope this is going where I think it is.'

Paula's response was markedly different. She snatched her emergency cigarette packet from the door pocket of the car and lit up.

Dave grimaced as the smoke blew across his face. He half-turned away from Paula towards Fielding. 'Her preliminary opinion is that the thumbprint on Bev's phone could have come from Tony Hill.'

'Could have?' Fielding was clearly disappointed. 'You can't do better than that?'

'It was a rush job. Obviously she'll be looking at it again.'

Paula's chest was tight with fear. These days, there was always room for doubt with fingerprints. No CPS lawyer would give the thumbs-up to a case that rested solely on fingermarks. But as a consolation, it was still rock-solid where juries were concerned. And would a jury be so wrong?

It was unimaginable to her, but what else but guilt could explain DNA *and* fingerprint evidence?

Tony had spent the half-hour of Paula and Fielding's absence racking his brains for an explanation as to how his blood had ended up on Nadia Wilkowa's cuff and he'd drawn a blank. It didn't help that he was feeling anxious. Stress was an enemy of recollection. Tranquillity, that was how you got the memories to flow. Not being wound up to a pitch.

When they finally returned, he practically jumped to his feet. 'This is crazy,' he said. 'Paula, we've known each other for years. You know I didn't kill anyone.'

'Sit down, Dr Hill,' Fielding said. 'This isn't about how well any of us knows you. It's about following the evidence where it leads us. And right now, it's only leading us in one direction.' She plonked her folder down on the table and drew a piece of paper out of it. 'Let's see what you make of this, shall we? You know what that is?'

'It's a fingerprint. Kind of smudged, but it's a fingerprint.'

'Actually, it's a thumbprint. The right thumb, to be exact. And so is this.' She proffered a printout of an official print card. 'Identical, I think you'd have to agree?'

This was starting to feel very uncomfortable. 'I have no expertise,' Tony said, his lips tight.

'You don't need expertise, you only need eyes. The print on the official record card was freely given by you just over three years ago. The other one was lifted from the back of Bev McAndrew's phone earlier today.'

There was a long silence. Tony could hear his blood pounding in his ears. The wheels were going round but they were gaining no traction. 'When did she go missing?' he asked, trying to buy time.

'She left work on Monday at the usual time. Shortly after half past five,' Paula said.

He ran a hand through his hair. 'I think I was at a meeting in Bradfield Cross on Monday afternoon ... I need to check my diary.'

'I'm not impressed with the absent-minded professor act,' Fielding said. 'Monday. This week. Where were you?'

Now it was time to find some steel. 'I already said. I need to check my diary.' He pushed the chair back. 'Are we about done here?'

'Not quite.' When she smiled, Fielding could look almost gentle. Nobody would have guessed, looking at her granite face then. 'Dr Hill, when did you last see ex-DCI Carol Jordan?'

Now he'd really had enough. He wasn't going to talk to this idiot any longer. He stood up. 'This interview is terminated. I'm done with answering your short-sighted questions. I've spent years trying to instil some understanding into police officers. And this is where it ends up.' He shook his head in disgust. 'Find somebody else to monster, DCI Fielding. I'm not playing any more.' He made for the door, but Fielding was ahead of him.

'Anthony Valentine Hill, I am arresting you on suspicion of murder. You do not have to say anything. But it may harm your defence if you do not mention when questioned something which you later rely on in court. Anything you do say may be given in evidence.'

He took a step back, turning to Paula, his face a mask of shock. 'Is she serious?'

'She's serious, Tony.'

He walked away from Fielding and sat down heavily in one of the chairs. 'Then, no comment.' Tony folded his arms across his chest and stared straight ahead. Inside, he was in turmoil. But on the outside, he would give nothing away.

Not until he'd figured out how to dig himself out of this hole.

42

Paula watched the duty sergeant walk Tony down to his cell. She'd processed him herself, making sure he was clear what he was entitled to. And that the duty sergeant knew she was looking out for her prisoner. 'You should call a lawyer,' she said.

'You can make the call from here,' the sergeant added, pointing to a payphone.

'I'll sleep on it,' Tony said. His face was drawn and tired and he seemed to have shrunk since he'd arrived at the station.

'I'm sorry,' Paula said.

He nodded. 'I know. It's OK. We're good.'

She desperately wanted to say more, but couldn't risk it. This was Fielding's nick, not hers, and she didn't know who to trust yet. Weary and unsure of what to do for the best, she headed upstairs, pausing for a cigarette break before facing Fielding and the murder squad. Cody was leaning against the wall by the door, blowing a stream of smoke upwards. 'Nice work,' he said.

'You think?'

'It's always good to get a collar early on. Gets the brass off your back and the media out of your face.'

'Even if it's the wrong collar?'

'Oh, I forgot. He's a mate of yours, isn't he? He's always been an oddball, from what the lads are saying.'

'It's a long way from oddball to sexual homicide. And I don't think he's capable of it.'

'Word is he lost the plot after the Jacko Vance business. That's why Jordan walked away from him. She knew he'd turned.'

All at once, Paula's moment of doubt became history. She stepped right into Cody's personal space and jabbed a finger into his chest. 'Where are you getting this crap from, Cody? Or are you making it up as you go along to wind me up? Jesus Christ,' she exploded. 'You sound like one of those tabloid reptiles who go in for trial by headline. Carol Jordan lost her brother. That's why she walked back from all of us. It's called grief, you twat.' She stepped back and turned away from him. 'It's got fuck all to do with this.'

'Take it easy, Sarge,' Cody said, his voice sarcastic. 'People'll think you've cracked an' all.'

'If I hear you or anyone else talking this kind of shit, I'll go straight to Fielding with it. That's a promise.'

Cody gave a soft, dark chuckle. 'What makes you think it's not coming from Fielding, Sarge?' Paula whirled round and crushed out her cigarette against the wall millimetres from his ear. He yelped as hot ash hit the sensitive skin. 'You mad bitch,' he yelled.

'You mad bitch, *Sergeant*. I'd advise you not to forget either part of that sentence, Cody.' She turned on her heel and stomped back inside, glad anger had replaced the fear and depression that had been building up all evening.

She found Fielding in her office, packing files into her

laptop bag. 'You should have told me you'd spoken to him about Bev McAndrew going missing.'

'I know. I'm sorry.' Paula waited for the bollocking. But to her surprise, Fielding walked away from it.

'I understand how it happened,' she said, sounding almost as weary as Paula felt. 'You're used to him being inside the tent, it was a natural thing to do.'

'What do you want me to do now?'

'Go home. Eat something. Sleep. We'll go back on the attack in the morning. Hopefully, the fingerprint techs will give us a definite yes rather than "could be". And we'll conduct a full search of his home and his office. Do you know if he has a storage unit or a lock-up or something as well as his boat?'

'No idea.'

'We'll check it tomorrow. I've got the grunts looking at the CCTV footage to see if we can pick him up anywhere relevant.'

Paula rolled her shoulders to loosen up the tightness that had been building there. 'Do you really think he did it?'

'I'm following the evidence, McIntyre. And that's where it's leading me. You're letting your emotions cloud your judgement.'

'Am I? I don't think it's my emotions. It's my knowledge and experience. I've worked with Tony Hill for years. He *saves* lives, he doesn't take them.'

'And I think you could be totally wrong. But it's good that you're digging your heels in. It gives me something to push against. It means we'll test our case properly and not get ambushed in court by the defence. Right now, though, we're just at the start. Away home now and come back in the morning refreshed and ready to go.'

'What about the media? Have we told them we've made an arrest?'

Fielding shook her head. 'I've told the squad to say nothing. Which probably means it'll be all over the internet by bedtime. But I'm saying nothing officially.' She fastened her case and shooed Paula out of the office. 'See you in the morning. With a bit of luck, we'll see his happy little face on the Trafford Centre cameras.'

And she was gone, leaving Paula all wound up with nowhere to go.

Home had never been like this. It was like walking into the middle of an intense TV drama. Torin was on his laptop at the dining table, a strange woman Paula presumed to be Rachel McAndrew was in an armchair with an iPad and a glass of wine and Elinor was ironing a white shirt. Ironing a shirt? Paula hadn't realised Elinor knew where the ironing board lived. But death – particularly sudden, violent death – always left people unsure of how to fill their time. The look of relief on Elinor's face told Paula all she needed to know for now.

'Hey, Torin,' Paula said. 'Hello, love,' to Elinor. And, 'You must be Rachel. I'm Paula. I can't tell you how sorry I am about Bev. We were very fond of her.'

Rachel put down her wine and stood up, extending a slim hand adorned with a couple of diamond rings. 'It's such a shock,' she said, her voice tremulous. 'And Elinor says we can't even bury her.'

Paula flashed a quick look at Torin, whose head lowered even closer to his screen, hair hiding his eyes. 'I've arranged for a Family Liaison Officer to come over tomorrow morning to take you through what's happening and explain how to go about the official side of things. He'll be here at half past nine.'

'Rachel's planning to stay at Bev's tonight, if that's OK with the police,' Elinor said. 'But Torin would rather stay here.'

285

Paula smiled. 'No problem, mate. I don't think I'd want to go back there just yet if I was you. There's no rush.' Torin's head bobbed in acknowledgement. 'I do have some news about the investigation which I wanted to share with you.' The atmosphere in the room quickened. Torin looked up, his eyes beseeching her. Rachel froze, her hand halfway to her wine. And Elinor gave her a tiny nod of encouragement.

'This evening we made an arrest in connection with Bev's death. And that of Nadia Wilkowa, another woman whose body was found earlier this week.' Paula held her hands up, palms out, urging caution. 'I don't want you to overreact to this. It's very early in the investigation and I'll be honest with you. I have serious reservations about the guilt of the person in custody. This happens sometimes in serious crime investigations. We arrest a suspect early on, with minimal amounts of evidence. That doesn't mean the investigation is over. In this case, the investigation's barely begun. But this arrest will be all over the media tomorrow and you should be prepared for that. It would be best if you don't speak to the media, but obviously that's up to you.'

'Who is it?' Torin demanded. 'Who did this to my mum?'

'The man we've arrested is called Dr Tony Hill. He's a psychologist who works at Bradfield Moor Secure Hospital and for years now he's also been working with us at BMP, drawing up profiles of serious offenders.'

'This man *worked* with you? And you had no idea he was a killer?' Rachel's outrage was obvious. It would only get worse, Paula suspected. Grief had to find an outlet somewhere.

'We don't know that he's a killer. Personally, I don't believe it. It goes against everything I know about the man.' But she had to be honest. She owed that to Bev's family. 'There is some evidence that points towards him though. We have to test that evidence and see whether we can actually build a case against him.' She looked to Elinor for support, but her partner was speechless, her face aghast.

'I don't understand,' Torin said. 'Did this guy know my mum from work? Why did he pick her?'

'We don't know, Torin. Right now, we have a lot more questions than we have answers. All I can say is that we're doing our job. None of this helps you to deal with your mum's death, I know. But I'm doing my best for her.'

'Great speech, Detective,' Rachel said. 'I think it's time I went over to Bev's.' To Elinor, 'Have you got a taxi number?'

'I could drive you over,' Elinor said. 'It's no trouble.'

'Thanks, but you've done more than enough for us,' Rachel said. It was a line that could have been taken either way and Elinor clearly got that.

Elinor called their usual taxi firm and Paula escaped to the kitchen. She was staring gloomily into the fridge when Elinor joined her. 'Taxi's on its way, thank goodness. She's hard work, Rachel. I made sandwiches for us all earlier. I'm afraid I used all the ham and cheese and salad.'

Talk of food was a displacement activity that displaced nothing for either of them. Paula closed the fridge. 'I'm not actually hungry. This has been one of the worst days of my working life. Not quite up there with the Temple Fields ordeal, but pretty damn close.'

'I can't believe it. Has Fielding lost her mind? Tony? If I had to compile a list of everyone I know in order of how likely they were to commit murder, I'd put him very near the bottom.'

'Same here. But she doesn't know him like we do. To Fielding, he's just another prospect in a sea of possibilities. But he is the scalp that will make her name. Can you imagine the headlines?' She shuddered. 'It's so ironic. One of the reasons she's convinced he's the one is that the victims look a bit like Carol Jordan. According to her armchair psychology, he's killing surrogates because he can't have her. But the truth is, the only person Tony would kill *for* is Carol.' Paula sighed and opened the fridge again. This time, she took out a pot of yoghurt. She stared at it for a long moment then put it back and closed the door again.

Elinor put her arms around her from behind and kissed the soft skin behind her ear. 'What are you going to do about it?'

'I don't know. I think Fielding's testing me. Am I good enough to be her bagman? If I put a foot wrong, she'll have my stripes, maybe even my job. So I have to be very careful not to be seen to be helping Tony. But I can't just stand by and let this happen to him. I understand exactly how the momentum builds behind an arrest.'

'The juggernaut of justice.'

'Exactly. People focus on anything that supports the arrest and dismiss any faint indications of other directions.' She leaned her forehead on the cool fridge door. 'I've never missed the MIT more.'

'Carol would know what to do.'

'Carol would never have arrested Tony in the first place. She'd have viewed the evidence against him as some kind of pointer towards the real killer. Or something.'

'You need her now. She'd be ferocious as a lioness protecting her cub.'

Paula gave a sad little laugh. 'Once upon a time, maybe. Now I'm not so sure. Whatever the glue was that held those two together seems to have come unstuck. And besides, she's not a cop any more.'

'All the better, surely? Paula, I know you. You need to do something or you're going to be awake all night, smoking too much and drinking too much coffee and twitching. And taking years off your life, which makes me very unhappy because I need you to be around for a very long time. Go and find Carol. Let her do the heavy lifting.'

Paula shook with silent laughter. 'You're crazy. You say "go and find her" like it was straightforward. She's gone off the radar. Even Stacey doesn't know where she is.'

'Stacey only knows machines. You know people.'

Elinor's words triggered something inside Paula's head. Not quite fully formed, but the teasing start of something. It was interrupted by the doorbell. 'That'll be the taxi,' Elinor said. 'I'll see Rachel off the premises. Don't move, I'll be right back.'

Preoccupied, Paula opened the fridge for a third time and took out a plastic container of leftover chilli. She flipped the edge of the lid open and stuck it in the microwave. By the time Elinor returned, she was forking it into her mouth, frowning into the middle distance.

'She's gone,' Elinor said. She sighed. 'It hasn't been an easy afternoon. She wants to take Torin to Bristol with her.'

'That's good, surely?'

'Except that Torin doesn't want to go. His arguments are very reasonable – his friends are here, his school, his band—'

'He's in a band?'

'Apparently he sings. Who knew? Also, he wants to be somewhere that holds memories of his mum. Not ripped out of the ground and transplanted to a strange city to live with people he barely knows.'

'Like you say, reasonable.' Paula was focusing on Elinor now, realising there was more going on than was being said. 'And?'

'It's a "but" really, not an "and". But he has no family here. And he's only fourteen.' She took a deep breath. 'He wants to stay with us, Paula. At least until his dad deploys back to the UK.'

Paula's eyes widened. 'Here? Living with us?'

Elinor pushed a stray strand of hair from her face. 'I don't know how I can say no.'

Paula's smile was wry and knowing. 'Even if you wanted to. Fuck, Elinor, this wasn't in my life plan. Somebody else's teenage kid.'

'Right now, he's a good kid, Paula. What happens to him next will determine if he carries on being a good kid. You know that. You see the results of fucked-up young men every working day. So do I. A&E is full of them. I think we should say yes.'

'What does Auntie Rachel say?'

'She's not happy. But then, I have a sense that Auntie Rachel isn't happy about much in her life. Ultimately, it's his father who has to make the decision. He might think the worst thing that could happen to his son is to be left to the tender mercies of a pair of big old dykes. But until that happens, I think we need to hang on to Torin. It's what he wants, and I think you in particular might be what he needs.'

Paula gobbled some more chilli, suddenly starving. 'I don't seem to have much say in this.' It was, they both recognised, an objection for form's sake only. More a gentle demurral than a righteous protest.

'Like you're going to start walking away from doing the right thing. Now finish up that chilli and get on the trail of Carol Jordan.'

Paula smiled. 'I had an idea about that.'

43

The cuisine that Marco Mather had learned from his mother was one of the healthiest in the world. At its heart, the Southern Italian food was the diet of peasants, too poor for obscure or luxurious items. It was based on a handful of easily grown vegetables and herbs, olives and their oil, cheeses made from the milk of hardy goats and sheep, and small amounts of game and poultry. But like so many other aspects of modern life, it had become corrupted by money.

That frugal but delicious diet had spread like a spare tyre to embrace all manner of richness. Estate-bottled olive oil used as a dip for enriched breads; cream and butter liberally added to sauces and ragus which contained more meat than their original creators would have eaten in a month; full-fat cheeses from grass-fed dairy cows; and an endless supply of tasty processed pig products. Italian food at its worst had become an invitation to obesity and furred-up arteries.

It was an invitation that Marco had embraced. The food

he created for their daily dinners was loaded with calories and cholesterol. Marie loved it, but she fought its effects by skipping breakfast and sticking strictly to so-called healthy options at lunchtime. Marco, working from home at his desk, had only his willpower to keep him from food during the day, and it generally let him down at least once between breakfast and bedtime. For a long time, his natural metabolism had kept his weight more or less under control. But as middle age crept closer, so the pounds were creeping on. His trousers were tighter and his thighs had begun to rub together as he walked.

And so he'd decided to lose some weight. He'd read several articles online and watched a documentary on TV about a new regime of exercise that involved short bursts of intensive aerobic exercise. The results were little short of miraculous. For less than two hours a week, his heart would be healthier, his weight would reduce and he'd live longer. He'd always resisted exercise in the past because it bored him. But surely he could manage a few minutes a day without losing his mind? It would be worth it, if it allowed him to continue cooking and eating the food he loved.

Marco had told Marie his plan, and she'd been delighted. She loved her husband and she hadn't wanted to make him feel bad about himself, she said. But she wouldn't mind if he lost a few pounds. So he'd ordered a state-of-the-art exercise bike and had it installed in the garage that morning. Now he was going to go for the burn. He hadn't done any exercise since he'd given up squash a dozen years before but he was confident he'd nail this.

He stripped to his boxer shorts, pulled on a pair of trainers and climbed aboard. He understood the importance of going flat out. He had to push himself to the very limit and go as fast as his legs could pump. He set the timer and started out, driving his legs up and down like pistons, pedalling as fast as he was able. In no time at all, his heart was hammering, sweat was bursting out in beads on his forehead and his breathing was ragged and painful. But he kept going. Surely to god he could exercise for five minutes?

Marco drove himself on, pushing forward, convinced he would break through the pain barrier to some zen-like state. But his distress just kept increasing till a spasm of pure agony seized his chest and rippled through his upper body. His arms were on fire, his chest gripped by an iron band.

He toppled from the bike, in the grip of a massive heart attack. Even if Marie had been there to summon the paramedics, it's doubtful whether they could have saved him.

And so, when a killer stole Marie Mather on the very street where she lived, there was nobody to notice she hadn't come home. Nobody to report her missing. Nobody to add her name to the list of victims.

Nobody to exonerate the man in custody.

44

Paula was glad it was dark as she drove out across the Yorkshire moors. It hid the interminable bleakness that always filled her heart with gloom. Other people saw splendour in the scenery, she knew that. But thanks to years of exposure to the worst of human behaviour, she saw it as a place where terrible things could go unwitnessed. A potential body dump. The landfill of loss.

Franklin had been reluctant to confirm what she'd guessed. 'Why would I know where your old DCI is hiding?' he'd said on the phone, sounding more amused than truculent. 'It's not like we were pals.'

'I had you down as somebody who knows when a mouse farts on his patch,' Paula said. 'So if you don't know where she is, I'd have to conclude she's not in West Yorkshire. And focus my attentions elsewhere.'

As she'd expected, the challenge to his capability did the trick. 'I never said I didn't know,' he replied.

'Any reason why you wouldn't tell me?'

'Is this a police inquiry, Sergeant? Or a personal one?'

'Does it make a difference, sir?'

'We're all entitled to our privacy and our family life, according to the human rights lawyers. If Jordan doesn't want to play nice with you lot any more, that's her choice. And it wouldn't be my place to deprive her of those rights.'

'And if it was an official inquiry?'

'I'd expect it to come through official channels.'

'I'm a detective sergeant, sir. How official do you need it to be?' There was a long pause. She could hear the rasp of him scratching stubble.

'Ah, fuck it,' he said. 'Why are we playing stupid games with each other? She's living at the barn. Her brother's barn. She's stripping it to the bare bones. There's nothing left to show what happened.'

'Thank you. I owe you a pint, sir.'

'You do. But I'll pass. I don't like you Bradfield bastards. That goes for Jordan just as much as the rest of you. So there's enough pleasure for me in grassing her up. Drive safe, Sergeant, we're not keen on dangerous drivers over here.'

He was gone before she could say more. And now it was after nine o'clock and the only thing between her and despair was the satnav. Every road looked the same, bordered by the wild grasses of the moorland or drystone walls that looked drunk but always seemed to stay upright. Occasional lights glimmered in the dark and now and again she'd pass a huddle of buildings claiming to be a village. Finally, a large building loomed on her right and her bossy navigator said, 'You have reached your destination.' Paula pulled into the parking area and turned off the engine. She felt sick.

Still, she forced herself out of the car and set off across the flags towards the barn. Security lights flooded the area, making her blink against her blindness. The stillness of the night was split open by a volley of barking that was barely diminished by the thick stone walls of the barn. A dog? Carol Jordan, the ultimate cat woman, had a dog? Had Franklin told her the truth? For a moment, Paula considered turning tail. But she'd come all this way. She might as well knock on the door.

As she raised her hand to the black iron knocker, the door opened far enough to reveal a familiar face. Carol Jordan did not look pleased to see her, and the dog whose muzzle was pushing against her knee didn't seem any more welcoming. A low grumble in the back of its throat would keep most sensible people at bay.

Paula tried a smile. 'Any chance of a cup of coffee? There isn't a Costa for miles.'

'Is that your best door-opener? Don't, for Christ's sake, abandon the job for a career in sales.' The door didn't budge. 'Give me one good reason why I should open the door?'

Paula reminded herself that Carol wasn't her boss any more. 'Because it's a bloody long drive and it's bloody cold out here. That's the smart-arsed answer. If you want the sincere one – you should open the bloody door out of friendship.'

Carol's eyebrows rose. 'You think we're friends?'

'You think we're not? We had each other's backs for years. I always thought we liked each other. Respected each other. I never even considered a future you weren't part of.' Paula flushed, wondering whether she'd gone too far. Carol's reserve in personal matters was as much part of her as her devotion to taking criminals off the streets.

Carol lowered her eyes. 'I'm not sure friendship is one of my strengths.'

'You'll never find out if you carry on running away from everybody who cares about you. Now, are you going to let me in before I freeze my tits off?'

Almost a smile. Carol opened the door and stepped back. She clicked her fingers and the dog lay down at her feet. 'Come in.'

The space Paula entered was a building site, a work in progress. A couple of industrial lamps in their metal cages lay on the floor, casting light and shadow in a complicated chiaroscuro, making it difficult to get a clear picture of what was going on. She clocked the sawhorses, a workbench, bare stonework and bundles of cable and wire sticking out at odd angles. 'Funny,' she said. 'I never had you down as a DIY queen. Or are you just getting in touch with your inner butch?'

'It's therapeutic. I'm undoing the past and making a future.'

She sounded like a cut-price version of Tony. 'Is there anywhere to sit?'

Carol gestured with her head for Paula to follow her. They went through a door and into another world. For a start, it was warm. The room resembled a small loft apartment. Bed, workspace, cooking area. No living area. Just a couple of office chairs in front of three computer monitors and a flat-screen TV.

The light was brighter here too. Paula could see Carol clearly, and as she'd never seen her before. Her hair was thicker and cut more bluntly than previously. There was silver among the blonde, glinting as it caught the light. Either she'd given up dyeing her hair or the years had finally caught up with her. She wore no make-up and her hands were scarred and scabbed from the snags and scratches of physical labour. Even under the thick sweater and jeans that she wore, it was obvious her upper body was more solid, her thighs stronger. In spite of it all, Carol looked healthier than she had for years. And Paula couldn't help remembering that she'd carried a torch for her former boss. Until Elinor had come along and reality had consigned fantasy to the dustbin.

'What's with the dog?' Paula held out a hand to Flash, who sniffed it disdainfully then turned away and followed his mistress as she filled the kettle and set it to boil. Carol readied a cafètiere with ground coffee. 'And where's Nelson?'

'I left him with my parents. He's too old for all this. The dog is a misfit who's here for the time being. We're both on trial, I think.' She turned to face Paula and leaned against the worktop. She pushed up her sleeves, revealing muscular forearms which she folded across her chest. 'So have you come to warn me too?'

'Warn you?'

Carol shook her head, disappointment on her face. 'Don't try to kid a kidder, Paula. John Franklin told me you were Fielding's bagman. Come to that, I saw you myself this morning at the crime scene. So let's start again. Have you come to warn me too?'

'Carol, I really don't know what you're talking about. Has Franklin been here? Today?' This wasn't making any sense to Paula.

'He stopped by this morning after Fielding handbagged him and took the case away.'

'Pissed off, was he?'

'Oddly enough, no.' The kettle boiled and she poured hot water on the grounds. The smell was tantalising. One thing Carol and Tony still had in common; you always got a better than decent cup of coffee. 'He said he was here to warn me.'

'What? To keep your nose out?'

'Warn me, not warn me off,' Carol said impatiently. 'He told me there's a killer on the loose who seems to have a thing for women who look like me.'

Paula was taken aback. 'Well, women who look like you

used to look. I'll be honest, you don't look like anybody's potential victim these days. Not that you ever did,' she added hastily, seeing the danger signs in Carol's expression. 'So, was that a surprise, Franklin showing up?'

'Completely out of the blue.' Carol smiled. 'I was gob-smacked. I'd always thought if there was any chance of me being murdered, Franklin would be out there selling tickets.'

'Only if it was happening well away from his patch.'

'True. So if you're not here to warn me to lock my doors and avoid the lonely graveyard at midnight, why are you here? I'm not naïve enough to think it's because you missed me.'

'But I do miss you. And not just because DCI Fielding is most emphatically not you.' Paula accepted a cup of coffee and blew gently to cool it. 'You made it clear you were done with Bradfield, done with the lot of us. And we all respected that. I respected that. Even though what I wanted was to be your friend. To take you out and get drunk with you. To listen to your pain. To bring you home and let Elinor cook you chicken pie and mash.' To her annoyance, Paula could feel her throat constrict with all the tears she hadn't shed with Carol.

'I understand that. What I did was the only thing I knew how to do. The last time I thought I'd lost everything, I ran away. And it worked. I was able to heal myself enough to come back into the world. That's what I'm trying to do this time.' She opened a cupboard and took out a bottle of brandy and poured a slug into her coffee.

'You drank too much last time too,' Paula said, feeling the crack of thin ice under her.

Carol's lip curled. 'Tony always did over-share with you.'

Paula shook her head. 'Tony never said a word out of place about you. I know you drank too much because you were still drinking too much when you set up the MIT. You

299

think we didn't know about the miniatures of vodka in your handbag and the quarter bottles in the desk drawer?'

Carol started as if she'd been slapped. 'And you never said anything? You knew I was drinking on the job and you never said anything?'

'Of course we didn't. Even Sam the Snitch had more sense. Besides, why would we? It's not like you were falling over drunk. It never interfered with the way you ran the team.'

'Christ, I never realised you all knew. Call myself a detective?' She turned away, embarrassed. 'So, why are you here? Really? Because if you'd come here with the olive branch of friendship, Elinor would have sent a Tupperware box of home baking with you.'

The time for bridge-building banter was over. Now it was time to cut to the chase. 'I'm here because DCI Fielding has arrested Tony for the murder of two women.'

Carol stared, open-mouthed, the cup halfway to her lips, disbelief growing on her face as the words sank in. She craned her head forwards as if she was straining to hear. 'Come again?' she said, full of obvious scepticism.

'We interviewed him under caution this evening and then she decided to charge him. And it's mad. I know it's mad, you know it's mad. But there's evidence. And Fielding can't see past that to the man. He needs your help.'

Carol put her coffee down and held her hands up. 'Whoa. Back up there. I'm not a cop any more, Paula.'

'You think I don't understand that? That's exactly why he needs you and not me. I'm on a knife edge here. I shouldn't be telling you this stuff. If Fielding finds out, it'll be all over for me. I'll have a dazzling career in Traffic.'

Carol frowned. 'So why are you here?'

'I told you. Tony needs your help. He's hopeless. Carol, you know better than anybody else what he's like. He thinks just because he's innocent that nothing bad will happen to him. And we both know how naïve that is.'

'I couldn't agree more,' Carol said, her voice the epitome of chilly reasonableness. 'But why would you think I'd leap to his defence?'

Now it was Paula's turn to be shocked. 'Because . . . ' She couldn't bring herself to use the l-word. 'Because he's your friend?'

Carol's face had grown bitter. Now her tone matched it. 'Look around you, Paula. I know you didn't see what happened here, but imagine the scene. Now imagine two people you love at the heart of that scene. That's what I went through because Tony failed them. He failed me. He didn't do his job and we paid the price. Me and my parents and my brother and the woman he loved.'

Paula shook her head in dismay. 'You can't blame Tony. He's a psychologist, not a psychic. How can you expect him to know the details of what Vance had planned? What Vance did was off the scale of vengeance. None of us, not one of us imagined for a moment that the people we loved were at risk. Carol, I know you're hurting. And I know how grief messes with our heads. Believe me, I know. But it was Vance who did this to you. Not Tony.'

Carol's mouth had a stubborn set to it. 'It's his job to think of the things that don't occur to the rest of us. And everybody else paid the price, not him. Michael and Lucy, Chris, that stable lad, my parents, me. Even Vanessa suffered more than he did.'

'And you think that doesn't torture him every day? You think he's not torn apart with guilt? I've watched him suffer his own sense of failure. Believe me, Carol, you can't load more blame on him than he does on himself. How long is this going to go on? His shame and your blame? Are you going to let this define the rest of your lives? Because from

301

where I'm standing, frankly, it's a colossal waste of two people's lives.' It was out before Paula knew she was going to say it. Challenging Carol wasn't something she'd been able to do in the past; the obligations of rank had always been the final stumbling block.

'It's none of your business, Paula.' Carol walked out of the room, through to the barn. The dog gave Paula a baleful look then went after Carol into the chill.

Paula hung her head and sighed. 'Blew that one,' she said under her breath. She waited to see whether Carol was coming back, but she was out of luck. So she returned the way she'd come. Carol was standing by a window, staring out at the dark. Paula could see her face in the glass. Her expression was as hard as the reflective surface.

'This is so unfair,' Paula said. 'Fielding's got everything on her side. Me included. And he's got nothing and nobody. He hasn't even got a lawyer.'

'I don't do pity, remember?'

Paula kicked out at a sawhorse in her frustration then shouted at Carol for the first time in her life. 'It's not about pity, for fuck's sake. It's about justice. The woman I used to know cared about justice.' The slam of the door behind her as she left was the only satisfying moment of the whole encounter.

45

Tony sat on the edge of the narrow ledge that passed for a bed in the Skenfrith Street custody suite, his elbows on his knees, his hands clasped. He'd been in police cells before, but only in the course of business. Talking to the damaged, the deranged and the demonised had brought him to places like this, but always with the door open. He'd often tried to put himself in the shoes of the captive, imagining how it must feel when that door slammed shut and they were alone. But he'd always started from a place of empathy – what it would be like for them. As opposed to how he would feel himself.

Mostly what he felt was uncomfortable. Being on his own in a small space didn't bother him. For a man who had learned to live on a narrowboat, it was no big deal. The noises-off didn't bother him either. Working in a secure mental hospital was an inoculation against unexpected and inexplicable human clamour. He wasn't hungry or thirsty yet, so that wasn't an issue. But there was no getting away from the discomfort. The bed was hard. There was a thin wafer of foam which he assumed was meant to be a pillow. It was lumpy and peculiarly distorted. Using it was like putting his head on a bag of liquorice allsorts. The physical discomfort made thinking much harder. And thinking was what he needed to do.

When the custody sergeant had closed the door behind him, Tony had almost expected him to throw it open and shout, 'Surprise!' That was how hard it was for him to credit what had happened. All through that bizarre interview with Paula and Alex Fielding, part of him had refused to take it seriously. He couldn't escape the notion that it was either a wind-up or a terrible mistake that he'd be able to put right in no time. Then it had dawned on him that Fielding was serious. Serious as only someone who didn't know him could be. Serious as only a detective driven by ambition could be.

Paula knew. Paula understood that whatever the physical evidence said, it was impossible to envisage him as a killer. But Paula wasn't the one making the decisions in that interview room. Paula was on trial too, her loyalty to the new boss under fire. Would she follow blindly where the evidence appeared to lead? Or would her fidelity to the old regime undermine Fielding's determination to get a quick and spectacular resolution to the case? On the walk down to the cells, she'd indicated she was on his side. But she had to be careful. For both their sakes, it was vital that she didn't get moved off the investigation. And there was only so much good that she could do by stealth.

Fielding scared him. That rush to judgement, that adamantine certainty that the evidence was king, that unwillingness to twist the Rubik's cube and look at things from a different angle – they all unsettled him, because there was no room for discussion. It wouldn't be enough for him to provide an explanation for the physical evidence against him. He'd have to find a reason to direct her hunter-killer instincts towards the real murderer.

Tony shifted awkwardly from one buttock to the other. If he hadn't let Carol down so badly, he'd never have found himself in this position. She simply wouldn't have allowed it to happen. No matter what cards might have been stacked against him, she would have taken his part, because she understood the limits of his capabilities.

He permitted himself a wry smile. Nobody knew his limits better than Carol. He'd always thought she could do better than him, that there must be other men out there who could give her more of what she needed than he had. But either she wasn't looking or she wasn't meeting the right men. Until her brother's death, she'd been happy to settle for their incomplete and inconclusive relationship. And then they'd found something that divided them so deeply nothing could bridge the gap. Not a shared history, not a mutual understanding. Not even love.

Impatient with himself, Tony jumped to his feet. If sitting or lying was torture, then he would pace. Six strides one way, ninety-degree turn then eight strides the other way. Six, eight. Six, eight. Stop brooding about Carol. She was gone. She wouldn't be there to pull him out of this particular pile of shit. It was over. He was on his own. Perhaps with a little help from his friend. Six, eight.

So. He had to explain the bloodstain. Others could find the verification of his story once he'd reached deep inside and accessed the truth. The thumbprint, too. That wasn't ringing any bells. 'I know I live in my head half the time, but you'd think I'd remember picking up somebody else's phone,' he shouted in exasperation.

Tony stopped pacing and leaned his forehead on the cool cement wall. He closed his eyes and dropped his shoulders. He deliberately relaxed his muscles from his scalp through his neck and arms. 'Think about blood. Your blood. About bleeding. Bleeding enough to stain somebody else,' he said out loud. There was the knee. The time when a crazed patient had gone on the rampage with a fire axe and had taken a swipe at Tony when he tried to talk him down. But that had been years ago, long before Nadia Wilkowa had ever come to Bradfield. A couple of times, he'd cut himself in the galley, unaccustomed to the occasional sudden movement of the boat. But there had never been anybody else there and besides, there hadn't been much blood. It had to be something that happened at work. In Bradfield Moor. He summoned up the hospital, as if he was offering someone a guided tour. The reception area. The locked doors, the faceless corridors. His office, the therapy rooms.

And then he remembered. Suddenly, it was all there, in crystal clear Technicolor detail. He threw his arms in the air. 'Halle-fucking-lujah!' The explanation of the thumbprint could wait. The DNA was the killer piece of evidence and now he knew how it had got there.

Tony grinned. Paula would be pleased. Now he just had to think of something that would lead them to the person who was actually killing women who looked like Carol Jordan.

46

While Tony was dredging his memory, another conversation went like this: 'Bronwen Scott here.'

'This is Carol Jordan.'

A pause. 'As in, DCI Carol Jordan?' Cautious, very cautious.

'As in ex-DCI Carol Jordan. I'm not a cop any more. But you, I presume, are still the best criminal defence lawyer in Bradfield?'

'That's quite an accolade, Ms Jordan. And I always thought you hated me.'

'I don't have to like you to appreciate your professional qualities.'

'So, to what do I owe this call? I'm assuming you didn't phone me at this time of night just to bolster my self-confidence. Don't tell me someone's had the temerity to arrest you?'

'I have a job for you. A client for you to represent. And a proposition in relation to that.'

'Sounds fascinating.' A long-drawn breath. 'But it's late. Won't it wait till morning?'

'I don't think so, no. Can you meet me in the car park opposite Skenfrith Street police station in half an hour?'

'Very Deep Throat. Why should I do this, Ms Jordan? What's in it for me?'

'A high-profile case. And the chance to fuck up BMP. I imagine no day is wasted for you if you get to fuck up an SIO.'

A throaty chuckle. 'You know which buttons to push, Ms Jordan.'

'I had an excellent teacher. Do we have an appointment?'

'It had better be good. It had better be very good.'

Carol smiled. 'I don't think you'll be disappointed.' She ended the call and changed down to third gear to negotiate a series of bends that climbed over the moor top before the descent into Bradfield. It hadn't been easy to maintain her composure during the phone call to the toughest criminal defence lawyer she'd ever jousted against. To say her feelings about the course of action she'd settled on were mixed was like saying the government had racked up a few debts. Her gut was churning and her hands were clammy on the wheel. Part of her wished she'd managed to ignore Paula altogether.

But she hadn't. When Paula had stormed out, Carol had barely paused before she gave chase. She caught up with her before she was halfway to her car. It didn't take much to persuade Paula back inside, where she gave Carol the kind of briefing that had been second nature when they worked together. The more she heard, the more Carol had been inflamed by the absurdity of what had happened to Tony. 'Not all evidence is created equal,' she'd protested. 'More often than not, it's coloured by its connections. You look at someone like Tony and your starting point is, this man didn't kill two women. So how is it that the evidence seems to point towards him? You don't just go, "Here's a bit of evidence, it must be you." That's not how you get justice.'

And so of course she had to wade in. It wasn't quite that simple, though. She couldn't entirely escape the notion that she'd been played by Paula. She suspected the detective had motives that went beyond unpicking Fielding's over-hasty decision. But if Paula thought she had set Carol on the road to reconciliation with Tony, she was in for a disappointment. This was about justice, pure and simple. The only sense in which it was about her and Tony was that their past history meant she knew him well enough to understand he wasn't a killer. On a personal level, she wasn't averse to the idea of him rotting in jail for something he didn't do, since the law had no way to punish him for what he had done. But that would leave a killer at large, and that was unacceptable. She might not be a cop any longer but Carol understood what justice was about.

That was more than she could say for Bronwen Scott. Having to get into bed with Scott was almost as hard as having to stand up for Tony. For years, Scott had been a thorn in her side, exploiting every weakness in the law to help the guilty. In theory, Carol held fast to the idea that everyone deserved a defence, no matter what their crime. But its manifestation in practice made her want to weep. She hated Scott for the maxim the lawyer regularly delivered with an air of injured innocence – 'Do your job, Detective. Then there would be no technicalities for me to exploit.' She despised Scott's cavalier ability to defend clients who were manifestly guilty. Most of all, she hated the way she felt when criminals walked free because Scott had played on sentiment and emotion in the teeth of evidence.

But now she no longer had the power of the job on her side, she'd have to exploit Scott's skills if she wanted to see justice done. Crucially, there was no doubt in Carol's mind that someone had to speak for the two dead women. Fielding wasn't doing that and because she wasn't, Paula couldn't. Somebody had to fill the breach. Getting Tony off the hook was merely the first step on a journey to the truth.

All these high-flown ideals were a perfect distraction. The more Carol wrapped herself in the flag of justice, the less she had to consider her feelings for Tony. The notion that she was reaching for a way to bridge the distance between them was one she would have dismissed with contempt if she'd allowed herself even to admit it as a possibility. It wasn't about forgiveness. It was simply that she didn't want him in her life.

Driving into Bradfield was a strange sensation. It had been months since she'd travelled city streets and although she could still easily navigate routes that used to be second nature she felt like a tourist following a map she'd learned by heart. This had been her home for years but she had cut her ties and already there were changes to the traffic flow. Nothing major; the odd lane change at junctions, an alteration of priorities at traffic lights. Enough to make her a stranger.

She pulled into the multi-storey car park in Skenfrith Street five minutes early. The sixties brutalist structure was stark in the fluorescent lights. It was past eleven and there were few cars left on the ground level. Carol parked her Land Rover Defender in the middle of a strip of empty slots and got out. Her footsteps echoed on the stained concrete like a clichéd movie soundtrack. She leaned against the front of the Landie, feeling a faint flutter of nervousness. She was a woman alone in a deserted late-night city-centre car park. When she'd been a cop, the simple fact of that status had acted as a protection. Now, although it made no sense, she felt distinctly more vulnerable. Even her choice of clothes contributed to that element of risk. She'd grown accustomed to the aura of strength and competence that came from her new work clothes. Donning her former work uniform of suit and blouse and low heels made her much more of a target for passing predators. She hoped Bronwen Scott wasn't going to be late.

Right on schedule, a set of tyres screamed as an Audi TT took the car park entrance a little too fast. It reversed into the space opposite Carol, like a pair of gunslingers facing off. Bronwen Scott's legs appeared first, gleaming in the light, black patent spike heels leading the way. Carol's eyes were drawn upwards to a pencil skirt topped with a tailored jacket over a camisole. Over it all, a loose, flowing camel coat. Her hair was dyed a hundred shades of dark blonde, shoulder length and glossy, and her immaculately made-up face showed no trace of the same years that had carved lines into Carol's. Although much of her practice was state-funded legal aid, the fancy clothes and the expensive car came from representing people who had not come by their wealth honestly, and every cop in the city knew it. The pursuit of justice was pushing Carol into the arms of strange bedfellows.

Scott stopped a couple of feet from Carol. 'Who'd have thought it?'

'That might possibly work in our favour,' Carol said.

'So what's all this cloak and dagger in aid of?' Scott swept her hair from her face in a practised gesture. Carol wondered what it must be like to devote so much attention to your appearance. She wasn't stupid; she'd seen the way men looked at her and she was aware that she was attractive. But it had never been how she defined herself, so when her looks began to lose the gloss of youth, she took it in her stride. But women like Bronwen Scott seemed to see ageing as a challenge, a war to be fought every day, taking advantage of every possible weapon, be it surgical or pharmaceutical. Carol had never seen the point of battles you couldn't win.

'There's a prisoner in the cells in Skenfrith Street who needs a good lawyer.'

'What's the charge?'

'Murder, times two.'

'Who's the arresting officer?'

'DCI Alex Fielding.'

'And what's your interest?'

Carol tilted her head back and studied the fluorescent tubes. 'Easily misconstrued.' She sighed and met Scott's curious stare. 'My interest is in seeing justice done. The man under arrest didn't do it. So there's a killer out there on the street who's going to kill again while Fielding's busy playing games with an innocent man.'

'I still don't see why you're bothered. I spend half my life clearing up the mess made by stupid cops who can't get past the first idea in their heads. What's special about this case? Apart from the fact that the accused man apparently can't pick up a phone himself?' Scott was beginning to sound irritated. That wasn't the goal. Time to get to the point.

'Tony Hill.'

Scott frowned. 'What about him? He's been keeping a very low profile since Jacko Vance.'

'He's under arrest. He's across the street in the cells. He thinks he doesn't need a lawyer because he's not done anything wrong.'

Scott cackled. 'One born every minute. You'd think he'd know better. Did you teach him nothing, all those years?'

'I think he needs you. Because there's some very tasty evidence stacked up against him.'

'Can he afford me?'

'Inheritance. Insurance. He can afford you.'

'Go on.' Scott was on the hook. Now Carol just had to reel her in.

'His blood on the cuff of the jacket of the first victim. His alleged thumbprint on the mobile phone of the second victim. And the key evidence, as far as Fielding is concerned, is that both of the victims look a bit like me.'

The tip of Scott's tongue slipped between her lips then she bit her lower lip. It was almost sexual. 'Interesting,' she said. 'And where is this coming from?'

'Do you remember Paula McIntyre?'

Scott made a sardonic face. 'Killer interviewer. Yes, I remember Paula very well.'

'She's Fielding's bagman now. She's always had something of an alliance with Tony. She doesn't like what's happening, but she can't put her head above the parapet or Fielding will shoot it off.'

'Makes sense.' Scott shivered and pulled her coat closer. 'So what do you want me to do about it?'

'I want you to go over the street and demand to see your client and do what needs to be done before Fielding gets her claws into him in the morning. They did an interview under caution and they plan to reinterview him and search his home and his office, according to Paula.'

'Will he do what he's told?'

Carol shrugged. 'That's debatable. I imagine it will depend on what you tell him.'

Scott shook her head, resigned. 'They never know what's best for them. Not even the smart ones. I suppose I should thank you for dropping this in my lap. So, thank you, Carol.' She laid a hand on Carol's arm, the dramatic scarlet nails drawing attention from her hand's betrayal of the attrition of age.

Carol looked down at the false gesture of intimacy and Scott withdrew it, though not hastily. 'I'm not done,' Carol said.

Scott cocked her head to one side. 'Of course you're not. I presume you want to be briefed?'

'More than that. I want to come in with you.'

Scott laughed, the sound echoing spookily round them. 'You know better than that, Carol,' she said merrily, as if it was the funniest thing she'd heard all day.

'Why not? I'm not a police officer. And you're the kind of superstar lawyer who's always got interns running after you, carrying your files and sharpening your pencils. What could be more natural than an ex-cop considering a career in the law?'

Scott was still grinning. 'Gamekeeper turned poacher with a vengeance. What's in it for me? How does it help my client?'

'I have the inside track. Paula's never going to trust you with confidential information. But spilling the beans to me? That's second nature to her. Plus you get all the benefits of a shit-hot investigator on your side at no extra charge.'

Scott shook her head, still unconvinced. 'It stretches the limits of credibility.'

'That's never stopped you before. Come on, you know you want to. If only for the look on Fielding's face. Think of it, Bronwen – you'll be dining out on that one for months. Especially when she's forced to release Tony without charge.'

'It's appealing, I'll admit. But we'd never get it past the custody sergeant.'

'I thought you liked a challenge?' Carol's smile dared Scott.

'Oh, fuck it.' Again the flip of the hair. 'Why not? I've not had a ruck with a custody sergeant for weeks. I'm getting rusty. Let me get my briefcase and we'll go and give them hell.'

They crossed the street side by side like a latter-day Cagney and Lacey. As they were about to walk into the police station, Carol paused and said, 'There is one thing you should know.'

Scott looked almost relieved, as if this was the dropping shoe she'd been waiting for. 'What?'

'Tony and I haven't actually spoken to each other since the Jacko Vance investigation. I said some pretty harsh things to him. It's possible he might not be too thrilled to see me.'

Scott smiled like a gratified cat. 'This just gets better and better.'

47

He stood in the garage doorway and stared at the freezer. He had high hopes of this one. She was, he reckoned, the right raw material for his project. He'd been too hasty, and that had led him into error. He'd been impatient to find the right replacement; he'd forgotten what it took to break a woman in from scratch. Like horses and dogs, it was always easier to work with one that had been taught some of the basics already.

That was where he'd gone wrong. That Polish bitch didn't even have a live-in boyfriend. She had no idea of what it took to be a perfect wife. How could she? She couldn't even speak English properly, for starters. He hated her stupid accent. If he'd realised she was a foreigner, he wouldn't have chosen her. Her looks had confused him, tricked him into thinking she was the one. That had always been what let Sirikit down. Her English was good, but she still had a bit of an accent, which grated on him. But more than that, she was dark. He wanted a blonde. He'd always wanted a blonde.

Ever since he'd seen Lauren Hutton in *American Gigolo* when he was barely a teenager, that was what he'd wanted. That was what he'd married, and the replacement would have to be blonde too.

It was naïve to think that a woman who didn't already know how to take care of a man could be broken in easily. The Polish bitch had fought him every inch of the way. He'd made it plain to her that, just like in *Star Trek,* resistance was futile. He'd tried every trick in the book, every technique he could think of before he finally had to concede you couldn't alter their fundamental nature. This one wouldn't give in and she wouldn't give up. In the end, the only satisfaction for him had been the final beating. He'd stripped everything from her that defined her and in the process he had made it clear what she really was – a lump of faceless, useless meat. No use even for sex. He'd washed her clean of any trace of him, made sure nobody else could get any use out of her then kicked her to death.

At least it had confirmed that there was, as he had suspected, genuine satisfaction to be had from finishing with the ones who let him down. He'd planned it for the very first one but he'd been thwarted. He'd fantasised about doing it, but the reality had outstripped the fantasy. That heady, drunken moment of absolute power when life finally leaked away was the best feeling he'd ever known.

But still. He was an optimist. He wanted to believe there could be as much delight in the perfect wife as there was in the perfect dealing out of death. And so he'd tried again. But the next one had been no better. He should have known. He'd hoped that the reason she was divorced was that her husband had been a poor excuse for a man, giving her no opportunity to demonstrate what she was capable of.

It didn't take long for him to realise she was probably divorced because she was a crap wife. He'd been hopeful when he'd tasted the steak she'd cooked. But the potatoes had been unforgivable. If she'd reached that age without being able to boil a potato properly, there was no hope for her. After that, the sex had been a formality. Even if she'd been the most exciting shag on the planet, it was too late for redemption. Perfection was always going to be out of her reach. All she was good for by that point was killing.

In spite of that, he was still hopeful. Sirikit had shown him that it was possible to find a woman who could be what he demanded. This latest one was married, that was a start. Just so long as she hadn't fallen into irreversible bad habits thanks to a weak and indulgent husband. He blamed other men for letting women get away with too much. It was like what they said about dogs. There was no such thing as a bad dog, only a bad master. Well, he was the good master. And this new one would be best in show, he felt it in his heart.

For now, she had to learn the first lesson. He was master. This time, he'd leave her locked away in the freezer for longer. Then she'd be properly grateful when he eventually let her out. Gratitude went a long way, in his experience. It was the same at work. You gave a little, and because people had such low expectations, you got a lot. It was one of the secrets of his success. Now all he had to do was teach it to the woman in the freezer.

48

The reception area of the custody suite was without comfort. It smelled, bizarrely, of stale sausage rolls and rotting fruit. Behind the scarred and untidy counter was a middle-aged man with a tonsure of chestnut stubble and a white shirt that strained over a barrel chest. The custody sergeant had a face like a rumpled Boxer, all creases and jowls. Carol almost expected him to slobber as he looked Bronwen Scott up and down. 'You're a bit late tonight, Ms Scott,' he growled. 'Will it not wait till morning?'

'The clock's running, as you well know, Sergeant Fowler. My client's facing very serious charges and we need to make a start at clearing his name.'

'Funny, he never mentioned having a solicitor. And he never made a phone call after he was brought down here. You developing telepathy as one of your skills?'

Scott leaned on the counter and produced a menacing smile. 'I don't think my means of communicating with my clients is any of your business. Now, I want to see my client.

And in an interview room, not some nasty little cell that smells of piss and vomit.' It was an impressive performance, Carol thought, remembering all the times Bronwen Scott's production numbers had driven her to distraction. Being on the same side was a lot more fun.

Sergeant Fowler made great play of consulting his watch and comparing it to the clock on the wall behind him. 'Let me see. DCI Fielding will be wanting to interview at nine, and your client is entitled to eight hours' rest, and it's half past eleven already. So I reckon that gives you an hour with your client, tops.'

'I'll take as long with my client as I need. If that means DCI Fielding has to rearrange her plans for the morning, that's the way the cookie crumbles, Sergeant Fowler. Now, are you going to produce Dr Hill?'

'One moment,' he said ponderously, his forehead corrugating. He scratched his armpit then pointed at Carol, who had been hanging back in the doorway. 'Is she with you?'

Scott gave a nonchalant glance over her shoulder. 'My intern? Of course.'

'Do you think I'm daft? Your intern?' He leaned forward, his mouth moving as if he was chewing a wad of tobacco. 'It's DCI Jordan, as was, right?'

'With the emphasis on "as was", Sergeant Fowler. I don't think our paths actually crossed while I was still working.' She stepped forward and produced her most winning smile.

'What am I supposed to call you, anyway?' he asked Carol.

'Ms Jordan will do nicely, Sergeant. It's my name. I don't have a rank any more.'

He scratched the band of stubble that ran round his head, frowning. 'Well, Ms Jordan. I can't let you sit in on an interview between a prisoner and his solicitor. You're just a civilian, you've no cause to be there.'

'I'm shadowing Ms Scott. I'm planning on a career in the law, Sergeant Fowler. It's a shame to waste all that hands-on experience. My role here is purely as an observer.'

'But you know him. You used to work with him.' He threw his hands in the air, a gesture that threatened his shirt buttons. He was clearly struggling for a valid reason why Carol shouldn't be involved. 'It's not . . . appropriate.'

'Oh, behave, Sergeant. Anybody would think you were still wet behind the ears,' Scott said. 'I'm always dealing with people I've encountered before. Defence witness one week, accused the next. And who do you think defends bent coppers? Criminal lawyers like me. So get down off your high horse and give Ms Jordan some credit for choosing an exciting new career path.'

'It's not as if I can leak confidential information to the defence, is it?' Carol wondered whether she was laying it on too thick, but Sergeant Fowler looked relieved at the thought.

'So can you fetch Dr Hill for us? The sooner we get started, the quicker we'll be done and the happier DCI Fielding will be in the morning,' Scott said in the kind of tone it was hard to argue against.

Fowler hauled himself to his feet and emerged from behind the counter. 'You can use the interview room at the end of the cell corridor. Follow me, ladies.'

He set off past the steel doors. Scott turned to Carol and winked. 'Overture and beginners,' she said under her breath. 'Let's do it, Carol.'

No turning back. She'd spent months literally working Tony Hill out of her system. And now she was about to discover whether she'd succeeded.

49

Tony had taken off his jacket and folded it under him to make the bed a more comfortable seat. Though it left a lot to be desired, at least he could sit cross-legged with his back to the wall in a relatively relaxed posture, eyes closed and hands loose in his lap. He didn't know whether he could sleep sitting up, but he was absolutely certain he couldn't do it lying down on that pallet. Still, buoyed up by his realisation of how his DNA had ended up on Nadia Wilkowa's jacket, he could finally chill a little.

The window in his cell door opened with a sharp metallic clang, startling him with a jolt. It clanged shut again before he had composed himself enough to work out what was happening. Then the door opened and the sergeant who had checked him into the cell stood in the doorway, hands on hips to make himself look bigger, eyebrows lowered to add to his threat level. All textbook stuff. 'Wakey wakey, Hill. Your lawyer's here for a conference.'

He understood the words but they made no sense. 'I've got a lawyer?'

'Don't you bloody start. I've had enough from her end. If you didn't have a lawyer, she wouldn't be in the interview room asking me to produce you, would she?'

Paula. She must have ignored him and decided to sort him out with a lawyer regardless. It wouldn't hurt to sit down in a more comfortable room and tell them that he really didn't need legal representation now he'd worked out how to explain the key evidence against him. Still, it would pass some time. So he unfolded his legs and stood up. He picked up his jacket and tried to put it on both arms at once, like Martin Sheen always did in *The West Wing*. As usual, he got into a tangle. It needed more practice, that was all. He caught the eye of the custody sergeant, who was struggling not to laugh. 'A man needs a hobby,' Tony said, stepping gratefully out of the cell into the corridor. He was about to head for the counter where he'd emptied his pockets earlier, but the sergeant blocked his path, directing him towards a door that stood ajar at the end of the corridor.

Feeling surprisingly jaunty, Tony pushed the door open. At first his brain denied what he was seeing. Bronwen Scott, he accepted that. She was the sort of person he'd expected to see. But the blonde head facing away from the door – it couldn't be. He was hallucinating. Or delusional. Then she turned her head and something inside him lurched and twisted. The ground beneath his feet seemed to tilt and he stumbled. 'Carol?' His voice held a mixture of wonder and doubt. So much for cutting her out of his heart. Apparently his heart hadn't got the message.

'You've got an hour,' Sergeant Fowler grunted as he closed the door firmly behind him.

Bronwen Scott got to her feet and greeted him with a wide smile. 'Dr Hill. I didn't expect to encounter you in cir-cumstances like this, but we'll have this sorted out in no time at all.'

He ignored her and walked round to the far side of the table like a sleepwalker. 'Carol?' He grabbed the back of the chair for support and subsided into it. He wanted to reach out and touch her, to confirm that he wasn't lost in some psychotic break.

Carol pushed her hair off her forehead, her eyes flinty, her face forbidding. 'I'm not here for you. I'm here because Paula knows how stupid you can be. You need Bronwen to get you out of this mess. Otherwise more women will die. If you'd thought about something other than yourself for five minutes, you would have understood that. So don't fool yourself that you're the big draw tonight. I'm here for Paula and for justice and for the women whose names we don't even know.'

Right then, he didn't care why she was there. All that mattered was that they were sitting in the same room again. The edifice he'd built to protect himself from his feelings for her was already a crumbling ruin. How could he have considered for a moment the possibility of excising her from his life? It was like rediscovering a limb he'd been managing without. A limb he'd thought amputated for ever. He couldn't keep the grin from his face, even in the teeth of her unflinching glare.

He was aware that Bronwen Scott was speaking but he had nothing to spare for her. He drank in every detail, checking it against the mental checklist he hadn't even known he'd been keeping. Her hair was styled differently – the lines more blunt, the shagginess thinned out more. The lines around her eyes were deeper, the new traces in her face from sorrow rather than laughter. Her shoulders seemed broader, the seams of her jacket straining slightly where before there had been ample room for a shrug. She'd always been self-contained; now she was like a door slammed in his face.

'Dr Hill?' Scott had raised her voice and finally penetrated. 'We don't have long. I need your version of events so
we can set about getting you out of here.'

'And finding out who killed those two women,' Carol
said.

'That's not my job,' Scott said briskly. 'And actually, Carol,
it's not your job any more either.'

Tony found his voice. 'Maybe not, but I'd put my money
on Carol without resources ahead of Alex Fielding and her
murder squad.'

Carol rolled her eyes. A familiar gesture but denuded of
the tolerant affection he'd grown used to. 'I couldn't be less
interested in flattery. Like I said, I'm here for Paula.'

Her disdain was hard to take. It made something inside
him clench in pain. But it was still better than not having
her in the room at all. 'What do you want to know?'

'Do you know why DCI Fielding has arrested you?' Scott
thrust herself back into the driving seat.

He nodded. 'Because she's one of those cops who can't see
past the evidence. You remember Alan Coren, the humorist?
He once told his son, "Don't write the first thing that comes
into your head – the dim kids will have had that idea. Don't
write the second either – the clever boys will probably have
thought of that one. Write the third idea – that will be yours
alone." Well, Alex Fielding's never bothered to give the third
idea house room.'

'Very entertaining, Dr Hill.' Now it was Scott's turn to roll
her eyes.

'Tony, please.' He knew he was showing off but he might
never get another chance to remind Carol of what he could
be.

'I appreciate you see the world through the prism of the
psyche, but could we focus on the evidential reasons why
Fielding arrested you? Tony?'

When he'd sat in the observation room and watched Bronwen Scott in action, Tony had often wondered how different she was with her clients than when she was an opponent. Tougher than he'd expected, was the first answer. She wasn't falling for his practised skills and she wasn't indulging him. Time to return her moves in the same style. 'The bodies of two murdered women have been found this week. For the record, I didn't kill either of them. They were both brutally beaten, to the point where their faces were unrecognisable. Their labia were shaved and glued together. There's no obvious connection between the two of them, although there might be a professional link. Nadzieja Wilkowa was single and Polish, she worked as a rep for a pharmaceutical company. Bev McAndrew was divorced, mother of a teenage son, and she was the pharmacist in charge at Bradfield Cross Hospital.' He stopped. 'You're not taking notes.'

'I'll get all this in disclosure from Fielding. At this point, it's interesting to have the background but I want to know where you come into the picture. And your version of events, of course.'

Carol raised a finger, indicating she wanted to speak. Scott nodded briskly. 'How much of this did you know before Fielding questioned you?'

She hadn't lost a yard of her pace, he thought, impressed with the question. 'I knew quite a bit about Nadia Wilkowa. And I knew Bev was missing. She's a friend of Paula's and she asked my advice about her disappearance. I wasn't much help. But in the course of that conversation, we talked about Nadia.' He gave Carol a pained smile. 'Actually, she took me to Nadia's flat.'

'Oh, Christ,' Scott said. 'So your prints and DNA are going to be all over the victim's flat?'

'I was gloved up,' Tony said. 'I'm not entirely hopeless.

There shouldn't be any obvious DNA traces. But DNA is one of the issues. There's a bloodstain on Nadia's jacket that has tested positive for my DNA.' Carol nodded wearily, but Scott merely looked resigned. 'When they interviewed me, I had no idea how that happened. But I've had time to think, and I can explain it.'

'I'm pleased to hear that. So how did it come about?' Scott leaned forward, fixing him with her attention.

'As I think you both know, I do most of my work at Bradfield Moor Secure Hospital. I deal with a wide range of patients who come to us because they are either a danger to themselves or a danger to society. Their lives are often car crashes and they're left stranded in the wreckage. When they first come in, they're often frightened and angry and violent. About a year ago, I was called out to assess a young man who had run amok with a machete in his school staff-room. Luckily, he'd been tackled by a very brave teacher before anyone had been seriously injured.'

Tony clasped his hands in front of him, running his thumbs over each other again and again. 'He'd been sedated before he came to us, but what I didn't realise was that he'd been growing increasingly agitated before I went in to talk to him. He seemed calm on the surface but as soon as I started asking him to talk about what had happened, he managed to free one arm from its restraints and he punched me in the face. My nose was bleeding copiously and I left the room to get it stopped and cleaned up.'

Carol gave the barest of nods. 'I remember you telling me about it.'

He looked straight at her. 'You know how clumsy I am, Carol. I stumbled out into the corridor and through a set of swing doors, not really looking where I was going, paper towels up to my face. And I crashed into a woman coming the other way. She put her arm up to protect herself.' He closed his eyes, replaying the scene. 'I'm pretty sure it was her left arm. I apologised. She said, no harm done and went on her way.' He opened his eyes. 'She was a pharmaceutical rep, right? That's what it said in the paper. So she had a reason to be there.' It sounded thin. Artificial. Even to his ears. But that was often the way with the truth.

'You bumped into a woman a year ago when you were having a nosebleed? And she still has your DNA on her sleeve?' Scott sounded almost amused, as if this was the most outrageous attempt at exoneration she'd ever heard.

'I'm just telling you what happened.'

'You think she went a year without having her work clothes cleaned? Without realising she had your blood on her jacket?'

'All I know is what happened. Now I've had my memory jogged, it's quite clear.'

Carol's investigative instincts cut in. 'Was the incident logged in the Bradfield Moor accident book?'

'It will have been,' Tony said. 'Because I needed an ice pack from the nursing team.'

'We need to check that date and then we need to cross-check it with Nadia Wilkowa's work diary,' Carol said, tapping a note into her phone. 'I'll chase that up with Paula.' He loved watching her doing what she'd always done best.

'It's a pity there's no way of telling how old the DNA sample is. That would have resolved it on the spot,' Scott added.

'Even more of a pity that the blood ended up on something that gets dry-cleaned rather than shoved in the washing machine. If it had been through the hot wash a dozen times, it would be so degraded it would be obvious that it wasn't made this week,' Carol pointed out, not to be outdone in the DNA knowledge stakes.

'Next time, I'll aim for the blouse. So you think we can

328

demolish the DNA evidence if we can prove the nosebleed incident?'

'It gives reasonable doubt a helluva knock, that's for sure,' Scott said. 'Was that it, then? Was that all she had?'

Tony shook his head sorrowfully. 'Then there's the thumbprint.'

Carol closed her eyes momentarily as if in pain. 'What thumbprint, Tony? I thought you said you wore gloves at her flat?'

'No, not on Nadia's stuff. My thumbprint is on Bev's phone.' He tried the pitiful puppy smile again. This time, both women scowled at him. 'I was completely baffled when they interviewed me about it earlier. Clueless. I've no recollection of ever clapping eyes on Bev in the flesh, never mind touching her phone.'

'Was it a clear print?' Scott asked.

Tony shook his head. 'It was a bit smudged on one side and a bit distorted by the shape of the phone. But when Fielding showed it to me, I could see the points of similarity.'

'Can you remember how many points of comparison were highlighted?'

'I think it was six.'

Scott smiled. 'I'm not worried about a fingerprint ID like that. I can put up half a dozen experts who'll discredit it. These days, unless you get a crystal-clear fingermark on a flat surface, you can knock the feet from under any prosecution expert witness. Fingerprint comparison is so subjective it's not even regarded as a science any more. All you have to say in court these days is "Shirley McKie" then watch the prosecution shrivel and die.'

'I don't understand,' Tony said. 'Who's Shirley McKie?'

'She was a Scottish police officer. Her fingerprint was wrongly identified inside a murder scene where she swore she'd never been. The Scottish forensic experts stuck to their guns and she was charged with perjury,' Carol explained. 'And then it all fell apart. Turns out that while it's true all fingerprints are unique, identifying them is riddled with human error.'

'So we can kick their fingerprint evidence right into the long grass,' Scott said. 'It's history.'

'That's good,' Tony said. 'Because as it turns out, I was in Bradfield Cross on Monday afternoon. When Bev went missing.'

Carol groaned. 'Why am I not surprised? Are you going to share it with us? Or shall we just play twenty questions?' She shook her head. 'Nothing changes.'

'Actually, Carol, you might be surprised on that score. But this isn't the time or the place for that conversation.'

'There is no time and place for that conversation. Monday?'

Slapped down again. Tony took a deep breath and picked himself up. 'I was at a meeting in Bradfield Cross Hospital late Monday afternoon. I tend not to agree with the consultant there, Will Newton. The man's a moron. I think he got his qualifications by saving up Coco Pops box tops. By the end of the meeting, I was furious. I stomped out of the meeting room. All I wanted was to get out of there before I said something that would only make everything worse.'

'Did you go anywhere near the pharmacy?' As usual, Scott was straight to the point.

'I don't think so. I was pissed off and I wanted to vent my energy so I walked home. I wasn't really paying attention to my surroundings. I don't think I passed the pharmacy but I don't know whether I passed Bev.'

Scott sat back in her chair and contemplated him. 'Please tell me that's all?'

'Well, the other things are circumstantial.' He spread his

hands. 'Nothing I've done. The sort of thing that could happen to anyone.'

'But only do happen to you,' Carol pointed out. 'You said, "things". Plural. What are we talking about here?'

'I was trying to be helpful,' he said. 'After Paula told me about Bev, but before we knew she was dead, I thought I'd take a look at the supermarket where she'd supposedly been shopping. I needed some bits and pieces and I fancied the walk, so I went over to Freshco at Kenton Vale.'

'It says on the custody record you live on a boat in Minster Basin. So you walked from the basin to Kenton Vale Road to pick up a few bits and pieces at the supermarket? That must be, what? Two miles?' Bronwen's deadpan delivery did nothing to hide her scepticism.

'He likes to walk. It helps him think.'

'She's right. I do. And it does. And what it made me think is that this is a careful killer. Because the CCTV in the car park at Freshco isn't great. There's plenty of holes in the coverage. According to Paula, the body dump for Nadia was in Gartonside, where it's scheduled for demolition and there are no cameras. And from what I can gather, Bev was found up on the moors in the middle of nowhere. So again, no cameras.'

'And? There has to be an "and", right? There generally is with you,' Carol said, bitterness still evident in her voice. She wasn't loosening up, he thought. He'd hoped they'd slip into old rhythms without realising it, but she was too watchful of herself for that. Time appeared not to have done much healing of her hurt.

'There is. I bought more shopping than I'd intended *and* I got the bus home. And that's when I realised buses have CCTV that films outside the bus as well as inside. Bradfield buses have fourteen cameras on each double-decker bus, did you know that? So I suggested to Paula that they take a look at the footage. Which they did.'

'Was it helpful?' Scott asked.

'Oh yes. They got a bit of Bev on one camera. And they caught a few seconds of the bloke who was following her. It wasn't much use for ID. Medium height, medium build, though he could have been a slim guy wearing bulky clothing. He was wearing a hoodie and he kept his head down. You can see he's wearing glasses, but that's about all. They told me they had footage of the man who abducted Nadia, and it was pretty much the same. There's only one distinguishing feature.' Tony looked down at the table. He hated this piece of information. In his head, it was the one that made him look guilty. 'He's got a noticeable limp. He limps with his left leg.'

'Oh, fuck,' Carol said. With feeling.

'You have a limp?'

Sometimes it was tempting to go for the crass one-liner. This probably wasn't one of those times. 'I had major knee surgery a couple of years ago. A patient attacked me with a fire axe. Someone else's patient, I always like to point out.'

'And you were supposed to have a second surgery to deal with the limp,' Carol said. 'I take it you're still dodging Mrs Chakrabarti?' She half-turned to Bronwen. 'He does have a limp. It's worse when he's tired. Such as, when he's tramped two miles across town to shop in a non-local branch of Freshco.'

Scott gave him a sharp, assessing look. 'I don't like the limp,' she said. 'That's the sort of circumstantial that the CPS gets very hot and horny over.'

'Lots of people have a limp,' Tony protested.

'No, actually, they don't,' Carol said. 'And if you'd done what you were supposed to, neither would you. Doing nothing just gets you into trouble, Tony. And not for the first time.'

She'd never held back. He'd always admired that in her. But it was hard to take when he was the target of her sharpest assaults. 'I'm sorry,' he said.

'Can we put the thrust and parry on the back burner for now, please?' Scott sounded almost as pissed off as Carol. 'What's the other circumstantial?'

Tony looked at Carol and gave a wry smile. 'Before I say this, in the interests of not getting my face slapped, I want to be clear that this is DCI Fielding's journey into absurdity. Not mine.'

'Fielding thinks the victims both look like me,' Carol said heavily. 'She's got a bee in her bonnet about it. She thinks Tony's killing women who look like me because I walked away from him.'

There was a long sticky pause. Then Scott said chattily, 'And are you, Tony?'

50

Patience was a virtue he'd learned young. His father had never tolerated tantrums or whining, so he'd understood at an early age that keeping his mouth shut and learning to wait was the key to minimising the pain of his existence. Therefore it was no hardship to him to extend the time she would spend in the freezer before he let her out to play.

But that didn't mean he had to sit around twiddling his thumbs. By now, her husband must be starting to panic. It was almost midnight – five hours later than she should have been home, given when she'd left work. At first, the husband would have assumed a hold-up in the transport system – a delay on the tram. An accident throwing the city centre into gridlock. Something relatively benign. But as the minutes ticked by and no text or phone call arrived, he'd have started to feel anxious.

What would he have done then, this Marco Mather, this man whose annoyingly handsome face smiled out of the photo in her purse? He'd have tried to phone her, of course.

But by then, her phone was not only turned off, it had its battery and SIM card removed. He'd put them back later, when it didn't matter if she was traced or not. But for now, he was taking every available precaution.

So, Marco would get a dead phone. What would his next step be? He'd probably call her friends to see whether she was with them or if she'd confided any plans to them. He'd draw a blank, of course. He wouldn't be able to phone anyone from work because she'd only just started her new job and she wouldn't have built up a social network yet. He wouldn't even know the names of her colleagues, never mind their phone numbers.

So he'd have to go to the Tellit Communications building, where the night security guard would explain there was nobody left in the office. If Marco Mather kicked off, the guard might even show him the computer record from when she'd swiped herself off the grid and into the lift.

He might think about the police then. But that would get him nowhere at all. Five hours late wouldn't earn a mention in the incident log. Not even in the light of two female murder victims in the same week. Because there was nothing to connect Marco Mather's wife to a Polish pharmaceutical sales rep or Bradfield Cross's chief pharmacist. There couldn't be because apart from the fact that they looked right, they were random selections. People said you couldn't judge a book by its cover, and unfortunately that was true. But he'd had to go by the cover. They were replacements, not substitutes. So they had to look right. They had to fit the fantasy in his head, the dream that had grown from those images of Lauren Hutton up on the screen. It was an exhausting process, but eventually he would find the right one. The one to replace the one who had cheated him out of serving up her just deserts.

But he was wandering off the point. Which was, what

would Marco Mather do? He was so tempted to go and see for himself. There would be a delicious pleasure in glimpsing him through a window, wringing his hands or crying on the phone.

Why not give in to temptation? There was no virtue in denying himself that pleasure, was there? So he pulled on a pair of latex gloves and picked up her keys. Just in case Marco had gone out to drown his sorrows and he got the chance to pick over their pitiful married life.

Less than quarter of an hour later, he'd found a parking space in the next street and, sticking to the shadows, he walked briskly round the corner. In spite of the limp one of his father's beatings had left him with, he could still move faster than most. At this time of night, the majority of the houses were in darkness, occasional slivers of light creeping through bedroom curtains, a few hall lights dimly seen through glass panels in front doors. This wasn't the sort of area where people stayed up late and had fun, he thought. Solid suburbia to the core; either they had to get up for work in the morning or else they'd retired and acquired the old persons' habit of early to bed and early to rise. Like they had something to get up for, he thought, imagining those unsatisfied lives where they'd settled for less than perfection. Not like him.

He wasn't entirely surprised to see plenty of lights on at the Mather house. The front room curtains weren't closed, and light leaked in from the bright hallway. He checked to make sure he was unobserved, then cut into their tiny front garden, slinking past the front door and peering in through the window. No sign of life. A couple of deserted sofas, a TV, shelves that seemed to contain DVDs and a few books. No clutter whatsoever. There were paintings, or prints, he supposed, all over the walls. He couldn't make them out in the dim light, but they looked colourful.

He slipped past the front door and down the side of the garage. A small window cast a parallelogram of light on the ground, and he ducked low to avoid being seen. Then he turned and edged his head forward so he could look inside. The usual crap-filled garage, he thought. Lawnmower, gardening tools. A tall freezer. Shelves crammed with tins of paint, household chemicals, assorted car products. He inched forward to improve his field of vision and saw something completely unexpected.

The top of a man's head, motionless on the floor.

Startled, he jerked back. When his heart stopped racing, he crept forward again, this time bolder than before. He could see the rest of the man's head from behind. Unsurprisingly, it was attached to a body. A body that was sprawled on the floor beside an exercise bike, one leg still trailing over the frame.

Marco Mather wasn't pacing the floor, panicking over his wife's absence. Marco Mather was dead.

Either that or he was going to be dead very soon.

51

Bronwen Scott enjoyed the moment then pushed her chair back. 'I need a quick word with the custody sergeant,' she said. 'Five minutes, Carol, any more and he'll start to get antsy.'

Tony and Carol stared at each other, stony-faced, waiting for her to leave. The door closed and they were alone for the first time in months. A scenario both had imagined but neither had expected. Tony cleared his throat. 'How have you been?'

'That's really none of your business.' The severity of her expression didn't diminish. He'd seen her look at colleagues she despaired of and criminals she despised in the same way.

'I think it is. You blamed me for what happened to Michael and Lucy.' Most people would have missed the infinitesimal flinch in her eyes at the mention of their names, but he didn't. Undeterred, he carried on. 'You probably still do. That gives me a burden of responsibility and I think our history runs so deep that you owe me the chance to discharge it.'

She shook her head. 'Even if I could translate that out of Tony-speak into something a normal person would understand, I suspect it would still be bollocks. I owe you nothing. No amount of twisted logic can change that.'

'So why are you here?'

She made a dismissive gesture with her hand. 'I told you. Paula feels the need to save you and she can't do it the straight way.'

He let himself consider whether she might be speaking the truth. He wanted not to believe her, but he had to concede it made more sense to accept what she was saying. 'But you agree with her, that I'm innocent?'

'I can imagine situations where you might kill. But I don't believe you're this kind of killer. And I think if you were pissed off enough with me to want to kill me, you'd get on with it. Not fuck about with surrogates.' There was a grim twist to her mouth that might almost have been a smile.

'You think somebody's really killing women who look like you?' Tony was genuinely curious. He thought he knew her well enough to predict the answer but he wanted to hear what she had to say.

She shrugged one shoulder. 'Other people seem to. Senior detectives with years of experience, some of them.'

'But you,' he persisted. 'What do *you* think?'

'I don't think they look that much like me.'

'There's a generic similarity. Same blonde hair, blue eyes. Same haircut. Similar build. Professional women who go to work suited up. Has it occurred to you that it's not them that look like you – it's you that looks like them?'

Carol frowned. This was how it had always played out between them. He said something impenetrable that she couldn't resist and she was hooked. It had been like that since the very first case they'd worked together, all those years ago. And here he was, doing it to her again. She wanted to get to her feet and walk out, but more than that she needed to understand what he was driving at. 'What do you mean – it's me that looks like them?'

'That's not quite right.' He spoke absently, as if thinking aloud. 'It's more that you all look like her.'

'Like who?' She almost howled in frustration.

'The one he wanted to kill.'

'Don't you mean "wants" to kill?'

Tony ran a hand through his hair. 'No. He's clever, he's organised and he's resourceful. If she was available to be killed, he'd have killed her and that would be an end to it.' He spread his arms wide as if trying to draw her in to embrace the idea. 'I think she's already dead. I think he was planning to kill her, working up to it. But somehow she thwarted him.'

'She killed herself?' Carol was intrigued now in spite of herself. She leaned forward, forearms on the table. He noticed the changes in her hands – scars, bruises, broken nails. What on earth had she been doing, this woman who he remembered barely being able to manage flat-pack furniture?

'Either that or she just died,' he said, distracted by his more private speculation.

'And this helps us how?'

'Find her, and you find him.' He shrugged. 'Obviously you're going to have to find her.'

Before Carol could respond, the door opened and Scott stuck her head into the room. 'Time to go, Carol. We'll see you in the morning, Tony. Chin up. She's never going to charge you.'

'So what happens now?' Carol asked Scott as soon as they were clear of Skenfrith Street police station.

'I'm going home to catch some zeds before I have to get up and go head to head with DCI Fielding,' the lawyer said. 'I recommend that you not show up for that conversation. It'll only get messy. Besides, you have plenty of other things to be getting on with. It'll be bloody ages before Fielding gives us disclosure on Nadia Wilkowa's work diaries. You're going to need to pull your strings and find out when this alleged incident happened at Bradfield Moor and whether Nadia was in the building that day to bump into Captain Clumsy.'

'You want me to go back to Paula?'

Scott broke her stride to give Carol an incredulous look. 'Well, duh. I want you to do whatever it takes to get the information that will clear my client. You always had the knack of coming up with the goods when you were working the other side of the fence.'

Carol gave a snort of bitter laughter. 'I did have one or two resources at my disposal.'

'You still do. Human resources. You've got friends. So has he. Use them.'

Carol suppressed a sigh. After the reaction she'd had from Sinead, she wasn't so sure how much reliance she could place on her old networks. How bitter would it be to have to rely on Tony's name to open doors? Tony, who was even more crap at intimacy than she was. 'I'll see what I can do,' she said wearily.

'And I'll line up someone to demolish her thumbprint evidence. We're going to leave her without a leg to stand on.'

They entered the dank car park and headed for their cars. Before they separated, Scott put a hand on Carol's arm. 'Did he say anything useful after I left you alone with him?'

Carol didn't know where to begin to explain the way Tony's mind worked to an outsider. 'No,' she said. 'It was private.' The words were out before she had time to think.

She walked to her car, thinking how hard it was to break the habit of mistrust.

She climbed into the Land Rover and took out her phone, keeping one eye on Scott, whose engine purred into life as soon as she'd settled herself into her seat. Carol waited till the solicitor had driven out of the car park, considering her options. It was late and she was tired, but the clock was ticking for Tony. There were strict limits on how long the police could hold him after arrest. If the defence couldn't blow apart the evidence against him, Fielding would charge Tony when the time ran out – or before that, if she could build a stronger case – and everything would become much harder. The police would stop looking for an alternative suspect. Mud would stick, even if Tony was subsequently cleared.

It dawned on Carol that she minded the idea of his name being blackened. She tried to convince herself that it was simply because it offended her sense of justice. She wasn't ready to accept that her history with Tony might mean there was a possible future for them. She was merely reacting as she would to the idea of any innocent person being unjustly imprisoned ahead of a trial for a crime they could never have committed. That was all it was. But that was enough to sanction any amount of unreasonable behaviour. Wasn't it?

52

The journey back in the car from the Mather house to his place wasn't long enough. He needed to savour what had happened, to replay it in his head and set it in stone so it would be the bedrock for what came next. This was so beautiful, you couldn't make it up. It was the perfect scene-setter for turning Marie Mather into the perfect wife. And the joy of it was that he hadn't had to do a thing himself.

He'd forced himself to stand at the garage window for a full five minutes, to be certain that Marco Mather wasn't moving. Five motionless minutes meant death or, at the very least, a deep unconsciousness he could take advantage of.

He'd debated whether to try the back door or to brazen it out at the front. There were a pair of mortise keys on her ring, but only one Yale. He guessed that, like most people, there would be a Yale and a mortise on the front door and a mortise on the rear. So, only one unfamiliar lock to fumble with at the back, and out of sight at that. On the downside, his limp made him less than stealthy, and gardens were notoriously cluttered with plant containers and hoses and bags of compost. Better to risk the front door than clatter around the pitch-black patio and rouse the neighbours.

Treading carefully, he returned to the front of the house and slipped the Yale into the keyhole, gambling that it would be the only lock engaged while Marco Mather was at home expecting his wife to return from work. It turned and the door swung silently open. He stepped inside confidently, for the benefit of anyone glancing out of their window on the way to bed. And he breathed in the smell of her home, nosing it like a wine connoisseur, relishing the faint scents of cooking herbs and the heady notes from the vase of lilies on a recessed windowsill. Yes, she had the basics of good taste, even if the lilies were a little florid for his liking.

Down the hall and into the generous dining kitchen. It was clearly the heart of the house, the sort of kitchen where cooking was observed like a religious ritual. A well-used *batterie de cuisine* was on parade and ready for use, a small array of battered cookbooks on the windowsill alongside pots of thyme, basil and oregano. His heart lifted. She was going to be the one. She'd cook like an angel and fuck like a whore.

The door to the garage was closed. He moseyed across the kitchen, helping himself to a baby tomato from a bowl sitting on a butcher's block. He popped it into his mouth and burst it with his teeth, enjoying the sudden explosion of flavour, sharp and sweet. Oh yes, this was going to be special.

There were no surprises on the other side of the door. Marco Mather was lying in exactly the same position. Only now he could see Marco's face. There was no doubt about it. The guy was definitely dead. And from the looks of him,

344

there had been nothing peaceful about it. Heart attack, at a guess. Fat bastard on an exercise bike, what did he expect? Greedy twat couldn't resist her excellent cooking and look where it had got him.

The beauty of it was that there would be no worried husband reporting his woman missing. No chance of some smart-arsed copper eager to make a name for himself connecting this to any other crime. Nobody would be looking for a woman who wasn't missing. He could phone her office in the morning. Pretend to be Marco. Claim she was sick. That would buy him plenty of time.

And he could use this to help bring her to heel. Once she saw Marco was dead, she'd know there was nothing to go back to. She'd have to make the most of what she had. It was bound to make her even more eager to please, to offer him the perfection he deserved. He was her future. He was her only future. She was a smart woman. She would understand.

To ram home the point to her, he took out his phone and took half a dozen photos from various angles. He thumbed through them, making sure they left no room for doubt. Then he left, turning off all the lights behind him. Nothing suspicious to alert friends or neighbours.

When he arrived home, he poured himself a Jack Daniel's and Coke and sat down at the breakfast bar, scrolling through the pictures of Marco Mather. He slowly savoured both his drink and the photographs, deciding how best to play the upcoming scene. He uploaded the photographs to his tablet. 'All the better to see you with,' he said.

At last, he rinsed his glass, dried it and put it away. Then he went through to the garage, snapping on the harsh white fluorescent tubes that bled life and colour from the scene. He unlocked the lid of the chest freezer and threw it open with a flourish.

The woman's face was a caricature of surprise and terror. Her hands jerked up to cover her eyes from the shock of the light. He could see her eyelids fluttering through the lattice of her fingers. Normally he liked to go on the attack right away, to catch them on the back foot. But for once, he was happy to wait, to enjoy the anticipation of her reaction.

Gradually, she grew accustomed to the light. One hand slipped down from her face to conceal her breasts. She peeked fearfully at him through the fingers of her other hand. 'You?' Incredulity made her voice tiny and tremulous.

'Here's the deal. If you scream, I hurt you. And I tape your mouth up so you can never scream again. Is that clear?'

Eyes wide, she bit her lip and nodded.

'I am the husband. And you are the wife.'

Tears brimmed and spilled from her eyes. 'I have a husband.' It was barely a whisper.

He shook his head, smiling indulgently. 'You used to have a different husband. Now you have me. There's no going back.'

53

Talking to Carol had left Paula too jazzed to go home. She hated to inflict her edginess on Elinor, especially when she was carrying particularly heavy burdens of her own. Like a bereaved teenage boy in the living room. So she'd headed into Temple Fields, where the gay village rubbed shoulders with the hookers and the lap-dancing bars. A lot of her colleagues thought of Temple Fields as Bradfield's badlands, but Paula had always felt at home here. She was old enough to remember when being gay meant you were an outlaw, not the darlings of a coalition government desperately trying to make itself relevant to anyone under forty. In those olden days, Temple Fields had been one of the few places it was possible to be openly gay, and she still relished the bustle and buzz of its streets in spite of some of the more recent memories her job had overlaid on those streets.

She headed for Darlings and pushed her way through the press of bodies to the bar. Armed with a bottle of Belgian beer, she pushed back through to the tiny patio at the rear of the pub. In the old days, it had been the yard where the empties were stacked. Now, it boasted outdoor space heaters and tall cocktail tables where the smokers could hang out even in the dead of winter. She spotted a couple of women she recognised and joined them, lighting up as soon as she'd put her beer down.

They swapped gossip, took the piss out of a new lesbian sitcom and diplomatically refrained from talking about their jobs. Two cigarettes later, Paula drained her bottle of beer, made her apologies and left, feeling like she'd turned the stress dial down to manageable levels.

The house was dark and silent when Paula let herself in. She dumped her bag and keys on the hall table then went through to the kitchen for another beer before bed. She took one from the fridge then crossed to the patio doors so she could go outside and smoke. Suddenly the shadows beyond the breakfast bar shifted and she almost dropped her beer in shock. 'Jesus,' she exclaimed, taking a step back, eyes wide with apprehension.

'It's only me,' Torin said as the darkness resolved itself into his shape.

Paula reached for the switches and turned on the low-level lighting under the cabinets. In the soft light, she could see he was wearing what passed for pyjamas these days – baggy plaid trousers and a grey V-necked T-shirt. 'You nearly gave me a heart attack,' she complained, reaching for the patio door and hauling it open.

'I'm sorry.' He looked as if he was about to burst into tears. 'I couldn't sleep.' He gestured at the half-empty glass of milk on the breakfast bar. 'My mum always said that milk helped you sleep. Something about the calcium. It's not working too well, though.' He hitched himself on to a tall chair.

Paula stepped outside with her beer, lit a cigarette and grimaced at the acrid taste that filled her mouth. Why was it that you only ever knew you'd reached the limit of daily cigarette pleasure when you went one too far? And what the hell was she supposed to say to this kid that wasn't some desperate cliché? 'You're going to have a lot of broken nights,' she tried. 'The only advice I can give you is not to fret over it. It's natural. Part of grieving.'

'What's going to happen to me, Paula?' His voice shook.

A lot of bad stuff. 'I'm not going to lie to you. You're going to have a shit time for a while. You're going to feel raw, like somebody scraped your insides with a spoon. You're going to feel like the tears are never more than somebody else's careless comment away. You're going to feel like nothing will ever be right in your life again. But I promise you, all of that passes. It's not that you stop missing your mum or loving her. Somehow it becomes bearable.'

'I don't know. It's like that would be letting her down.'

She remembered that feeling only too well. When her colleague Don Merrick had died, it had felt like every day on the job was part of a long process of failing his memory. 'What would be letting her down would be to not live your life as fully as you possibly can. You've got a helluva touchstone there, Torin. When you're confronted with hard choices, you can always ask yourself what would have made your mum proud.' Paula took a last drag and crushed out the half-smoked cigarette in the ashtray Elinor reluctantly allowed on her precious deck. She came back inside and sat in the chair next to him.

'I want to kill the man who did this to her,' he said, staring bleakly at his milk.

'I know.'

'But what's worse is knowing that, even if he was standing in front of me, I wouldn't be able to. I'm just a kid,

Paula. And there's nothing I can do to make him feel the misery he's made for everybody that knew her.' He banged his fist on the table. 'I feel pathetic.'

'We're doing everything we can to bring him to justice. It won't be the kind of wild justice that we all crave when we're hurting, but it will deprive him of everything that makes life worth living for most people.' She put her hand over his. 'And you're already in a better place than him because you've got people all round you who care about you. When we catch him, his friends will melt into the darkness. His family will disown him. He'll have nothing. You'll always have more than him.'

Torin didn't look convinced. 'I wish my dad was home.' He gave a jerky laugh. 'Listen to me. Fourteen years old and I want my daddy, like I was a little kid.'

'Of course you want your dad. It doesn't matter what age you are when you lose a parent, you want somebody you love to take care of you. I'm sorry your dad can't be here, but we're going to do our best for you, Torin. Don't bottle up how you're feeling. Don't worry about what we think of you, because what we think is that you're a great lad.'

All at once, his shoulders were shaking with sobs, huge gulping moans that filled the room with his anguish. Not knowing what else to do, Paula got up and gathered him in her arms. It was like hugging an alien; the feel of his body, the faint boy-smell of his skin, the vibration of his grief in her own chest were all foreign to her. She'd thought the best thing she could do for Torin was to nail his mother's killer. Now she understood this was a case that was going to make far greater demands on her than that.

And then her phone rang.

54

Sleep was a distant stranger for Tony. Simply being in the same room as Carol had sparked his engines back to life. He had imagined so many scenarios where the weight of grief and loss had driven Carol to destruction, and now he'd seen her apparently intact the relief made him feel buoyant in spite of being locked in a smelly cell with no prospect of walking free just yet.

He ran an inventory of what he'd clocked. She'd always cheated time, looking younger than her years, but now her history had caught up with her. In his eyes, she was as attractive as ever, but the bloom had started to fade into something that told a darker story. She did look as if she was sleeping well though. The dark bruises under her eyes that had been a regular feature when she'd been up half the night trying to find a resolution to serious crimes had faded out, but her blue-grey eyes still had a weariness to them.

Carol had never been vain, but the one aspect of her appearance she'd always taken trouble with was her hair.

Naturally thick and blonde, it was always styled to look informally shaggy, but she'd once explained to Tony that it took a lot of skill to make it appear so casual. Now, whoever was cutting it lacked the necessary proficiency and it looked untidy. And the silver she'd kept at bay with clever colouring had asserted itself, changing the shade from honey to ash. The alteration he saw in her spoke volumes to Tony. Carol had lost her pride in herself. She no longer saw value in who she was and what she did.

And what exactly *was* she doing? Her body shape had undergone some subtle changes too. Her shoulders were broader and she wasn't carrying any spare weight round her midriff. She'd abandoned the silver twelve-piece Turkish puzzle ring she used to wear and her hands carried the marks of physical labour, yet she'd always been the first to insist on getting someone in when there were any problems with the house. As far as he was aware, she barely knew what a screwdriver was for. Whatever displacement activity she had chosen as her form of therapy, she had moved well outside her previous comfort zone.

And here he was, well outside his own comfort zone, completely reassured by the arrival of a woman who was adamant in her desire not to give a damn about him. Her very presence gave him hope. And now that he had genuine hope, it was possible to examine honestly the hopeless position he'd been in previously. He wondered what he represented to Alex Fielding to make her so swift and sure in her condemnation of him. Was it simply that she sensed a sensational scalp? A headline-grabbing arrest and conviction? It seemed a giant leap to believe him capable of such crimes. After all, BMP had consulted him for years. He'd been trusted to maintain confidentiality and to produce profiles that could be relied on by its officers. He was aware that a significant number of powerful officers thought he was odd, to say the least, but as far as he knew, they didn't consider him potentially lethal. But for Fielding to have gone on the attack like this, she must have been confident of support from the top brass.

And, realistically, that meant no matter what Paula believed, she couldn't rescue him from behind the barrier of her official position. If she hadn't already broken the rules for him, he'd have been lost. Fielding would almost certainly have charged him in the morning and the magistrates almost never granted bail on a murder charge. Definitely not on a double murder charge, regardless of who the accused was. Oscar Pistorius would have had no chance of making bail in a British magistrates' court.

Without Carol, he had been lost. With Carol, he stood a chance. And the best thing he could do to help her set him free was to focus not on her and how she'd changed and what was going on inside her head, but on the man who was killing a subset of women that she fitted into.

He got to his feet and started pacing. Profiling, that's what he was supposed to be good at. He needed to think about this killer in those terms. He'd written the introduction to his profiles so many times he knew it by heart. As he paced, he recited it aloud like a mantra to put his head in the right place. 'The following offender profile is for guidance only and shouldn't be regarded as an identikit portrait. The offender is unlikely to match the profile in every detail, though I would expect there to be a high degree of congruence between the characteristics outlined below and the reality. All of the statements in the profile express probabilities and possibilities, not hard facts.

'A serial killer produces signals and indicators in the commission of his crimes. Everything he does is intended, consciously or not, as part of a pattern. Discovering the underlying pattern reveals the killer's logic. It may not appear logical to us, but to him it is crucial. Because his logic is so idiosyncratic, straightforward traps will not capture him. As he is unique, so must be the means of catching him, interviewing him and reconstructing his acts.'

He stopped and rested both palms flat on the chilly wall. He wished he had a set of the crime-scene photos in front of him; his memory, like his eyesight, was not quite as sharp as it used to be, and a lot had happened since he'd flicked through the photos Paula had shown him. Some things were still vivid, however. The smashed face of the victim. The primitive markings of the bruises that covered her torso. The shaving of her genital area and the sealing of her labia.

'Mixed messages,' he said. 'The destruction of her face looks frenzied. The bruising on her body is organised. You didn't stamp on her at all, which you almost certainly would have done if you'd been in a frenzy. So, as with the facial destruction, in spite of appearances to the contrary, there's a reason. Here, it's because you are careful not to leave forensic traces. You're determined not to be caught and you're smart enough to have developed a strategy to deliver that result. You knew about the limitations of the CCTV coverage but still you took care to make sure you couldn't be identified. The things we think we know about your appearance we may not know at all. You're wearing glasses but they might have plain lenses. You've got a limp but you might be faking it. You look reasonably strapping but you could just be wearing bulky clothes on your upper torso. The only thing we will be able to say for sure, once some techie has done the biometrics, is how tall you are, give or take an inch.'

He pushed off from the wall and began pacing again. 'So how do we use these contradictions to provide investigative value?' He started numbering points on his fingers. Pinkie. 'First, the victims resemble each other. Similar height and build, blonde, blue eyes, professional women, not in a relationship. As far as we know. You're going for a type that means something to you. You want them to fit a specific niche in your picture of the universe. And when they don't, you destroy their faces.' Six, eight. Six, eight, brow furrowed in thought.

'You destroy their faces because it turns out they don't live up to the template. They look right but they don't act right. So they don't have the right to belong in that cohort any more. They've forfeited the right to be on the team. Let there be no mistake about it. They're worthless. They're history.'

Ring finger. 'So it's not a frenzied attack at all. It's more in sorrow than in anger. And now the other stuff makes sense. You kick them to death to teach them a lesson. How dare they fail you? How dare they trick you into thinking they were the one and then not be the one? You're sending a message, only there's nobody there to read it. If only she knew it, you're sending a message to the next one. "This is what will happen to you if you don't pass muster."' He paused, frowning. 'It's savage, it's lethal, but you never lose control, do you?'

Middle finger. 'And that's the thing with the washing and the shaving and the superglue. It's not just about removing forensic traces. It's another message. It's like stamping the carcase "not fit for human consumption". You're warning the rest of us, don't get taken in, this one isn't even worth shagging. You're protecting other men from the mistakes you made. You're the good guy, you're providing a service, making sure nobody else wastes time on them.'

Tony scratched his head with both hands, as if creatures were crawling over his scalp.

'So what is it that you're looking for? It's more than auditioning a girlfriend. I think you're looking for a replacement.

355

You had your perfect woman and something went wrong. And before you could make her pay the price for her fall from grace, she got away. And you can't find peace without her so you need a replacement.'

He threw himself down on the bed, forgetting it was so hard. He yelped and sat up again. 'I didn't think it through when I told Carol to find a dead woman who looks like her. But that's it. She's either dead or on the missing list. Because if she was around to be killed, he wouldn't need to bother with anybody else. And he didn't kill her then, so although he kids himself he's looking for a replacement, what he's actually looking for is an excuse to kill them. He kept Nadia alive for three weeks. He believed he could mould her but then he had to kill her when she couldn't make the grade. But killing her was such a kick he's convinced himself that it's a waste of time trying to get them to toe the line. He's run out of patience when it comes to training them because, whether he'd admit it or not, he'd rather kill them than keep them.' Index finger. 'He's not looking for a replacement now, he's looking for satisfaction, and unless he gets a perfect replica more or less straight away, he's going to be just like Mick Jagger. Trying and trying.'

All of which was interesting but not helpful when it came to catching a killer. What Carol – and Paula – needed was something a bit more concrete. 'You're not young,' he said thoughtfully. 'Bev was in her late thirties and you thought she was a possibility. Which probably puts you between thirty-five and fifty. You're authoritarian and arrogant, contemptuous of others. You let people know when they don't come up to scratch, which has probably hurt your career. And that makes you even more resentful. You're practical. You turn up with a taser and whatever is in that case.' He paused for a moment then smacked himself in the forehead. 'Of course. It's a portable anaesthetic kit. Like paramedics use. You're putting them under so they don't make a noise in the boot of the car. That's what you're doing.' He patted his pockets for his phone out of habit. Then it dawned on him he couldn't call Carol or even text her to share his revelation. Disappointment rippled through him, leaving him frustrated and annoyed.

'Focus, you moron,' he chided himself. 'Just make sure you remember it in the morning. And as for you, you clever bastard – you're probably in a white-collar job, though not a highly qualified professional. Not a doctor or a lawyer. Maybe a middle-manager of some sort. But you think you're better than that. That's why you're leaving them where they'll be found. You want us to pay attention, to take you seriously.'

Tony stood up again and walked the perimeter of the room, trailing his fingers along the wall as he went. 'You're local. Both your victims are from Bradfield. I think you're picking them at random. You see them on the street or on the bus and they look right and you stalk them to see whether they'll do. You acquired and killed Bev very soon after Nadia, which makes me wonder whether you've got a little list of possibles.

'You've probably got a house with a garage or a private area for parking cars. You're taking their cars somewhere, then going back for your own later. Then you dump theirs. We need to find out where those cars end up. Burned out? Left with fake plates in long-term parking? What are you doing with them?

'The other thing is, you need to be able to contain them. Keep them captive without being overlooked or overheard. No nosy neighbours wondering what the screaming is all about.'

It was thin, he had to admit. But with the limited resources at his disposal, he'd made a start. He was beginning to have a sense of what kind of man this killer was. And if he was right about the portable anaesthetic machine, Paula might be able to develop that into a viable lead.

He sat down on the edge of the bed, feeling the adrenalin finally ebb away, leaving him weary and depleted. But the despair was gone. Carol might not know it yet, but her arrival at Skenfrith Street signalled the installation of the caissons. Now the real work could begin on rebuilding the piers that would hold up the bridge that needed to be built between them.

For the first time in months, he actually believed it might be possible.

55

Marco would save her. Marie kept repeating the words like a sacred invocation. Marco would save her. She whimpered and shifted her position. It didn't matter how often she rearranged herself, some part of her body complained. How could anyone do what he'd done to someone they knew? She wasn't some stranger he'd dragged off the street. She was a person with a name and a place in his world. It made no sense in Marie's universe, where life was comfortable and people behaved in predictable, conventional ways. She wasn't stupid. She knew there were lots of people who lived in chaotic, illogical, even violent ways. But until today, she thought people like that were safely contained outside the neat borders of her life.

After this, nothing would ever be the same for her again. She'd look at the world in a different way once Marco had saved her from this hell. Right now, he'd be talking to the police. They'd be looking for her. They had all sorts of ways of tracking people down these days. There was CCTV everywhere. They'd be talking to people from work, people who got on the same tram as her morning and evening. The newsagent. Someone must have seen something. Or else he'd crack, this madman. He'd give something away without even realising it. And then they'd be on to him.

She wasn't going to think about what he'd done to her. The way he'd slapped her and dragged her across the concrete floor, ripping her skin in a painful graze from hip to knee. The kicks and punches he'd aimed at her when she'd tried to explain in as placatory a way as she could that she had no idea how to cook a steak because Marco was the cook in their house. He'd laughed incredulously then he'd gone mad with his fists and his feet.

But she wasn't going to dwell on that. She was going to hold fast to her hopes. Marco would save her. He wouldn't rest till she was home. And there would be no need to tell him about what had happened after the beating. He wouldn't press her for details. She'd never have to relive that horror. The pain, the humiliation, the things Marco had never dreamed of asking her to do – she would make herself forget them. She would be strong, because that's who she was. She wasn't whatever this beast wanted to make of her. She was Marie Mather, wife of Marco. Who would save her.

A moan escaped from her bruised lips. She had to be strong. She couldn't give in. She had to be the woman Marco loved. She had to be worthy of him. Because Marco would save her.

Then the lid was thrown open and her resolve wavered at the sight of him looming over her again. 'What was it you said earlier? Something about your useless wanker of a husband coming to save you?'

Although she was so scared she thought she might throw up, Marie managed to choke out, 'He will.'

He leaned forward and laughed viciously in her face. He

produced a tablet computer and turned it to face her. At first, she couldn't make sense of what she was seeing. And then it dawned on her that this was Marco. Sprawled over their garage floor. It made no sense. The beast leaned into the freezer and held it closer so Marie could see it more clearly.

Her mouth dropped open in horror. 'No,' she said, disbelief raising the volume.

He dragged his finger across the screen to bring up the next photo. 'Oh yes. Like I said, you used to have a different husband. But now he's dead.' As he spoke, he eased the taser out of his pocket. If he was going to need it, now was probably the time.

'You killed him? You killed my Marco?'

'I didn't have to. His cooking killed him. Your demands killed him. I'm not going to let you do that to me.'

She was oblivious to his words, completely focused on the image on the screen in front of her. 'No,' she said, this time more loudly still. 'No.' It was a shout now, suddenly deadened as the freezer lid slammed back down and plunged her into darkness.

Marco wasn't going to save her after all.

56

It was almost like old times, Carol thought. Sitting round a
table at midnight with Paula and Stacey, drinking coffee
and going over a live case, trying to come up with a line of
inquiry that would do the business for them. Except it
wasn't. She was kidding herself. Old times had never
included Tony in jail, Chris in various kinds of therapy, a
teenage kid upstairs and Elinor Blessing in the kitchen
making the coffee. Kevin and Sam, the other members of
the MIT, had moved onwards and upwards too; she had no
idea where they were or what they were doing. This, she
had to accept, was a new chapter with scant connection to
the past.

'Thanks for joining us,' she said to Stacey.

Stacey flipped open a slender laptop. 'Paula explained
about Tony. I wanted to help.'

I deserved that. 'Of course. He was always ready to put himself out for us.'

Elinor came through with a tray of steaming mugs.

'Coffee all round. I'd worry about it keeping you awake, except that you're all cops and it has as much effect on you as on doctors.' She handed out the drinks and put a plate of chocolate digestives on the table. 'Lucky for you I got fresh supplies of biscuits in. Torin seems to inhale them.'

'How is he doing?' Carol stirred milk into her coffee and reached for a biscuit.

'I don't know him well enough to be certain,' Elinor said. 'He's obviously deeply upset but I think he doesn't really know how he's supposed to react. He's got no experience of grief to draw on. It's like he's not sure what he's feeling.'

'Still in shock,' Paula said, keeping his secrets. 'I don't think it's begun to sink in yet.'

'Poor boy,' Stacey said.

Carol tried not to show her surprise at Stacey displaying empathy with a carbon-based life form. Then she remembered Paula's revelation that their former computer guru had been seeing Sam Evans socially. Maybe even romantically. Yet another reminder that this was not old times. 'Arresting the wrong person's not going to help,' she said.

'I've already said I'm sorry about that. I did try to persuade Fielding to wait, but I think she's got one eye on the brass. Trying to make an impression.' Paula shook her head. 'And Tony doesn't help himself.'

'I never thought I'd be grateful for Bronwen Scott,' Carol said. 'All we have to do now is demolish your case, Paula.' She held up a hand as Paula opened her mouth to protest. 'I'm not blaming you, I know it's DCI Fielding who drove this. I just said "you" because you're the only one here officially involved.'

'Exactly,' Stacey said. 'I'm not actually here.'

'And I'm not either,' Elinor said. 'Someone has to do the sleeping.' She kissed Paula on the cheek. 'I'm going to leave you to it. Don't stay up too late, ladies.' She patted Carol on the shoulder as she passed. A day ago Carol would have flinched at the contact. Now, it felt good.

They all waited politely till Elinor left the room, then Carol said, 'I take it as a given that none of us believes Tony could be responsible?' Paula looked outraged, Stacey rolled her eyes. 'OK, I had to ask. So I'm tasked with undermining the case against him enough to make Fielding back away from charging him.'

'And you don't have much time. She's going to want to reinterview him first thing and my guess is that unless Bronwen Scott gives her a very good reason not to, she's going to charge him at the end of that interview.'

'Would demolishing your DNA evidence be a good enough reason?' Carol asked sweetly.

Paula sat up straight. 'What do you mean?'

'He's remembered how it got there.' Carol revealed what Tony had told her earlier, leaving them both shaking their heads in disbelief. 'Stacey, Paula told me you've found your way into Nadia Wilkowa's data. Is that right?'

Stacey nodded. 'It wasn't hard.' She tapped a couple of keys and angled the screen so they could both see a diary page. 'I merged the data on her laptop and her phone so we have as full a picture as possible of her day to day life. So ...' She clicked on something and the display changed. 'On any given day I can tell you what her business appointments were, whether she had any personal appointments, what texts she sent and received and her emails.'

'Did I ever tell you how much you scare me?' Carol gave Stacey a thumbs-up.

'Just make sure you stay on her good side,' Paula muttered.

'So can you pull up dates she had appointments at Bradfield Moor?'

Stacey reclaimed the laptop. They waited while the keyboard whispered under her fingers, then she turned it to face them. 'Five times since she started the job. She had meetings with Joanna Moore, the Medical Director.'

'Can you email me those dates? I need to compare them with the incident log at Bradfield Moor. One of those dates should correspond to an occasion when Tony was punched in the face by a patient and had a nosebleed.'

Stacey snorted. 'Nothing changes, does it?'

'The thing is, I do actually remember that incident,' Carol said. 'His nose was swollen like a strawberry for a few days. It was last year some time. I can't be more precise than that.'

'I swear to God, you couldn't make him up,' Stacey muttered.

'Will they let you see the log?' Paula asked.

'If I have authorisation from Tony, I don't think they can refuse. I'll get on to that first thing tomorrow. On the downside, he was at a meeting with Will Newton in Brad-field Cross on Monday. He stomped out at the end because he was so pissed off. He walked home to work off his bad mood, so he's not got any kind of alibi for when Bev went missing.'

Paula groaned. She gave Carol a direct look. 'The "no alibi" isn't exactly a surprise. He misses the life he had when the MIT was still running. He doesn't really have much social contact without us.'

Carol knew the true opinion lurking behind Paula's words but she wasn't willing to engage with it. 'See what you can do.'

Paula dipped her head, acknowledging her failure to get Carol to open up with a wry twist of her mouth. 'You want me to get one of my firm to check the hospital CCTV and the street cameras?'

Carol nodded. 'You'll get a better response if you do it offi-cially than I will if I try to get anything out of hospital bureaucrats. Meanwhile we'll be finding expert witnesses to knock down your fingermark evidence. Because obviously, it's not Tony's.'

'This isn't enough,' Stacey said, twirling a strand of her sleek black hair round her finger. 'Explaining the blood and the thumbprint would probably convince a jury there was reasonable doubt, but it's not going to hold Fielding back from charging him.'

Paula's expression was grim. 'I've barely got my feet under the table, but I'd say you're right. If we're going to get Tony off the hook before she charges him, we're going to have to find a stronger suspect.'

Carol leaned forward, hands flat on the table, intense and focused. 'Tony has a theory based on the way the killer treats his victims.' She looked at Paula. 'You know how Fielding has this mad idea that Tony's killing women who look like me because I walked away? Well, Tony suggested that he's not killing women because they look like me. It's that we all – me and the two victims – we all look like the woman he actually wants to kill.'

'So what's stopping him killing the woman he really wants to kill?' Stacey drummed the pads of her fingers softly against the laptop casing, alert and interested now there was some fresh meat on the table.

'Tony thinks she cheated him out of it. Suicide, accident, whatever. But she might be dead already. And quite recently. He thinks if we can find her, we find the killer.'

Paula stood up abruptly and lit a scented candle that immediately filled the air with the festive scent of cinnamon and cranberries. Then she flipped open her cigarette packet and sparked up a cigarette from the candle flame. 'Bloody hell,' she said at the top of the in breath. 'And how does he propose we do that?'

Carol pulled a face. 'He didn't get that far.'

'Surprise, surprise.'

Stacey frowned. 'That's an interesting challenge. It's not like you can google "dead blonde Bradfield" and expect anything useful.'

'A few tasteless blonde jokes maybe,' Paula sighed. 'But that doesn't help us any.'

'I thought I might trawl through the *Sentinel Times* archives. The hard copies, not the online version,' Carol said. 'I think they still keep them on file at the central library.'

'If that hasn't gone in the local government cuts,' Paula said gloomily.

'It's not exactly exhaustive,' Stacey pointed out.

'Maybe not, but funeral directors recommend a death notice as part of the package and the overwhelming majority of people still go for it,' Carol said. 'It's the best we can do.'

'And I'll try and persuade Fielding not to charge Tony in the morning.' Paula cracked a yawn and rolled her shoulders. 'I'm sorry, girls, but I'm going to have to go to bed.'

Carol stood up. 'Lucky you. I've got the best part of a forty-minute drive before I get to sleep.'

'There's a sofa bed here,' Paula said. 'We seem to be the unofficial home for waifs and strays.'

Carol smiled and shook her head. 'Thanks, but I've got to get home for the dog. I'm new to this game. I don't know how long you can leave them alone without them freaking out.'

'Where did you leave her?' Paula looked worried.

'In the main barn. There's nothing to chew except sawhorses and scrap wood.'

'Probably just as well.'

'I'll bring her with me tomorrow. She can sleep in the Land Rover and I can take her for a walk at lunchtime.'

'Are you sure that's legal?' Stacey asked, looking concerned.

'I don't see why not. The weather's not exactly warm and I'll obviously leave a window open. And I'll walk her whenever I can.'

Paula pushed herself to her feet. 'It'll be fine. I'm glad you came, Carol. Tony needs you on his side.'

All the relaxed bonhomie drained from Carol's face and her shoulders tightened. 'I'm not on his side. I'm on the side of justice being done. That's all. And when it's done, I'm going straight back to my own life. I'm done with him, Paula. I'm done with Tony.'

57

Day twenty-seven

It was infuriating. Why were women so stupid? You didn't have to be Einstein to work out that, if your husband was dead, you'd better make a good impression on the man who was willing to take his place. But that didn't seem to have penetrated her thick skull. He'd left her in peace all night so she could get Marco out of her system and get used to her new reality, but he might as well not have bothered.

He'd set his alarm especially early so he could provide her with her first lesson before he set about the business of the day. But when he opened the lid of the freezer, she barely reacted. No panic, no terror, no offer of obedience. She remained huddled at one end of the freezer, knees against her chest, arms wrapped around her head. He shouted at her but she didn't flinch. It didn't seem to register at all. He'd heard about catatonic states, but he couldn't believe he was seeing one for real. He was convinced she was putting on an act, so he slapped her a couple of times to snap her out of it.

But all he achieved was to sting the palm of his hand. She made no attempt to protect herself or to fight back.

He tried tasering her and throwing her on the floor of the garage but she remained where he dropped her, sprawled in an ungainly way across the concrete. He shouted at her to get up, but she stayed where she was. He booted her in the midriff; she rose and fell like a sack of meat. She made no protest, not even a whimper.

He didn't have time for this. Not now. So he tasered her again and threw her into the freezer. 'You need to buck up your ideas,' he said. 'You could have a great life with me. Or you could end up in the mortuary like the other ones. It's your choice. When I get home tonight, I expect you to have had an attitude readjustment. Marco's dead. Get used to it. You can join him or you can join me. I'd say it's a no-brainer. But people make shitty choices all the time. Still, you're supposed to be a clever bitch. Show me how smart you really are. Choose life, bitch. Or pay the price.'

Then he'd slammed the freezer shut. Rage burned like acid in his throat. Who the *fuck* did she think she was? Failure was one thing, but defiance was another. That's where the first one, the original, had gone wrong. When things came to a head between them and he made it clear her behaviour was unacceptable, she'd flouted his instructions to improve herself. She'd thought she could go against him. Take his children and walk out the door. She'd thought she was escaping.

Instead she'd driven so bloody badly that she'd ended up in a pile-up on the M62. That she was dead was fine with him, even though there would have been more satisfaction in dealing out death himself. But she'd destroyed his kids with her treachery. His kids. His son and his daughter, still in the process of being moulded into a pair of children anyone would be proud of. And she'd taken herself beyond revenge at the same time. He'd cheerfully have killed her again and again and again for the affront of leaving him. The outrage of taking his children from him was worse; for that, he'd have tortured her slowly, grimly, gruesomely for as long as he could possibly make it last.

Well, this one would discover the price of defiance soon enough. First, though, he had to go to work.

58

The dog had greeted her so rapturously on her return that Carol felt obliged to take her for a walk. She hadn't fancied stumbling over the rough pasture in the dark, so she'd stuck to the margin of the field where the ground was relatively even. Flash didn't seem to mind. She raced off in random directions before returning at regular intervals to make sure Carol hadn't lost her way. 'A bit like my brain,' Carol said once she'd recognised the pattern.

Even when she'd finally gone to bed, her mind was still racing, running over the same problems in the hope of finding a solution. In the end, she'd pummelled the pillows one last time and managed to drift off to the sound of the World Service. When the alarm roused her a few hours later, the same thoughts were still rattling round her head.

There was no time to take the dog for a run; she had to meet Bronwen Scott at eight so they could go over things once more with Tony before Fielding arrived to interrogate him again. Scott had redoubled her suggestion that Carol avoid the interview itself. 'I'm sure Fielding will know by then that you're on the team, but I don't want to feel she's got something to prove because you're in the room.' It was a good point. It was also a way of protecting Paula.

Carol might not have known much about dogs, but even before Stacey had weighed in, she had realised it wasn't acceptable to leave the dog alone for long periods of time. They were supposed to keep each other company, after all. So she opened the rear door of the Land Rover and spread a couple of blankets on the floor. Flash jumped aboard as if it was routine. Carol added a litre-bottle of water and a plastic bowl to her dog-walking kit of leash, training treats and plastic bags, and they were ready to roll. One way or another, she'd find time to walk the dog.

She beat Scott to Skenfrith Street by five minutes but she didn't go inside, thinking it more sensible to wait at the car-park entrance. Scott was perfectly groomed as ever, immaculate in a fitted charcoal-grey suit over a sharply tailored blue-and-white pinstriped shirt. The narrow skirt, coupled with teetering heels, showed off her legs to distracting advantage. Carol felt like a frump in her best black trouser suit and flatties, both from the Hobbs' sale a couple of years ago. This time, they were shown to an interview room away from the custody suite, fitted with recording equipment and a long narrow wall mirror. It had the familiar grey walls and the mingled smell of stale bodies and cleaning chemicals. Without thinking, Carol headed straight for the chairs that weren't bolted to the floor. Scott laughed. 'Old habits die hard, Carol. You're on the wrong side of the table.' As Carol made to stand up, Scott waved her back down. 'It's OK, it's only us here. Stay where you are for the time being.'

Scott sat down and put on a pair of rectangular glasses with thin black frames. They made her look like a sexily strict headmistress. She opened a file and studied the contents page by page. When Tony was shown in a few minutes later, she closed the file and stood up. As he approached the table, she moved towards him and put a hand on his arm. 'How was your night?'

He looked across at Carol, who had not moved. 'It passed,' he said, moving past Scott to sit down opposite Carol. 'I don't know how long we've got here, but there are a few things I need to say. I think he's local. Given that men tend to go for women younger than them and he chose Bev as a possible surrogate, I'd say he's at least thirty-five. One thing that bothered me was that the women don't seem to have tried to escape or draw attention to themselves after he loads them in the car. I'd have thought if there had been any reports of pedestrians hearing someone kicking or shouting in the boot of a car Paula would have said something about it. So I wondered if what he's got in that metal case is a portable anaesthetic kit. Like paramedics carry. That would explain both why he's carrying the case and the women's apparent passivity. It's because they're unconscious. So maybe it's worth checking if any of the local hospitals have lost one?'

'Given the professions of the victims, he might even be a paramedic,' Carol said.

Tony ran a hand through his hair. 'I don't think so. I'd put him in a white-collar job. But you could be right,' he added hastily.

Trying to suck up. Pathetic. Carol made a note. One for Paula to suggest to Fielding, maybe. To make it look like she was on her boss's side. She looked across at Scott. 'Could I have a sheet of paper?' Scott tore a blank page out of her legal pad. 'I need you to write me a letter of authority to Bradfield Moor, asking them to give me access to any entries in the incident log involving you. We've got the dates when Nadia

Wilkowa had appointments there and if we can match them up, we can undermine Fielding's case.'

Even before she'd finished speaking, he was writing. 'If we can do that, they'll have to let me go, right?'

'Not necessarily,' Scott said. 'Especially since somebody's bound to leak to the internet or the local media that they've arrested someone as high profile as you.'

'High profile? Me?'

'In crime terms, you're the bee's knees. A profiler gone rogue? It doesn't get any better than that.'

He looked shaken. 'They're going to put me all over the papers, right? Like that poor bloke in Bristol who got demonised for nothing more than having a weird hair-style.'

Scott sighed. 'Probably. So far, I've not had any calls. But Fielding kept this very quiet and the overnight custody sergeant is notorious for hating the media. That won't last once the dayshift briefing happens. You're almost certainly going to get screwed over. All the Jacko Vance stuff will be raked up again.' She nodded towards Carol. 'They might come after you too.'

'I'll enjoy that,' she said grimly.

Tony signed the letter and passed it across to Carol. 'Ask for Maggie Spence, the Assistant Director. She likes me, she'll be helpful.'

'Unlike your boss,' Carol said drily. She knew the history between them. Power never forgives those who know its dirty little secrets.

A wry smile. 'Hard to believe how much pleasure this will give him.' He swept his arm to encompass the depressing room.

'They'll have a search warrant by now,' Scott said, impatient to get on with the serious business of the morning. 'They'll be going through your home and your office. If there's anything you don't want them to find, now's the time to tell us.' She cocked an eyebrow at him.

Tony shrugged, spreading his hands in a gesture of openness. 'Good luck to them. If they find the data CD for Tomb Raider 3, I'd be eternally grateful.' He gave a strained smile. 'I really don't have any dark secrets. Hidden shallows, that's me.'

Carol had had enough. She pushed her chair back and folded Tony's letter away in her bag. 'Unless there's anything else you think I need to know, I'm going now. I've got inquiries to make and the clock's ticking. And my dog needs walking.'

'Dog?' Tony looked bemused.

'I'll fill you in later,' Scott said to her retreating figure.

Tony's spirits sank as Carol walked out of the interview room. Bronwen Scott made him feel nervous and inadequate; a woman for whom he could never have enough right answers. He watched the door close then said, 'She's got a dog?'

Scott looked baffled, but in an amused sort of way. 'I have no idea what Carol's domestic arrangements are.'

Tony pulled a face. 'Neither do I, apparently. So, what's going to happen now?'

'Fielding will interview you again. Unless she's got something new we don't know about she'll just try to rerun yesterday's questions and you're going to go "no comment" to everything she puts to you. She'll try to unsettle you, to provoke you. But you mustn't let her get to you.'

'I'll pretend she's a patient. They generally try to divert attention from what's ailing them by asking me questions. I'm quite good at avoiding the answers.' He stared down at the table. 'I know I shouldn't take this personally, but it's hard not to feel hurt by how quick off the mark Fielding has been to arrest me. Call me sentimental, but I'd have expected her to cut me a bit of slack. I mean, I've been at the heart of so many investigations, I'd have thought they'd think twice before they jumped to the conclusion that I'm a serial killer.' He met her eyes, his expression pained.

'Fielding's showing the brass her independence. And maybe trying to take some of the gloss off Carol's achievements at the same time. That's why she's so keen on having Paula on the team. Ficlding wants to be seen as the rehab unit for officers contaminated by the maverick tendency.'

Tony managed a tired smile. 'And I thought I was the psychologist. So, do you think they're going to charge me?'

'I think she's going to keep you hanging on till the last possible minute. She'll get another DCI to authorise an extra twelve hours' detention, which will take us up to tomorrow morning. Then she'll either charge you or let you go, or, if she thinks she's got enough with the DNA and the thumbprint, she'll go to the magistrates for an extension. At which point we'll wheel out all the undermining evidence that Carol will have assembled plus something from the fingerprint expert my office is lining up, and they'll order your release. Probably on police bail. If we hang on and do it that way, your exoneration is more public.'

'That sounds good.'

Scott held one hand out flat and swivelled it at the wrist. 'Yes and no. The exoneration is more public, but the downside is that the media and the twittersphere will have had a full twenty-four-hour news cycle to rip you to shreds.'

'They're going to rip me to shreds anyway by the sounds of it, so the more publicly I'm taken off the hook, the better, surely? Or are you thinking the mags won't let me go?'

Scott twisted her mouth in an expression of uncertainty. 'I'd be very surprised if they backed Fielding on this one once her so-called evidence is thoroughly undermined.'

Before Tony could respond, the door slammed open. Fielding stood in the doorway, a tiny ball of barely contained fury. Her mouth was tight, her eyes narrowed and her hands curled into fists. 'A word, Ms Scott,' she said. It wasn't a request.

Scott took her time, pausing to give Tony's shoulder a quick squeeze. 'I'll be right back, Tony.'

She'd barely closed the door behind her when Fielding stepped into her personal space and hissed, 'What the hell do you think you're playing at?' Today, Fielding's accent had abandoned charm in favour of blunt threat. It would have made nobody want to visit Scotland.

Scott smiled sweetly and looked over Fielding's shoulder to where Paula stood, frowning with worry, trying to melt into the wall. Scott nodded a greeting to Paula then made a deliberate show of looking down at Fielding. 'You're going to have to give me more of a clue, DCI Fielding.'

'You know exactly what I mean, lady. Bringing Carol Jordan in here to meet your client under the pretence of being your intern. Do you think my head buttons up the back?'

Scott's expression was of amused condescension. 'I don't understand why you're so upset. Carol isn't a serving officer. She's entitled to explore new career options. She approached me asking for the opportunity to shadow me to decide whether a career in the law might be for her. I was willing to take that at face value and not assume she was trying to infiltrate my office on your behalf.'

'On *my* behalf?' Fielding sounded like a gasket about to blow.

'It wouldn't be the first time your colleagues have tried to undermine my attempts to provide my clients with the best possible defence.'

'That's a disgraceful allegation,' Fielding spluttered.

'No worse than your imputation of inappropriate motives to me and Carol.'

'So why was she here, if not to try and compromise my operation?'

'How could she do that? Are you suggesting your officers are going to sneak around behind your back and leak things you should be disclosing to the defence anyway? All out of some misplaced loyalty to a retired colleague? It must be depressing to have such little faith in your team, DCI Fielding.' Scott turned away, her fingers on the door handle.

'I trust my team,' Fielding spat, her words like sharp little darts aimed at Scott's heart.

'Good. Then shall we get on with our "no comment" interview? And perhaps I could have disclosure of the fingermark evidence?' The last word and the last smile to the defence, Scott thought as she sailed back to her client's side.

59

Bradfield Moor Secure Hospital perched on the side of a hill on the north-western side of the city at the point where cultivated greenery gave way to the untamed hodge-podge of moorland vegetation. The buildings were angled so they faced down the hill at trees and roofs and lawns and shrubberies and flowerbeds rather than the weatherbeaten grasses and stunted shrubs of the peat bogs above. Tony had once described it to Carol as a Victorian metaphor directed at the patients within. 'They're supposed to turn their backs on the jungle of madness and become part of the ordered consensus below,' he'd said. Typical Tony, she thought, then felt irritated with herself for enjoying the richness of his take on the world. Now he was the one implicitly accused of madness and she was the one with the task of restoring him to the mainstream.

The hospital had extensive grounds and once she had cleared the security gates and parked well away from the buildings, Carol clipped the leash on Flash and let her out of the Land Rover. The sky was grey and heavy with the promise of rain, but it was still only a promise. She walked down the driveway in the teeth of a stiff breeze and when she was sure there was nobody around, she let the dog run free. As she'd done the night before, Flash ranged across the terrain but kept returning to her mistress without being summoned, before taking off on another zigzag run. Carol let the dog run for quarter of an hour, then put her back in the Landie with a bowl of water and a handful of treats.

By the time she reached the main entrance, she could feel a few drops of rain. 'Not a moment too soon,' she muttered, pushing the door open. The reception area was the usual institutional beige and grey, but someone had taken a little effort and imagination to make it more appealing. There were attractive photographs of tranquil mountain scenery around the walls and a pair of large blue glazed pots containing an assortment of house plants. Too heavy to be lifted and thrown, of course, Carol recognised. Off to one side was a doorway without a door leading to a seating area where visitors could wait before being processed and allowed in to see inmates. Behind the glassed-in reception desk, one woman was on the phone, another at a computer.

Carol stood patiently waiting for one of them to pause in their vital tasks to deal with her. It took a couple of minutes, but the woman on the phone eventually finished her conversation and slid open a panel in the glass. 'Visiting hours don't begin till noon,' she said, not unkindly. 'They should have told you that at the main gate.'

'I'm not a visitor.' Carol produced the old warrant card that had got her on to the premises and flashed it at the women. 'I'd like to see Maggie Spence.'

'Have you got an appointment?'

'No.'

'Can you tell me what it's in connection with?'

'It's confidential.'

The woman at the computer glanced up at the word, like a dog picking up a scent. She frowned momentarily, then her face cleared. 'I've seen you with Dr Hill,' she said, smiling. 'Molly, this lady works with Dr Hill when he's doing his profiling.'

Molly squeezed a smile out. 'I'll see if Mrs Spence is available.' She slid the panel shut and returned to the phone. A brief conversation, glancing at Carol a couple of times, then she replaced the phone and reopened the panel. 'She's coming through.' She produced a clipboard and handed Carol a pen. 'If you wouldn't mind signing in?'

Carol completed the formalities and was pinning a visitor pass to her jacket when a heavy door to one side of the desk clicked open and a woman emerged. Somewhere in her mid to late fifties, Maggie Spence looked like a woman for whom comfort was the headline priority. She wore loose khaki chinos topped by a baggy blue T-shirt and a hand-knitted multicoloured cardigan. A pair of scarlet-rimmed glasses perched on the end of a nose that wouldn't have looked out of place on Santa Claus. Her plump face was lined with the tell-tale tracks of smiles rather than frowns. Seeing Carol, she gave an automatic grin. 'Hi, I'm Maggie Spence. I gather you wanted to talk to me?' She extended a hand and Carol found her fingers enveloped in a warm grip.

'I'm Carol Jordan,' she said. 'Thanks for seeing me. Is there somewhere we can talk?'

Maggie glanced at the visitors' waiting area. 'Molly said it was confidential, right?' Carol nodded. 'This is too public, then. Come with me and we'll use my office.'

Carol followed as Maggie used a swipe card to lead her through a series of locked doors and short hallways to a neat little room with a view across the grounds to the distant moors. Apparently the staff were allowed to enjoy the wild grandeur of nature. Maggie's office was crammed with books, files and paper, but unlike Tony's, everything was organised in neat piles. The only wall space not fitted with shelves was covered by a colourful patchwork hanging that appeared to be an impressionistic image of a mountain landscape. Maggie waved Carol to a chair and settled herself behind the tidy desk. 'So, what's all this about?'

Carol took Tony's letter out of her bag. 'I'm here under false colours, I'm afraid. I'm not a police officer any longer. I'm working with Bronwen Scott, who is a criminal defence lawyer.'

Maggie leaned forward and opened her mouth to speak. But Carol held up a hand. 'Please. Hear me out?' Maggie subsided, but the smile was gone.

Carol cut to the chase. 'Tony Hill was arrested last night on suspicion of committing two murders. You know Tony. You know how absurd that is. But there is some circumstantial evidence and a cop who has decided this is how she's going to make her name. I'm working with his lawyer to establish his innocence.' She pushed the letter across to Maggie. 'He's asking for your help.'

Maggie looked stunned. 'Tony? Arrested? Are you sure?'

'I've just come from Skenfrith Street police station. I know it's hard to believe—'

'Hard to believe? It's surreal. I've never met a man with more compassion. The idea that he could intentionally kill anyone is ridiculous.'

'Unfortunately, not everyone knows him like we do. And he doesn't come across like most blokes.'

Maggie gave a little snort of laughter. 'No kidding. All the same. Working in here, you think you've heard everything. And then you walk in and tell me Tony Hill's suspected of murder. Incredible. Poor Tony.' She picked up the letter and pushed her glasses up her nose. She read it carefully then put it down on the desk. 'All right. We have some data protection issues here. I can't let you have access to our incident log because of our duty of confidentiality to staff and patients. But because I have Tony's permission, I believe I can give you copies of entries in that log that relate to him, provided that I redact the names of the patients involved. Will that give you what you need?'

Carol nodded. 'I don't need much in the way of detail. All I'm interested in are the dates and the nature of the incidents.'

Maggie nodded. She pulled her keyboard towards her and started hammering the keys with the energy of someone who had learned her skills on an old manual typewriter. Every now and again she paused and massaged her forehead with her fingertips. 'Luckily everything's online these days,' she muttered. 'And searchable.'

After a few minutes, she said, 'I'm going to cut and paste all the incidents involving Tony into a separate document then I can redact any identifying features relating to patients and I can print it out for you. That fine?'

Carol nodded. 'Perfect.'

The tip of Maggie's tongue slipped out between her lips as she concentrated on what she was doing. Finally, she looked across at Carol and smiled. 'That's it. Four incidents. I expect you already knew about the knee?'

A swirl of recalled emotion caught Carol unawares. She had a vivid recollection of the axe attack that had left Tony lying in a hospital bed and its aftermath. No need for redaction there. Lloyd Allen's name was carved on her memory. 'I was around at the time,' she said calmly, hiding what was going on beneath the surface.

Just then the door swung open behind her. Carol turned in time to catch the arrival of Aidan Hart, Clinical Director of Bradfield Moor. It had been at least a year since she'd seen him last and time was definitely not on his side. He didn't look as if he'd gained weight, but somehow, his face had grown pasty and jowly. Although he'd barely turned forty, there were deep lines between his eyebrows, and the whites of his eyes looked liverish. She'd never considered him attractive – particularly given what she knew about him – but now he was becoming positively repulsive. 'What the hell is going on here?' he demanded. For a psychologist, his interrogatory techniques seemed somewhat lacking.

Maggie was clearly inured to his belligerence. 'I'm just sorting out something Dr Hill asked for,' she said calmly.

'On whose authority?' Hart moved further into the room, using his height and bulk to dominate the women.

Maggie was undominated. She picked up Tony's letter and waved it at him. 'On Dr Hill's authority. He has the right to access his own records.'

Hart looked around him theatrically. 'I don't see Dr Hill here.'

'His letter authorises Ms Jordan here to access the information on his behalf.'

'He can't do that. It's a data protection issue.'

Maggie shook her head. 'I've redacted everything that could identify patients or other staff.'

'I'm not prepared to release any of our records to a third party, however redacted they are. She's not a police officer any more, you know. She's here under false pretences.'

'No, she's not, she told me that.'

Hart's crocodile smile crept across his face. 'She didn't tell the gatehouse staff or reception. She used police ID to bypass our security.'

Carol shrugged. 'I needed photo ID. That was all I had. I never said I was a serving police officer.'

Two stripes of scarlet appeared on his cheeks, as if a child had drawn on his face with lipstick. 'Don't split hairs with me, Miss Jordan. I'd like you to leave now.' He was wholly focused on her, but beyond him, Carol could see Maggie's fingers move stealthily on the keyboard.

'Not without what I came for. It's completely uncontroversial. We could easily get a court order.' Carol wasn't going to give up without a fight.

'Get one, then.' He threw the door open. 'Maggie, show Miss Jordan out, would you?'

'No point in making a fuss,' Maggie said, taking Carol's elbow and steering her to the door. Hart watched them leave, then, as Maggie opened the first locked door, he turned and marched off in the opposite direction. Maggie looked after him and smirked. 'I figured something as menial as seeing you off the premises would be beneath him. He is the absolute antithesis of a class act. I don't know how Tony puts up with him. I don't know how *I* do, come to that.'

As she talked, she led the way towards reception. But just before they emerged into the foyer, she turned abruptly into another office. A young man in a nurse's tunic sat at a desk, working on a spreadsheet. He looked up when they walked in and grinned. 'You owe me a drink.' He leaned across the desk and picked up a few sheets of paper from the printer tray.

'Thanks, Stephen.' Maggie accepted the papers and handed them to Carol. 'There you are. Tuck them away so the snitches on reception can't see them. Now it really is time to go, Carol.'

'Thanks. Nice move,' Carol said as she followed Maggie into the corridor. 'I have the impression you've done that before.'

'We look after each other here,' Maggie said. 'Aidan only looks after number one. Tell Tony, chin up.'

On her way out, Carol made a point of glaring at the

receptionists. Anything else would have looked suspicious. She didn't so much as glance at the papers until she was out of sight of the security guards on the front gate. Then she pulled in to the first woodland track she came to for a read. It wasn't easy to make sense of the redacted reports, but when she compared them with the dates Nadia Wilkowa had been in Bradfield Moor, one thing rapidly became clear.

Tony had been treated for a nosebleed following an incident with a patient on a day when Nadia Wilkowa had been there. 'You fucking beauty,' Carol said, kissing the sheet of paper. The first piece of evidence against Tony had been perfectly undermined.

60

The absence of their bosses didn't let the workers at Tellit Communications off the hook. They knew their computers recorded every detail of their working lives. Their keystrokes were counted, their phone calls timed, their absences from either form of communication logged and monitored. The workers were so wrapped up in what they were paid to do that they barely looked around them. So Rob Morrison had been in his office for a good twenty minutes before Gareth Taylor appeared in his doorway.

'Marie Mather's husband phoned earlier,' he said. 'I was the only one in, so I picked up the call. Apparently she's been taken to hospital with a suspected burst appendix.'

Rob winced. 'That sounds painful. Did he say how long she'd be off?'

Gareth shook his head. 'He said he'd phone again when he had a better idea of the prognosis, but not to expect her in for the rest of the week. He sounded fucking terrified,' he added with a sneer.

'That's not a great start to a new job,' Rob said.

'I don't suppose she planned it.' Gareth pushed off from the door jamb and turned back to the busy room. Unobserved, Rob gave a sly smile. Marie Mather's big ideas had definitely been put on ice and he wasn't in the least sorry about that.

Paula had felt her phone vibrate against her thigh while they'd been conducting their miserable 'no comment' interview with Tony Hill but she'd known better than to take it out in front of Fielding. The DCI was obviously right on the edge of losing her temper and Paula definitely didn't want to be her target.

The interview had run into the sand when Fielding had started repeating questions. Bronwen Scott had leaned back in her chair and smiled with the weary charm of one who has seen it all before. 'Charge my client or release him,' she'd said.

Fielding had thrown her pen on the table. 'We're continuing our inquiries. We have search warrants for Dr Hill's home and his office, and officers are conducting those searches right now. So we won't be releasing your client just yet.' She'd pushed her chair back and stabbed a finger at the recording equipment. 'This interview terminated at 11.17 a.m.' Then she'd stalked out of the room, leaving Paula to make an apologetic face and follow. She took the chance to glance at her phone and see a message from Carol Jordan. 'Think the metal case might be portable anaesthetic unit? Check any missing? Check paramedics?'

Chiding herself for not having thought of that, Paula hurried to catch Fielding. 'Bloody woman,' Fielding snarled, climbing the stairs with the energy of fury. 'And bloody Carol Jordan.' She stopped in her tracks and turned on Paula and lowered her voice to a growl. 'Don't even think about leaking to Jordan.'

'I'm not stupid,' Paula said. 'But I did have a thought while you were asking Dr Hill about hospitals. That metal case the killer is carrying in the CCTV footage? What if it's portable anaesthetic apparatus? When he tips them into the car boots, he puts the box in and leans over them. We can't see what he's doing. What if he's putting them under so they can't escape or give the alarm?'

Fielding's face lit up. 'That's a bloody great idea, McIntyre.' She clapped her on the shoulder. 'Hill could easily have figured out how to get his hands on one of them. Head upstairs to the incident room and get that actioned right away. I want a check on hospitals that Nadia Wilkowa visited, see if they've had any portable anaesthesia units stolen. Paying particular attention to Bradfield Moor and Bradfield Cross. Although Tony Hill's credentials could get him in anywhere.' She looked almost gleeful. 'Bloody brilliant! Well done, McIntyre.' She bounded off up the stairs leaving Paula in her wake, feeling stricken. The suggestion was meant to shake Fielding's certainties. Instead, it seemed merely to have reinforced them.

'Bloody hell,' Paula muttered, heading up to the incident room. If they uncovered any stolen anaesthetic sets, that would give fresh life to the investigation. At least she could set the guys on to checking out paramedics rather than solely focusing on Tony. She wondered whether the search teams were suitably baffled by Tony's life – psychology textbooks, computer games, superhero comic books, case notes and cryptic memos to himself. She couldn't imagine they'd find anything to link him to the victims or the crimes. Wasting police time, that's what this was.

Somehow, she didn't think anybody would be charging Fielding.

61

Buoyed up by her success at Bradfield Moor, Carol was eager to get to the Central Library so she could pursue the next stage in her investigation. But her life wasn't quite as simple as it had been a few days before. She couldn't just drive straight to the library and immerse herself in bound copies of the newspaper for as long as it took; she had Flash to consider.

She texted Bronwen to fill her in on the outcome of her inquiries at the hospital then let Flash run free again while she walked several hundred yards up the track and back again. As before, the dog ranged far and wide but always returned at intervals to make sure Carol was still there and, presumably, in one piece. After this second run, Carol considered the dog could be left in the Landie for a while. Later, she could take the dog down to the canal and let her have a walk along the towpath, safe from the city traffic.

Carol left the Land Rover in a multi-storey near the library, cracking the window open to give the dog air. She'd always been a little intimidated by the massive Victorian building. Its highly polished marble columns, staircase and wall panels came in colours she associated with the sort of old-fashioned butcher's shop where the meat had lost its first bloom. There were no books in the grand entrance hall to absorb sound, and every noise seemed magnified by the hard surfaces, echoing in a swirl of footsteps and snatches of speech.

She hurried up the stairs to the octagonal gallery where the local collections were kept. Bookshelves lined the walls from floor to ceiling, starting with ancient leather spines at one end and travelling through a chronological catalogue of book bindings to privately published memoirs bound with adhesive cloth tape.

At the far end stood a line of angled wooden tables, designed so that a person could sit and browse the large bound volumes of the newspaper collection. Here, this year's copies of the *Bradfield Evening Sentinel Times* were fastened together week by week, clamped in place between long thin wooden batons. Carol found an empty chair and logged in with her tablet to the library's wifi. Then she settled down with the previous week's papers, working backwards from the day before Nadia Wilkowa's disappearance.

She pored over the news pages, checking even the shortest snippet of news. Then she moved on to Births, Marriages and Deaths. She'd settled on fifty as a sensible upper-age limit for her target. Whenever she found a woman in the right age group, she turned to her tablet and went to the online edition for the day in question. A few months before, the *BEST* had started offering those who placed notices in the BMD section of the paper the opportunity to post a digital photograph in the online edition. It was a clever marketing ploy – it cost the paper nothing, but it generated a huge amount of goodwill. Now, when people died, their families and friends chose their favourite photo and up-loaded it to the BMD pages online. So Carol was able to ascertain quickly whether the dead women were blondes.

It was a slow, painstaking process. By lunchtime, she only had two potential candidates. One had died, aged forty-four, 'after a long battle with cancer. Beloved wife of Trevor, mum to Greta, Gwyneth and Gordon, gran to Adele. Much missed by her dear friends from the Fleece darts team.' Her blonde looked as if it had come from a bottle. Somehow Carol didn't think a killer with the control-freak tendencies Tony had outlined would allow his wife to join a pub darts team.

The other was, on the face of it, more promising. The woman was thirty-five and she'd died with her two small children in a motorway pile-up on the M62. Carol reckoned from her colouring that she was a natural blonde. There was no BMD announcement, just a news story about the accident. A lorry driver had been critically injured and two other motorists hurt in the late-night collision. An eye-witness said the lorry had appeared to swerve without warning across the outside lane before smashing into the crash barrier. The photograph of the woman showed her holding a baby on her lap with a toddler cuddled into her side. To Carol's eye, she didn't look very relaxed. But people often didn't in posed photos.

According to a short follow-up in the following day's paper, the woman had been taking the children to visit their grandparents in York. Ironically, she'd set off late in the evening to avoid the traffic. So said a police spokesman who gave the standard spiel about the dangers of driving while overtired.

Carol couldn't find the news stories in the online edition, so she took photocopies. She decided to walk the dog then return and do another month. That would make three in total. She reckoned that was far enough back.

It was a relief to be out in the fresh air and Flash showed her pleasure at Carol's return with extravagant tail wagging and a long pink tongue aimed at her owner's face. Carol avoided it with an exclamation of disgust and let the dog jump free. Ten minutes' brisk walking brought them to the Minster Basin. Carol tied Flash to a table outside one of the pubs and went inside to get a glass of wine, a bowl of water and a bag of crisps. She gave the dog some water and shared her crisps. She let her gaze wander idly across the boats in the marina, stopping short when she spotted a stern she recognised. There couldn't be two boats with that name, not painted in the same design. How in the name of God had Tony managed to get the narrowboat from Worcester to Bradfield? A man who could barely navigate from his own front door to work?

Even as she stared, a stocky man with a shaved head and a tight suit made from an unfortunate shiny grey material backed out of the main hatchway. He was carrying a laptop, its connection cable trailing behind him. He stumbled ashore and put the computer in the boot of a Toyota saloon. Then he returned to the boat. Either Tony was being burgled or this was Fielding's search team. She didn't mind which, but it might be fun to freak them out.

She untied the dog and the pair of them crossed the cobbles to the boat. The dog was reluctant at first, but with Carol's encouragement she jumped aboard, followed by her owner. 'Hello?' Carol called.

Almost immediately, the bald head reappeared, a frown on his pink face. 'Who the—' And then recognition dawned. He looked over his shoulder. 'Harry?'

'What are you doing on my friend's boat?' Carol demanded. Flash obligingly gave a couple of brusque barks.

'We're—' This time his shout was more frantic. 'Harry?'

'What?' The voice came from below.

Baldy's face creased with the effort of working out what to say. 'It's DCI Jordan,' he finally settled on.

'Ex-DCI Jordan,' Carol gently reminded him. 'You still haven't explained who you are and what you're doing on Dr Hill's boat.'

'We've got a warrant,' a nasal Scouse voice said.

'Might I see it?' Carol said sweetly. 'And your ID?'

Baldy turned away from her and held a brief muttered exchange with his colleague. He swung back to face her and presented two sets of ID and a search warrant. Carol gave them a quick once-over and handed them back. 'Thanks. You can't be too careful these days. Shame you've had a wasted journey,' she added.

'What do you mean, a wasted journey?' Baldy was wary.

Carol smiled. 'She'll have to release him. Her case is falling to bits around her ears.' She shook her head. 'They should never have disbanded the MIT.' Then she turned away and leapt ashore, dog at her heels. Pathetic, really, but she'd enjoyed herself. A pleasant interlude before heading back to the library.

By half past three, she had added one more possible to the pile. Another natural-looking blonde who'd died from cancer aged thirty-three. Unmarried but with a partner, according to the death notice. Three sisters and two brothers, a slew of nieces and nephews. Carol checked she'd copied the page to her laptop then packed up.

The question now was what to do with the results of her inquiries. There wasn't any point in sharing them with Bronwen or even Paula; this was something for Tony to ponder. She wondered whether the custody sergeant at Skenfrith Street would allow her to speak to Tony, in her assumed role as assistant to his lawyer.

There was only one way to find out.

62

Stradbrook Tower had been the city council's final mistake of the sixties. Paula reckoned they must have been the last local authority in the country to commission a tower block for council tenants. It had been the destination of last resort for residents for over ten years, but in the early eighties the council gave up trying to force their tenants into the damp-ridden condensation-plagued flats. The block had stood empty for a few years, then a bright spark in the housing department had realised it was relatively close to the mushrooming campus of Bradfield University. A deal was done, six months of remedial work was carried out and now the flats were home to hundreds of students.

It was still a sore point with the locals, who felt, not unreasonably, that the flats could have been made habitable for them rather than the privileged scions of the middle class. Or spoilt rich bastards, as they preferred to think of them. And so the area around the tower block had become the perennial site for the ceremonial burning of stolen cars. From where she was standing, Paula could see three burnt-out wrecks. The one nearest to her had belonged to Bev McAndrew.

The ANPR system had picked it up a little after two in the afternoon, careering out of the car park at Bradfield Central station. By the time they'd alerted BMP, it had traversed the city centre, heading out past the university towards Stradbrook Tower. Control had scrambled the nearest Traffic car, which had arrived in time to see two lads, heads covered by hoodies, jump out of the car and toss lighted petrol bombs inside as they fled.

Flames filled the car, and before the traffic cops could even release their small fire extinguisher from its clips, it exploded with a low boom. It was such a regular occurrence that nobody so much as ventured out on to their balconies to watch.

'There goes our trace evidence,' Ficlding said. 'Wee fuds.'

'But not at Tony Hill's hand,' Paula pointed out.

'We don't know that.' Fielding scowled. 'We don't know what he told Carol Jordan to set in motion.'

Paula fought to hide her scorn. 'Carol would never destroy evidence,' she said. 'That would be a betrayal of everything she believes in.'

'Isn't that what working with Bronwen Scott is? You lie down with dogs, you get up with fleas.' Fielding turned on her heel and walked over to the sheepish traffic cops. 'Find out who those wee thugs were,' she said. 'I want to know how they knew to steal that car.'

Carol still wasn't accustomed to wearing a visitor's pass in a police station. It felt wrong to sign in when she arrived at Skenfrith Street, to have to wait till someone came to escort her past the front counter, to be confined to the places where she was led. At least she'd had the good sense to phone Bronwen Scott's office and have them pave the way for her solo prisoner visit. It had, she suspected, saved her a degree of humiliation.

While she was waiting in the tiny airless room they'd been in the previous night, Carol powered up her laptop and opened the details of the women in the death notices. She took out the photocopies of the news stories and set them down beside the laptop. Then she softly drummed the pads of her fingers on the blank metal flanking the mousepad. Realising what she was doing she stopped abruptly, cross with herself. There was no need, no reason, no point in nervousness. Whatever their history, there was no future for her and Tony. She was doing this simply to save Paula from being caught up in a career-wrecking miscarriage of justice. This wasn't about Tony. Businesslike efficiency, that was what she needed now. Not twitching like a teenager.

The door opened and Tony walked in. As with all prisoners held in police cells, his appearance had started the downward slide away from respectability. His hair was unruly and unkempt. He had a day's growth of stubble, an oddly pathetic patchwork of dark and silver. He wasn't young any more, she thought with a stab of sadness. Because that meant she wasn't either. His clothes were crumpled and creased and he'd begun to look more criminal than the average citizen.

His face lit up when he saw Carol on her own. 'It's good to see you,' he said. 'I've never had a problem with my own company, but time passes slowly when you've nothing to read.'

'And no computer games to play.' There was no lightness in her tone, no room to interpret her remark as friendly. 'I looked through the newspaper archive. Obviously, it's not definitive . . . '

'But almost every family still puts a death notice in the paper. Undertakers steer them in that direction, and it's a shortcut to let friends and workmates know the funeral details.'

'And the *Sentinel Times* publishes photos in its online edition.'

He grinned. 'Of course. I wondered how you were going to weed out the blondes. I'd forgotten about that. Imagine what a miserable job that would have been until recently – calling up the recently bereaved and going, "Was your wife blonde? And was it natural?"'

She couldn't help a wry smile. She'd taken part in some crass inquiries over the years, because sometimes that was the only way to secure the information they needed. She wasn't sorry about this particular forward march of technology. 'So, there are two death notices and one news item that seem to me to fit the bill.' She turned the laptop to face him and slid the photocopies across.

He read everything through once, then repeated the process more slowly. He rubbed his chin, the rasp of his hand across the stubble clearly audible. Then he pushed the photocopies back towards Carol. 'No death notice that corresponds to this?'

She shook her head. 'Not that I could find. Her parents live in York, though. So maybe it was in the local paper there.'

Tony looked grim. 'If it was, it will have been put there by her parents. Not by the husband.'

'What makes you say that?'

'I think this might be the one.'

'Why?'

He shifted the laptop so they could both see the screen. 'This one first. She had enough freedom to be out there playing darts in a pub. If I'm right, this guy is a control freak. He's

399

never going to let her out of the house with a bunch of other women to have a social encounter that doesn't include him.'

'That's what I thought too. And the other death notice?'

'Look at her family group. Five siblings and a football team of nieces and nephews. Obviously a close sibling group. A man as controlling as this wants his victim to be isolated, not at the heart of an intimate family group.'

'We don't know that they're close,' Carol objected.

'We don't, that's true. It's a reasonable assumption, though. But even if they weren't, the killer I have in mind wouldn't acknowledge their existence. He wouldn't include them in the death notice at all. No, Carol –' he stabbed the photocopies with a finger – 'check this out. No death notice. No quote from the grieving widower.'

'Maybe he was too grief-stricken.'

Tony shrugged. 'It's possible. But look at this photo. She's strung as tight as a bow string.'

'Some people don't like having their photographs taken.'

'She's posing with her kids. Most women are so concerned about how the kids are coming across and whether they're behaving that they lose their own self-consciousness. I think she's anxious. I'd go so far as to say scared. That's the kind of expression you see on the faces of victims of abuse. Terrified of putting a foot wrong, of provoking the rage that's always just round the corner.'

'I think you're reading a lot into a photograph.' Without even thinking about it, Carol had fallen back into her old patterns with Tony. She was the test-bed for his ideas. He threw them at her and she poked them and prodded them and pronounced them fit for purpose. Or not.

'It's one small part of a bigger picture, Carol. Who sets off after eleven at night with two small children to drive to York? To visit parents who are definitely past the first flush of youth and probably like to be tucked up in bed by then?'

'It says there. She wanted to miss the traffic.'

'If you want to miss the traffic, you leave at eight, not eleven,' Tony scoffed. 'You set off at eleven in the car with the kids because you're in fear for your life.'

There was a pause while Carol considered his words. Finally, she said, 'It's a long shot.'

His shoulders slumped. 'It's always a bloody long shot. But it's paid off more often than I have any right to expect. Carol, I'm penned up in this bloody awful place. I'm accused of two murders that I didn't commit. If long shots are all I have, I'll take them.'

'I understand that. But it's probably whistling in the dark.'

The mask slipped and she caught a glimpse of his despair. 'Carol, I need you to help me. For whatever reason, Fielding sincerely wants to nail me. And I don't know anyone who has a better chance of getting me out of this mess than you. I know you still blame me for Michael and Lucy, but I didn't hold the knife. Yes, I made a mistake. I set my focus too narrowly. And believe me, nobody could give me a harder time for that than I give myself. But I don't think any reasonable person could have figured out what Vance's agenda was at that point. I don't believe there's another profiler around who would have worked it out. I did my best and it turned out crap. Don't think I don't know that.' His eyes were glistening with tears, his voice cracking with emotion. 'Carol, you've been the most important person in my life since I first got to know you. I would take a bullet for you. I'd have taken a bullet for Michael, for your sake.' He gave a wry smile. 'Maybe not for Lucy, mind.'

His words twisted in her gut like a knife. The dark gallows humour struck a chord in spite of her determination not to give him an inch. 'Don't be a smartarse,' she said, surprised to find her own voice catching in her throat.

'We all make mistakes, Carol. Sometimes they're more expensive than others. But I don't deserve to lose you,' he said, spreading his hands in appeal.

Abruptly she slammed the laptop shut and grabbed it. 'I'll check it out,' she said gruffly, stumbling to her feet and heading for the door. She wasn't willing to let him back into her life. Not now, not ever. No matter what he said. No matter how well he manipulated her emotions. And that was all that was going on here. It wasn't real. Just Tony playing her for his own benefit. It didn't change anything. Michael and Lucy were still dead. Well, she'd show him she was a better person than him. She'd do the right thing because it was the right thing. Not for his sake. For its own sake.

Carol had no recollection of leaving the police station. The blur resolved itself as she reached the Land Rover. She climbed inside and leaned her forearms on the steering wheel, staring straight ahead, trying to recover herself. After a couple of minutes, she composed herself enough to take out her phone and send a message to Stacey:

> Everything you can give me on Gareth Taylor from Banham village. ASAP.

Now it was simply a question of waiting.

A moment's inspiration was never enough in police work. Generally, it had to be followed up by the painstaking slog of asking questions and making checks. And then sometimes it paid off. Paula might have scored the credit for inserting the idea of a portable anaesthetic machine into the investigation, but it had taken a hardworking detective constable bashing the phones all day to come up with the strongest lead.

He bounced up to Paula's desk with all the abandon of a small boy who's won a treasure hunt. 'I've got a stolen portable anaesthetic machine for you,' he said, waving a piece of paper at her.

She couldn't help feeling a lift in her spirits. Sometimes the slightest forward motion in an investigation felt like a giant stride. 'Good work. Where was it nicked?'

'There was an emergency services conference five weeks ago at Manchester University. They had an exhibition hall full of stands for equipment manufacturers. Everything from ambulances to satellite radios. And a company that makes portable anaesthetic units had one that went a bit too portable, if you get my meaning?' He grinned at her as he handed her the details of the exhibition. 'It went missing overnight from their stand. They'd been using it to demo how it works on site.'

'Did they report it to us?'

He shook his head. 'The organisers persuaded them there was no point. They refunded their exhibitors' fee, so the company weren't out of pocket and the organisers didn't have to deal with the embarrassment of having cops crawling all over their exhibition. That's why it didn't show up on our records.'

'Fantastic. Well done. So, does anybody have any idea who might have nicked it?' Even as she spoke, Paula knew it was too much to hope for.

Now he looked crestfallen. 'If they have any suspicions, they're not letting on.'

'Have you got a map of the layout of the exhibition?'

His eyebrows rose in surprise. 'Of course. No, I haven't. I didn't think of that. I'll track it down.'

'And a list of accredited attendees. One other thing – what about the gases that the machine uses? Did the thief get those as well?'

He nodded. 'Apparently the machine was loaded up with the real thing. Bloody stupid, if you ask me.'

Paula sighed. 'If you don't expect to be a victim of crime, you don't always take the sensible precautions. Still, nice work. Let me have a look when you've got that exhibition map. Plus a list of delegates and exhibitors.'

He took off, bounce restored at the prospect of having something useful to do. Once the PC had done his job, she'd have to persuade Fielding to check whether it was possible that Tony could have attended the conference or the exhibition. Paula couldn't help hoping he'd have a cast-iron alibi for the days in question. It was a pity she couldn't reveal the ultimate source of this latest development to her boss. Demonstrating Tony's usefulness to the investigation might remind Fielding of his value to BMP but it probably wasn't the best way to improve Paula's career prospects.

63

Stacey's speed had always been a thing of beauty. Work-ing at less than full stretch thankfully hadn't blunted her skills. Within half an hour of Carol sending her text, Stacey had replied with a hyperlink to a cloud-based appli-cation. Tapping the link took Carol to the fruits of Stacey's searches.

Under Gareth Taylor's name was a list: date of birth, National Insurance number, driving licence details, passport number, address, vehicle registration number, bank details and current account balance, and the name of his employer, Tellit Communications. He had no criminal record and a first-class degree in computer science. Photographs from his passport application and his driving licence were next. Then came a separate list of details for his late wife. A note from Stacey read, Can't find a UK bank account. No employ-ment history after marriage. NHS records for both coming later. At the bottom of the report, there was another note from Stacey.

Tellit are more than just a mobile phone company.
They deal in a wide range of electronic
communication. Among their contracts are the
comms system used by the ANPR cameras and also
one of the main systems used by fire and
ambulance services. Working for Tellit could give
GT access to a vast range of data. His actual job
seems quite low level for his skills. But sometimes
the side benefits of data access outweigh that!

Carol read the note with an increasing surge of excitement. A viable suspect. She didn't know much about Gareth
Taylor, but already she had more belief in him as a potential
killer than in Tony. She forwarded the link to Paula, adding
a note: Check with ANPR for any sightings of Taylor's
vehicle near body dumps, or homes and workplaces of
victims. Am going to stake out Tellit office/Taylor's
house.

The address Stacey had supplied for Gareth Taylor's workplace was on the other side of the city centre, so Carol
decided to change car parks. But before she did, she called
Stacey. 'Brilliant job,' she said as soon as Stacey answered.
'Does Tellit have a staff car park?'

'I'll get right back to you.'

Five minutes ticked past to the sound of Carol beating
time on her steering wheel. Then her phone beeped. The
text from Stacey read, No dedicated car park. But discount
parking in Ramshorn Street multi-storey.

Ten minutes later, Carol was cruising the car park, looking
for Gareth Taylor's red BMW. She found it on the third floor
but she couldn't find another slot with a view of his car. She
sat for a moment with her engine idling, wondering what to
do next. Now she knew where his wheels were, she could
always leave the car park and set up outside. But she'd have

to be careful where she chose. Leaving the multi-storey, drivers could turn left or right. If she parked facing the wrong way, she could be stranded, given the appalling turning circle of the Land Rover. Or she could circle round inside the car park, taking temporary station in areas that weren't, strictly speaking, parking spaces.

In the end, she settled for a side road a little further down the street. She could emerge quickly enough on his tail from there, she reckoned. The Land Rover was about as far from an ideal surveillance vehicle as it was possible to get, especially in the city centre, but the one advantage it possessed was its height. She could stay several cars behind Taylor and still remain in touch with his car. At this time of day, nothing moved faster than a crawl in town anyway, so it wasn't like she was going to lose him at the lights.

All the same, Carol knew she would have to find another solution if the surveillance ended up lasting any length of time. Wrong vehicle, not to mention that she was sitting on a double yellow line. She daren't leave the Landie in case she got ticketed, clamped or towed. Now she was beginning to realise how much she'd taken for granted when she had still been a copper. How in hell did private eyes manage any kind of effective stake-out?

Luckily for her nerves, she didn't have long to wait. Barely twenty minutes had passed when the scarlet nose of Taylor's BMW stopped at the exit barrier. He turned right, and Carol fell in behind him with three cars between them.

Their progress across town was slow, the rush-hour stream of buses, cars, vans and trams clogging the tight mesh of streets that had been built for horses and carts two centuries before. But as they left the city centre and moved into the outer suburbs, the traffic thinned and Carol had to work a bit harder at staying in touch but unobtrusive. From the route Taylor had taken, it looked as if he was heading home.

Carol couldn't help wondering where he was in his murderous cycle. Did he have another victim lined up? Was there already another woman in captivity? It was clear that he kept them before he killed him. Might he be headed back to an imprisoned victim right now?

The short-term answer to her question came just before the ring road, when he pulled off into an out-of-town development packed with the traditional selection of carpet warehouse, fast-food outlet, discount sofa store, white goods and computer emporia and a sprawling DIY megastore. For a brief uncomfortable moment she was right behind the BMW. She hung back while he parked in a distant area of the car park then watched as he jinked through the lines of parked cars to arrive at the DIY store entrance. He paused to retie his shoelace, and as he set off again, she could see he had a slight but noticeable limp. Just like Tony.

'Yes,' Carol hissed triumphantly. She left the Landie in the first available slot and ran after him. By the time she made it through the door, he'd vanished from sight. She hurried up to the aisle that bisected the shelves at the midway point and walked briskly along, scanning in both directions as she went.

She spotted him in the locks and home security section, checking padlocks and chains. It was a terrible cliché, but she supposed clichés only reached that status because there was truth in them. She turned down the next aisle, then came up behind him, pretending an interest in brass and chrome door furniture. He didn't turn his head. He selected a heavy padlock and started walking towards the rear of the store. Carol followed, keeping her distance and constantly ready to turn aside and examine whatever was on the shelves.

He was making for the trade counter, she quickly realised. Even though this was a different chain from the store she used for her own building requirements, they all had a similar layout. Taylor clearly knew his way around, making straight for the doorway that led to the timber-cutting area. He must be ordering or collecting made-to-measure wood, she thought. She found a vantage point where she could keep an eye on the doorway without looking suspicious, and stared unseeing at a catalogue of bathroom fittings.

Time trickled past, but Taylor didn't reappear. At first, Carol wasn't concerned. She knew from experience that it could take a while to straighten out a customer's requirements, especially if several different pieces were being ordered. But after ten minutes, she began to feel uneasy. This wasn't right.

At last, after twelve minutes had passed, she walked into the timber-cutting area. Behind the counter, a man in company livery was going through a sheaf of paperwork, comparing it to a computer screen. Another assistant leaned against a rack of different woods, deep in conversation with Gareth Taylor. *Fuck.* Carol crossed to a bin of scrap wood and rummaged through it, as if she were looking for something in particular. She pulled out a piece of plywood, pretended to check something on her phone, tutted and replaced it, then walked out. *Fuck.*

She returned to the bathroom fittings, cursing herself for her lack of patience. All she'd had to do was wait, but she couldn't even do that. Tony's words echoed in her head. 'We all make mistakes, Carol. Sometimes they're more expensive than others.' She pushed him to one side in her head, hoping this wasn't going to be one of the truly expensive ones.

Another fifteen minutes crawled by. And then the man from behind the counter appeared in the doorway, reaching above his head to grasp a metal shutter. Galvanised, Carol hurried over as he hunkered down to padlock it shut. 'Are you closed?'

He looked up at her. 'Aye. We close at half five. If you want some timber cutting, you'll have to come back in the morning.'

'Damn,' she said. 'I wondered – is there a loading entrance here, so I don't have to trail my wood through the store?'

The man straightened up. 'Not officially, like,' he said. 'But we've got a roller shutter at the rear for deliveries – we let people drive round and load up.'

She turned away, hollow with anger and disappointment. Not only had she made Taylor suspicious, she'd lost him. He'd clocked that she was taking an interest and he'd shaken her off. He could be anywhere now, doing anything. And she had nothing on him except a limp and Tony's theory based on a dead wife. Even Bronwen Scott would struggle to make something out of that.

Carol trudged to the exit, all her earlier exhilaration gone. Maybe she should call Paula and the pair of them could work out what to do next. But the way things were going, if justice was going to be served, Carol wasn't going to be the waitress.

At least driving a Land Rover Defender meant you never mislaid your vehicle in a car park. The high Landie stuck out even among the pick-up trucks and fat clumsy 4x4s. Head down, thinking hard, she set off. Given how full the car park was and how busy the store had been, it was surprising how few people were in sight. A cluster round the burger van, but mostly it was deserted. Unsurprisingly, Gareth Taylor's red BMW was no longer parked where it had been. She'd obviously lost him.

As she approached the Landie, Carol raised her arm over her head and pressed the door release button. It was always a bugger, this remote. You had to be right next to the driver's door before it conceded and the locks clicked open. She decided to let the dog out for a quick pee before they set off for wherever they were going next, so she turned away from the driver's door to walk round the back.

That was the only reason she saw Gareth Taylor coming at her with the taser.

64

Carol's message had given Paula a dilemma. Tracking Gareth
Taylor's car using the ANPR system wasn't a problem in
itself. But in the byzantine world of contemporary police
administration, every search had to be justified. And somewhere down the line, she'd have to explain why she'd asked
for this particular search at this particular time. An alert
defence lawyer might well pick up on the fact that she had
actioned a search at a point when Gareth Taylor's name had
never appeared in the official investigation. 'Woman's intu-
ition' wouldn't cut it, she knew that much.

As usual, when faced with intractable problems, Paula
sought refuge in nicotine. She sneaked out of the incident
room and huddled in a quiet corner of the car park, inhaling
and thinking. She couldn't see any point in coming clean to
Fielding. Her DCI was so committed to the idea of Tony Hill
that she would reject any lead emanating from him as automatically tainted. But if Paula left her own paper trail in her
notebook, pointing the finger at the defence as the source of

a tip-off, she might just get away with it. It would have to be a paper trail, though, since there were no texts from Bronwen Scott in her phone and she wasn't about to give Carol up as her source.

Satisfied that she'd come up with something that would cover her back, Paula returned to the incident room and sanctioned the ANPR request. Because she was Fielding's bagman, nobody questioned her authority and the data wheels started turning. She was about to go in search of her boss when DC Pat Cody called her over. 'Got a funny one here, skip,' he said, tapping his screen with a chewed ballpoint.

'What's that?'

'We put out a routine request for any female misper reports. A bloke phoned in this afternoon. Control passed the details on to us. I don't know if it's owt to do with us, but it's a funiosity, as my gran used to say. His name's Rob Morrison and he's Director of Operations at Tellit Communications' Bradfield office.'

'Tellit?' Gareth Taylor's workplace. Anything unusual connected to Tellit set the alarms flashing on Paula's radar.

'You know, the mobile phone and data network company? Apparently they started a new Director of Marketing this week, a woman called Marie Mather. She didn't turn in for work this morning but one of the staff took a call from her husband saying she'd been rushed to hospital with a suspected burst appendix. This Morrison guy decided to send flowers, so he rang Bradfield Cross to find out what ward she was on. And they've never heard of her. He tried the cottage hospital and they said the same. Her mobile's turned off, there's no answer to her home phone and the number he has for her husband goes straight to voicemail.' Cody scratched his head with the end of his pen then stuck it in his mouth like a cigar.

'She might be skiving off. Having a fun day out with her old man,' Paula said, not believing it for a moment.

'She might, except that she's just started this important new job. "Strategic", your man Morrison called it. And here's the thing. She's thirty-one, blonde, blue eyes, medium height and build and a professional woman. She fits our victim profile to a T.'

Paula felt a buzz of adrenalin surging through her. 'Which would mean that the suspect we have in custody isn't the killer.' She couldn't help smiling at that realisation.

Cody made a face. 'Not necessarily. I called this Morrison bloke. She left work about an hour before Hill checked in here. If he's keeping them before he kills them, he could have stashed her before he walked in here.' His turn to smile. 'That's the kind of brass neck a proper serial killer would have, isn't it?'

'Only in a film,' Paula said repressively. 'Have you told Fielding about this yet?'

He shook his head. 'It's not long in.'

'OK. Send a couple of uniforms over to her home address to see whether Mr and Mrs Mather are having a duvet day. Meanwhile, check with Bradfield Cross admissions. Maybe Mather is her own name and she was admitted under her married name. See whether anyone was brought in with a suspected burst appendix. Let's get our ducks in a row before we bother the DCI with this.' She didn't quite know what to make of this latest information. But if there was any chance at all that it might exonerate Tony, she'd strip Marie Mather's life to the bone.

Years of frontline policing kicked in and, faced with danger, Carol acted instinctively. She gave a banshee yell and lunged towards Taylor, aiming to knock him off balance. But he was equally quick off the mark and fired the taser before she covered the few feet between them. Her cry was cut off abruptly but her momentum carried her forward and he held out his arms to catch her before she hit the ground. He staggered under the impact but managed to keep his footing, thudding into the side of the Land Rover.

Taylor quickly looked around, but nobody seemed to be paying them any attention. He half-dragged, half-carried Carol round to the rear of the Landie, his brain efficiently processing the options. As soon as he'd got the big back door open, he'd be secure from prying eyes. He could chuck her in the back and improvise. If there was nothing to tie her up with, he could bang her head on the floor and knock her out for long enough to get her back to his place. That would show the bitch the kind of man she was dealing with. Who the fuck did she think she was, tracking him across the city like he was a common criminal? Well, he had her now. He'd soon show her who was boss. Finding out who she was and what she thought she was doing would be an unexpected pleasure.

He reached up and pushed the door handle upwards. It was stiff, and he grunted with the effort. As he struggled with the catch, Carol regained control of her limbs. She blinked repeatedly for a few seconds as he tried to get the taser aligned in his hand. The she snapped back into full consciousness. The arm that had been hanging loose at her side swept up in a long looping punch that connected with Taylor's ear.

He yelped, instinctively clapping his hand to the side of his head and letting the taser fall to the ground. Carol saw it fall, but he still had one arm gripping her close and she had no chance of reaching it. She pulled her arm back for a second punch but he saw this one coming and grabbed her wrist.

But Carol didn't mind fighting dirty. She ducked her head

and clamped her teeth round his wrist, clenching her jaw as hard as she could. Simultaneously, she brought her knee up sharply between his legs, making satisfying contact with his balls. *Bastard, bastard, bastard.* Taylor's breath shot out in a long squeal and he let her go. But as he let her go, he rammed his fist hard into her gut, forcing the air out of her lungs in a searing rush. Reflexively, she released her bite and gasped for air. They reeled around each other like a pair of late-night drunks.

Carol lunged to the ground, aiming for the taser. But he wasn't giving up. As her hand closed around the black plastic, he stamped hard on her wrist, numbing everything below it. He leaned over her and grabbed the taser. 'You fucking bitch,' he gasped as he pressed the trigger. Her body jerked and twitched then lay still.

This time he'd get the Land Rover door open before he lifted her up. He strained at the handle again, pushing it upwards. But as soon as the catch released, the heavy metal door catapulted towards Taylor, the edge catching him in the middle of the forehead. He clutched his head and staggered, tripping over Carol's prone body and crashing to the ground. A flying bundle of black-and-white fur flew through the air and struck him in the chest, taking him down. Taylor heard the deep terrifying growl of a hostile dog as he hit the tarmac. He took his hand away from the bump on his forehead and saw gleaming white teeth bared inches from his face. He screamed.

Groggy but almost in control of her limbs, Carol pushed herself upright and shouted 'Help!' at the top of her lungs. What the fuck was she supposed to do now? She had no handcuffs, no authority. Taylor was squirming at her feet, screaming at Flash, who had him pinned down, front paws on his chest, slavering mouth dripping on his face. A couple of blokes had peeled away from the hot-dog van and were running towards them. Carol reached inside the Land Rover and pulled out the lovely new tack hammer she'd bought only a few days before. It wasn't heavy, but she knew she could do some serious damage with it if she had to. With her free hand, she pulled out her phone and called Paula. She had a funny feeling it was going to be a long night.

65

Day twenty-eight

When she got Carol's call, Paula wasted no time on explanations. She yelled for Cody and ran for her car, gunning the engine till he piled in next to her. She tore out of the car park with a screech of tyres. Unlike TV cop shows, she didn't let the crisis go on playing itself out till she personally made it to the scene. She called up the control room on her radio and had them send the nearest patrol car to the DIY store car park.

The patrol car arrived to find a terrified man cradling a bleeding wrist sitting on the ground beside a Land Rover. An angry-looking blonde toting a hammer that looked more like a toy was standing over him, a taser sticking out of her jacket pocket. A black-and-white dog stood at her side, lip curled in a snarl. Around them stood a horseshoe of blokes in puffa jackets and football shirts, some of them munching on burgers.

'Fucking twatted her with a taser, didn't he,' one of them volunteered as the two uniformed officers rolled up, hands at the ready on their utility belts.

The woman half-turned and the driver, a grizzled veteran of the traffic division, drew his breath in sharply. 'DCI Jordan,' he said. 'Ma'am.'

'Not any more,' Carol said. 'This is Gareth Taylor. I think DS McIntyre wants to interview him in connection with two murders.'

'This is grotesque,' Taylor yelled. 'She attacked me, not the other way around. Who's got the taser, for God's sake?'

Everyone ignored him apart from the dog, who growled. Carol continued, unruffled. 'But he's just committed an assault and an attempted abduction, so I suggest you cuff him and stick him in the back of your car until DS McIntyre gets here.' She smiled sweetly. 'Not that I'm telling you how to do your job, officer.'

The traffic officer's smile mirrored hers. 'Couldn't have put it better myself, ma'am.' He went to drag Taylor to his feet, but the man protested his innocence loudly, struggling against the cop. 'Do you want me to add resisting arrest to the charge sheet?' the officer snarled, hoicking him up by his arms, not caring about the shout of pain from Taylor. He snapped a pair of cuffs on him, not bothering to avoid the bleeding bite-mark on one wrist. Then he frogmarched him to the traffic car and stowed him in the rear seat, effortlessly ignoring Taylor's litany of complaint. Carol sat down on the tailgate of the Landie, looking relieved. The dog jumped up beside her and licked her ear, as if in consolation.

The officers moved among the men, taking down names and addresses and bare-bones preliminary statements. And that was when Paula rolled up with Cody. She practically ran to Carol's side. 'Are you OK?'

Carol nodded. 'I'm fine. Look at those guys. It's gradually dawning on them that they've just been involved in something that's going to earn them pints in the pub for years to come. I can hear them now: "Did I ever tell you how I took on a serial killer?" Though the real hero is the dog. Flash saved me.' She rumpled the dog's mane. 'You've got him on assault and attempted abduction at the very least.'

'Well done,' Paula said. 'That's all we need to get warrants for his house and his car and his workplace.'

'Even someone as single-minded as Fielding can't ignore this,' Carol said.

Paula shook her head. 'Unless she thinks they were in it together, him and Tony.'

'I think that would be a bridge too far, even for her.'

'I wouldn't bank on it.'

'Are you going to take him in and interview him?'

'I'll get Cody to take him in. I want to be with the team that does the house search—' Her phone rang and she reached for it. As she listened, her face grew grave. 'I understand. You need to notify DCI Fielding directly, I'm pursuing another line of inquiry right now. And make sure CSI are on standby.' Paula ended the call and closed her eyes, taking a deep breath.

'Trouble?'

'This case gets uglier all the time. We thought we might have a third missing woman so I sent a patrol car to her home address. They've just radioed in to say they've spotted what appears to be the dead body of a white male through the garage window. Sounds like Marie Mather's husband got in the way of what that bastard wanted.' She jerked a thumb over her shoulder towards the patrol car. 'Nailing him is going to be a pleasure.'

In one sense, Banham village was the last place people would expect to find a serial killer. It straddled the Yorkshire–Lancashire border, changing its allegiance with every local government reorganisation since the War of the Roses. Grey stone cottages formed a tight triangle round the village green, a Norman church at the apex. Beyond the village centre were clusters of houses that had accreted like cankers over the past three hundred years, a mishmash of styles that had evolved its own distinctive character over the centuries. It had avoided being swallowed up by the urban sprawl of Bradfield thanks to the deep cleft of a valley that separated it from the main thrust of urbanisation. Banham wasn't the easiest commute in the area, but it was definitely one of the most desirable.

On the other hand, if you wanted to keep a woman prisoner undisturbed, it was a much better option than anywhere in the city. For Banham was only a fake village. It had none of the sense of community that knit together real villages. Here, nobody looked out for each other. Nobody knew each other's business. Nobody knew when their neighbours went on holiday or where they were going. There was no epicentre – no pub to run quizzes, no village hall, no WI or Autumn Club or Brownie pack. The detached cottages and houses were separate and inviolate. It was the sort of place people lived when they wanted to impress. It was also the sort of place where nobody lived for more than a few years.

Driving into the village, Paula reckoned that once upon a time living somewhere so anonymous might have appealed to her. Nobody knowing she was a cop, nobody questioning the women who occasionally drove up to her house at weekends and stayed over. But that was when she allowed anxiety to circumscribe her life. She hadn't felt like that for a very long time. And part of that was because of Carol Jordan and her MIT.

Taylor's house wasn't hard to spot. It was stone-built, like most of the houses in Banham. Even though it was probably only about thirty years old it was solid and well-proportioned. Unless he had another source of income, it must have stretched Gareth Taylor to afford it. The white CSI van sat in the driveway and a liveried BMW was parked on the roadway outside. A huddle of people in white Tyvek suits milled around in the drive, waiting for her as she'd instructed them to do. She wanted to be here every step of the way. All they had on Taylor so far was circumstantial. A car repeatedly showing up on the ANPR records was suggestive. But it wasn't proof. Going armed with a taser and using it on Carol Jordan was suggestive but it wasn't proof, particularly since, by her own admission, she'd been following him. Working in the same office as Marie Mather was suggestive but it wasn't proof. Having a limp was suggestive but it wasn't proof. If she was honest and impartial, there was still more solid evidence against Tony than there was against Taylor right now. If she was Fielding, she probably wouldn't be releasing Tony just yet.

Paula suited up, put on shoe covers, then nodded to the officer carrying the door ram. In one smooth sweep, he delivered a massive blow to the heavy front door. The wood splintered and gave up its lock, which clattered down hard enough to leave a dent in the parquet. Softwood tarted up to look like hardwood, Paula thought. *How very Banham.*

There was nothing untoward about the hallway. An attractive Afghan-style runner sat precisely in the middle of the floor. A console table held a bowl with keys and a vase of authentic-looking silk sweet peas. Photographs of glittering waves and frolicking dolphins lined one wall. Paula advanced cautiously. A door on the right opened on to a living room that looked as if it had been styled for a magazine feature. Some might say uncluttered; Paula thought sterile. On the face of it, nothing to interest them. But they would come back to it. No stone unturned. Just that some stones were definitely more promising than others.

Next off the hall, a dining room. Again, not much in the

way of homely touches. The only personal item in the room was a large studio portrait of Taylor and two children hanging opposite the door. Neither child looked particularly happy to have Daddy's hands heavy on their shoulders. Paula told herself off for projecting. Really, there wasn't much you could tell from a photo.

At the end of the hallway an archway led into the kitchen. Paula caught her breath. At her shoulder, the lead CSI swore softly. 'Arrogant twat clearly never expected to get nabbed,' he said. 'Look at this. There's forensic traces bloody everywhere. Blood, fingerprints . . . There's a clump of hair on the floor over there by the bin. And look at those metal eyes screwed into the door frame and the wall. First time I've ever seen a kitchen that looked more like a dungeon.'

Paula hung back while the CSIs placed metal trays across the floor to create a walkway that would preserve any evidence. This was the kind of result that was like a double-edged sword. As an investigator, it hit the jackpot. As a human being, it made her heart heavy. Now she could imagine what her friend had endured and it was a horrible thought. While she waited, she directed the other CID officers upstairs. 'Take a quick look around,' she said. 'Just an Open Door search to make sure Marie Mather isn't on the premises.

'Does that door lead to the garage?' she asked, pointing to the frame where the metal eye was fastened.

The CSI glanced out of the window, orientating himself. 'Looks like it. You want to take a look?'

'We've still got a missing woman, so yes. Soon as you like.'

The final chequered plates were laid down, providing a route to the door. The lead CSI opened it with a flourish and Paula crossed the threshold. At first glance, it was a regular suburban garage. Tools and garden equipment, all hung up neatly in their allotted spaces. A workbench and a stack of folding garden chairs. A chest freezer.

And then you looked more closely and saw the pre-torn strips of duct tape hanging from a shelf. And the trails of blood and what looked like skin snagged on the rough concrete floor. And the metal eyes screwed in strategically in three places. 'Oh, fuck, the freezer,' Paula said softly and started across the garage.

'Wait,' the CSI shouted. 'You're fucking up the evidence.'

'There's a woman in that freezer!' Paula shouted over her shoulder, breaking into a run, blood and adrenalin pounding in her head. She pulled the lid up. The rubber seal released loud as thunder in her ears. And there was Marie, curled in the foetal position, in a pool of blood and piss. Blonde and bruised and battered. Still as death. Paula reached in and felt warm flesh, the flutter of a pulse under her jaw. 'Get her the fuck out of there, she's still alive.'

'We need photos,' the CSI shouted at her.

'I'm right here,' the videographer said. 'Step away a second, Paula.'

All her instincts screaming against it, Paula did as she was asked. But only for as long as it took her to count to five. Then she was yelling at them all to help her, to call an ambulance, to get Marie Mather out of what was intended to be her coffin and back into life.

Back at Skenfrith Street, Fielding was steadfastly ignoring the fact that she still had Tony Hill in custody even though the compass needle was swinging round to point unwaveringly elsewhere. This was supposed to be her big day, the press conference where she got to announce the arrest of a high-profile double murderer. In her head, it was the point where she put down a marker that she was destined for the top.

Instead, she'd had to listen to Bronwen Scott's pitiful attempt to explain away the evidence against Tony Hill with an improbable story of nosebleeds and a collision in a corridor. It was obviously a fabrication that would fall to pieces under scrutiny, but checking it out would waste time while the clock was ticking. It was clearly a ruse to postpone charging him, so she'd have to let him go on police bail. And that would give that bitch Scott time to line up her so-called experts to cast doubt on the fingermark.

And now McIntyre was off on a tangent of her own. Some nonsense based on nothing that Fielding could put her finger on. A bagman was supposed to be unquestioningly loyal, but Fielding was beginning to think McIntyre had loyalties that were nothing to do with her. How else had Carol Jordan turned up with Bronwen Scott in the middle of the night when Hill hadn't even made a phone call? When this was all over, McIntyre was going to be shipped out to another firm and Fielding was going to find a bagman who understood what a privilege it was to be so close to the heart of an investigation.

And then McIntyre herself hustled into the squad room. Fielding opened her office door in time to hear her sergeant say, 'Hussain, Wood – we've got more data in from ANPR. See if we can put Taylor anywhere near the acquisition sites or the body dumps. And one of you check with the local lads and see if they've given anyone a tug yet for joyriding Bev McAndrew's car. I want to know where it was nicked from.'

Fielding took a deep breath. 'McIntyre? In here.'

Paula closed the door behind her. 'We found Marie Mather.'

Fielding looked stunned. 'Why did nobody tell me?'

'I've just come from the hospital,' Paula said. 'I imagine the team assumed I would tell you. Which I'm doing now.' Her tone bordered on the insolent.

'You should have called me right away.'

'I was more concerned with getting Marie Mather to hospital. She's still alive. Barely, but at least she's in with a chance now. And if she makes it, she makes our case for us.'

'Which team?' Fielding clutched at the last available straw. There were search teams going through Tony Hill's home and office. As well as the one McIntyre had called out to Gareth Taylor's house.

'Didn't I say? We found Marie in a chest freezer in Gareth Taylor's garage.'

There was a long silence. *Wrong, wrong, wrong.* The word echoed in Fielding's head like a bell tolling.

Paula had her hand on the door, getting ready to leave. 'I think you should release Dr Hill now,' she said gently.

'You do it,' Fielding said brusquely. 'You're such good pals. And you've worked so hard to get him off the hook.'

Anger finally flared in Paula's eyes. 'Just as well someone did, since he's innocent.'

'We followed the evidence, McIntyre. I'd have been irresponsible if I'd released him earlier.'

'We followed it down the wrong road, ma'am. And I'm busy right now. I have to interview the victim of a serious assault who will only talk to me. So I suggest you do it yourself.'

66

C arol had been confined in an interview room for hours. First, in spite of her protestations that she was absolutely fine, they'd had to wait for a doctor to confirm that she was well enough to be questioned. Then there had been a certain amount of discussion about the dog. Carol had refused to leave Flash locked in the Land Rover indefinitely and the dog team had pointed out it was nothing to do with them. Eventually, before she'd disappeared upstairs, an exasperated Fielding had said Carol could keep the bloody dog with her and claim it was a guide dog if anybody complained.

Then Carol had refused to be interviewed by anyone except Paula, which meant she had to wait till she was free.

When Paula finally sat down with Carol, it was almost midnight. Paula set down two tall cardboard cups. 'Not cop-shop crap, proper coffee-shop coffee from the all-night stand by Central Station.' She dug a paper bag out of her pocket. 'And a couple of muffins. Slightly squashed, I'm afraid.'

'Caffeine and sugar. That should do the trick,' Carol said.

She broke off a chunk of her muffin and dropped it at her feet, where Flash wolfed it before it hit the ground. 'Has Fielding released Tony yet?'

'I think she's doing it now. Me, I'd have done that the minute we arrested Taylor, but she wasn't taking any chances. Or so she said.'

'I hardly know the woman, but I'd say she's not someone who takes it well when she's proven wrong.'

Paula gave a grim little smile. 'I've a funny feeling I'm not going to be her bagman after tonight.'

'I'm sorry.'

'I'm not. I don't want to spend my time running around with a brush and dustpan after someone who can't keep an open mind.' She shrugged. 'There's other firms. I'm good at my job, people know that. Now, we have to figure out a way to spin this that doesn't drop anyone in the shit.'

Carol grinned. 'Just like old times.'

Paula shook her head. 'No way. Old times was me and Tony figuring out how to avoid you going ballistic at one or both of us for bending the rules.'

Carol's smile disappeared. 'I suppose so. Well, one thing we all know for sure. That won't be happening again.'

In another part of the building Bradfield's Chief Constable was wondering why he'd been so keen to take on this job. He believed he'd put together an efficient and effective team, but he'd just had to listen to the woman he thought his best DCI explain how she'd let a bee in her bonnet drive her over the edge of professionalism into a kind of stubborn madness. In the old days, he could have rammed a lid on her fuck-up with a fair degree of certainty that it would never leak out to the public. But these days, with a twenty-four-hour rolling news cycle and a ravenous social media, the chances of keeping things quiet were nil. You could only cling to the hope that something else would make a louder noise to distract the twitterati.

James Blake exhaled heavily and pushed himself to his feet. He opened a cupboard and stared longingly at a bottle of cognac. What he wouldn't give for a large drink right now. But he still had a truly horrible encounter to deal with, and he daren't go into it smelling of drink. He closed the door and pulled himself up to his full height. He knew he could be imposing in a certain way, and God knew he needed that now. He slipped into his executive bathroom and checked himself in the mirror. There was something old-fashioned about his looks, he knew that. His wife said he had the air of a man who should be astride a horse leading a pack of hounds in pursuit of a fox. And although his background was relentlessly lower middle class, he played up to that image. He'd cultivated an accent several degrees above his natural station, he tended to wear country tweeds with double-vented jackets over Tattersall checked shirts, his pink cheeks were always freshly shaven, his hair treated with some expensive unguent from Floris. He'd moved to Bradfield from Devon, where he'd fitted in better, but had felt constrained by the lack of serious crime.

Well, this was where serious crime got you. Standing in your office in the middle of the bloody night waiting to be eviscerated by a woman who could stand as the dictionary definition of 'bitch'. James Blake tightened his stomach muscles and stalked back into his office. He crossed to the door, opened it and gestured to the waiting pair. 'Do come in.'

Paula walked Carol down to the Skenfrith Street car park and her Land Rover. She watched her tail lights disappear then lit a cigarette, shivering in the damp night air. She'd barely smoked half of it when her phone rang. When she saw it was Elinor, she was tempted to send it straight to voicemail. She imagined the arrest was on the news and she couldn't talk about it yet with Elinor or Torin. But loyalty won over expediency and she took the call. 'DS McIntyre,' she said, using their standard code to make it clear they were in work mode.

'This is only a quickie. I saw the news and I know you must be up to your eyes. But I thought you'd want to know.'

'Know what?'

'We've spoken to Torin's dad again. Actually, Torin did most of the speaking. They've had a really good chat. He talked about how he feels about his mum. He really opened up. And then I was able to talk to Tom. The upshot is that Tom would be very grateful if we'd have Torin to stay until he's finished his tour of duty in Afghanistan.'

Paula could hear the genuine pleasure in Elinor's voice. She wasn't entirely sure how much of that delight she shared, but she was willing to go along for the ride. She'd never dreamed of a quiet life. Which was probably just as well. She stubbed out her smoke and walked into the warm fug of the station. 'I'm glad,' she said. 'I think Bradfield's the best place for him right now.'

'I love you, DS McIntyre. I'll see you later.'

Paula grunted. 'I doubt it, the way things are going.' She walked back into the squad room. And the moment's respite was over.

Because then an eager detective constable with an unruly mane of ginger curls raised a hand, as if she was in a GCSE maths class. 'Sergeant, you know how we were wondering how he knew it was safe to dump Nadia's body in that squat?'

'Yeah?'

'Well, I've been taking another look at the reports. Taylor's wife's maiden name was Waddington. And one of the lads who live in the squat is called Waddington. It's not that common a name. What's the betting they were related?'

'Good work. Check it out,' Paula said. She glanced across to Fielding's office. Empty. No surprise there. Hussain and Wood were communing with their computer screens and Cody was on the phone, his expression grave. He put the phone down and smacked his fist on the desk. Startled, everyone looked up.

'She didn't make it,' he said angrily. 'Marie Mather. She was bleeding internally. They couldn't stabilise her. Fuck.'

Paula stood in the middle of the room, feeling like a failure. All the things that had gone wrong with this case felt like a personal rebuke. She should have resisted Fielding more forcefully. She should have confronted Gareth Taylor as soon as Carol came up with his name. Certainly as soon as there was any suggestion that Marie might be missing. Like all cops, Paula carried the burden of what she might have done differently. Marie Mather's death had just added major weight to that burden.

Tony's first thought after release had been a fierce longing for his own bed. But Bronwen Scott had been waiting for him. She'd whisked him off to a quiet corner and given him a brief rundown on what had happened in the previous few hours. 'Carol did the business, and Paula picked up the pieces,' Scott had said, a feline smile of contentment on her face.

'What about Fielding?'

Scott's smile widened. 'Fucked. I see a great future for her in Traffic.'

'I'm glad they've stopped him.'

Scott appeared to have lost interest. 'Yes, yes. That's always good.'

'So, can I go home now?' He tried not to sound like an overtired plaintive child, but he suspected he'd failed. Twenty-eight hours in custody could do that to a man.

Scott laughed. He'd always wondered what writers meant

when they described a laugh as a tinkle. Now he knew. A brittle, musical sound. 'Sorry, Tony, but there's still work to be done. We're going to see Blake.'

'The Chief? Why?'

'Because you're going to be suing BMP for a very large sum of money for wrongful arrest, false imprisonment and damage to your personal and professional reputation.'

'I am?'

'You are.'

'I don't believe in suing public institutions. It's a waste of taxpayers' money that could be better spent doing other things.'

She looked at him as if he were mad. 'Fielding fucked you over. They've damaged your reputation, and that's what you live by. You deserve to be compensated.'

He shrugged. 'I don't think there was malice involved. Fielding just got a crazy idea in her head and dug herself in too deep.'

'Nevertheless. This is payback time. BMP owe you.'

'I don't want—' He'd been about to say 'their money', but then a better idea occurred to him. 'OK,' he said. 'Let's go and see Blake.'

So here they were, walking into Blake's office, a sanctum like a gentlemen's club. Tony wondered if you could buy a room spray that smelled of leather and cologne and cigars, because he'd have sworn that's what it smelled like.

'Come in, sit down,' Blake said, waving expansively at a group of leather tub chairs set around a low table. 'I do hope this hasn't been too traumatic an experience, Dr Hill. But of course, our officers do have to follow the evidence,' he said before they were even settled.

'That's what they're supposed to do,' Scott said, ice in her tone. 'But not at the price of making preposterous decisions. Every fragment of circumstantial evidence against Dr Hill was readily demolished by my team within a handful of hours. Arresting him and holding him in custody was completely unnecessary.' Blake tried to speak but she held a hand up. 'Dr Hill is a Home Office-accredited police consultant. He's devoted his professional career to helping police solve cases like this, for heaven's sake. You know where he lives and works. Even if there had been solid evidence to link him to these crimes, he was never any kind of flight risk. This has been preposterous from start to finish.' She exhaled sharply through her nose.

Blake shifted in his chair, crossing his legs at the ankles. 'However, matters have been resolved very quickly. I hope we can put it all behind us.' He steepled his fingers and gave an avuncular smile. 'Then it will all die down and reputations won't be unduly damaged.'

'I don't think you understand,' Scott said. 'We're looking for substantial compensation here. Wrongful arrest, false imprisonment and damage to Dr Hill's professional reputation. This is a major lawsuit, Mr Blake.'

Blake made a strangled mumbling sound. 'There hasn't been any significant publicity,' he pointed out.

'We haven't given our side of the story yet,' Scott said sweetly. 'We have an extraordinary tale to tell. A man of spotless reputation is thrown in the cells on the scantest of evidence. The police are so incompetent that I have to turn to a retired officer for help. And within twenty-four hours, we civilians not only destroy the case against Dr Hill but also expose the identity of the real killer. I imagine this one will run and run across the traditional and the digital media.'

Tony sat up straight, galvanised by this unexpected turn of events. To judge by the expression of shock that had crossed Blake's face, he hadn't expected that line of attack either. He looked like a man staring down the barrel of the end of his career. 'That's a shocking distortion of the facts,' he blustered.

'In what respect?'

Tony could tell Blake was on the point of closing the meeting, which wasn't what he wanted. He had an agenda of his own, and now was the time to pursue it. He cleared his throat and said, 'There is one way to avoid a costly and embarrassing lawsuit.'

They both swung round in their seats to stare at him. 'I don't think this is a good idea,' Scott said.

'Of course you don't,' Tony said. 'You're a lawyer. Conflict's your bread and butter. James, there's no denying that this has not been BMP's finest hour. I believe this whole debacle would never have happened if the MIT had still been up and running. When Carol Jordan's brother was killed, you shouldn't have let her go. You should have clasped her to your bosom and helped her through it, not cut her loose.'

'DCI Jordan had handed in her resignation before that happened. Which you very well know, Dr Hill.' Blake was like a dog with its hackles up.

'It doesn't matter. You should have taken care of her. But it's not too late. It's obvious from what's happened here that she's still got what it takes to make a difference. Here's the deal. You go to Carol Jordan and you offer her whatever it takes to get her back on board. I'm not saying you have to eat dirt and publicly reinstate the MIT. But you bring Carol back and find a way to put that team back together, and you'll hear no more about this.' He smiled at them both. Scott looked ready to thump him.

Blake, however, had the air of a man reprieved. 'What if she says no?'

Tony gave an apparently guileless smile. 'You need to make sure she doesn't.'

67

Day twenty-nine

When she finally got home and read Paula's message about Marie Mather, Carol's first instinct had been to pour herself a drink. But instead of knocking back the very large vodka in a oner, she sat staring at the glass for a long time. She took off her jacket and slung it over a hanger, then gave the glass her full attention. Stepping back into the world had given her pause. There was nothing wrong with what she was doing here in the barn. But she'd let that become an end in itself and the past few days had shown her that wasn't enough.

She'd only been on the periphery of the investigation but that had been enough to remind her that she had a talent for justice. Not to exercise that talent was wrong. Not just because of the end result; the lives that would be changed because she wasn't there to do what she was best at. But because it was bad for her to ignore the things she was good at, the things she could be proud of.

If she carried on like this, Jacko Vance would have scored

the ultimate victory. He'd set out on his campaign of vengeance with the aim of making her life not worth living. She hadn't been able to see past her grief to understand how well he'd succeeded. But the last few days had helped her to comprehend what had happened to her.

If she carried on like this, Jacko Vance would have won.

It wasn't only her professional life that had been poisoned by his actions. He'd managed to estrange her and Tony. Vance was the worst kind of clever psychopath; he'd understood how things would play out downstream of his actions. He'd worked out how to cause them maximum pain. And she'd walked right into the trap. She'd blamed Tony when really, the only person to blame was Vance himself.

Carol raised the glass to eye level and stared long and hard at the drink. It was time for her to make some changes. Her life wasn't over yet.

Slowly and steadily, Carol stood up and poured the vodka down the sink.

Dawn broke in a sky that seemed almost as watery as the canal basin. Grey, pearl and eggshell ran into each other in an uncertain muddle of sky and cloud. Tony sat on the roof of his boat up by the bows. His hands were folded round a cup of instant soup that had stopped steaming a while ago. His face was drawn and tired, his eyes gritty with lack of sleep. He'd returned to the boat shortly after one in the morning, so tired his very bones hurt. But as soon as he'd climbed into bed, sleep had slipped from him, leaving him restless and weary. He'd tried to fight the wakefulness, but he'd eventually given up and come outside to watch the orange glow of street lights lose their hold on the sky.

He'd had the sort of experience he could learn from, no doubt about that. He would better understand some of his patients as a result. Still, it was something he could have done without. Except that it had brought Carol back into his life, however briefly. He took her words at face value – that she wasn't there for him but for the sake of justice. It had always been what drove her. He wasn't arrogant enough to think that was a smokescreen for her true feelings. He knew her true feelings. She blamed him and she couldn't bear his presence. And yet, if he could be certain she'd be there every day, he'd have settled for a life sentence.

He'd felt on the verge of tears ever since he'd returned to the boat. He knew it was partly because he was tired but it was also because he'd lost her again.

Even as that thought crossed his mind, the boat rose and fell with the familiar sudden lurch that came from someone boarding. He almost didn't want to turn round because he couldn't bear the disappointment of seeing Paula at the other end of the hull. But he did turn, because he wanted to think of himself as someone who could be strong.

And there she was, standing at the stern, dressed for business in the same suit she'd been wearing the day before. Different shirt, though. Her hair was rumpled and her eyes were bleary with tiredness. But she was there and that was all that mattered to him.

He scrambled to his feet and couldn't think of a single thing to say that wasn't banal.

Carol spoke first. 'Do you know anywhere we can get a decent cup of coffee this time of the morning?'

He gestured to the open hatch. 'I have coffee.'

She shook her head. 'Neutral territory.'

He glanced at his watch. 'The only place I know is the all-night coffee stand at Central Station.'

She nodded. 'I'll see you there in ten minutes.' And she jumped ashore, a black-and-white dog at her heels as she strode across the cobbles with more energy than he could have managed.

Tony scrambled along the boat and locked the hatch, leaving his mug on the roof. He stumbled ashore and ran across to where his car was parked by the tapas bar. He reached Central Station with three minutes to spare and bought coffee for them both. He stood by the coffee stand, a cardboard beaker in each hand, waiting.

The dog still by her side, Carol rounded the corner and gestured with her head to a bench opposite the station entrance. He joined her there, silently handing over her drink. He still didn't know what to say. 'I heard you'd got a dog.' Hell of an ice-breaker.

'Always the master of the irrelevant.'

'It's not irrelevant. It means something.'

She sighed. 'And what does it mean in Tony world?'

'It means you've decided to let yourself form an emotional attachment. And that's a good thing.'

'If you say so.' She sipped her coffee. 'You blackmailed Blake,' she said.

'I did.'

'Why did you do that?'

'Because I'd rather someone like you was investigating serious violent death in this city than the Alex Fieldings of this world. And because everyone should practise the craft that they're best at.'

'You're still a psychologist, then?' There was an incredulous edge to her voice that cut him.

He sighed. 'It's the only thing I'm equipped for.'

'Scary thought.'

Sitting side by side, he couldn't see her face. There were no clues in her tone. Time was, she would have said things like that ironically, as a joke. 'Did you say yes?'

'I told him I'd think about it.'

'You should say yes. You got me out of jail.'

Now she sighed. 'I'm used to having the full weight of a

professional team behind me. I made mistakes in the last twenty-four hours that might have got me killed. Marie Mather might still be alive if I'd done things differently.' She buried her free hand in the dog's luxuriant coat. 'It forced me to realise that I'd been blaming you for not being flawless. And none of us is flawless.' Another sigh. 'I was so angry with myself for what happened to Michael and Lucy that I had to turn my anger somewhere else and you were the easiest target.'

He tried to speak and found he couldn't. He took a swig of coffee and tried again. 'I knew that. And I also knew the only way back for us was if you worked it out for yourself.'

'You think there is a way back for us?' A train rumbled over the bridge and disappeared into the station.

He shifted round so he could look at her. 'You're here, aren't you?'

**Now turn the page for
your free Val McDermid short story!**

Keeping on the Right Side of the Law

Just imagine trying to get a straight job when you've been a villain all your life. Even supposing I could bullshit my way round an application form, how the fuck do I blag my way through an interview, when the only experience I've got of interviews, I've had a brief sitting next to me reminding the thick dickheads on the other side of the table that I'm not obliged to answer? I mean, it's not a technique that's going to score points with the personnel manager, is it?

You can imagine it, can't you? 'Mr Finnieston, your application form was a little vague as to dates. Can you give us a more accurate picture of your career structure?'

Well, yeah. I started out with burglary when I was eight. My two older brothers figured I was little enough to get in toilet windows, so they taught me how to hold the glass firm with rubber suckers then cut round the edge with a glass cutter. I'd take out the window and pass it down to them, slide in through the gap and open the back door for them. Then they'd clean out the telly, the video and the stereo while I kept watch out the back.

All good things have to come to an end, though, and by

the time I was eleven, I'd got too big for those toilet windows, and besides, I wanted a bigger cut than those greedy thieving bastards would give me. That's when I started doing cars. They called me Sparky on account of I'd go out with a spark plug tied on a piece of cord. You whirl the plug around like a cowboy with a lasso, and when it's going fast enough, you just flick the wrist and bingo, the driver's window shatters like one of them fake windows they use in the films. Hardly makes a sound.

Inside a minute and I'd have the stereo out. I sold them round the pubs for a fiver a time. In a good night, I could earn a fifty, just like that, no hassle.

But I've always been ambitious, and that was my downfall. One of my mates showed me how to hotwire the ignition so I could have it away on my toes with the car as well as the sounds. By then, one of my brothers was doing a bit of work for a bloke who had a secondhand car pitch down Strangeways and a quiet little backstreet garage where his team ringed stolen cars and turned them out with a whole new identity to sell on to mug punters who knew no better.

Only he wasn't as clever as he thought he was, and one night I rolled up with a Ford Escort and drove right into the middle of a raid. It was wall-to-wall Old Bill that night, and I ended up in a different part of Strangeways, behind bars. Of course I was too young to do proper time, and my brief got me out of there and into a juvenile detention centre faster than you could say 'of previous good character'.

It's true, what they say about the nick. You do learn how to be a better criminal, just as long as you do what it tells you in all them American self-help books in the prison library. You want to be successful, then hang out with successful people and do what they do. Only, of course, anybody who's banged up is, by definition, not half as fucking successful as they should be.

Anyway, I watched and listened and learned and I made some good mates that first time inside. And when I came out, I was ready for bigger and better things. Back then, banks and post offices were still a nice little earner. They hadn't learned about shatterproof glass and grilles and all that bollocks. You just ran in, waved a shooter around, jumped the counter and cleaned the place out. You could be in and out in five minutes, with enough in your sports bag to see you clear for the next few months.

I loved it.

It was a clean way to earn a living. Well, mostly it was. Ok, a couple of times we ran into one of them have-a-go heroes. You'd think it was their money, honest to God you would. Now, I've always believed you should be able to do a job, in and out, and nobody gets hurt. But if some dickhead is standing between me and the out, and it's me or him, I'm not going to stand there and ask him to move politely aside, am I? No, fuck it, you've got to show him who's in charge. One shot into the ceiling, and if he's still standing there, well, it's his own fault, isn't it? You've got to be professional, haven't you? You've got to show you mean business.

And I must have been good at it, because I only ever got a tug the once, and they couldn't pin a thing on me. Yeah, OK, I did end up doing a three stretch around about then, but that was for what you might call extracurricular activities. When I found out Johnny the Hat was giving one to my brother's wife, well, I had to make an example of him, didn't I? I mean, family's family. She might be a slag, but anybody that thinks they can fuck with my family is going to find out different. You'd think Johnny would have had the sense not to tell the Dibble who put him in hospital, but some people haven't got the brains they were born with. They had him in witness protection before the trial, but of course all that ended after I went down. And when I was getting through my three with visits from the family, I had the satisfaction of knowing that Johnny's family were visiting his grave. Like I say, families have got to stick together.

By the time I got out, things had changed. The banks and building societies had wised up and sharpened up their act and the only people trying to rob them were amateurs and fucking eejits.

Luckily, I'd met Tommy inside. Honest to God, it was like it was written in the fucking stars. I knew all about robbing and burgling, and Tommy knew all there was to know about antiques. What he also knew was that half the museums and the stately homes of England – not to mention our neighbours in Europe – had alarm systems that were an embarrassment.

I put together a dream team. And Tommy set up the fencing operation, and we were in business. The MO was simple. We'd spend the summer on research trips. We'd case each place once. Then we'd go back three weeks later to case it again, leaving enough time for the security vids to be wiped of our previous visit. We'd figure out the weak points and draw up the plans. Then we'd wait till the winter, when most of them were closed for the season, with nothing more than a skeleton staff.

We'd pick a cold, wet, miserable night, preferably with a bit of wind. That way, any noise we made got swallowed up in the weather. Then we'd go in, seven-pound sledges straight through the vulnerable door or window, straight to the cabinets that held the stuff we'd identified as worth nicking. Here's a tip, by the way. Even if they've got toughened glass in the cases, chances are it's still only got a wooden frame. Smack that on the corner with a three-pound club hammer and the whole thing falls to bits and you're in.

Mostly, we were off the estate and miles away before the

local bizzies even turned up. Nobody ever got hurt, except in the pocket.

They were the best years of my life. Better than sex, that moment when you're in, you do what you do and you're out again. The rush is purer than you'll ever get from any drug. Not that I know about that from personal experience, because I've never done drugs and I never will. I hate drug dealers more than I hate coppers. I've removed my fair share of them from my patch over the years. Now they know not to come peddling their shit on my streets. But a couple of the guys I work with, they like their Charlie or whizz when they're not working, and they swear that they've never had a high like they get when they're doing the business.

We did some crackers. A museum in France where they'd spent two million quid on their state-of-the-art security system. They had a grand opening do where they were shouting their mouths off about how their museum was burglar-proof. We did it that very night. We rigged up pulleys from the building across the street, wound ourselves across like we were in the SAS and went straight in through the skylight. They said we got away with stuff worth half a million quid. Not that we made anything like that off it. I think I cleared fifteen K that night, after expenses. Still, who dares wins, eh?

We only ever took stuff we already knew we had a market for. Well, mostly. One time, I fell in love with this Rembrandt. I just loved that picture. It was a self-portrait, and just looking at it, you knew the geezer like he was one of your mates. It was hanging on this Duke's wall, right next to the cases of silver we'd earmarked. On the night, on the spur of the moment, I lifted the Rembrandt an' all.

Tommy went fucking ape. He said we'd never shift that, that we'd never find a buyer. I told him I didn't give a shit, it wasn't for sale anyway. He thought I'd completely lost the plot when I said I was taking it home.

I had it on the bedroom wall for six months. But it wasn't right. A council house in Wythenshawe just doesn't go with a Rembrandt. So one night, I wrapped it up in a tarpaulin and left it in a field next to the Duke's gaff. I rang the local radio station from a call box and told them where they could find the picture. I hated giving it up, mind you, and I wouldn't have done if I'd had a nicer house.

But that's not the sort of tale you can tell a personnel manager, is it?

'And why are you seeking a change of employment, Mr Finnieston?'

Well, it's down to Kim, innit?

I've known Kimmy since we were at school together. She was a looker then, and time hasn't taken that away from her. I always fancied her, but never got round to asking her out. By the time I was back in circulation after my first stretch, she'd taken up with Danny McGann, and before I worked up the bottle to make a move, bingo, they were married.

I ran into her again about a year ago. She was on a girls' night out in Rothwell's, a gaggle of daft women acting like they were still teenagers. Just seeing her made me feel like a teenager an' all. I sent a bottle of champagne over to their table, and of course Kimmy came over to thank me for it. She always had good manners.

Any road, it turned out her and Danny weren't exactly happy families any more. He was working away a lot, leaving her with the two girls, which wasn't exactly a piece of cake. Mind you, she's done well for herself. She's got a really good job, managing a travel agency. A lot of responsibility and a lot of respect from her bosses. We started seeing each other, and I felt like I'd come up on the lottery.

The only drawback is that after a few months, she tells me she can't be doing with the villainy. She's got a proposition for me. If I go straight, she'll kick Danny into touch and move in with me.

So that's why I'm trying to figure out a way to make an honest living. You can see that convincing a bunch of suits that they should give me a job would be difficult. 'Thank you very much, Mr Finnieston, but I'm afraid you don't quite fit our present regulations.'

The only way anybody's ever going to give me a job is if I monster them into it, and somehow I don't think the straight world works like that. You can't go around personnel offices saying, 'I know where you live. So gizza job or the Labrador gets it.'

This is where I'm up to when I meet my mate Chrissie for a drink. You wouldn't think it to look at her, but Chrissie writes them hard-as-nails cop dramas for the telly. She looks more like one of them bleeding-heart social workers, with her wholemeal jumper and jeans. But Chrissie's dead sound, her and her girlfriend both. The girlfriend's a brief, but in spite of that, she's all right. That's probably because she doesn't do criminal stuff, just divorces and child custody and all that bollocks.

So I'm having a pint with Chrissie in one of them trendy bars in Chorlton, all wooden floors and hard chairs and fifty different beers, none of them ones you've ever heard of except Guinness. And I'm telling her about my little problem. Halfway down the second pint, she gets that look in her eyes, the dreamy one that tells me something I've said has set the wheels in motion inside her head. Usually, I see the results six months later on the telly. I love that. Sitting down with Kimmy and going, 'See that? I told Chrissie about that scam. Course, she's softened it up a bit, but it's my tale.'

'I've got an idea,' Chrissie says.

'What? You're going to write a series about some poor fucker trying to go straight?' I say.

'No, a job. Well, a sort of job.' She knocks back the rest of her pint and grabs her coat. 'Leave it with me. I'll get back to you. Stay lucky.' And she's off, leaving me surrounded by well-meaning like the last covered wagon hemmed in by the Apaches.

A week goes by, with me trying to talk my way into setting up a little business doing one-day hall sales. But everybody I approach thinks I'm up to something. They can't believe I want to do anything the straight way, so all I get offered is fifty kinds of bent gear. I am sick as a pig by the time I get the call from Chrissie.

This time, we meet round her house. Me, Chrissie and the girlfriend, Sarah, the solicitor. We settle down with our bottles of Belgian pop and Sarah kicks off. 'How would you like to work on a freelance basis for a consortium of solicitors?' she asks.

I can't help myself. I just burst out laughing. 'Do what?' I go.

'Just hear me out. I spend a lot of my time dealing with women who are being screwed over by the men in their life. Some of them have been battered, some of them have been emotionally abused, some of them are being harassed by their exes. Sometimes, it's just that they're trying to get a square deal for themselves and their kids, only the bloke knows how to play the system and they end up with nothing while he laughs all the way to the bank. For most of these women, the law either can't sort it out or it won't. I even had a case where two coppers called to a domestic gave evidence in court against the woman, saying she was completely out of control and irrational and all the bloke was doing was exerting unreasonable force to protect himself.'

'Bastards,' I say. 'So what's this got to do with me?'

'People doing my job get really frustrated,' Sarah says. 'There's a bunch of us get together for a drink now and again, and we've been talking for a long time about how we've stopped believing the law has all the answers. Most of these blokes are bullies and cowards. Their women wouldn't see them for dust if they had anybody to stand up for them. So what we're proposing is that we'd pay you to sort these bastards out.'

I can't believe what I'm hearing. A brief offering me readies to go round and heavy the kind of toerags I'd gladly sort out as a favour? There has to be a catch. 'You're not telling me the Legal Aid would pay for that, are you?' I say.

Sarah grins. 'Behave, Terry. I'm talking a strictly unofficial arrangement. I thought you could go and explain the error of their ways to these blokes. Introduce them to your baseball bat. Tell them if they don't behave, you'll be visiting them again in a less friendly mode. Tell them that they'll be getting a bill for incidental legal expenses incurred on their partner's behalf and if they don't come up with the cash pronto monto, you'll be coming round to make a collection. I'm sure they'll respond very positively to your approaches.'

'You want me to go round and teach them a lesson?' I'm still convinced this is a wind-up.

'That's about the size of it.'

'And you'll pay me?'

'We thought a basic rate of two hundred and fifty pounds a job. Plus bonuses in cases where the divorce settlement proves suitably substantial. A bit like a lawyer's contingency fee. No win, no fee.'

I can't quite get my head round this idea. 'So it would work how? You'd bell me and tell me where to do the business?'

Sarah shakes her head. 'It would all go through Chrissie. She'll give you the details, then she'll bill the legal firms for miscellaneous services, and pass the fees on to you. After this meeting, we'll never talk about this again face to face.

And you'll never have contact with the solicitors you'd be acting for. Chrissie's the cut-out on both sides.'

'What do you think, Tel?' Chrissie asks, eager as a virgin in the back seat.

'You could tell Kimmy you were doing process serving.' Sarah chips in.

That's the clincher. So I say Ok.

That was six months ago. Now I'm on Chrissie's books as her research assistant. I pay tax and National Insurance, which was a bit of a facer for the social security, who could not get their heads round the idea of me as a proper citizen. I do two or three jobs a week, and everything's sweet. Sarah's sorting out Kimmy's divorce, and we're getting married as soon as that's all done.

I tell you, this is the life. I'm doing the right thing and I get paid for it. If I'd known going straight could be this much fun, I'd have done it years ago.